All Our
HIDDEN
GIFTS

All Our HIDDEN GIFTS

Caroline O'Donoghue

WALKER
BOOKS

First published in Great Britain 2021 by Walker Books Ltd
87 Vauxhall Walk, London SE11 5HJ

2 4 6 8 10 9 7 5 3 1

This book has been typeset in Bembo, Frutiger, Open Sans, Rosewood

Printed and bound by CPI Group (UK) Ltd, Croydon CR0 4YY

British Library Cataloguing in Publication Data: a catalogue record for this book is available from the British Library

ISBN 978-1-4063-9309-5

www.walker.co.uk

To my family, for being interesting.

And to Harry Harris, for waking up the Housekeeper first.

CHAPTER ONE

THE STORY OF HOW I ENDED UP WITH THE CHOKEY CARD Tarot Consultancy can be told in four detentions, three notes sent home, two bad report cards and one Tuesday afternoon that ended with me being locked in a cupboard.

I'll give you the short version.

Miss Harris gave me in-school suspension after I threw a shoe at Mr Bernard. It was payback for him calling me stupid for not knowing my Italian verbs. To this, I responded that Italian was a ridiculous language to learn anyway, and that we should all be learning Spanish because globally, more people speak Spanish. Mr Bernard then said that if I really thought I was going to learn Spanish quicker than I am currently learning Italian, I was deluded. He turned back to the whiteboard.

And then I threw my shoe.

It didn't hit him. I'd like to stress that. It merely hit the board next to him. But no one seems to care about that, except me. Maybe if I had a best friend – or really, any close friend at all – I'd have someone to vouch for me. To tell them that it was a joke, and that I would never knowingly hurt a teacher. Someone who could explain how it is with me: that sometimes frustration and rage surge through me, sparking out in ways I can't predict or control.

But that friend doesn't exist, and I'm not sure I would deserve them if they did.

In-school suspension starts on Tuesday morning, and Miss Harris meets me at her office and then leads me to the basement.

In the four years I've been at St Bernadette's, the sewage pipes have frozen and burst twice, not to mention the annual flooding. As a result, the two tiny classrooms down here are covered in grass-green mould, and a damp, mildewy smell permeates everything. Teachers try to avoid scheduling classes down here as much as they can, so naturally it gets used a lot for detention, exams and storing extraneous junk that no one can be bothered to throw away.

The holy grail of this is the Chokey, a long, deep cupboard that makes everyone think of the Trunchbull's torture room in *Matilda*.

Miss Harris waves a dramatic arm at the cupboard. "Ta-da!"

"You want me to clean out the Chokey?" I gasp. "That's inhumane."

"More inhumane than throwing a shoe at someone, Maeve? Make sure to separate general waste from dry recyclables."

"It didn't hit him," I protest. "You can't leave me to clean this out. Not by myself. Miss, there might be a dead rat in there."

She hands me a roll of black plastic bin bags. "Well, then, that would go in 'general waste'."

And she leaves me there. Alone. In a creepy basement.

It's impossible to know where to start. I start picking

at things, grumbling to myself that St Bernadette's is like this. It's not like normal schools. It was a big Victorian town house for a very long time, until at some point during the 1960s, Sister Assumpta inherited it. Well. We say 'Sister', but she's not really one: she was a novice, like Julie Andrews in *The Sound of Music*, and dropped out of the nunnery, and started a school for "well-bred girls". It probably seemed like a good idea when the number of "well-bred" girls in the city was about a dozen. But there's about 400 of us now, all bursting out of this crumbling house, classes rotating between draughty prefabs and converted old attic bedrooms. It's obscene how expensive it is to send your daughter to school here. I have to be careful about how much I complain in front of Mum and Dad. The other four didn't have to go here, after all. They were bright enough to make it through free schools unaided.

St Bernadette's costs about two thousand euro a term, and wherever the money goes, it's not on health and safety. I can't even step into the Chokey at first because of all the broken old desks and chairs that are stacked up inside, blocking the entrance. A fresh waft of rot and dust hits my nose every time a piece of furniture comes free. I try to carry each piece out and make a neat pile in the corner of the classroom, but when chair legs start coming loose in my hand, smacking against my legs and laddering my tights, it gets less orderly. I throw my school jumper off and start hurling rubbish across the room like an Olympic javelin champion. It becomes cathartic after a while.

Once all the furniture is gone, I'm amazed to see how much space there is in the Chokey. I had always thought it was just a big cupboard, but it's clear it used to be some kind of kitchen pantry. You could fit three or four girls in here, no problem. It's good information to have. There's no such thing as too many hiding places. It needs a lightbulb or something, though. The door is so heavy that I have to prop it open with an old chair, and even then, I'm working in near darkness.

The furniture, however, is just the beginning. There are piles of papers, magazines and old schoolbooks. I find exam papers from 1991, *Bunty* annuals from the 1980s and a couple of copies of some magazine called *Jackie*. I spend a while flicking through them, reading the problem pages and the weird illustrated soap operas that play out over ten panels. They're ridiculously dated. The stories are all called something like "Millie's Big Catch!" and "A Date With Destiny!"

I read "A Date With Destiny". It turns out Destiny is a horse.

When I reach the back, things start getting really interesting. A couple of cardboard boxes are stacked against the wall, covered in a thick, chalky dust. Pulling the top one down, I open it and find three Sony Walkmans, a packet of Superkings cigarettes, a half-empty bottle of crusty peach schnapps and a pack of playing cards.

Contraband. This must have been where all the confiscated stuff ended up.

There's also a single hair slide with a little silver angel on it, looking very pure and holy next to the fags and booze. I try it on briefly and then get worried about nits, so throw it in a bin bag. Only one Walkman has a tape in it, so I stick the headphones on and press play. Amazingly, it still works. The cassette starts turning. *Holy crap!*

A playful, plodding bass line thrums in my head. Dum-dum-dee-dum-de-dum. A woman's voice whispers to me, childlike and sweet. She starts singing about a man she knows, with teeth as white as snow, which feels like a dumb line. What other colour would she expect them to be?

I listen, clipping the Walkman to my skirt. Most of the songs I don't recognize, but they all have a grungy, arty edge to them. Songs where you can hear the bad eyeshadow. I can't remember the last time I listened to something and didn't know exactly what it was. I'm not even sure I want to find out. It's sort of cool not to know. I listen to it over and over. There are about eleven songs in all, all either by very high-pitched men or very low-voiced women. I pop open the cover to see that it's a homemade mix. The only decoration is a white strip label that says, "SPRING 1990".

I try to lift another heavy box, but the damp cardboard splits at the bottom and comes crashing down on me, smacking me full force in the face. Something must hit against the door because the chair I was using to prop it open suddenly topples over, and the Chokey door slams shut.

I'm plunged into stinking darkness. I grapple around for the doorknob, and realize that there isn't one. Maybe it's not a pantry after all. Maybe it's just a closet.

The music keeps playing in my ears. Now it doesn't seem fun and bouncy. It's creepy. Morrissey is singing about cemetery gates. The tape gets stuck as I pound on the door, a little hiccup at the end of the word "gates".

"HELLO?" I shout. "HELLO, HELLO! I'm STUCK in HERE. I'm STUCK IN THE CHOKEY!"

"… cemetery gAtEs, cemetery gAtEs, cemetery gAtEs, cemetery gAtEs…"

The cupboard, which had felt so roomy just minutes ago, now feels like a matchbox about to be set alight. I have never thought of myself as claustrophobic, but the closer the walls press in on me, the more I think about the air in the room, which already feels so thick and stale that it might choke me alive.

I will not cry, I will not cry, I will not cry.

I don't cry. I never cry. What does happen is actually worse. Blood rushes to my head and, even though I'm in complete darkness, I see spots of purple in my vision and I think I'm about to faint. I grapple around for something to steady me, and my hand falls on something cool, heavy and rectangular. Something that feels like paper.

The battery is starting to die on the Walkman. *"… cemetery gAtEs, cemetery gAtEs, cemetery gAaaaaaaaayyyyyyyyy…"*

And then nothing. Silence. Silence except me screaming for help and banging against the door.

The door flings open, and it's Miss Harris. I practically fall on top of her.

"Maeve," she says, her expression worried.

Despite my panic, I still feel smug at how concerned she looks. *Take that, bitch.*

"What happened? Are you OK?"

"The door closed on me," I say in a burble. "The door closed, and I was stuck and I…"

"Sit down," she orders. She fishes in her bag and brings out a bottle of water, unscrews the cap and hands it to me. "Take small sips. Don't be sick. You're panting, Maeve."

"I'm OK," I say at last. "I just panicked. Is it lunch now?"

She looks really worried now.

"Maeve, it's four o'clock."

"What?"

"You mean to say you haven't taken lunch? You've been here this whole time?"

"Yes! You told me to stay here!"

She shakes her head, as if I'm the magic porridge pot that keeps spewing porridge relentlessly until you say the magic word for it to stop.

"Do you know," she says, walking into the cupboard (I briefly consider closing the door on her), "it's amazing what you can do when you apply yourself. I had no idea there was so much space in there. You're a magician. Well done."

"Thanks," I reply weakly. "I guess I'll become a cleaner."

"I think you should clean up in the bathroom and go home," she says, and I realize what a state I must look. I'm covered head to toe in dust, my tights are ripped and there are bits of cobweb stuck to my school shirt. "Are you sure you're OK?"

"Yep," I say, a little snappy this time.

"I'll see you in the morning. We can figure out what to do with all this furniture then." She makes her way to the door, fixing her handbag back on her shoulder. She takes one last look at me, then tilts her head to the side. "Huh," she says at last, "I never knew you were into tarot cards."

I have no idea what she's talking about. Then I look down. There, clutched in my hands, is a deck of cards.

CHAPTER TWO

I LOOK AT THE CARDS ON THE BUS HOME. I CAN'T WORK OUT what the pattern is supposed to be. Some of the cards have titles, like the Sun and the Hermit and the Fool, but others have numbers, and suits. But not hearts, clubs, spades and diamonds. The suits here are rods, which are long brown sticks, as opposed to fishing rods; cups, which look more like wine glasses; swords, which are just swords; and pentacles, which are little stars on discs.

Most of the cards are drawings of people, the colours in brilliant reds and golds and purples, each character engaged in deep concentration with whatever task they're doing. There's a man carving a plate, but, like, he's *really* carving it. No one has ever applied himself like this dude is applying himself. He is the eight of pentacles, the card tells me. I wonder what he's supposed to mean. *You will carve a plate today?*

I've seen tarot cards before, obviously. They come up in films sometimes. A fortune teller draws the cards and says something vague, and you, the viewer, are convinced she's a con artist. Then she says something specific to make you sit up and pay attention: "And how does your husband *Steve* feel about that?" Or something.

I flick through them quickly, noticing that each card is marked by a very similar system to ordinary cards. Every suit is marked ace, two, three, four, five, and so on until ten. There are royal families, too: pages, knights, queens, kings. My old best friend Lily would love these. One of our first made-up games was called Lady Knights and mostly consisted of us pretending to ride horses around her back garden, defeating dragons and saving princes. Maybe she's still playing Lady Knights in her head, but we don't speak any more.

As I think about Lily, another card catches my eye. One that seems different from the other cards, and makes my stomach swoop when I touch it. My eyes go bleary for a second, like I've just woken up. Is that a woman's face? I pull it out to look, but there's a noise at the back of the bus that forces me to turn around. It's a clutch of boys from St Anthony's. Why are boys so unbelievably loud on the bus? They're passing around something, then screaming with laughter. It's not a nice, joyful sound, though. It's mean. I catch a flash of something and see that they also have cards.

Now that's weird. The one day I find tarot cards is also the day the St Anthony's boys take up tarot?

Suddenly, Rory O'Callaghan gets up from his seat and saunters up the aisle, even though I know his stop – the same as mine – isn't for ages. "Hey, Maeve," he says, pausing near me. "Can I...?"

"Sure," I say. Today keeps getting stranger and stranger. Here I was, just thinking about Lily and over comes her older brother. Rory and I have known each other since we were small kids, but we've never been friends. Remote, impressive and seldom seen, he was like a comet through my childhood.

He sits down, and I see that his face is completely red, his eyes shiny. I don't ask what happened. Rory has always been a bit of a target. His big, soft features and solitary habits make him an outsider at a school like St Anthony's, where if you don't play football or hurling, you might as well be dead. It probably doesn't help that the O'Callaghans are Protestant in an almost entirely Catholic city. They're not religious; no one is, not really. But their being Protestant gives them an air of slight Britishness. A kind of polite, re-tiring energy that boys will prey on.

"Rory!" one of the boys shouts down. "Hey! Rory! Roriana! Roriana Grande! Come back!"

Rory blinks his big hazel eyes, which really do look a bit like Ariana Grande's, and turns to me. "So, how are you?"

"I'm OK," I say, shuffling the cards. I like the way the cool cardboard feels. It's very nice if you're the sort of person who doesn't know what to do with their hands.

Rory blanches when he sees the cards. "Oh, crap. You have them, too."

I'm puzzled, and put the cards face up, showing him the swirling illustrations. "Tarot cards?"

At that moment, one of the boys comes sprinting down the bus. "Hey, Roriana Grande, has your girlfriend seen these?"

The boy, whose name I don't know, shoves some cards under my face and all at once, I get the joke. They're not tarot. They're the kind of gross, porn playing cards you get on holidays. Naked girls with huge boobs and thongs so tight they'd give you thrush. And stuck to every face is a photocopy of Rory's school photo. Rory pretends to look out of the window, knowing that if he grabs for them or reacts in any way, they'll get exactly what they want.

This is, quite simply, the most awkward moment ever experienced on the Kilbeg bus.

"Wait a second," I say, my voice studious, like I'm cross-examining someone on their term project. I look at the boy. "So you photocopied, cut out and glued Rory's photo onto fifty-two playing cards?"

He laughs and gestures at his friends in an "aren't I hilarious?" expression.

"Wow, you must be totally *obsessed* with him," I say loudly, and the boy gives me a dirty look and returns to the back of the bus. Rory and I sit in silence. Out of the corner of my eye, I notice that his fingernails are painted pink. Not loud, hot fuchsia. But soft pink, the colour of a ballet slipper. So close to his actual skin colour that, at first, you'd hardly notice it.

When we get off at our stop, he walks in the opposite direction, with barely a murmured "Bye."

My house is a good twenty minutes away from the bus stop, but it's a nice route, and on days like this I actually look forward to it. I have to walk alongside the riverbank, the huge blue-grey water of the Beg on the left-hand side of me, the stone walls of the old city on my right. Kilbeg used to be the city centre a hundred years ago, because the docks were here. It was a trading port, one of the most important in all of Ireland, and there are still plenty of old market squares and cattle posts left over from those days. There's even a drinking fountain, dry for decades now, where people used to tie up their horses. Back in primary school I did a project on the riots that took place here during the Famine, when the landlords shipped the grain out of the country even though the Irish were all starving. I got a prize. My first ever, and probably my last.

Our house seems big from the outside, but not when you realize that at one time all seven of us lived here. Yes, *seven*. Mum, Dad, my oldest sister Abbie, the two boys Cillian and Patrick, Joanne and then me. People always ask me what it's like having so many siblings, unaware that there's fifteen years between me and Abbie, thirteen years between me and Cillian, ten between me and Patrick, and seven between me and Jo. It's more like having a load of parents.

"Hey," calls Jo from the kitchen. She's baking. It's something she's into at the moment. She broke up with her girlfriend a couple of months ago and is living with us while she finishes her Master's degree. I really don't want them to get back together, although Mum thinks it could be on the cards. It's so boring when it's just me and Mum and Dad.

"Hey, you're home early," I respond, dropping my bag in the hall and making my way into the kitchen. "What are you making?"

"Ugh, there was some mad Christian protest happening right outside the library window, so I came home." She sucks a little bit of batter off her finger. "Pistachio and almond blondies."

"God. What were they protesting? And why do you always have to bake things that taste like salt?"

"They're not salty," she says, crushing the nuts up with the end of a wine bottle. She's always despairing that there's no proper equipment in this house, but with five kids and a career, Mum could never really be bothered. "They're *savoury*. And they were protesting about the Kate O'Brien exhibition, saying the taxpayer shouldn't pay for art about queer people. As if there would be any good art *left*."

She cups her palms and scoops the nuts into a mug. "How was in-school suspension?"

"It was ... fine."

"Did you apologize to Mr Bernard, like I told you to?"

"No."

"Maeve!"

"It didn't *hit* him!"

"That's not the point. You should at least apologize for acting up all the time and purposefully disrupting his class."

I hate that. Acting up. Why are people always in a hurry to categorize you being funny as you being a sociopath? When a girl is quiet, they just say: "She's quiet. It's her personality." If she's a massive overachiever, they just say she's ambitious. They don't question it. Jo was so completely anal about school that she gave herself stress-induced psoriasis during her Leaving Cert, and all anyone had to say was that she was goal-orientated.

"And anyway," she says, sprinkling the mug of nuts into her blondie mixture, "I don't see why you find languages so hard. You're verbal enough. You just have to memorize the right verbs in the important tenses. Everything else is simple."

Just? You just have to memorize them?

Does she not realize how impossible that is?

And yet, other people do it. All the other girls I hang around with got at least eighteen or nineteen out of twenty in the last vocab test, while I struggled to make it past ten.

Just before I started at St Bernadette's, Mum took me to a special examiner to see if I was dyslexic. I think everyone was really hoping that I was.

"I just know she has some hidden gifts," Mum told the examiner, trying to convince herself as much as him. "She was the earliest to speak of all my kids. She was talking at eleven months. Complete sentences."

They wanted an explanation for my underachievement. Especially the boys, who are both so science-y. They called up every day with new theories on why I was falling behind so much. "Have we considered that it might be her hearing?" Cillian suggested one weekend when he was home. "Maybe she can't actually hear what the teacher is saying."

Ironic, seeing as the only reason I know he said this was because I overheard him from the next room.

I'm not dyslexic, or blind, or deaf. Unfortunately for everyone, I'm just thick.

I lick my finger and start dabbing the worktop, picking up crumbs of pistachio and putting them in my mouth.

"Maeve. Gross. Stop. I don't want your spit in these blondies."

"Why? Who are they for?"

"No one. God, do I need an occasion to not want spitty blondies?"

"They're for Sarra, aren't they?" I say, needling her. "You're meeting up with Sarra."

"Shut up," she says, sweeping the nut crumbs into her hand and then folding them into her mixing bowl with a wooden spoon.

"You are!" I say, triumphant. "Well, don't expect her to appreciate them. She'll probably say she loves them and then cheat on them with some brownies."

Joanne stops mixing. Her face is going red. Oh God, I've done it now. Sometimes I forget that, even though we've all known about the cheating for so long that it feels like old news, Joanne still relives it every day. I might be over her being cheated on, but she certainly isn't.

"Hey," I say. If I can make her laugh, then we can both have a giggle about it, and Sarra's memory will be thrown over our shoulders like lucky salt. "Brownies are horrible. Probably the most overrated baked good in the world. And slutty, too."

Joanne says nothing, and just spoons the mixture into her baking tray.

"If you like brownies you're probably an asshole," I try again, watching her guide her tray into the oven.

"Jesus Christ, Maeve, will you just leave it?"

Suddenly she's shouting, so angry that she loses her concentration and burns her forearm on the side of the oven. She screams and instinctively clutches her skin, dropping the entire tray of batter on the floor. I grab the kitchen roll and start trying to clean up the sticky yellow globs.

"Stop!" she shouts, pushing me away. "Just get out. Get out, get out, get out! Go to your room."

"I'm trying to help, you cow," I say, my eyes tingling already. *God, don't cry. Don't cry.* Nothing worse than being the baby of the family and crying. "And you can't tell me to go to my room. You're not Mum, so piss off."

Now Joanne is crying. Sometimes I think that she spent

21

so long being the baby of the family that she's even more sensitive than I am. She had her baby status taken away from her, after all, while I'm desperately trying to leave it behind.

The kitchen door swings open and Mum's there, holding the dog's lead and looking exhausted by us already. The dog charges in and dives for the batter, stuffing as much as he can into his mouth before Mum starts shrieking about his irritable bowel syndrome.

"GRAB TUTU!" she yells. "Maeve, get Tutu AWAY! Tutu, STOP! Tutu, BAD! Joanne, is there butter in this? I am not cleaning up rancid dairy diarrhoea. Do you have any idea how that's going to smell?"

We lock Tutu outside while we clean up the mess and Joanne tearfully explains what a bitch I am.

"I can't believe you," I snap at her. "You're in your twenties and you're snitching."

Then I say a bunch of horrible stuff about her and Sarra that I instantly regret but will also never apologize for. Tutu and I go to my room, two outlaws.

There are fifty WhatsApp notifications on my phone, but all of them are from groups I'm part of. Niamh Walsh and Michelle Breen @'d me a few times, asking what Miss Harris made me do during my first day of suspension.

I cleaned out the Chokey, I write back.

Lots of emojis.

What a bitch, someone says.

I found so much crap, I type. I send a picture of the Walkman with the grungy mixtape.

They all register their surprise, but quickly move on to something else. There are at least fourteen of us in this

WhatsApp group, so it's hard for everyone to keep up. I find myself wishing, not for the first time, that I had a best friend to talk to.

I had one, once. But that whole thing with Lily is over. It's been almost a year and a half, now.

Then I remember the cards. The brilliant reds and purples, the serious expressions and strange symbols. I pull them out of my bag and start sifting through them, laying them out in numerical order.

1. THE FOOL.

   A guy with a dog and a flute. He's kind of hot
   in that long-haired Prince Valiant kind of way.

2. THE MAGICIAN.

   A guy at a table, mixing a potion.

3. THE HIGH PRIESTESS.

   A woman with a moon on her head. She
   reminds me of Miss Harris, beautiful and stern.

I peer at each one, hoping that I'll get some kind of psychic vision if I make close-enough eye contact with the people in the cards. Nothing happens. Eventually, bored of my own ignorance, I open my laptop and search: How to teach yourself tarot.

And then, the evening disappears.

CHAPTER THREE

"Hey, guys, welcome to my channel. I'm Raya Silver of Silverskin Magic, and today we're going to learn how to give a standard three-card tarot reading."

The woman in the YouTube video is sitting cross-legged in a wicker armchair, impossibly gorgeous in the New Orleans mystic shop that is also her family home. Raya has two kids, a dog, a cat and a third eye.

It has been two hours, and I am obsessed with her.

I've learned a lot. I've learned that the "face" cards – like "Death" and the "Magician" and the "High Priestess" – are like main characters of the tarot, and they're called the Major Arcana. The rest of them are suits, just like in regular playing cards, and they're the Minor Arcana. Cups represent emotions. Swords represent the mind. Rods represent passion. Pentacles represent money.

"Swords, cups, rods, pentacles," Raya's e-book says. "Head, heart, loins, feet."

"I want you to get warmed up with a nice juicy shuffle," she instructs, her cards slipping through the air and into her fingers like silk scarves. I mimic her movements, and the cards splay out of my hands, falling onto the bedspread. I'm still trying to get the hang of my shuffle technique.

"Or, if you're reading for someone else, get them to shuffle.

The cards are living, breathing things. They need to soak up all the energy from whoever you're reading for. Then, ask the client to cut the deck into three with their left hand, and put it back together. Fan the cards out so they have plenty of choice."

I do as she says.

"Now pick three. They represent past, present and future."

I pick carefully and turn all three over. The Moon, the Chariot and the Tower. The Moon is just the Moon, a big luminous, pearly illustration. The Chariot is a man on a two-horse chariot, and the horses look mad as hell. The Tower is the only one I'm anxious about. It looks horrible. A medieval tower is broken in half, orange flames licking the stone. Two people are falling out of it, plunging to their deaths. It gives me a chill. But I trust Raya. She says there are no truly bad cards, that there's a good side to everything, and I believe her.

Pausing the video, I consult my Kindle to see Raya Silver's descriptions of the cards. All of Raya's interpretations are friendly, text message-length and written in ordinary language, not in some weird obtuse magical language. It's why I like her so much. She feels like a friend.

> THE MOON: The Moon rules over our periods, so there's a lot to be mad about here. This card represents deep subconscious energy, maybe even stuff that you are suppressing. Remember, all evil has to come to the surface eventually!
>
> THE CHARIOT: Woahhhh! Slow down! Your chariot is about to veer off the track – or are you going so fast that it just looks like chaos to

25

everyone else? Ask yourself whether you're in control of your situation or not

THE TOWER: OK, I know this looks bad. Real bad. But sometimes old structures need to come tearing down so you can build something new.

I unpause the video, and Raya instructs me on how to put these three cards together. *"Use your intuition,"* she says breathily. *"Let the cards talk to each other."*

I gaze at them, and ask myself how I'm feeling. The moodiness of the Moon has definitely been a thing for me lately. A profound loner energy has ruled over this year at school. The last two years, if I'm honest. It seems like everyone's deeper in their cliques than ever, and I'm lagging behind, no best friend, no firm group, no academic success. Then there's the Chariot, the guy trying to keep his cool while his two horses go crazy. Yeah, that feels like me.

"Speak your truth," Raya says. Her voice is breezy, but her chocolate-brown eyes are focused and direct. *"Speak it out loud."*

"I'm not very happy at the moment," I say aloud, and to my complete surprise I feel a tiny hot tear come into the corner of my eye. I quickly blink it away. "And I'm trying to make out like I'm fine, but I'm not."

"Go to your place of fear," Raya Silver says, as though she can hear me. "Say what you're afraid of."

"If I don't sort myself out, things are going to get really, really, really bad," I say, and before I have a chance to get upset about it, Dad calls me down for dinner.

When I get downstairs, it's just Dad at the table. Jo has gone out – probably to Sarra's house – and Mum is correcting exam papers in Abbie's old room, so she's eating in there.

"I heard you were giving Joanne hell," Dad says disapprovingly, shoving me a plate of lasagne.

"If that's *her* side of the story…"

"You should be nice to your sister. She's going through a hard time."

"I am nice," I say. "I can be nice."

"You're better than nice, Maeve. You're good. There's so much good in you. You just need to show it."

"What's the difference?"

"Nice people," he says, stroking Tutu, who is pawing at his lap for scraps, "will smile and listen and say, 'Oh no, how terrible' when they hear a sad story. Good people do something about it."

Dad is the youngest in his family, too, so he tends to have a bit more sympathy than everyone else. But he was the one genius in a family of idiots, and I'm the one idiot in a family of geniuses. It's not exactly the same.

We talk for a while, and he asks me if school is going any better, and I lie and say it is.

"How's Lily getting on?" he asks, pushing his food around. "Do you still talk?"

"We're not friends any more, Dad," I say quickly, and take my tarot cards out of my pocket.

"What are *those*?"

"Tarot cards," I respond. "Do you want me to give you a reading?"

"I don't know. Will you tell me nasty things about my future?"

27

"Tarot doesn't tell the future," I say, mimicking Raya Silver's calm, guru-like voice. "They only help you analyse your present."

"Jesus. Are you in a cult now? I heard on the radio that all the young people were joining a cult, but I didn't think they'd nab *you*."

"No. I'm just interested in the cards. They're part of history, you know. They were used in Italy in the fifteenth century."

"So you're into history *and* Italian now? I think I like this cult."

"Here," I say, handing them over. "Shuffle these bad boys. Get your juice into them."

"My *what*?" Dad looks appalled.

"Your energy! Get your energy into them! Cards are made of paper, Dad. Paper is made from trees. They're conscious."

"Uh-huh," he says, clearly bemused. "And when did you get these cards?"

"Today," I answer. I get him to shuffle and split the cards into three piles. Then I fan the cards out like Raya did. "Pick three."

He picks three. Ten of Rods, Two of Cups, the Fool. I study them.

"It looks like you're working really, really hard," I say, pointing at the man with a bunch of rods on his back. "And that you might be neglecting Mum in the process. The cards are suggesting you go on a holiday or an adventure together so you can feel, y'know – in love again."

My dad's face goes dark. "Piss off," he says. "It did not say that."

"It did!"

"Has your mother put you up to this?"

"No!" I say, gleeful. "Why? Am I right?"

"Je-eeee-eee-sus!" He starts raking his hands through his thin, sandy hair. "Well, I guess we're going to Lisbon then."

"Lisbon?"

"Your mum has been on and on about us going to Lisbon. Flights are cheap at the moment. And I've been working like a madman."

"Go!" I say, truly excited to have been right. "Go to Lisbon!"

"Who's going to make sure you get to school every morning?"

"I'm sixteen! I can wake myself up for school. And Joanne will be here."

He takes our plates to the sink and rinses them off. "My God," he says, still dazed. "I guess I better check Ryanair."

I shuffle the cards again, delighted by my success. "I find it very interesting," he says, before leaving the room, "that you can learn all these cards in an evening, and still haven't quite mastered your times tables."

"Shut up! I know my times tables! I'm sixteen, Dad, not eight."

"What's sixteen times eight?"

"A million and three."

"Wrong. It's 128."

"Oh, look," I respond, drawing my cards. "It's the Death card. I'd hurry up about booking those flights."

He leaves, and I'm alone with my deck of Chokey cards. Thinking that, despite his stupid maths joke, it is a little

29

weird that I've managed to learn the cards so well in an evening. But it's not like learning everything else. It doesn't fall out of my brain the minute I move on to something else, like school stuff does. It sticks, like song lyrics. Like poetry. Like feelings I already had but finally have a map for.

CHAPTER FOUR

THE NEXT DAY MISS HARRIS MAKES ME SPEND MOST OF MY lunch break finishing the Chokey. I don't even really mind. Dad gave me some replacement batteries for the Walkman, so I'm enjoying the job now, eager to see the Chokey looking clean and orderly, and I attack it while singing to 1990s goth music. I keep the cards zipped into the front of my school bag and try to resist the temptation of playing with them.

Five minutes before the bell goes, she declares the Chokey a success, and tells me to go to the common room and eat something. After yesterday's door-slamming incident, she's clearly afraid of me getting hurt and it being all her fault.

Most of the girls have walked into town to buy their lunch, but a few people are still lounging around the classroom and avoiding the February cold. Lily O'Callaghan is sitting on her own with a book, her long dark-blonde fringe brushing into her eyes. I can see red swollen spots around her temples, acne breakouts where the grease from her hair touches the skin. How often is she washing her hair these days? Lily isn't dirty, per se; it's just that she doesn't really like to live in her body. She doesn't like to notice it. If she could just be a brain in a jar, reading books and drawing, she'd be much happier.

She looks up and gives me a tight smile, fiddling with her hearing aid as I walk past. I spot a clutch of girls I know and quickly join them, bustling past Lily without a word.

Why do I do this? Why am I so awful to her, when we've been through so much together?

I go and sit with the gang. Michelle has a new make-up palette from this American brand endorsed by all the most famous drag queens, apparently, and she's very excited about it. It's hard to see why. The colours look exactly like the kind of thing you'd get for twenty quid in Urban Decay, which I make the mistake of saying, and then everyone laughs and Michelle looks annoyed.

"Sorry," I say, when I see that her ears are red. Michelle is ginger so any tiny changes in her mood are highly detectable. I sit silently for a while and listen to them talk. It gets boring quickly. I start fidgeting, and I shove my hands into the pocket of my school blazer to find the tarot cards sitting there. *What?* I was sure I had left them in my school bag.

My face must look confused, because the girls stop and look at me.

"What's up?" Michelle asks. "You look like you've just smelled a bad fart."

"Nothing," I say, straightening my expression. "Hey, do you want me to read your tarot cards?"

"My what?"

I show her and the rest of the girls crowd around.

"You can't actually read them, though, can you?" asks Michelle.

"A bit," I say. "I practised last night."

Michelle shuffles and draws. The Queen of Rods, the Three of Cups and the Ace of Pentacles.

Just like last night with Dad, everything slots together perfectly. It all seems so simple what these cards are trying to say. I weave the story for Michelle. About how her creative passion for make-up and her love for her friends are the twin forces in her life, and how they are going to be her path to success.

Michelle is clearly impressed. "Wow. Maeve, it was only last night that I made a YouTube channel for my make-up."

There's an audible gasp, and I can already tell that the tarot cards are going to be a big deal.

"No!"

"Yes! Look! Let me show you!"

She pulls out her phone and brings up the YouTube app. She's telling the truth: there, with zero subscribers and a grey circle for a photo, is a YouTube channel called "SweetShellFaces". Michelle is burning with embarrassment at showing us, but clearly wants to underline the uncanniness of the reading.

"Don't be embarrassed. The cards think it's a good idea."

"Really?"

"Positive. Look at these!" Then I outline how the Queen of Rods is all about female creativity, the Three of Cups about friendship, and the Ace of Pentacles is financial success.

From that moment, lunches are taken over with tarot readings. Everyone seems to think it's magic, that I'm psychic, but as much as I would like to believe my own hype, I know that's not the case. It's just a case of knowing the cards and knowing these girls really well. When the three of swords comes up for Becky Lynch, I know that the pain of the card is referring to her parents' divorce. When the Death card comes up for Niamh, everyone screams, but I know that the card is pointing to the fact that Niamh recently had to give up her horse because her family moved from the super rural countryside to the middle of the city.

"Gypsy isn't going to die, is she?" she asks tearfully. The whole room leans in, high on the drama.

"No," I say, after a breathy pause. I can't pretend like I'm not high on the drama, too. "It's just, you need to accept that the Gypsy part of your life is over, so that something new can begin."

Soon, the whole year knows about my tarot cards. I'm waiting to use the toilet one morning when Fiona Buttersfield walks right up to me and asks for a reading.

"Hey," she says. "You're that girl."

"Fiona," I reply nervously. I'm a little intimidated by Fiona Buttersfield. We only have one class together, but she's kind of a celebrity in our year. Fiona is one of those Saturday-stage-school kids who manage to make it not embarrassing. She's been doing it for so long that the older kids have all gone on to college, but they still let her hang around and even be in their plays.

"Fiona's your name, too?" She looks confused.

"No, your name is Fiona. *My* name is Maeve."

"I know what *my* name is."

"Do you want something, or...?"

"I heard you were doing tarot readings."

"Uh..." I stall a bit and try to wonder whether or not I could really read for someone I don't know. "Do you want one?"

34

She nods. "I want a career reading."

"I see," I respond. "Well, come and find me at lunch-time."

"No way," she says, folding her arms like I've just asked her to take her knickers off. "You're not supposed to do readings in public. Don't you know that? They're supposed to be private."

"You already seem to know a lot about this."

"My tita used to do readings back in Manila," she says, and then clocks my confused face. "My *aunt*."

"Oh, right. Why don't you just ask her, then?"

"Because she'll tell me to do something boring, like law or medicine."

"Right. OK." The bell goes for class, and I'm still bursting to go to the toilet. I push into one of the cubicles and pull down my tights. Fiona lingers outside.

"So will you do it?"

"Yes!" I call, conscious that she can hear me pee. "The Chokey, lunchtime!"

"I'll cross your palm with silver!"

For a moment, I'm sure I've misheard her. "What?"

"I'll pay you!"

At lunchtime, Fiona is at the Chokey. I still have the key Miss Harris gave me, and we sit cross-legged on the floor with our phone torches on, our faces ghoulish in the darkness.

As I shuffle, I can't help but look at her curiously. It's a genuine surprise to see her here. She's not a mean girl, exactly, but definitely distant. I can't say I blame her. Her mum is Filipino, and as one of the few non-white people in our school, she gets a few comments about her looks. Last year when we got back from summer holidays, a few of the other girls asked her to hold her bare arm out against theirs, so they could all compare tans. Her shiny black hair is complimented constantly, but almost always with a weird qualifier. Something like: "Well, I bet it's because you eat a lot of fish."

I pass the deck back to Fiona, asking her to shuffle and separate. She picks her cards. I take one look at them. For a second, I don't say anything.

"Are you … OK at the moment?" I ask tentatively.

"What do you mean?"

"Your cards just seem a bit … sad."

"I asked you about my career."

"Yes, but…"

I wave my hands over the cards. Five of Cups. Sadness, anxiety, loss. Three of Swords. Heartbreak. Nine of Swords. Worry.

Her lip twitches. I've always seen Fiona Buttersfield as a bit full of herself. Someone too good to mingle with the unsophisticated masses.

"It just seems there are other things on your mind that aren't your … uh, career."

She gazes at the cards for a long moment, and I assume she is about to call off the reading.

"I've got this boyfriend," she finally says. "He's older."

"Oh," I say. I try to keep my cool. Like: *Oh yeah, sure, I have plenty of older boyfriends, too.*

"He's twenty."

"Wow."

"We met in the theatre," she says, putting a little breathy voice on. There's something intensely annoying about the way she says "theatre". Like there's no "r" in it. The-ah-tah.

"He wants me to…"

"Have sex?" I venture.

"Yes," she responds, grateful.

"And you…"

"I don't know!" She suddenly explodes, raking her fingers through her hair. "But, you know, we've been going out for three months. It would hardly be scandalous."

"Uh-huh," I say again, thinking, *This is already way above my pay grade*. I'm an amateur tarot reader, not a therapist. I do my best. "Well, the cards are clearly trying to tell you something here."

"What?"

I pick up the Nine of Swords. "This is a picture of a woman who is literally crying in bed at the thought of a man getting into it."

And she laughs. Not a fake little titter, but a real, full laugh.

"Shut up, it does *not* mean that."

"Just tell him you're not ready."

She twists her mouth and looks at the card again. "To tell you the truth, I don't think I'll ever be ready. I don't know if I even fancy him that much. But he's in the theatre group, and they're all older…"

I think for a moment. "Well, you could always say that romance is distracting you from your … your *craft*."

She nods, considering this. "That's not a bad shout."

"Or you could break up with him."

She smiles and looks at the ground. "That's not a bad shout either."

At that moment, there's a knock on the cupboard door, and there are two first-year girls standing outside.

"We heard you were telling fortunes," the braver one says.

Fiona pushes past me. "She is," she says. "Two euro, ten minutes."

She whips her head around back to face me, her smile full of mischief. "I'll take care of appointments if you give me free readings. Deal?"

"Deal," I say, uncertainly.

"Every star needs her own psychic."

She's trying to sound casual, but underneath the bravado I'm starting to spy something that I can only recognize because I possess it myself. Fiona is lonely. Every star needs her own psychic, and every girl needs someone to talk to.

And that's how the Chokey Card Tarot Consultancy begins.

That night, I spread every card out on my bedroom floor. I decide to test my knowledge, to make sure that I can remember every one. If I'm going to go into business with this, I need to know that I won't be stumped, regardless of what card comes out. I point at them, saying each meaning aloud as though I were weaving a magic spell.

"Ace of Cups, compassion! Two of Cups, romance! Three of Cups, friendship!"

How is this all so easy?

Once I've been through every card at least three times, something weird happens. There's a spare card, stuck to the World, the final card of the Major Arcana. It has no number or suit, the way all the other cards do. It shows a woman with long, black hair and a knife in her mouth. She's wearing a long white dress. I've seen her before, I think. My eyes flicked to her briefly that day with Rory on the bus, but she hasn't popped up since.

Her teeth are bared in an expression of playful wickedness. Some kind of long-limbed dog, like a greyhound or a whippet, is standing forlornly next to her, his head leaning against her leg as if for balance. Underneath the illustration of her is just one word:

HOUSEKEEPER

I search the e-book for the term Housekeeper and nothing comes up. I check Google for Housekeeper card and there are no relevant matches.

The longer I look at her, the more unsettled I feel. She's not the grimmest card in the deck by any means – the Ten of Swords, for example, is a dead guy with ten swords sticking out of his back – but the Housekeeper is different.

My stomach starts to churn with an ill-placed sense of guilt, the kind you get when you're sure you have upset someone but you don't know how. The blood in my fingers feels fizzy and electric, and I'm suddenly hyper-aware of my own skin. Each flayed cuticle, the dry corners of lip. I'm stuck in a staring match with this card, one I can only lose.

She is, after all, a drawing. It gives her the competitive edge on staring contests.

"Maeve!" Joanne is calling up the stairs.

"What?"

"Are you coming down for food or what?"

"Coming!" I get up, collect all the splayed cards and put them back into an orderly deck.

Except for her. The Housekeeper, who must be some kind of weird Joker card that has no place in a real reading.

I take her out. I open my desk drawer, wedging her carefully between pages of Abbie's old French phrasebooks that she sent over.

I head downstairs, eat pad thai, and don't fight with Jo for the rest of the evening.

CHAPTER FIVE

AFTER A FEW DAYS I'M SO KNACKERED FROM READING PEOPLE'S tarot that I spend every free period lying on the floor of the Chokey while Fiona counts out our earnings.

"Sixteen euro!" she says with glee. "And that's just today and yesterday."

Usually I would be delighted at the concept of more money, especially as Mum and Dad haven't adjusted their allowances for inflation since Abbie was a teenager. I'm too tired to celebrate, though. I keep my eyes closed.

"Cool."

"You should invest it back into the business," Fiona says. "There's a shop in town where you can buy witchy stuff."

"Witchy stuff?"

"Yeah," she says. "My tita says the woman in there throws you out if your aura is bad."

The shop is called Divination, and I head there after school. It's pokey and fragrant, thick incense filling the room. Crystals, dream catchers and bottles of homemade perfume fill every surface. As I'm waiting for the shop-keeper to finish selling someone a deodorant stone, I start picking up and examining things, trying to be as respect-ful as possible while simultaneously sure that most of it is bollocks.

"Hello there," the shopkeeper says brightly. She's in her mid-fifties and wearing red cotton harem pants, a chunk of amber hanging around her neck. Her hair is bright blonde and tied into a ponytail, a red satin scrunchy making her whole head look strangely girlish.

"Can I help you with something?"

"I need crystals," I say, and take out the fourteen quid I made today from readings. "How many can I get with this?"

"That depends. What do you need them for?"

"What do you mean?"

"You need different crystals for different jobs, pet."

I pick up a glittering piece of grey and purple stone the size of a potato. "How much is this one?"

"Thirty-five euro."

"Wow," I say, quick to let it drop out of my hands. It lands on the display with a thud.

"Amethysts are a powerful protective stone. Plus, they need to be a certain price if we're going to source them ethically," she says. She doesn't seem too offended by my ignorance, thank God.

"I'm sorry," I say. "It's just, I've started doing tarot readings lately, and I thought it would be nice to have some stones around to help my … uhh, clients … relax."

"Congratulations," she says, smiling. "Tarot readings are a lot to take on. I don't do them any more. The older you get, the more crowded you get with other people's energy. After I turned forty, every time I gave a reading I woke up with a crick in my neck. Other people's bad juju, you know. It's really a young woman's game."

"Oh," I say, thrown by the idea of ingesting people's energy. "Is that ... a *thing* that happens?"

"It depends."

"On what?"

"Sensitivity. Empathy. The kind of people you read for. They bare their heart to you, uncork all this bottled up junk they've been working on for years and years, then they give it to you. And it sticks. That's why I burn wild sage in here," she laughs. "It's less about cleansing the customers. It's more about protecting me *from* the customers."

"I think I know what you mean," I say. I decide I like her. I stick out my hand. "I'm Maeve Chambers."

She sticks out her hand, and for some reason, instead of saying her own name, she laughs at mine. "You have three 'e's in your name," she says, with mild interest.

"So?"

"Names are powerful. Three 'e's means when you fall in love, it's for real. My sister Heaven was the same."

Heaven. Of course someone who owns a witchy shop has a sister called Heaven.

I leave to get the bus twenty minutes later with a pocket full of rose quartz, orange-tipped calcite and tiger's eyes. She also throws in a few incense sticks for free.

"Remember to cleanse the space you read in regularly," she says chidingly. "And take care of yourself! Don't get stuck with other people's gunk!"

"Thank you," I say, unsure.

"Go raibh maith agat."

The 5.15 bus is quiet. Too late for school kids, too early for rush hour. I have my thin plastic headphones from the

43

Walkman on, the Spring 1990 tape playing in my lap. I find it oddly comforting, like white noise I can turn my brain off to. I see Rory O'Callaghan sitting on his own and it seems rude to not sit next to him after yesterday. We both say "hey" at the same time, and then lapse into silence. He is still clearly embarrassed by the incident from yesterday, so I don't mention it.

I look down at his nails. They're still painted that ballet slipper pink.

"Oh cool," I say, reaching into the paper bag in my coat pocket. "I have a stone the same colour."

I show him the rose quartz. He chucks it between his hands as though it just came straight out of a forging fire.

"Hey! Be careful! Those things aren't cheap."

"You spent money on this?" he says, clearly amused. "It doesn't have a string or a clasp. You can't even wear it."

"It's a rose quartz. It's for…" but then I can't remember what it's for. "It's for something important."

"Are you into this now? Crystals and incense and all that?"

I pull a stick of incense out of my pocket and brandish it like a wand. "Er, you could say that."

"Wow," he rakes his hand through his long, curly fringe that obscures his eyes so much of the time, pulling it back towards the crown of his head. "Maeve, you are the last person in the world I envisioned getting into New Age stuff."

His eyes are a bright hazel, that rare colour where the green and gold shine with equal lustre. There's an intense prettiness to Rory that gave him a spooky, Victorian-ghost-child look when we were kids but now is weirdly engrossing to look at.

"Me? Why am *I* the last person you'd picture?" I ask, incredulous. "Not … Vladimir Putin?"

"Putin, now see, Putin has that sort of evil where you could see him sacrificing a virgin on an altar to win another election, y'know?" Rory says playfully. "Putin is definitely more witchy than you."

"OK, so Putin is witchier than me," I concede, trying to think of more un-witchy celebrities. "What about … the Rock? No, no, sorry, take it back. The Rock is definitely witchier than me."

"Oh yeah." Rory smiles. "I mean, he's named after something from the ground. He's like earth goddess levels of witch."

We go on like this for a bit, trying to think of the un-witchiest celebrities. Eventually, when I have run out of famous people and Rory has run out of reasons that they're more magical than I am, I finally tell him about the Chokey cards.

"Oh, right, those. You had them a few days ago, didn't you?"

"Yeah," I say, careful to avoid mention of the other cards we saw that day.

"Well, go on, show me then."

He pulls three cards. The Page of Cups, the Hanged Man, the Ace of Rods.

"Well…" I start, flexing my fingers. "This Page of Cups guy right here? He represents dreams and subconscious stuff that is on the verge of coming to the surface."

I point at the page, who is holding a fish in a cup. "That's what this fish represents."

45

"Do I have to get a fish now?"

"No, you just have to work on … ideas that haven't quite formed yet. The Hanged Man, he's hanging by his foot, do you see?"

I hold up the card. Rory nods at the man who is upside down, tied to a tree by his ankle.

"He's stuck between things. Not able to commit to one thing or the other. Or maybe he's just stuck in an awkward position that he can't figure out a way to get out of."

Rory's expression suddenly changes. His face, already pale, now takes on a greyish tinge. "What do you mean by that?"

"Um … I don't know. What do you think?"

Rory says nothing.

"It's supposed to be a two-way street, these readings. You talk to me and we figure out the cards together."

"What does the last card mean?" he says, his voice stern.

"Don't you want to talk about the Hanged Man first?"

"No. What does the last card mean?"

"The Ace of Rods? It's like pure potential, pure fire. It's about you finding drive to do what you want to do. Whatever the Page and the Hanged Man are cooking up, the Ace of Rods will help you get to it."

Silence. Rory arranges his face into visible boredom. "This is dumb," he says finally.

"No, it isn't."

"It is. How do I know you're not making this shit up as you go along?"

"Because I'm not. What are you so annoyed about? It's a very mild reading. The Hanged Man isn't a bad card, Rory. He's not literally hanging."

46

"Whatever," he says. His gaze goes to the window. When the bus gets to Kilbeg, we go our separate ways with another mumbled goodbye. I'm halfway home before I realize that he still has my rose quartz.

CHAPTER SIX

I HAD HOPED THAT MY ABILITY TO MEMORIZE THE TAROT cards would spell a breakthrough for my memory generally, and that school would get easier. It doesn't. But school suddenly gets a lot more bearable when my whole day is arranged around tarot readings. People have gone nuts for them. Morning and lunch are spent in the Chokey now, and notes are constantly being passed to me and Fiona to make appointments.

I put my new crystals on the shelves of the Chokey, and even though I'm pretty sure that the lady in Divination was being overly cautious with her whole "energy" thing, I still burn my incense after every reading. I go a little heavy on it though, because by 3 p.m. all the teachers are complaining about the smell rising up through the building, but no one rats on the Chokey Card Tarot Consultancy. Even people who aren't that interested in the tarot are in love with the fact that we, as a year, have a secret. Something that sets us apart.

Fiona runs the appointment book with an iron fist, never letting anyone skip the queue or bargain their way into a better time slot. She always keeps ten minutes for herself, at the end of the day. I don't even tell her much. We draw cards but she mostly just lies on the floor and tells me how she's going to study Drama in Trinity, but that there are only seventeen places a year, and how she *has* to get in.

But despite all that, I like Fiona. She always does brilliantly in exams, but never makes a fuss about it, and she's not a lick-arse with the teachers either. And she doesn't bother herself with gossip, like everyone else does. Most of the girls who come in for a reading have the exact same questions: what their best friend is thinking, and what their best friend is saying. Moira Finch and Grace Adlett have both been in three times, just to set the record straight on why, exactly, they're no longer speaking to one another.

Some girls have incredibly benign readings and they still leave the Chokey weeping and shaking. It's all show, of course. Everyone wants to be the one who had the life-changing, future-telling, you'll-never-believe-it reading.

Fiona's on the floor again, rubbing a piece of orange-tipped calcite between her hands.

"My older brother's a doctor. He lives in Boston," she groans. "My mum thinks acting is for egomaniacs."

"Both of my brothers are engineers," I sympathize. "And my sister Abbie works for the EU, in Belgium. No one can believe that I can't pass Italian."

"Ugh, that sucks. Who cares about Italian?"

"I know, right?" I say, relieved to hear her say it. "We should all be learning Spanish."

"They speak Spanish in most of LA, you know. And there's lots of Spanish words in Tagalog."

"Really? You see, that's exactly my point."

We're friends, kind of. I think. It's hard to say.

Things get complicated, however, when Tarot Time bleeds into class time. The girls I can't fit in during my lunchtime sessions start dropping by my desk between lessons. Mr Bernard is almost always five or ten minutes late, and people take full advantage of this. They crowd around me, pleading for a reading.

"It's better if we do it in private," I say, hesitant at the gaping audience of girls too cheap to pay for a reading, or too spooked to go into the Chokey alone. "It's supposed to be a private thing."

"I don't mind!" Rebecca Hynes says gamely. "People can watch!"

"But ... I need to ... y'know, conserve my energy."

It's true. I'm beginning to feel what the Divination Lady was saying. I miss my aimless old lunch breaks, listening to Michelle talk about nose contouring. I'm starting to feel heavy at the end of every day now. I get home and don't watch Raya Silver videos any more. Two days in a row I fall asleep on my bed in my school uniform until Mum calls me for dinner.

But I still give the readings. It's hard to say no. I don't want people to think that I have ideas above my station, just because I have a deck of cards now. I have to stay nice, stay likeable, stay funny. With my grades looking the way they do, being funny is the only thing that keeps people interested in me at all.

So, when I give my classroom readings, I ham it up a bit. I play to the crowd.

"The Lovers!" I say, as if the words were fresh strawberries. "Now *this* is an interesting card."

"Is it about love?" Rebecca Hynes says, all excited. The girls crowded around exchange giggles and nudges. The only girl not peering to see the reading is Lily. I glance at her through the clutter of heads and shoulders and watch her hand reach to her hearing aid.

Is she turning it *off*?

"It is about love," I say to Rebecca, though that's not strictly true. The Lovers is more about finding harmony between two opposing forces than proper romantic love. But who wants to hear that?

"You're going to meet your soulmate," I say.

"When? Where? How?"

I stick out the deck to face her. "Ask the cards. Ask them. Ask them who your soulmate is."

I see Fiona's face from across the room. She's more annoyed by people abusing the tarot than me. She rolls her eyes at me and picks up her phone. My WhatsApp beeps. I look down at it quickly, the screen half-shielded by my pocket.

Hamming it up, much?

I grin and decide to ham it up even more. "Rebecca, you have to ask the cards with an open heart. Ask them who your soulmate is."

"Who is my soulmate?" Poor, stupid Rebecca Hynes asks the cards.

"LOUDER!"

"WHO IS MY SOULMATE?"

"The forces of magic can't hear you, Rebecca!"

"WHO IS MY BLOODY SOULMATE?" she yells.

She yanks a card from the deck. It's the Devil card.

"Satan!" I shout, trying to look afraid. "Your soulmate is Satan!"

At that moment, Mr Bernard walks into the room and the whole circle gathered around me screams in sudden panic.

"What? What's all this? What's going on here? Maeve?"

I sneak my cards away. "Nothing, sir," I say sweetly.

"*Andiamo! Andiamo!*" he commands, gesturing everyone back to their seats.

CHAPTER SEVEN

I DON'T SEE RORY FOR A FEW DAYS, BUT BY THURSDAY I'M next to him on the bus again.

"Heya," he says. "I have your thing."

He fiddles at the collar of his shirt and pulls out a long, brown string that he has fixed to my rose quartz.

"Thanks," I say, as he drops it into my hand. I'm embarrassed by how warm it is from the heat of his skin. "You're kind of into jewellery, aren't you?"

It's an innocent-enough question, but the way it comes out feels loaded and awkward.

"Yeah, I am," he answers, casually enough. "I like …"

He stretches his hands out and shows me his freshly painted nails. They are aquamarine now.

"… plumage," he concludes, with a self-effacing grin.

"I don't blame you," I say, observing his blue-green fingers. "I mean. I'm not really into make-up or jewellery or anything, but I feel like … the only reason I'm not is because everyone expects you to be, as a girl, y'know? Like, whenever I put it on, I'm so aware of how I'm supposed to be wearing it. It kind of ruins the whole experience."

He nods, looking at me as if I've started speaking a language he hasn't heard since childhood.

"Sorry, I'm talking out my hole. That probably doesn't even make sense."

"No, it does," he says, his voice completely firm. "It really does. I guess neither of us wants to do what's expected of us, then."

We're quiet for a moment, both observing the other in a completely new light.

"Hey," I say, still feeling the warm, pink stone clasped in my palms. "Why don't you just keep this?"

"What? No. It's yours."

"No, really. As I said, I don't wear jewellery."

I lift it over his head and it dangles outside of his jumper. He quickly tucks it under his clothes.

"Thanks, Maeve."

We're quiet for another few minutes as the bus rolls on, and when we get off, he lingers.

"Do you have to go straight home?" he asks.

"No," I respond. "Why?"

"I just … can't be arsed going home straight away."

"Oh. OK," I say, my stomach surging. "Well, where do you want to go?"

We walk along the Beg for a while, kicking stones and branches, not talking much. He doesn't seem to have anywhere in particular in mind. I've been down this walk before, with other boys. No one important. They're constantly looking around for somewhere private, secluded, somewhere they can touch me and I can let them. It's happened twice before. Never full sex though. Just enough so that I can feel like I'm keeping up with everyone else.

I wonder if Rory has had sex. He is seventeen, for what

it's worth. I start to blush thinking about it, then rewrap my scarf around the lower half of my face.

We get to a long, narrow underpass where some people have abandoned beer bottles and cigarette packets. This has been a hideout for teenagers for years. There's graffiti on the tunnel walls that mourns the passing of each generation's tragedy: Kurt Cobain, Amy Winehouse, Mac Miller. We sit and look at it for a little while, and talk about how pop stars and rock gods and icons are just people, people who die.

"God, we're being so goth," Rory laughs, wrapping his arms around his knees.

"Do you know what would be even MORE goth?" I say, reaching into my school bag. "A homemade mixtape."

"Holy crap," he says, as if I just pulled a severed human foot out of my bag. "Spring 1990," he reads. "Does it work?"

"You bet it works."

I play the mixtape. We take an earphone each, and I'm amazed by how many songs Rory knows.

"The Cure!" he says when "The Lovecats" comes on. "Oh, wow! And the Pixies!"

"I didn't know you knew so much about music."

"Duh. Maeve. I play guitar. I'm in a band. You knew that."

"How on earth would I know that?"

"I thought Lily would have—"

I cut him off. I don't want to talk about his sister. "I didn't know, OK? Now tell me all the song names."

He tells me all the song names. I write them down in my phone.

The cold ground starts spreading a creeping chill up my back. I stand up.

"I should go home," I say.

"Yeah, me, too."

There's a silence for a moment. I'm so confused by this surreal little afternoon with him. We've never spent this much time alone together in our lives, even though I've been having sleepovers at his house since I was six years old. There's this weird nervousness I get around him, offset by a sense of over-familiarity. Like I could say anything and he would just smile, and smile, and say something funny.

Do I *fancy* Rory?

It's too big a question, somehow. Usually when I fancy someone, I'm absolutely sure of it. It's a gut thing. Not this weird muddle of adrenalin and friendship.

"Well, see you soon," I finally say. I lurch a hug on him, an awkward clash of our bodies that is all odd angles.

"OK, yeah. See you tomorrow, probably."

And then, something incredible happens.

He cocks his head to one side, and gives me the strangest smile. A sideways smile that doesn't exist in the realm of ordinary friendship. A smile that makes my legs burn and my throat tickle.

"Maeve," he says, and his voice is low, lower than I've ever heard it. He is very close to me now. I can see the roots of his lashes where they connect to his skin. "C'm'ere."

Is he going to kiss me?

Am I about to be kissed by Rory O'Callaghan?

Well, Jesus, why not?

I close my eyes, and wait for it.

And then, nothing. No touch. Just a sound.

"My name," he says, "is Roe."

My eyes flicker open.

"Huh?"

"I want you to know what my name is," he says simply, all the magic and intimacy of the previous moment either completely disappeared or, worse, totally imagined. "So you can call me it."

"Roe. Roe," I repeat. "You want to be called Roe?"

He nods. "It's my name. I chose it."

"Wow. OK, Roe," the word settles on my mouth. "I like it," I say, truthfully. "It's kind of mysterious."

Roe turns to go and gives me one last rueful smile. "All the witches in stories know things by their true names, don't they?"

And then he leaves me to gape at the river.

CHAPTER EIGHT

"YOUR BOYFRIEND SOUNDS HOT." SAYS FIONA. "I'M JEALOUS."

Fiona is lying on her back in the Chokey, five minutes before our first class. I almost never see the girls she had with her the first day. I sense that, like me, Fiona knows a lot of people but doesn't have any particularly special friendships. For the first week of the tarot phase, five or six girls would be here in the morning, but now that most people have had their tarot read at least once, the sessions have eased off. Fiona still shows up every morning though.

"He's not my boyfriend," I say, defensively. "We didn't even kiss."

"I like the name thing. Has he asked you to use different pronouns?"

"No."

"Has he text you since?"

"I don't think he has my number."

"Hmmmmm. How about we ask the cards? Can we do that?"

"Sure," I say, shuffling them. When I'm not in class, I'm shuffling. It's soothing. It helps empty my mind when, at night, all I can hear is the voices of the girls in my class, each one of their problems clamouring in my ear like clowns trying to push through a car door.

"Cards, cards, cards, what should Maeve do about her fancy man?" Fiona plucks one at random from her upside-down position on the floor.

"Here we go," she says brandishing it at me. "Upside-down man."

"It's the Hanged Man!" I say, grabbing hold of it. "That's the card Roe drew the other day on the bus!"

"Woah."

"He got super weird about it. He didn't want to talk or anything. I just told him about how the Hanged Man was about being suspended between two states."

"Or genders," says Fiona thoughtfully. "Maybe he's enby – non-binary. Roe is kind of a gender-neutral name."

"I guess," I say. "I'm not really sure what that means, though."

"I think it can mean different things for different people. I have an actor friend who is enby."

"I get it, Fiona, you have actor friends."

"Don't be a gowl." She grabs an old textbook and hits me with it. The bell sounds.

"We should get to class," she says, and neither one of us moves.

"What do you have now?" I ask.

"English. You?"

"Bio."

There is a small, self-conscious quiet while we both ponder asking each other the same question.

"Yeah," I say, and lie on the floor with her, my jumper a cushion. The Chokey is really quite cosy, once you get used to the smell. "Skip."

⬟　⬟　⬟

That afternoon, no one shows up to teach History. This happens a lot at St Bernadette's. Sometimes teachers just don't appear because of a scheduling conflict or a sudden emergency. They usually rush in with a supply teacher for the first years, but they tend to be a bit laissez-faire with the fourth, fifth and sixth years. Twenty minutes after the bell goes, we're still alone, no adult supervision.

"Maeve," Michelle says. "Do my tarot."

"I've done your tarot, Mich. Three times."

To tell you the truth, I'm getting a little bored of this now. I like being famous for something, but I hate how everyone expects me to be a performing monkey. It's always been like this, with me. If I think I'll get a laugh for something, I'll do it. That's how I ended up throwing the shoe at Mr Bernard. Tarot hasn't elevated my reputation, but set it in stone.

"Do mine," says Niamh. "You haven't done mine since Wednesday."

"Your tarot hasn't changed that much in two days, Niamh. Anyway, I left them in the Chokey."

"Maeve, you liar. You haven't left them in the Chokey. They're right here," Michelle fishes them out of my blazer on the back of my chair.

What?

"Did you put them in there?" I ask snappishly. "Were you messing with my stuff?"

"Jesus, no. God, you're so cranky," she huffs. "We're just *bored*."

"I can't keep reading for the same people over and over,"

I respond, peevishly, and consider the matter closed.

"Lily hasn't had a reading yet," she says.

"She hasn't asked for one," I snap.

Lily is sitting where she always sits, at the very far left of the top row. Her head's in another one of those weird books that I tried to get her to stop reading in first year. She hasn't engaged with any of this tarot stuff. Partly because I'm sure it frightens her, and partly because she doesn't talk to me any more.

"Lily doesn't want a tarot reading."

"Sure she does," Niamh says, before calling out to Lily. "Hey! Lil! Do you want Maeve to do your tarot?"

"Lil!" Niamh shouts again, and because Lily still can't completely hear what she's saying, she gets out of her chair and crosses the room to us.

"Hi," Lily says shortly. "What is it?"

"We were just wondering if you want to get your tarot done."

"Why were you wondering that?"

"Well, because you're the only girl in the year who hasn't got hers done yet. We thought you'd be curious."

Niamh isn't a mean bitch all the time. She's actually pretty nice. But like a lot of girls she has a lot of Mean Bitch Potential that comes out around easy targets like Lily O'Callaghan.

Lily tucks her hair behind her bad ear, something she always does when she's nervous. It's like she remembers all of her weaknesses at once and compulsively needs to show you them, the way a dog shows you the soft pink skin on his belly.

"I'm not curious," she says. She still hasn't looked at me yet. She doesn't, if she can help it.

"See?" I say to Niamh. "She doesn't want to. So drop it."

"Are you scared?" goads Niamh. It's a cliché, but it's a cliché for a reason. It works.

Lily's lip twitches.

"No," she says.

"Then just pick three cards. Any three," says Niamh, grabbing the Chokey cards from the table.

Lily delicately picks her cards with her thumb and forefinger, holding each one by her fingernail as if to minimize contact with them. She places them face down on the table.

"Are you going to turn them over, Maeve?" Lily asks, and suddenly there's fire in her voice. Then, she looks me right in the eye. "You're used to turning on people, aren't you?"

There is a loud, audible gasp. Lily just *called me out.*

It feels like everyone in the room is looking at us. Even Fiona has put her phone down and given up the "over it" look she usually adopts for class time.

It's impossible to know what to expect from Lily. I blush with shame thinking of yesterday evening, when I closed my eyes and waited for her older brother to kiss me. Did he tell her? Are they close? They weren't a year ago, but they might be now. They're both weird enough, after all.

I flip Lily's first card over. It's the Five of Cups, aka, a picture of a woman crying with some knocked-over cups around her.

Lily looks straight at me. "What does that mean, then?"

I suddenly feel frightened of her. Where is the prissy,

babyish Lily I used to know? The one who used to beg me to tell her ghost stories, but then cry if they got too scary?

"Sadness," I say with a wince.

Lily and I were both put in the slow-reading class in primary school. We were six and still struggling with "C-A-T" and "D-O-G". When our mums realized how close our houses were, they became friends. The whole arrangement was magic for me and Lily. We had weekly sleepovers, went on family holidays together, tore around the wildlife park while our mums sat and chatted in the cafe for hours and hours. We both got out of the slow-reading class, but we stayed best friends.

Until secondary school came, and who you were friends with was now much, much more important.

Or. At least. I thought it was.

"Sadness," Lily repeats sceptically. "That sounds a bit *general*."

"What do you mean?"

"People are always sad. People can be sad for lots and lots of reasons," she says coolly. "Why am I sad?"

Because I abandoned you.

I can hear Niamh and Michelle getting bored and annoyed by how slow this is going. Do they remember, how me and Lily used to be friends?

"You're sad because..." I flip the next card over. The Three of Swords. Heartbreak. "Because someone dumped you."

There's a shriek of laughter. "Oh my Godddddddd," says Michelle. "YOU had a BOYFRIEND?"

"That's a pretty amazing accomplishment, Lily, well done," says Niamh with patronizing sincerity.

Lily's face goes red. For a moment, I'm sure that she's going to say any number of things that she knows about me, and that whatever tenuous popularity I've gained over the last few weeks will dissolve into nothing. Even though we haven't been proper friends in over a year, our mums still talk a lot.

No one has ever looked at me with the kind of hatred that Lily O'Callaghan is looking at me with right now. I can feel it burning through my bones like acid.

"Flip over the last card, Maeve," she says tightly.

I flip it over. At first, the letters don't even make sense. They take a few seconds to form in my head, and I'm momentarily transported back to being six years old and sounding out every letter of "boat".

H O U S E K E E P E R

My mouth opens and closes in complete shock. How can the Housekeeper card be here, when I know for a fact it's locked in my top drawer? I definitely took it out.

"What does it mean?" asks Lily, all her fire turned to smoke. She's always been a huge believer in magic, equally fascinated and terrified by fairy forts, changelings, witches, banshees. She would seek these things out, but then frighten herself with her own belief. Even if Lily and I were still friends, there's not a chance she would have asked for a tarot reading willingly. Her respect for the occult is too high to want to actually engage with it.

"I don't know," I say, and she can tell right away that the tremor in my voice is real. "It's the extra card."

"Tell me what it means," Lily says. Her eyes are locked with the illustration, the woman with the knife in her teeth

64

and the mangy greyhound at her side. "It's bad, isn't it? Tell me what it means, Maeve?"

"There are no bad cards!" Fiona, who has apparently been watching this whole exchange, interjects. "Isn't that what you always say, Maeve? No bad cards?"

"Yeah," I say hoarsely. "No bad cards."

Lily looks as if she's about to burst into tears. "Tell me, Maeve. I'm not too much of a baby to know."

"I don't know what it means," I say again.

Lily's face reddens, her nostrils flaring. Pure, molten rage is surging past the anxiety in her voice. She hates me for doing this to her. For putting her on the spot like this, for making her fear something I *knew* she would.

"This is so like you," she snarls, and girls who weren't even paying attention to the reading look up.

"This is so *Maeve*," she finishes, her teeth gritted.

"Lily," I say, keeping my voice low in an attempt to hush her. The panic and guilt I feel at involving Lily is being compounded by the sheer terror of seeing a card I know I removed. "Stop. I genuinely don't know what it means, OK?"

But Lily doesn't want to stop. She's slow to anger, but when she does, she won't be told to shut up.

"You'll do anything for a bit of attention, won't you, Maeve? But then, when all eyes are on you, you've got nothing to back it up."

The girls around us go "ooooooooooh" and I hear one "me-ow!" near the door.

"I can't believe we were ever friends," Lily says, staring at the Housekeeper. "You're not a good friend, Maeve."

Fiona winces with the brutality of it, her face heavy

with pity for me. Over her shoulder, I see Michelle and Niamh exchange a look. A look that says: "Wow, if even *that* loser doesn't want her for a friend, why are we hanging out with her?"

I can't just let Lily say that to me, not in front of everyone. I have to fight back with *something*.

"I wish I had never been friends with you," I snap. "Lily, I wish you would just disappear."

Lily looks at me like I've slammed her fingers in a car door. She takes one step back, her eyes brimming, and bites down on her lip.

The bell goes, and everyone starts moving on to their last lesson of the week. I have Civic Studies now. Lily has Geography. After class, I look around for her, gnawing my fingernails. I can undo this, can't I?

How could I have told Lily that I never wanted to be friends with her? The truth is, I haven't laughed — really, clutch-your-guts *laughed* — since Lily and I stopped being friends. I miss her, and I have missed her for a long time. Even before I severed her off like a bad limb last year, I had been putting distance between us since we started secondary school. I used to think this was normal. Normal to grow apart, normal to grieve the distance. It was a healthy grief, the grief you feel for Barbie dolls and pony figures when you become too old to play with them and still be socially acceptable. But Lily isn't some object that can be chucked to the back of a toy chest. She's a person. A great one.

I can't find her after school, and I don't see Roe on the bus, either.

I spend all weekend worrying about her, asking Mum

faux-casual questions about Mrs O'Callaghan and whether they've spoken lately. They haven't. Mum and Dad go to Lisbon on Sunday night and Joanne and I get takeaway. We eat it in front of an episode of *The Masked Singer*.

At around ten o'clock, the power cuts suddenly and the room goes dark. I jump up, yelping like a dog in a thunderstorm.

"Jesus, Maeve. Relax. It's only blown a fuse."

"I know. Sorry. I just got a fright."

Our house is old and badly wired, so this kind of stuff is relatively common. Jo stands on a chair in the pantry and flips a switch in the fuse box. The lights come back on immediately, but the TV doesn't. Jo gets up and fiddles with it, but quickly realizes she doesn't know what she's doing, and gives up. We sit in front of it, completely out of ideas.

"I guess the TV's broken," she says lamely. "Dad's going to have a field day with this. 'I leave you alone for two minutes', etcetera, etcetera."

I look at our reflections in the shining black screen. Two sisters who look nothing at all alike. Joanne looks and moves like a professional tennis player. She's all lean and muscular, with big cheekbones and a vaguely Nordic air about her. Her blonde-streaked hair is always in a ponytail. She looks wholesome, like the sort of person who should always be eating carrot sticks. I have an aesthetic that Mum likes to call "straight off the Armada", which means that I've got a lot of dark, wiry hair and a unibrow that I have to pluck every other morning if I want it to stay invisible. My brother Cillian looks like this, too. "Maeve and Cill are more Mediterranean," she always says, which is remarkable considering no one on

67

either side of our family is from anywhere but Ireland.

"Are you OK?" she says, poking me with a chopstick, suddenly moved to speak after hours of companionable silence. "You haven't said a word all weekend."

"I'm fine," I say blandly.

"Do you want to practise your tarot on me?"

"No, thanks. I'm kind of over it, now."

"Over it? Already?"

Maybe I'm overreacting. Lily is sixteen now, after all, same as me. She's probably grown up a lot over the past year. Her overactive imagination and her easiness to scare are probably things she's left behind, but I keep thinking about how fierce she was during the reading. She gave as good as she got, and forced me to consider her as an equal, rather than a childish old friend. It felt like an ocean had moved within her since I last spoke to her, an ocean that's made us drift even farther apart.

I feel sick every time I look at the cards. I've leafed through them a couple of times, to try and weed out the Housekeeper card, but she's disappeared. Does Lily have it? Did she pocket it in all the excitement?

I'll apologize on Monday. I'll even give up the tarot consultancy, and I'll be nice to Lily, and then maybe we can think about being friends again. Now that me and Roe are friends, we could all pal around together.

Except Lily doesn't come to school on Monday. She doesn't come in on Tuesday, either.

It's not until Wednesday that the police show up.

CHAPTER NINE

THE FIRST I HEAR ABOUT THE POLICE IS FROM NIAMH, WHO saw them waiting outside Sister Assumpta's office that morning.

HOT COP, she WhatsApps the group. **THIS IS NOT A DRILL. There is a HOT COP in the building.**

As you can expect from an all-girls Catholic school with only one male teacher — if you can really call Mr Bernard a man, or a teacher — everyone goes nuts. Three people message, **PICS!** at once.

Niamh sends through a picture of two Gardaí in luminous jackets. One is a blonde woman, stocky and fair, with a tiny little ponytail at the base of her neck. The other is apparently the Hot Cop in question: a very tall, very thin, tawny-haired man of about thirty-five.

Niamh, Michelle pings back. **You call THAT a hot cop? We need to talk about your taste.**

Why are there Gardaí in school? I text, but no one responds. It's just Michelle and Niamh now, getting increasingly defensive over what constitutes as an attractive man.

Are you going to go up to him, Niamh? someone else asks.

I will in my HOLE.

Several laughing emojis.

I text Fiona the same question. No response. She's busy

this week with some new performance troupe she's formed with her older acting pals. There were pictures of her in wartime fishnets on Instagram Stories all yesterday evening.

I keep typing out messages to the group that I don't send. I'm too afraid to say what I really think is happening: that this is about Lily, and her absence over the last few days.

Morning classes tick by. Maths, then Geography. We are learning about soil creep. *"The slow movement of rock and soil down a slope."* That's what the book says. I try to keep up with the teacher but my eyes keep skittering over that one sentence. *"The slow movement of rock and soil down a slope."* The words on the page are merging with some internal gut instinct, and I feel as if I'm about to be crushed under the weight of a heavy, endless mass.

Then, it happens. Ten minutes before the end of class, there's a knock on the classroom door. Miss Harris enters, flanked by Hot Cop and Blonde Cop.

"Hello, girls," she says, trying to keep her voice bright. "This is Detective Garda Sarah Griffin and Inspector Matthew Ward. I know you'll all be keen to have your morning break, but they just have a couple of questions for you before you do. It's about Lily."

I can feel the hovering glance of twenty-one pairs of eyes all on me. I don't think anyone had truly noticed Lily's absence until now, and I imagine most of them forgot about the Housekeeper card by late Friday evening. But now that they've heard her name, they're starting to put it all together.

"Good morning, everyone," says Griffin. "Unfortunately, your classmate Lily O'Callaghan has been missing since Sunday night. While we won't go into the details here, her family are all very worried, and we would very much like anyone who knows Lily well or who spoke to her at school last week to please step forward with any information you have. I cannot express enough how even the smallest conversation could be helpful to us."

You can literally hear the sound of a roomful of girls catching their breath at once. An inward suck of tension, of air being pulled through teeth.

Griffin's eyes flick over the room. I can see her mentally logging this. Something to write in her notebook later. Her stare hops from girl to girl. She's figuring out who she's going to pull aside if no one puts their hand up.

The Garda Niamh fancies starts to talk. "Now, I don't want any of you to panic," he says, his voice kind. "In the vast majority of cases, girls of Lily's age and description tend to have run away from home. Usually they come back on their own. But we want to make sure that Lily is safe, so if anyone knows about a boyfriend, or a friend – or an ... *organization* – that Lily might have been a part of."

Detective Griffin suddenly looks at her subordinate sharply, as if the word "organization" was not part of their agreed script.

More girls glance over their shoulder. A few nudge each other and look at me. If I don't say something now, I'm going to be outed. Griffin is going to triangulate these stolen glances and realize that I am at the centre of them. I put my hand in the air.

Miss Harris's eyes widen. She's only been here a couple of years. I don't think she actually knows that Lily and I used to be best friends.

71

"Maeve?"

"Hi," I say slowly. "I think I might know something about Lily."

All three adults blink at me and then look at each other in an expression of "huh, we didn't think it would be that easy."

"I think it might be my fault," I say.

And I am led from the room, the heat of their stares molten as a dragon's breath. Thankfully, I'm in the hallway before the tears start.

I'm led into Sister Assumpta's office, a bright airy room where they bring rich parents and ex-alumni when they're looking for donations to fix the roof. I've never been in this room before, though of course I see snatches of the lemon walls and the over-stuffed couch whenever I pass it, usually to get told off in Miss Harris's pokier office.

Now I'm in here and I don't know what to do with myself. No one has a directive, either. Stand up? Sit down? If I were being punished my natural instinct would be to stay standing, but the air around me is so tense with concern and gratitude that my knees feel weak. My bones have been replaced by a stack of almost-empty shampoo bottles, ready to be kicked over in the shower.

"Now, Maeve," Miss Harris says, touching my arm as she sits down on the couch. "Why don't you sit down next to me, grab a tissue, and just breathe for a second."

I flop down, still streaming tears. Jesus Christ. What must she think of me? Through my tears, I can see a slight furrow emerging on her forehead. She's confused by this. She probably has a list in her office of sensitive girls and I very much doubt my name is on it.

I take a tissue all the same, huffing the contents of my nose into it. I grab another. And another. From the corner of my eye, I see Sister Assumpta in all her ancient glory hobbling into view.

There's a joke about Sister Assumpta that they keep her in this office with the phone unplugged because it's cheaper than sending her to a retirement home. It's not exactly a nice joke, but it started long before I was at St Bernadette's and it will continue until Sister Assumpta dies. Which, it seems, she has no plans on doing. Just as every human civilization thinks that it will be the one to witness the Apocalypse, every wave of girls that comes through this school is convinced they are going to be the one to witness Assumpta's passing.

Sister Assumpta is a tiny woman. She is somewhere between sixty-five and a hundred and three years old, depending on the weather. In winter she seems like the oldest person to ever have lived, clad in layers of knitwear and thermal socks that she straps to her hands.

During our first month of secondary school, Lily and I were hanging around in an empty classroom during lunch. Sister Assumpta suddenly flung open the door with a vigour I haven't seen in the old woman before or since. She pointed a bent finger at the two of us.

"You two," she said. "Come with me."

We were so new to St Bernadette's that we weren't sure whether we had broken some rule without knowing it. We also still thought that Sister Assumpta had power, which she doesn't.

We followed her outside, to where her 1963 sky-blue Volkswagen Bug was parked under a tree.

"She still *drives*?" Lily asked in a whisper.

I stifled a giggle. "How is that *legal*?"

As she unlocked the car, we got a chance to gaze at the inside, and quickly realized that this beautiful little Bug hadn't been driven in some time. The window had been left slightly unrolled, and the car had filled up with piles of fallen leaves, some the dark orange of old pumpkins, some as green as a traffic light. The car clearly hadn't left the school car park in years.

Sister Assumpta popped open the boot and pointed to three decaying cardboard boxes festering inside. "Carry these in," she said shortly. "Lift from the legs. You're good strong girls, now. That's it."

We followed her back to the school and dumped the boxes in what would become Miss Harris's office but then was just a big closet. As soon as Sister's back was turned, I opened a box and picked out a velvet jewellery case. There were about twelve cases, maybe more. I clicked open one and found endless strings of costume jewellery. Plastic pearls, glass diamonds. Stuff that probably wasn't worth much individually, but together, probably came to a few hundred euro.

We talked about it for months. The VW Bug filled with leaves, the masses of cheap jewellery, the crooked finger. The feeling that we were just one small part of some vast plan our school principal had, and perhaps was still completing. We wrote stories about it. Lily would start with two sentences, then fold the paper down, then I would write two sentences. Before long we had an ongoing saga, an epic romance about an ex-nun and a Brazilian count. Every time we saw Sister Assumpta after that, we would explode into giggles, and we never told anyone why.

Seeing Sister Assumpta now, this tiny deranged little ex-nun with her sock hands and her ankle-length navy skirt, everything starts to dawn on me.

Lily is gone. An entire life of memories, private jokes and pet names are up in smoke, and I'm the one to blame. Did the tarot reading on Friday really upset her so much that she couldn't face coming to school on Monday? Did she run away?

I start howling again. Crying, it turns out, is very hard to stop once you start. Sister Assumpta is peering at me through her enormous owl glasses, utterly mystified.

"This is a private office," Sister A says, clearly annoyed. "I didn't say you could have police in here."

"I know, Sister," says Miss Harris. "But these are rather special circumstances, so I didn't think you would mind."

"There's a girl crying in here," says Sister A. "Why is there a girl crying in here?"

"This is about Lily O'Callaghan, Sister," replies Miss Harris, trying to keep her cool. "The missing girl."

"Who?"

"Look," Detective Griffin says finally. "We really can't take a statement from Maeve unless she has a parent or guardian present, and she's clearly very upset. How about we spin her home, we can talk to her parents, and Maeve can speak to us there? Where she's comfortable?"

"Isn't that Harriet Evans' little sister? The youngest one?" Sister Assumpta pipes up again.

"No, Sister," Miss Harris replies, exasperated. She turns

75

to Griffin. "I think that would be a good idea."

So that's what we do. Everyone's on morning break, crossing the yard to access the car park behind the building. There are girls in my year artfully lounging against walls and mossy, mildewed benches. They straighten up as they see me being dog-walked by two Gardaí, standing on tiptoes to watch me leave.

A breathtaking silence falls over the yard. Everything seems to slow down and mute itself. Even the skipping rope that some of the younger girls are swinging becomes soundless.

Then, I hear it. A lone voice calling like a shotgun across a desert plain.

"Witch!"

Griffin's head cocks.

"WITCH!"

Griffin gazes around at the yard, trying to locate the source of the sound. It's too late though. There are too many of them.

"WITCH! WITCH! WITCH! WITCH! WITCH!"

And it keeps going until we get into the squad car, and leave St Bernadette's.

CHAPTER TEN

WE'RE A MILE AWAY FROM THE HOUSE WHEN I REMEMBER that Mum and Dad are in Portugal, and I have no idea whether Jo has classes today. I unlock the front door and Tutu jumps on everyone. Usually I wouldn't feel the need to apologize about the dog. But now, within the rigid formality of having two Gardaí in my house, everything feels like proof of my obvious guilt. The jumping dog, the dirty plates in the kitchen, the gnarled brick of butter still left out on the table from breakfast. Everything around me feels like evidence of what a scruffy, scrubby little urchin I am. A bad housekeeper, and a bad friend.

"Jo!" I shout up the stairs, hoping she's home. No response. I smile at Griffin and Ward apologetically.

"Joannnnnnne!" I shout again, charging up the stairs.

"What?" She opens her bedroom door crankily, dressed in joggers and towelling her wet hair. Oh, thank God she's home.

"There's ... uh. There's police here."

"Excuse me?"

"Downstairs. I have to give a statement. Lily is missing."

"Lily *O'Callaghan*?" Joanne claps her hand to her mouth, her eyes already moist. "For how long?"

"Sunday night. Look, just come downstairs, will you?"

77

Joanne comes down and I shakily make introductions. Detective Griffin gives a modified version of what she told the class. She gives Jo more detail, though, more relaxed without the eyes of twenty teenage girls boring into her.

"The last Lily's parents saw of her was on Sunday night. She went to bed at around ten, but according to her brother it wasn't unusual for Lily to stay up drawing or reading until one or two in the morning."

Her *brother*.

"The O'Callaghans say they didn't notice any particular changes in her behaviour that weekend, although maybe a little more quiet than usual, on reflection."

"Lily was always quiet," Jo says. "She's just like that."

"That's the impression we're getting. In any case, her mother didn't realize she was missing until around 8 a.m. on Monday morning, when Lily didn't respond to numerous calls. Eventually Mrs O'Callaghan opened the bedroom door, and she was gone. She didn't take anything with her. No clothes, no bag. She didn't even change out of her pyjamas, by the looks of things."

Jo and I are silent, both of us imagining Lily trudging down her suburban road in pyjamas. I find myself wondering, strangely, what kind of pyjamas Lily wears now.

"We're looking for anyone who can give us information about Lily," Griffin concludes. "And Maeve volunteered herself."

"But, Maeve, Lily hasn't been round here in ages. You two fell out last year, didn't you?"

Griffin gives me that look again. That sharp, enquiring look that says, *Well that's interesting.*

"Yes, but … we spoke again on Friday. I gave her a tarot reading. I didn't want to, and neither did she, but the girls in school sort of … made it happen."

"I'm sorry, tarot reading? Like, the cards?" Ward asks.

"Yeah," I reply. "I've been giving tarot readings for everyone in our year. I found a deck in school and I learned the card meanings. It wasn't a big deal. Or, I didn't think it was. Anyway, I gave Lily a reading and she got upset. Then she didn't come back to school."

"What did you tell her in the reading? Did you say she was going to die, or something?"

"No, not at all. I would never. The cards don't predict the future, they show your present." I don't know why I'm delivering my little rehearsed speech on tarot readings to a detective. As if she cares.

"What did Lily's reading say?"

"It said she was very lonely. And heartbroken."

"Lonely? For a boyfriend? Did she have an ex-boyfriend she was in contact with?"

"No," I shake my head firmly. "Lily wasn't like that. The reading was about me. I…"

I splutter again. Jo asks if I want some water, and I shake my head. I take another run at the sentence.

"I used to be Lily's best friend. And then we stopped – *I* stopped – being friends with her."

"Did you have a fight?"

I bury my face in my hands. No, we didn't have a proper fight. I wish we had. A fight presumes that both parties are equally at fault.

The truth of the thing is that I froze Lily out, plain and

simple. I started getting friendlier with some girls who were technically higher up the social pecking order, and, for a while, I thought Lily could climb with me. Me, Michelle, Niamh, and Lily would all sit around at lunch. I knew the girls didn't like Lily as much as I did, but I thought that could change once they got to know her. They would see how funny she was, how utterly original.

But it didn't work out like that.

"What are you staring at, Lily?" Niamh asked one day when she caught Lily staring at them taking selfies together. "You're always looking at us."

"I was just thinking, how cool would it be if you took all these selfies, and they aged and got all disgusting, but you stayed the same? And every time you opened your phone, you just saw this gnarled tree-stump face. Like in *The Picture of Dorian Gray*. But with phones."

I laughed at that. I hadn't read *The Picture of Dorian Gray*, but Lily had, and she had told me the plot. We acted it out. We were still into "acting things out", even though we were definitely too old for games like that.

"You're weird," Niamh retorted. At first, she said it warmly, as if giving her the benefit of the doubt. But she kept saying it. The last straw came when we started hanging out with some boys from St Anthony's at the old tennis courts after school, and Lily licked Keith Delaney.

"Maeve," Niamh rang me that night. "We need to talk. It's about Lily."

"About the licking," I countered, knowing already what this was about. "She was just doing this game we play sometimes."

The Licking Game was a thing we had invented a few

years earlier. It started when Roe told us that it was impossible to lick your own elbow, and we spent about two days trying. That spun into a years-long game of trying to lick things in difficult or risky places, even if it was just putting your tongue on it for a second. We would go into Waterstones on a Saturday and pretend to browse from across the store, keeping one eye on each other, and then slowly – so, so, slowly – put our tongue on whatever book we were pretending to read. Then we would leave the shop, holding each other and screaming with laughter.

It's one of those "you had to be there" things, I suppose.

So when Lily, after hours and hours of patiently waiting for something fun to happen at the tennis courts, gently tapped her tongue on the back of Keith's neck, it was her way of saying: *Hey, can we just have some fun, already?*

When I lamely tried to explain Licking to Niamh, she was silent for a time. "Look, Maeve," she said, "*we* never asked to be friends with her, and *we* don't want to hang around with her any more."

And that was it. I started snubbing Lily at school, turning my back on her, refusing to meet her eye when she spoke to me. I told Joanne to tell her I was out when she phoned the house looking for me. Eventually, Lily got the hint. The Licking of Keith Delaney turned out to be her final act as my best friend.

I turn my face back to Griffin. "No, we didn't have a fight. We just grew apart."

"Can you put a date on that, Maeve? When you stopped being friends."

"Just … just before the Christmas holidays. Last Christmas. So, around fourteen months ago, I suppose."

Ward looks irritated. He is writing everything down. "So, Maeve, are you saying that you have no relevant information about Lily from the last year? Did she have any … any chat rooms she visited? Any *special* friends?"

Griffin cocks an eyebrow at him. "I'm not sure if 'chat rooms' are quite the thing any more, Ward. And anyway, this *is* relevant. Tell me more about this tarot reading, Maeve. Is there anything else that happened?"

I bite my lip. "Yes. A card came up. One that didn't belong to the rest of the pack."

"Can you show me? Do you have your cards now?"

I dig them out of my school bag, sitting on the floor next to me. I flip them over so they're face up.

"See, all these cards, they each have a place. They belong to a suit or a pattern. But this one card, it came up only for Lily. It was this scary-looking woman called the Housekeeper. She was all on her own."

"What does the Housekeeper mean?"

"I don't *know*. That's why Lily got freaked out. She believes in this stuff. More than most people. More than me. When I told her I didn't know the card, she got scared. I was scared, too, because I thought I had taken the Housekeeper out of the deck."

"Can you show me the Housekeeper now?"

"That's the thing," I say, biting my lip. "I don't know where it's gone."

There's a quaver in my voice, as if I'm afraid the card is going to walk through the door.

"So you were frightened, and that made Lily frightened," Griffin says. "Her brother mentioned that she was quite susceptible to that kind of thing."

My heart jumps at the word "brother" again. Roe. I have been so upset at the thought of Lily in danger I had completely forgotten about Roe, and how he must feel about all of this.

"Yeah. I was always kind of … the leader, I suppose," I say lamely. "Lily always feels what I feel."

"So this is why you were so jumpy all weekend," Jo says. "You were feeling bad about Lily."

I nod.

"That's why all those girls were chanting 'witch'," reasons Griffin.

Another nod.

"There's something else," I say, and I can feel the three adults physically lean towards me, wanting to catch my words as though I were spitting tickets like an arcade game. My eyes flicker to Jo, hoping that she will protect me when I tell the final piece of information, the thing that will reveal just what a cruel and terrible friend I really am.

"Me and Lily had sort of … an argument on Friday. She said some mean stuff to me, and then I said some stuff to her."

"What kind of stuff?"

"She said … she said she didn't know why we were ever friends, and I said I wished we never had been."

A thick, porridge-y lump forms in my throat. "And then I said that I wished she would just disappear."

Griffin, Ward and Joanne all look at each other, wide-eyed.

83

"And now she *has* disappeared," I say, my eyes filling up again. "Lily's missing and it's all my fault."

Jo puts her arm around me.

"Mae," she says affectionately. "It sounds like you've freaked yourself out over some spooky nonsense. It's OK. It's not your fault. Whatever has happened with Lily, it's not as if you were bullying her, or preying on her in some weird way. You were every bit as freaked out as she was. I remember a sleepover where they played with a Ouija board and Maeve rang Mum to bring her home."

At this last bit she smiles at Griffin and Ward, in a sort of "girls will be girls" way.

"Listen to your sister, Maeve. There's no point beating yourself up about this. The way to help Lily is to tell us everything you know about your best friend. Anything could be helpful."

My best friend. Present tense. Who treats their best friend like this?

I talk, and they write. They ask endless questions about Lily, none of them specific. They sound like they've been taken from *The Big Book of Teenage Problems*.

"Did Lily ever have any problems with bullying? Catty behaviour among the other girls?" Griffin asks. "Was she concerned about body issues? Drink or drugs?"

Drink and drugs: that's easy. No way. Once, we decided to drink a bottle of vodka, neat, while on her trampoline. Just to see what happened. We got about a third into the bottle before Lil vomited down the side and vowed never to drink again.

Body issues: maybe. It doesn't feel likely, though. The

summer we were twelve Lily shot up five inches. She went from being a kind of monkey-faced kid to a somewhat gawky teen, the tallest girl in our year by a good inch or two. It never seemed to bother her. She has that vaguely alien look you see on certain Russian fashion models, the ones that aren't necessarily pretty but seem to be picked for photograph shoots that require disjointed positions wearing sack dresses.

Bullying: well, that's a little more complex. The girls at St Bernadette's could be bitches, sure, and even the kids at primary school were cruel. There were weird prying questions about her hearing aid on good days and outright insults on bad days. Here's the thing about Lily, though – she genuinely doesn't care. People say that all the time, but for her, it's true. Whenever anyone was mean to us for being in the slow-learning class, she would just roll her eyes. "Don't worry about that, Maeve. It's just *noise*."

Because, for her, it was. Lily is an expert lip-reader, entirely self-taught from birth, so no one caught on about her hearing issue until relatively late. She learned to listen for the right sounds by tuning the wrong sounds out, and it had a permanent effect on her personality. If someone's saying something she doesn't want to hear, she simply decides not to hear it.

I wish I could be that way. I wish I didn't care what people like Michelle or Niamh thought of me.

"I think that's quite enough," says Joanne, after what feels like hours of questioning. "Maeve needs to do her homework and eat dinner. You can phone me if you have any other questions."

The Gardaí sneak a look at my phone on the coffee table.

"You're to contact *me*," she repeats protectively.

Ward flips his notebook closed, and they get up to leave.

"You've been amazing, Maeve," Ward says, smiling at me. You can see why Niamh thought he was handsome. "You've certainly ruled out a lot of things."

As Joanne walks them to the front door, I hear Griffin talking out loud, mostly to herself. "Frankly, she ruled out so much I'm not sure what's left."

CHAPTER ELEVEN

THE NEXT MORNING, I TRY TO CONVINCE JO TO LET ME STAY
home from school. No dice.

"If Mum were here, she'd let me stay home," I plead.
My classmates yelling "witch" across the yard is still echo-
ing in my ears, vibrating like a can kicked around an alley.

"No," she says firmly. "I'm out all day and I don't want
you home, watching the Kardashians and getting depressed.
You'll only start blaming yourself, and I won't be here to
talk you out of it. I will drive you in though. How's that for
a compromise?"

"Fine," I say grouchily, even though I know she has
a point. In fairness to Jo, she did a pretty good impression of
an ideal sister last night. I talked all night about Lily, about
the tarot consultancy, and how our friendship fell apart
when I started being friends with Niamh and Michelle.

It's not something I've talked to anyone about before.
Mum and Dad did ask why Lily had suddenly stopped
coming over, but I always responded huffily, trying to imply
that there was a fight that involved both of us and not just
me. Lily's mum tried to bring it up with mine a few times.
I heard them talking about it.

"It's such a shame, isn't it?" Mrs O'Callaghan would say
tersely.

"They'll come back around. Girls always fall out and make up again," Mum would respond.

To this, Mrs O'Callaghan would say nothing. She was too clever and too kind to say, "Well, not Lily. It must be that nasty cow of yours who's the problem," but I could tell she was thinking it whenever she passed me in the hallway or at the school gates.

"Look, Maeve," Jo says, with her arm around me. "You shouldn't have frozen Lily out the way you did. But it's clear you feel terrible about it, and have for a long time. When Lily comes back, you're going to apologize to her, and ask, very nicely, if she wants to be pals again. In the meantime, you can't take responsibility for her disappearance."

"But I was the one who gave her the reading, Jo. I upset her. *I said she should disappear.* Then she went missing."

"But didn't you give twenty other girls tarot readings? And they weren't all rosy, were they? I bet some scary cards came up there, too."

"I suppose," I say, and rest my head on her chest.

"The thing is, Mae, Lily has always marched to the beat of her own drum. Even when she was a really little kid. She's always been the sort of girl you saw in a crowd and thought, *Oh yeah, she's going to do something different.* Now, whether that's run away and join a cult, or solve world hunger using three toothpicks, I was never quite sure."

I'm silent as we drive to school, turning this over and over in my head. Jo's right about Lily. The air around her has always been charged with something else. She's like a walking electromagnetic field. And there I was, her lumpy friend who could just about grab on to the lowest rung of popularity, and abandon someone truly great in the process. Why wasn't I unique and strange? Why couldn't I solve world hunger with three toothpicks?

The fact of the matter is this: I dumped Lily, but she would probably have been better off dumping me.

"I'm going to come in with you," Jo announces when we get to the school gates.

"What?"

"I want to talk to Miss Harris. I don't want the police to be hauling you out of class, trying to tap you up for more Lily information. I could tell that Detective Griffin's not done with us, not by a long shot."

Every morning Miss Harris stands outside the front door of the school until the bell rings, but she crosses the car park the moment she sees us.

"Good morning, Maeve. And you must be Joanne," she says brightly, sticking her hand out to shake Jo's.

"Yes," Jo says nervously, and I remember, briefly, that she's only twenty-four. To me, she's a grown up, but to someone like Miss Harris, she's as much of a child as I am. "Maeve's parents – uh, our parents – are away on holiday at the moment. I'd like to have a word about Lily O'Callaghan and Maeve's place in all this."

Miss Harris nods. "Yes, I think that's a good idea. Maeve, I was hoping to speak to you before class anyway. Would you like to come this way?"

Jo is amazing in Miss Harris's office. She's all firm and crisp, telling Miss Harris that I had nothing to do with Lily's disappearance and that a sixteen-year-old girl shouldn't be brought into something so serious. Then she says a bunch of embarrassing stuff about how I'm "not as tough as I look", a sentence that is completely annoying because there's no good way of responding to it. I can't say, "Yes I am!" because it makes me seem petulant, but I can't say, "You're right, correct, I am a hairless worm, please go on..." either.

"I quite agree," Miss Harris says tightly. "I think it's best if, for the good of Maeve and for all the girls, we minimize her involvement in this. I've been teaching in girls' schools a long time, and once something gets in the water, it's very hard to control it. Fads start, and they're quickly followed by a kind of mania. One that brings out the worst in people. I believe the story going around is that Maeve is ... a witch?"

I flush red. "Yes," I say. "I mean, no, I'm not one, but that's what they said yesterday."

"And that you have been reading tarot cards for the other girls on your lunch break?"

"Er ... yeah. It was harmless, though. Ask anyone. It was just a bit of fun."

For them. It was a bit of fun *for them*.

"Even so, I've decided that from now on, there will be an official ban on tarot cards, and, more broadly ... occult-ish things. So no cards, no spells, no Ouija boards, no incense. No sage."

At this, Miss Harris produces a shoebox full of things that I had been keeping in the Chokey. Everything I bought in Divination, all that I had thoughtfully arranged to turn the cupboard into my own little magic shop, has been reduced to a couple of bits rattling around in a cardboard box.

I've never felt like more of a child.

"Do you have the tarot cards with you today, Maeve?"

"Um, yes. They're in my school bag."

"Can you take them out, please?"

I unzip my bag and take them out, the cool weight of them still comforting and solid, despite the trouble that they have caused.

"Give me the tarot cards, Maeve."

"What? Why?"

"They're banned from school. And I'm concerned that some of the girls will start asking you for readings outside of school."

"I'll just say no," I protest.

"You won't say no," Miss Harris says, and a coldness comes into her voice. Like she knows how easily I can be pressured into doing things if it means that people will like me. "So I'm not giving you the option to say yes."

I can see that Jo wants to rush to my defence, but that silently, she agrees with Miss Harris.

I feel betrayed.

"Please, Miss," I plead. "They're mine."

"Actually, they're not yours. You found them in the basement cupboard. They're school property, and frankly, Maeve, I should be giving you a Behavioural Correction for using the cupboard without permission. You purposefully didn't return the key to me. Please return it now."

Me and Miss Harris have never been best friends, but I've always thought that deep down, she sort of liked me. Or, at the very least, she had faith that I was a basically OK person. The way she's speaking to me now though goes

91

beyond gently chiding a misbehaving student. It's like she thinks I'm a criminal.

I fish the key out of my pencil case and give it to her without a word. Miss Harris opens her bottom desk drawer and places the tarot cards in there, locking the drawer with a little key.

"Now, I believe you have Geography first, don't you? You can head there now, unless you have anything else to say."

Jo gives me a small "I've done everything I can do" smile and gets out of her chair. "I'll be at home later. Give me a text if you need a lift from the bus stop."

I don't want Miss Harris to know she's won, so I saunter out of the room like I couldn't care less, my school bag flung over one shoulder. I can sense the lack of the tarot's weight immediately, and suddenly I feel like my tether to the earth's surface is very fragile. Like I might float away and disappear, just like Lily did.

Before I leave the room, I turn around to face Miss Harris again. "Miss," I say, shy all of a sudden. "Have Lily's parents asked about me at all? Because, y'know, I'm happy to talk to them, like I did to the Gardaí."

"Oh yes," Miss Harris responds. "They had ... quite a lot to say. I wouldn't worry, Maeve. The Gardaí has passed on any relevant information. I think it's best if you let the O'Callaghans have their space, for now."

Roe's face swims into my head and my pulse quickens. Is he still wearing my lump of rose quartz under his clothes? I picture it hitting the bare skin of his chest and feel a blush creeping up my neck.

Poor Roe. Poor Mr and Mrs O'Callaghan. I keep picturing Mrs O'Callaghan's face when she finds Lily's bed empty. The hammering on the bathroom door, her confusion turning to panic. The raw, ripe fear of realizing her only daughter is missing.

Classes are a nightmare. I had been afraid that, after yesterday's "witch" chant, the others would keep well away from me out of terror that they, too, would disappear in the middle of the night. The reality is much worse. People are clamouring to speak to me, but only want to talk about Lily, about witchcraft, about the tarot. There are rumours of a curse. There have been wild stories about Miss Harris finding Lily O'Callaghan voodoo dolls in the Chokey cupboard. There's another about how Lily is not missing at all, but dead. That she killed herself after being taunted by me on Friday.

They gather around me at lunch, desperate to be the one who shakes more information out of me. As angry as I am to have my tarot cards confiscated, I kind of see why Miss Harris needed to do it.

"Maeve, I've been so worried about you," Niamh says, tugging at the shredded sleeve of my school jumper. "People were saying you used to bully Lily, but I told them that was bollocks. You were her friend, weren't you? In primary school, I mean?"

Why is Niamh saying this, like she had nothing to do with the fact that me and Lily are no longer friends? How can she look at me, her eyes pricked with tears of concern, as if she is completely innocent in all of this?

"It's just so sad," she continues. "I couldn't sleep last night because I was so worried about Lily."

Suddenly, I can't take it any more. I can't sit here and look at Niamh pretending to cry because she's upset about a girl she despised from day one.

"Niamh, are you *freaking high*?"

Oh God. I'm shouting now. Why am I suddenly shouting?

"You didn't give a shit about Lily. In fact, you're the reason I pretended not to give a shit about her, when she was the best friend I've ever had. And now you're going to pretend like you're so concerned?"

Niamh blinks at me, her tears thick now, running down her pretty face in even streams.

"Why are you yelling at me? I'm on *your* side."

"There are no sides! I didn't do anything."

Silence. Every single one of my classmates are staring at me.

"Right," Niamh counters, coolly. "You didn't do *anything*, Maeve."

At the end of the day I pick up my school bag to find that someone has written *W I T C H* on it in permanent ink. I pretend not to notice it, not wanting to give anyone the satisfaction of seeing me squirm.

It's only when I'm on the bus home that I realize whoever wanted to call me a witch changed their mind. The "W" is crossed out and, with a very sure hand, has been replaced with a "B".

CHAPTER TWELVE

THE NEXT MORNING I HAVE MATHS FIRST THING. MATHS HAS always been my worst subject, made even more difficult by the fact that Lily and I are in the same class.

Or, we were.

As soon as I step through the door the air is tinged with a prickling static. There's an immediate silence. Usually when you're talking about someone and they enter the room, you quickly change the subject and start talking in a fake, halting way about what your dog did last night. This is different. This is a silence that wants to make itself known. A deathly quiet that lets you know that you were being talked about, and everyone wants you to know it.

I trudge through the room, looking straight ahead. I don't allow myself to blink, terrified my eyelid will push a stray tear out of my eye and let it roll down my cheek. Proving my terror. Proving my guilt.

Just get to your seat, Maeve. Get to your seat.

But I can't get to my seat. My chair, the back-row gap wedged between Michelle and Niamh, is currently being filled by Aoife O'Connor. None of the girls look at me.

I will not say anything. I will not confront them. I will not *beg* for friendship.

My eyes shoot around the room, looking for somewhere

else to sit. Thinking: *OK, I'll just take Aoife's old seat.* But someone else is in Aoife's old seat. There's a hot pulse of terror pounding in my head, so forceful that I'm sure my eyes must be bulging out of my skull. I keep scanning the room. There should be at least two empty seats, what with Lily missing and me on my feet, but there's only one. Maybe they dragged the other one into the corridor outside to prove a point. The kind of bitchy, silent point you only get in a girls' school of this size and calibre. I take the empty seat.

The seat that, last week, belonged to Lily O'Callaghan.

There's nothing I can do except trudge to Lily's old desk in the front row, feeling each pair of eyes on me, the white heat like a bulb that has just popped out of its socket.

And there, carved into the ancient wood, alongside the hearts and the crossbones and the fancy Superman "S" left by students of years past, is a new offering:

S O M E   F R I E N D.

This, I learn over the next few days, is the part of the story my classmates are the most hypnotized and disgusted by. Not just that Lily is missing. Not just the tarot cards. But the fact that Lily had been my best friend, that I had ditched her, then bullied her, wished she would disappear in front of everyone and now – as far as anyone could tell – she has either killed herself or run so far from the city that she might as well be dead.

No one actually says this to me, of course. But I catch snatches of conversation as I pass girls in the hallway.

"… *her best friend!*"

"…*well, I never saw them together but Becca went to their primary and…*"

"Their mums! Their mums are still friends!"

"Did you hear? What she said? To her friend? HER BEST FRIEND?"

"... she's always been a bit of a bitch of course, but once she started getting a bit of attention for that witchy shit, she got really nasty..."

"Her BEST friend!!!"

One day after coming back to lunch I noticed a gang of first-year girls crowded around my bag, and I leapt on it, baring my teeth at them.

"What were you doing?" I snapped, thinking they were filling the pockets with something smelly, like mouldy fruit or tuna.

"Nothing," a pink-eyed twelve-year-old says, stuttering the entire time. "W-we were just d-d-daring each other."

"Daring each other? To do what?"

"To ... t-to touch your b-bag."

It was the first time I became aware that I wasn't just the talking point of my year. The whole *school* was in on this. I had become a legend. Miss Harris asked me to be extra nice to the younger girls. One was apparently afraid to come to school.

But the younger girls I can handle. It's the ones my age and above that are the most worrying. Since Lily's disappearance, all of their parents have started freaking out about letting them go into town after school, and suddenly there are traffic jams at the school gates because no one wants their daughter to get the bus home. A girl in the year above shoulders me into the wall as I'm walking to assembly.

"My mum took away my phone," she said. "Thanks a lot, Chambers."

Mum and Dad come back from holidays on Friday. Jo has filled them in about Lily already, and I suspect, about how life has been for me at school. Their bags are stuffed with trinkets for me: earrings that look like miniature blue tiles, Portuguese custard tarts that have been slightly squished by air travel.

"I know we're taking things easy with the … New Age stuff," Dad says, sheepishly. "But I found myself in one of those crystal shops, and ended up stumbling out with this."

He extracts a long, golden thread with a hard, black pendant on the edge of it, accompanied by a single red bead. "She told me it was a protection charm," he says. "Azabache. Or, jet. But I like azabache. They give it to babies in South America when they're born. Helps ward off the evil eye."

"Thanks, Dad," I say, smiling weakly. Imagining him trying to make conversation with a crystal-seller is enough to make my heart glow with a sense of hope. My parents are home. Things have to get better, don't they?

He drapes the necklace over my head and the stone lands in the centre of my chest, settling at my breastbone. I run my finger over the smooth black stone, the shape and size of a thumbprint and immediately think of Roe.

Talk eventually turns to the O'Callaghans. Mum has already texted Lily's mum from Portugal.

"Have you spoken to her?" I ask hopefully.

"No," she says sagely. "You don't phone at a time like this. Especially if you're not family. You need to give people space, but let them know you're there."

"That family needs grace," Dad says, shaking his head.

"That family," Mum says, standing up to take out our biggest frying pan, "needs lasagnes."

I help Mum make the lasagnes all night. I grate the cheese, chop the garlic, run to the shop to get big pasta sheets. In the morning, she drives me to school in the car and we hit the O'Callaghans' house on the way. The shortness of the trip – just three streets, two left turns and you're there – is a nauseating reminder of just how often I used to make this journey. I have been down this road on Barbie rollerblades, on light-up trainers, on the sunshine-yellow bicycle I begged for that was stolen two months later.

We park outside their semi-detached house, identical to every other house on the road except for the fact that I spent half of my childhood inside it. I hold the two tin-foil-covered lasagnes – one meat, one vegetarian – in my lap.

"Right," she says. "Pen. Notepaper."

I rip out a page from my spiral-ring notebook and hand her my best pen. She scribbles something about reheating at 180 degrees, adding that she's "on call" for anything they need.

She signs off with *love always, Nora Chambers* and then takes a long look at me, sitting low in the passenger seat

… *and Maeve*, she writes.

CHAPTER THIRTEEN

THERE ARE SEARCHES FOR LILY. PEOPLE WALKING AROUND the riverbank and marshlands with flashlights and dogs. Items of her clothing sniffed at. Mum doesn't let me go. I hear her and Dad arguing about it in their bedroom. He thinks it will make me feel proactive; she thinks it will traumatize me. What I think seems not to matter.

Dad goes both nights and returns home only after I've gone to bed. I hear his steps creaking on the old staircase and then the sound of a long, exhausted sigh when he enters their bedroom.

My brother Pat comes home for the weekend, back for the wedding of two school friends, and the house is momentarily distracted by the big silliness of him. I spend a long time sitting in the beanbag in his bedroom, showing him the list of songs I cribbed from the Walkman.

"Oh wow, it's happening," he says, scanning the list with raised eyebrows. "At long last."

"What?"

"You're developing *taste*."

He picks through his vinyl collection and extracts a big, square record with a red-haired woman on it.

"Maeve, I think it's time you met Jenny Lewis."

Suddenly, I'm plunged into a world of loud women with

guitars, an endless family tree of people Pat talks about as if they were beloved ex-girlfriends. Courtney and PJ and Carrie and Jenny. Kim and Joni and, for some reason, Prince.

"Prince wasn't a woman," I say.

"Prince wasn't anything. Prince was just Prince."

Every album and song that Pat passes on to me makes me think of Roe. I want to tell Pat about him, but I can't get the words out right.

I don't say anything. Instead, I just lap up the music Pat gives me, eager to memorize his opinions so I can possibly repeat them to Roe later, at some faraway point on the horizon when Lily is back and we can go back to our bus conversations. Pat, of course, thinks it's because his taste is superb.

"Come in and listen any time you want," he says, plucking at the strings of his old bass guitar. "Just *leave* everything in here, yeah?"

But then Pat goes, and real life is the dreary act that follows him. The days pass with a sluggish melancholy, and the school-wide iciness towards me doesn't even begin to thaw. People avoid conversation with me in the line for the loos. They just raise their eyebrows and then look right through me.

The rhythm of my schedule is still completely the same: I take the bus to school, I go to classes, I take the bus home. Yet everything feels coloured by an unsettling shadow, like the bluish cast on a duck's egg. Missing posters go up, and every time I see Lily's face on a telephone pole, I feel as though I've bitten into ice cream. I don't see Roe. The girls in school stop asking me questions, and instead just stop talking when they see me approach. It would all be completely unbearable if it weren't for Fiona.

I start eating lunch in the art room in the attic of the building, a room people tend to avoid because of how perpetually freezing it is. On Wednesday, Fiona silently enters the room, sits down, and opens a Tupperware container. We don't say anything for a few minutes.

Eventually, I crack.

"Your lunch smells good."

"Thanks," she says, flushing a little. "My mum has the week off, so she's making me lunches."

"That's nice of her."

"Yeah…" she replies, uncertainly. "Except I brought in a goat stew yesterday, and you'd swear I brought in a dead My Little Pony or something. Everyone made this big thing about it."

She sounds exhausted. I don't blame her.

"You can *buy* goat here?"

"Oh yeah. My mum gets it from a Jamaican shop in town."

"There's a Jamaican shop in town?"

Fiona gives me a wry smile. "There are a *lot* of shops white people don't know about."

Fiona's first name is Irish, her second name is English, her skin is brown and her patience for other people's bullshit is limited. I've always admired the way she can gently cut people down for being ignorant, but it also intimidates the hell out of me.

"Well, it smells great," I say. "I wish my mum made me lunch."

102

She offers me some. It's delicious.

We have different class schedules, but we fall into the pattern of eating lunch together in the art room. I roll pieces of modelling clay between my fingers while she uses different highlighters to colour in her shoelaces, making a striped tricolour of pink, yellow and blue.

I'm grateful to her for not abandoning me like everyone else has, even though I'm not sure what she gets out of the arrangement. She's pretty, talented and fun.

And me? I'm the girl who used to have tarot cards, and who killed her best friend.

"Hey," she says, threading her newly-rainbowed laces back through her white Converse. "It's a teacher training day tomorrow. We're off at one."

"Oh yeah. Cool."

"Do you want to go into town?" Fiona asks, her voice casual.

The question cuts like a beam of light through a grey fog. Fiona wants to be proper friends. After-school friends. *Town friends. I blink at her in vague disbelief.*

Look. I'm not a total cretin. It's not as if I don't get invited to parties or trips to town. But I'm almost always invited as part of a larger group, my presence the end product of someone saying, "Oh, and invite the Bernadette girls" or "Invite Michelle and her friends". I don't know when the last time was that someone wanted to hang out with just me.

Yes, you do, Maeve. It was Lily, and it was over a year ago.

Clearly, I'm taking too long to respond, so Fiona rushes in, full of anxious qualifiers.

"It's just that, there's auditions for *Othello* in a couple of weeks, and I really think I could do Desdemona, but I really need someone to practise lines with. To do Othello's bit. So. Don't worry if you're busy, or whatever. I can ask someone…"

I can't help but crack a smile. "This is a really long-winded way of saying you want to get off with me."

"Oh my God, don't be such a philistine."

"It's grand. Let's do it. Wait, doesn't Othello murder Desdemona at the end?"

"He sure does. Maybe I should ask someone else. What with *your* track record…"

Fiona slaps her hand over her mouth almost the minute she says it. I gape at her.

"Sorry. That's not funny. I have like, stupidly inappropriate humour sometimes." She goes bright red, pinching the bridge of her nose. "I'm such a liability. I'm sorry, Maeve."

It takes me a moment to gather myself. "So they're still saying that, then."

"No."

"Fiona."

"OK. Yes. But they're a bunch of cows just looking for a story. They're bored. Christ, they're *boring*."

I chew at the dry skin under my thumbnail, not sure what to say. Fiona starts apologizing again, clearly upset. "This is what Mum always gives out to me about. No filter. Jesus. Look, it's fine, we can forget about tomorrow."

"Fiona, calm down. It's OK," I say, smiling at last. I'm finally beginning to understand, I think, why she wants to be my friend. I've been too in awe of her prettiness and her poise to notice our similarities. Namely, that we both have foot-in-mouth syndrome. "Let's go into town tomorrow."

The next day I meet Fiona in the car park and I am glad, so glad, that I remembered to bring a change of clothes with me. She's abandoned her uniform in favour of grey jeans, an emerald-green leotard designed to look like a mermaid's tail, and an oversized biker jacket with wide sleeves and deep, zippy pockets. It's clear to me now how she snagged an older boyfriend. She looks about twenty.

I, meanwhile, am in a stripy jumper from Next and a pair of leggings I keep having to pick dog hair off. It's painful enough standing next to her in my street clothes, but I don't think I could manage it if I was in my uniform.

We walk down the hill and into the city, streams of girls descending with us in pairs and trios. For the first time since my tarot reading with Lily, I feel a pink bubble of joy expand in my throat.

"Let's do something dumb," I say, swinging my giddy body off a lamp post. "Like try on wedding dresses."

"Wedding dresses?" She laughs. "Who would let us into a wedding dress shop? They're all appointment-only."

"Not if we go where they sell the crappy wedding dresses."

Fiona's eyes sparkle with possibility. "Go on."

"Let's go to Basement."

Perhaps at one point in its long history, Basement was really just a basement. At this moment in time, it's a four-floor building, and is home to some of the most questionable clothing choices you can imagine. Polyester evening gowns, eight-inch clear heels, neon rave wear, Halloween costumes that attempt to avoid copyright infringement by calling themselves "Bat Gentleman" and "Wonderful Woman". No one's quite sure how they make rent, but once I was looking through a rack of second-hand army coats and a tile fell out of the ceiling.

"I *love* that shop," Fiona says excitedly. "I convinced Mum to take me in there one time, and she dragged me out by the ear when she saw all the bongs for sale."

"They have a whole section for crazy evening wear and gross wedding dresses. Let's go try them on. We can run your lines for Othello after."

I've only actually been in Basement once, back when Abbie was getting married and someone had told her they found an original Vera Wang in there. They were, it turns out, messing with her.

We stop to admire the window display before going in. There's a female mannequin in a gas mask wearing a neon tutu, walking a male mannequin on a lead. The male mannequin is wearing a leather harness.

"Oh my God," Fiona says, trying not to laugh. "Is this a sex shop?"

"I think they just like to push the envelope."

"They're pushing it all right," she says, looping her arm through mine and pulling me through the door. "She is *pushed*."

A man with green hair and huge holes in his earlobes nods at us as we stride to the back of the store. We find an old theatre trunk full of yellowing lace and a sign that says, *Broken Dreams – 50% off*. There is a shower curtain draped across one corner as a makeshift changing room.

Fiona ends up in a puffy-sleeved 1980s monstrosity, the satin fabric slit to reveal her entire thigh. I'm in a giant meringue, the layers of taffeta itching my leg. We can't stop screaming at each other, collapsing into giggles every time we discover a new hideous feature.

"You look like you should be carrying a big brick phone," I say. "So you can be an eighties power business bride."

"And you need –" she examines me – "a hat. You need one of those stupid hats that sit at the front of your head. I'm going to ask."

She pushes past me and runs barefoot to the counter. I hear her voice, giddy and shrill. "Hi, sorry, excuse me, do you have any hat—? Oh."

The "Oh" sounds worried, defensive. I stick my head out of the shower curtain, anxious to go to the front of the shop in my stupid dress. A group of men are talking to the green-haired boy. They're about the same age, but the way the men are dressed makes them seem decades older. Or, not older, but from an older time. They're in navy-blue suits, and have a sort of 1960s masculinity that makes me think they're going to say something from *Mad Men*, a show I have not watched but feel I understand the vibe of.

Two of them stop to leer briefly at Fiona. One, a young-looking guy with short blond hair, is speaking to the green-haired boy.

"So, as you can see, sir, you'll find that in Section 18 of the Irish Criminal Act, any person who commits, in public, any act that may offend modesty or injure the morals of the community can receive a fine of up to six hundred euro. Or, if the court decides, they may be sent to prison for up to six months. It's really in your best interest to comply."

The man is American. My knowledge of American accents isn't good enough to know where it's from exactly. It's that kind of clear-water accent that you only expect Americans in adverts to have, as opposed to Americans in films. The kind of adverts that always end with *"side effects include nausea, depression and diarrhoea…"*

"Piss off," Green Boy retorts.

"Sir, I really must stress that this is *the law*, OK, and that your store – and your window display – is in direct contradiction to this country's moral heritage."

"This country's moral heritage?" Green Boy sneers. "What would you know about the morals of my country?"

"With all due respect, this is still a Catholic country."

"Is this a wind-up? Jesus feckin' Christ, man. Have you been living under a rock or what? I dunno what kind of Ireland you came here for, but we're more or less done with the Bible-bashing bullshit. Equal marriage? Repeal the Eighth? News to you, mate?"

Green Boy keeps getting louder, but the Americans stay icy, polite. I expect Fiona to come running back, but she doesn't. She stands there, her body language wary, curious. I feel afraid for her, suddenly. I start quietly slipping my jeans on underneath my huge skirt, the taffeta rustling noisily as I do.

"I suppose," I say, and rest my head on her chest.

One of the older men hears it and turns around, taking in Fiona and me for the first time.

"Sir, do you really think it's appropriate to have school-aged children in your store?" He turns to Fiona. "Shouldn't you be in school?"

"It's … uh, it's a half-day."

"And don't you think you should be doing something more productive and … *wholesome* with that time?" His eyes scan her body. The dress that was so funny a few minutes ago now feels like proof of some terrible crime. "Where do you go to school?"

"St Bernadette's."

"And is that a Catholic school, honey?"

"Umm, kind of."

"How do you mean, *kind of*?"

"Like our principal is a nun, but I don't believe in God." In saying the word "God", Fiona seems to regain some kind of courage. "And this shop rocks. There's nothing wrong with this shop. Morally or any other way."

Green Boy permits Fiona a tiny smile. This spurs her on even more.

"And don't call me honey. Not if you're going to call him *sir*."

He smiles at her, his lip curving tightly inwards.

"Of course," he says, then turns his attention to Green Boy. "If you're not going to listen to me, I'm afraid I'll have no choice."

"No choice?" he spits back. "What are *you* going to do?"

They stare at one another wordlessly for a second, and I suddenly remember nature documentaries about alpha predators.

"Well. I must be going. Have a nice day, girls. Why don't you take a pamphlet from one of our boys here?"

A waxy blue brochure is thrust into my hands, and they're gone. *Children of Brigid,* it says in big, proud letters. There are photographs of teenagers being baptized in picturesque out-door lakes.

"Vomit," I say, breaking the silence that had fallen between me and Fiona. I pass it to her.

"Gross," she replies, her voice still faintly shaken. "Still, at least the blond one was good-looking."

"They all kind of looked the same to me."

"Let's go run those lines," she says. "This wedding dress is giving me a rash."

"Yeah," I agree, the fun of dressing up now strangely deflated.

CHAPTER FOURTEEN

WE END UP IN BRIDEY'S, A STICKY OLD CAFE WHERE A POT OF tea for two people is only a euro, and a slice of apple tart is two. It only has two kinds of customer: old people, and arty types who are on the dole. We sit on a musty green sofa, the tinned apples sliding across my tongue. I read Othello and Fiona does Desdemona. It doesn't seem that great a part, if I'm honest: a lot of her thrashing around and saying that she would never be unfaithful. There's no denying it, though: Fiona is good. She does something with her voice, making it tremble in some places, making it strident in others. I hear her giddy voice.

"*Yet I fear you, for you are fatal then!*" she says, grasping my hand. "*When your eyes roll so: why I should fear I know not, since...*"

She pinches the bridge of her nose again. "Give me the line."

"*Since guiltiness...*"

"*Since guiltiness I know not; but yet...*"

Another nose pinch.

"*But yet I feel...*" I prompt her. "C'mon, you know this."

"*But yet I feel love?*"

"No."

"Come on, just give me the whole line."

"Fine," I say, standing up and gesturing with the sheets of paper. I put on a crazy theatrical voice, like a drunk Ian McKellen. *"Since guiltiness I know not, but yet I feel I fear!"*

"Maeve," a voice comes from behind me. A voice that's all too recognizable. I turn around.

"Roe."

We stare at each other wordlessly for a moment. He isn't in his school uniform either. He's wearing a scarlet bomber jacket that would almost look sporty if the collar wasn't leopard print.

"Hey," I say. "How are you?"

Roe doesn't respond. He just blinks at me. It isn't until Fiona jumps up to shake his hand that he makes any move at all.

"Hi, you're Roe, right? I'm Fiona. I'm so sorry about what's going on with your sister. I'm sure you must be having a terrible time."

Everything she's saying is technically correct and totally polite, but the way she's saying it is so rushed and manic that it's only adding to the mounting pressure between us.

But it does its job. It snaps Roe out of his shock at seeing me. He takes Fiona's hand for a quick shake, then drops it and turns back to me.

"Hey. Not good, actually," he says. "I'm not exactly sleeping very well, as you can probably imagine, and Mum spends her evenings crying so loudly that I've started doing my homework in here. But I see you've taken this, too. Should have seen that coming."

"Roe, I'm so sorry about Lily. But you have to believe me, that tarot reading I gave her—"

"Jesus, Maeve —" he runs his hands through his dark curls, and scrunches them tightly in his fist at the crown of his head — "you think this is about your fecking tarot cards? You abandoned her. You were her only friend and you knew she was vulnerable and you left her wide open. Now there's some weirdo..."

His voice cracks at this. There are purple lines under his eyes, a spiderweb of anxiety on his pale skin.

"Now there's some weirdo who probably has my sister bundled into a van somewhere, doing God knows what to her. Do you know the stuff I've had to hear about, in the last week? Have you ever had a total stranger in your house, talking to your parents about sex trafficking? They went through her *things*, Maeve. Her sketchbooks. Her fantasy novels. Trying to make out like she ... like *she's* the freak, just because she likes drawing. Because she likes making stuff up."

I suddenly remember Lily's sketchbooks. Giant mechanical birds. Steam-punk piglets, with cogs for noses. The most startling, creative stuff you can think of, and I haven't even seen them in a year. I can't imagine how amazing they are now.

"I'm sorry, Roe. I don't know what to say, except I'm sorry."

"I'm only her brother. What the hell was I supposed to do? You're not meant to be close to your sister. Not at this age. I always thought we'd come back together when we were older. That's how it's supposed to go. But now I'm never going to see her again. Because you ... because you had *better* people you wanted to be friends with."

"You *will* see her again, Roe. You will," I protest, my eyes filling with tears. What in the hell have I been playing at? Running around town with Fiona Buttersfield while Lily's life is in danger?

"But worse than that," he says, his voice harsh again, "is that I thought *we* were friends, Maeve. *I* could have really used a friend. But I didn't hear a peep out of you."

"The school *told me* not to get in touch," I protest. "My parents, too. They said not to talk to you. That you were going through enough. I wanted to call you, Roe, honestly. I've been going out of my mind."

"Whatever, Maeve. I have to go find somewhere *else* to study," he says. "Believe it or not, I still have a Leaving Cert this year. It was nice to meet you, Fiona."

And with that, he's gone.

I sit back down, staring straight ahead.

"Maeve," Fiona says tentatively. "He's just mad. He didn't mean that."

"No, he does," I say. "He really, really does." I drop my face into my hands, and start to cry.

Fiona puts an arm around me, rubbing my back with her hand. She doesn't say much, which I'm grateful for. A new onslaught of snotty, soupy tears pours out of me whenever I order myself to stop.

"Sorry," I say through choked sobs. "I'm sorry. You can go. Just leave."

"Pal, I'm not going to *leave* you here. Not after that."

"I deserved it, though."

"Maybe. He didn't have to go in on you, though. Christ."

I hold some coarse paper napkins to my eyes, the cheap paper scratching at my skin.

"What happened between you and Lily?" Fiona asks quietly.

I bite my lip, trying to find the words. How can I explain how bad a friend I am to the first real friend I've made in years?

"We used to be best friends. We grew up together. But we had one of those intense, weird best-friend relationships where things that were funny or interesting to us were weird and gross to other people. And when we were in third year, I decided that I would rather be popular than be friends with Lily. And I started, sort of … cutting her off."

Fiona doesn't say anything, just raises her eyebrows silently.

"Just, you know, not inviting her to stuff. Hoping that if I was just casually mean to her, she'd get the hint and find some other people to be friends with. But she never did. So last year, I…"

I trail off. Is Fiona really ready to hear about what a horrible person I actually am?

"Look," Fiona says, her arm still around me, "I don't know why Lily is missing. I don't know if she'll come back. But whether she does or doesn't, you can't beat yourself to death over how you acted when you were thirteen. Yes, it was stupid and shallow. But, once again: you were *thirteen*. I got *nits* when I was thirteen."

"Nits? At thirteen?" I say, mock-horrified, still sniffling through tears. I squash the urge to correct her. Maybe I started distancing myself from Lily at thirteen, but I dealt

115

the killing blow only a year ago, at fifteen. There are girls in some countries who are *married* by fifteen.

"Hey, I'm not judging *you*, friend-dumper," she nudges me. "Or are you going to dump me now, too?"

"Nah," I reply, nudging her back. "You can stay."

We leave Bridey's some time later. The dark February evening is already settling in, navy as the school uniforms balled up in our bags. Fiona's arm is looped through mine, protective and strong.

"It's only half four," she says. "D'you wanna swing by Basement again? I saw a basket of weird earrings I wouldn't mind going through."

"Sure," I say, and we turn through the cobbled side-street until we're back at the crumbling behemoth of a shop again.

Only this time, we're not alone.

Outside the shop is a throng of people, forty at least, all shouting and holding signs up.

"Are they singing?" Fiona asks, her ear cocked to the air.

"They're chanting," I reply, utterly dumbfounded.

Each syllable punches through the air, falling into a hard, practised rhythm. We inch closer, keeping our arms linked, our grip tightening on each other. We don't speak, keeping our ears trained on the crowd.

"OUR! MORALITY! IS NOT! FOR SALE! OUR! MORALITY! IS NOT! FOR SALE! OUR! MORALITY! IS NOT! FOR SALE!"

"What in *hell*? Where did this come from? Is this…?"

"Yes," I agree, before she even has the words out. "I think it is."

116

"Those guys? Those Americans? Are they here?"

I stand on my tiptoes. I'm a good bit taller than Fiona, so I can see above heads a little easier. I don't see the Americans. What I do notice is even more disturbing.

"Everyone here is *our age*."

"Yeah," she nods. "And look at the signs."

I peer closer. They all say "de-Basement" and have a big red "X" over the word. Clever.

At the front of the crowd, Green Boy is trying to confront the crowd while an older woman – presumably the owner – talks frantically on the phone, keeping a worried eye on the crowd.

Fiona and I edge closer to the front, the chanting still vigilantly on beat.

"OUR! MORALITY! IS NOT! FOR SALE!"

Protesting, in one form or another, is a thing you get used to in this city. Here and all over Ireland, I expect. During the abortion referendum a few years ago, the streets were littered with photos of baby hands, baby feet, baby heads. Baby anatomy threading through the street lamps People with loudspeakers yelling about the rights of the child. Before that, it was the marriage-equality referendum. Joanne took me to a protest where a man stood on a stage and talked about the rights of the family, the importance of marriage, the eyes of God. I held Joanne's hand and we shouted at him until we were hoarse.

But this is different. This isn't a referendum. It's a shop.

Why are these people so young? Why are they protesting about a clothes shop that sells the occasional rubber harness and novelty bong? This kind of stuff has been part of the city for as long as I can remember. Clothes shops that sell photocopied zines and bad CDs at the till. Music shops that sell green *LEGALIZE IT!* T-shirts. The city is big enough to have a few different alternative "scenes", small enough that the most talented people in that scene eventually leave. Some of my earliest memories are of Pat coming home in a rage because the singer in his band was leaving to pursue a career in Dublin. Or London. It was always either Dublin or London.

Then Pat left. And Cillian. And Abbie. Now it's just me and Jo, and I'm sure she'll be gone pretty soon, too.

"Do you want to hold a sign?"

A short, toothy girl of about eighteen is trying to shove a placard into my hands.

"It's just, I really need a pee," she continues.

"Piss off," I say, shoving it back towards her. She teeters, and Fiona puts an arm out to stop her falling. She gives me a sharp elbow in the ribs.

"Excuse me, why are you protesting this shop?"

"Aren't you protesting, too?"

"No. We like this shop."

"Well, do you know that they sell drugs to kids here?"

Me and Fiona look at each other in utter astonishment.

"What?" we say in unison.

"Yeah. The whole thing is a front."

"Who told you that?"

"It's all online. It was on the Facebook group. The See-Oh-Bee group," she adds shortly, seeing our blank looks. "Look, are you going to hold this or not? I really need to pee."

118

"No."

The girl glares at us, tucks her sign under her arm and stalks into the McDonald's on the other side of the street. As my eyes follow her, I catch a flash of scarlet at the corner of my vision and feel a spark run through me.

Roe is standing outside the McDonald's, staring at the mob with his mouth open. Our eyes meet. I put a hand up, palms flat, fingers straight. A gesture that is both "I see you" and "I'm not a part of this". He watches me for a second, then looks away.

A few seconds later, the girl with the sign emerges from the McDonald's looking furious. My guess is that they wouldn't let her use the toilet without buying something. She looks at Roe in his red bomber jacket trimmed with leopard print, his school bag covered in badges, his hair long and curly. Everything in her body language is hotly, avidly disapproving.

Leave him alone, I demand silently, my inner voice sharp and protective. *Don't say a word to him.*

The girl watches him for a moment, spits on the ground in front of him, and then crosses the street to rejoin the protest.

"Come on," Fiona says. "Let's get out of here before someone sees us with these nutters."

"Sure," I say. When I glance back to find Roe, he's gone.

CHAPTER FIFTEEN

IT'S IMPOSSIBLE TO FORGET ABOUT LILY. BUT WITH FIONA around, it becomes possible to forget about witchcraft, the tarot and the Housekeeper card. I get email updates from Raya Silver's Patreon account that I delete immediately.

"Why don't you just buy more cards?" Fiona asks.

Why don't I? They're not very expensive, after all, and I'm sure the woman in Divination would be delighted to help me pick out a new packet. But I feel frightened of that side of me now. Of the *WITCH* branded into my rucksack. Frightened that those first years who are afraid to come near me have a very good reason.

Because it's not just that I was good at memorizing cards, or telling people what they wanted to hear. When the cards were in my hands, I felt like I had discovered some part of myself that was better off hidden. Something troublesome and strange, thorny and not completely under my control.

"… she's always been a bit of a bitch of course, but once she started getting a bit of attention for that witchy shit, she got really nasty…"

There was a truth to that, I think. When I had the cards, the girls in my year seemed silly and small. Their problems boring, their fights stupid. They exhausted me. Something about the tiny spark of power the cards gave me made me feel apart from the rest.

I couldn't feel any more distant from my year group than right now. People are still deeply invested in Lily's disappearance. Fliers with her face on are everywhere, a photo from our Junior Cert results. I wonder if they cropped me out, or whether Lily had cut me out long before.

Girls start coming to school with wild, exciting stories about being followed home from school by a vast and inconsistent variety of strange men. At first the guards were interested in these stories, but it became clear pretty quickly that the younger girls were getting weirdly swept up in the strange romance of being kidnapped. No one ever wanted to be like Lily, but now suddenly, everyone sort of does. There is a kind of glamour to being "chosen", I think. I understand it, but it still makes me feel sick.

On Saturday morning, Fiona texts me and asks if I want to come to a party at her house.

What kind of party? I ask.

Just some food and music with my aunts and cousins

I don't know how formal the party is, but I figure it's only polite to wear something nice, so put on a light-blue knit dress that I last wore a year ago to a christening. Fiona opens the door and I can smell meat and garlic and onions. My mouth starts to water.

"You're here!" she says, delighted. "Wow, nice dress. You're going to want an apron."

"Why?"

"My mum's food is basically barbecue. You *will* have stains."

"How come you're not wearing an apron?"

"Because I'm a *professional*."

121

I kick off my shoes and Fiona leads me into the kitchen, where a bunch of women are hovering over hot trays, yelling at one another about where a certain kind of bowl is.

"Mum!" Fiona says, putting her arm around a pretty woman that I assume is her mother. "This is Maeve. Do we have anything she can put over her dress?"

"Maeve!" her mum says, putting both arms on my shoulders. "We've heard so much about you! I'm Marie. It's always a thrill when Fifi brings home someone who isn't at that stage school."

Fiona makes a face, and I can't tell if she's more annoyed by "Fifi" or her stage school being dissed. Her mother catches it.

"*Ni*, it's true. They're all so pretentious. So serious. Maeve, I hear you're fun."

"I *try* to be fun," I reply.

"Do you sing?"

"No."

"See, more of this. I married an Irish man, thinking that the Irish are so musical, and he doesn't sing either. Well, he does now. Fifi, where's your daddy?"

"Upstairs."

"Get him down! Maeve, have you met everyone? Fiona, introduce Maeve to your titas."

I meet everyone. Fiona has two titas, Sylvia and Rita. They have two brothers who still live in Manila, who they talk about like they have just popped out and will be back any minute now. Clutches of cousins and family friends move in and out of the kitchen, grabbing plates of meat and rice, then wandering back into the living room to

122

play *Mario Kart*. Fiona's dad arrives, surprisingly introvert-ed compared to her outgoing mother, and then joins the other husbands standing and drinking beer at the kitchen's perimeter.

I'm just finishing my second plate of food and my fourth game of *Mario Kart* when Fiona taps me on the arm. "C'mon," she says. "Follow me through the kitchen."

We glide back through the kitchen, where a karaoke machine has been set up and two of Fiona's aunts are singing "Vogue". Fiona walks into the room, claps and sings along, and then seamlessly wraps her hands around a bottle of red wine and hides it under a dishcloth. She winks at me, and I follow her up the stairs and into her room.

"Slick," I say, impressed.

"Like cat shit on a linoleum floor," she replies with a grin.

She tips the wine into two plastic cups.

"Thanks, Fifi."

"Shut your damn mouth."

"Your family are very cool."

"Oh God, don't. If you say that around my mother, she'll get her sax out."

"Her *saxophone*?"

"Drink your stupid wine."

The wine tastes like dirt and blackberries, bitter and stinging on my palate. I cough.

"You don't drink wine?"

"No, I do. Just usually … white."

Lie. One the rare occasions that I drink, it's usually some vile vodka mix sipped out of a Coke bottle. I take another gulp, and it goes down easier this time.

"Mmm. Earthy."

I peer over my cup to see that Fiona is also grimacing slightly, and that she doesn't really drink wine either. I catch her eye and we both burst out laughing, delighted that we were both willing to put on a show for the other.

Fiona opens her laptop. "So I looked up Children of Brigid, and there's not that much out there. Just the closed Facebook group that weird girl mentioned. I mean, who even *uses* Facebook any more?"

"See-Oh-Bee. CoB! Children of Brigid. OK, sorry, I just got it."

"Thank you, Miss Chambers, for joining the rest of the class."

"Shut up. I got there eventually. Did you request to join?"

"Are you joking? Imagine if people saw – they're a fundamentalist protest group."

I suddenly think of Jo, and the day she left college early because there was a protest of some queer exhibition. It seems likely that these are the same crowd, and that they're after more than just cool shops.

"Well, we could make up some fake profiles, and ask to join as them."

So we drink wine, and we create fake Facebook profiles. We steal photos from obscure Tumblr pages and call ourselves Mary-Ellen Jones and Amy Gold. We spend a long time trying to make our profiles look like ordinary, real girls and it becomes a sort of game. We try to out-normal each other, turning the traits of other people into jokes about the kind of girls we will never be. We're being a little cruel, but

124

I can tell that these jokes are as much a balm to her as they are to me.

"OK, OK," Fiona says, giggling while typing. "I'm going to put, 'Love my besties for ever'."

"How about that Marilyn Monroe quote people always use? What is it? 'If you can't handle me at my worst' – or some crap?"

"'If you can't handle me at my worst, then you sure as hell don't deserve me at my best'," she says. "Oh yes, that's gold. I'm putting that."

Suddenly, we hear a thick pop of brass travelling up the stairs and I jump.

Fiona's mum has brought her sax out.

I phone Mum, who says she'll collect me at eleven. I brush my teeth with my finger in Fiona's upstairs bathroom before she arrives to try to disguise the smell of alcohol, and say goodbye to her family.

Marie hugs me tight. "You know you can stay for a sleepover if you like? You can call your mother, if she hasn't left already?"

"That's OK," I reply, beaming at her. "But I'll be back! If you'll have me."

"Anyone who eats is allowed to come back. It's why those actresses haven't got a second invitation."

"Mum!" Fiona scolds.

"Fifi, it's *true*."

Luckily, Mum doesn't seem to notice that I've had half a bottle of red wine, or if she has, she's decided to forgive me for it. She looks at me a little suspiciously on the ride home, her brow furrowed as I talk animatedly about Fiona's family, telling her that we should have more family parties. I keep reminding myself to slow down, to not slur my words, to hide as best I can that I'm on the slightly-wrong-side of tipsy. She stays silent.

"You know," I say, slightly huffy with her, "I thought you'd be glad that I was out on Saturday night. *With* parental supervision."

Mum continues to say nothing. We are pulling into the driveway of our house.

"They're *such* a nice family," I continue. "And Fiona's mum Marie plays the saxophone!"

"Maeve," Mum finally says, turning off the ignition. "There's been some news."

In an instant, my sloppy wine buzz turns into pure nausea.

"Good news? Bad news?"

"Neither, really. Just news. It seems someone saw Lily on the night she went missing."

We sit in the car, and Mum tells me everything Lily's mum told her. At around 5 a.m. on the morning Lily went missing, a milkman was doing his rounds near the Beg when he spotted a very tall girl with dark-blonde hair wearing a coat over her pyjamas. She was not alone. Walking with the girl was a woman with black hair. The milkman, who was used to bumping into all sorts of unusual characters at that hour of the morning, waved hello to the pair. The woman turned away, hiding her face, but the girl looked straight at him. The girl looked like she had been crying.

"The milkman apparently assumed that they were mother and daughter, and that they were fleeing some sort of domestic violence," Mum explains. "Which is why he re-membered them. They stuck in his head, and apparently he was worried about them for quite a few days afterwards. He felt very guilty for not offering to do more, to drive them to a refuge or something, so when he heard a description of Lily on the radio he came forward."

"Oh my God," I say, sickness rising through my stom-ach like a tide.

"So, obviously, the next question for everyone is who this woman is. According to the milkman, Lily – or, who we *think* was Lily – seemed to be upset, but still going with this woman quite willingly. She also didn't have a bag with her. If this was a planned runaway, wouldn't she have wanted to take something with her – a toothbrush – at least?"

I assume that Mum means this as a rhetorical question, but when I look at her I realize she wants answers. From *me*.

"Jesus, Mum, how would I have a clue? You know I haven't been proper friends with Lily in a long time."

"I know, love, I know. And I want to keep your name out of this as much as we can, but, unfortunately, you're the only person who knew Lily very well. She's a very insular kid. Even Rory seems to have been oblivious to what was going on in her head."

I almost ask, "Who's Rory?", forgetting that "Roe" is a title only shared with a trusted few.

"I don't know, Mum. What do you want me to say? Like, Lily can be odd, but I don't know why she would just follow a stranger into the street."

"What about the woman? Do you have any idea who

that could be? Is there anyone she was talking to, even online or something?"

"Mum, I keep telling you, *I don't know.*"

"I'm sorry. It's just —" she tightens her grip on the steering wheel, even though the motor is off — "when a man takes a teenage girl from her bed, you expect it, you … you know what that's about. But when a *woman* takes her…"

She stares through the windscreen in silence, blinking hard. Wondering, I think, how she could have possibly raised five children and have nothing like this even cross her mind before. For a moment, I think about what it must be like to be her. To think you've seen everything that could hurt children, and then have to contend with something new.

"Mum," I say, putting my hand on her back. "It will be OK, won't it?"

She nods and folds me into a hug, holding me tight.

"Let's go inside," she says. "You *honk* of wine."

Crap.

"And no, I'm not thrilled about it, but I'm glad you're not getting rat-arsed in a field. If you're going to drink, please try to only do so in houses where there are at least two parents and at least one saxophone."

I trudge up the stairs to bed with a pint glass of cold water in my hand. I tell myself that I won't be able to sleep, but as soon as I pull my dress off and put my head on the pillow, I'm out.

The wine sends me into a heavy, drunken slumber that lends itself naturally to heavy, twisted dreams. Dreams where a dark-haired woman remains constantly in my field of vision, but always just out of my grasp. I can never look at her face-on. I only get flashes. A lock of straggling black hair that doesn't curl or wave even though it's soaking wet. A mouth that is full but completely unlined, devoid of any spiderweb lines of cracked skin.

I am following her down the path I walked with Roe, the path that stretches alongside the Beg, tripping behind her and screaming at her to turn around. I keep wanting to call out to her, to command something of her, but my mouth can't find the words. Who is she? What is she? I grapple at it, like my mind is pawing at a cliff edge that keeps falling away. She's something. Something in a home. A maid? A cook? Something in a nursery?

Finally, we reach the narrow underpass where Roe and I almost kissed, but didn't. Where he told me that witches know things by their true names. At this memory, the word "housekeeper" shoots across my brain like a burning comet.

She starts to turn around, and I see the curve of a slightly piggy, upturned nose, and the beginnings of a smile. My mouth starts to fill up with water, dirty river water that tastes like mud, metal and weeds.

I wake up with a pain in my stomach so deep that I have to stumble to the bathroom, holding my belly as though my guts are about to explode out of it.

The vomit is fluorescent pink and tastes like acid, and with each new retch, I vow to never drink red wine ever again. I clutch the side of the bowl, shivering as chunks of barely digested meat are ejected out of me. My thick, frizzy hair keeps spilling forwards, flecks of vomit sticking to it like paint splatters.

Once my stomach is totally empty, I run the ends of my hair under the tap, brush my teeth and wash my face with Mum's expensive wash. I almost feel OK again, except for a thudding, pulsating headache that's ringing through my skull. I'm still trying to analyse the dreams, but it's like trying to transport water from one hand to the other. With each pass, another detail falls away. The feeling, however, stays strong. The woman from the cards has taken Lily. She's a demon, or a ghost, or a witch, and she sprung to life through the reading I gave Lily three Fridays ago. That's who the milkman saw. That's what has taken her.

Back in my bedroom, Tutu has taken advantage of the open door and is lying with his head between his paws, his tail thumping supportively. I pull back the covers and he burrows in, his doggy sense of empathy clearly detecting that I need help.

I settle back into bed and open my bedside cabinet, hoping that there's a Nurofen Plus in there. I dig around, my hands flailing at old colouring pencils, Post-it notes and popped-open Strepsil packets. My palm finally falls across something square and bulky. The precise weight and length of it is so familiar to me, and yet, so terrifying in this context.

The Chokey cards are back.

CHAPTER SIXTEEN

THE NEXT MORNING, I COME DOWNSTAIRS AND MUM, DAD and Jo are at the kitchen table. The Sunday papers are strewn around them, a pot of coffee steeping on the sideboard. Jo is reading the culture supplement, Dad has the magazine, Mum has the style. They all look so cosy, so blond, so part of the same unit. How can I tell them that a pack of cards that were confiscated from me almost two weeks ago are somehow now back in my possession? How do I tell them that a character from the same deck of cards took Lily away?

Do I even *believe* that, though? *Can* I believe that?

"Morning," Dad says gravely. "I hope I don't have to have a word with you about last night. The sound of you retching at 2 a.m. better be lesson enough."

"Yeah. Sorry. Honestly, I only had about three glasses. I don't think I'm a red wine person."

"Three glasses of wine is a lot, Maeve. It's not like having a bottle of beer or something. Wine goes to your head quickly."

"I know. Sorry," I mumble again, then turn to Mum. "So, you know those tarot cards that Miss Harris too—"

But I don't get to continue, because Jo, apparently, has something to say. She glances across at me disapprovingly, her nose wrinkled and annoyed.

"You woke everyone up," she says dismissively. "Also, where did you even *get* the wine from? Were Fiona's parents just giving you…"

"No," I say guiltily. "Fiona nicked it from their table."

"Right. So you went over to a new person's house and stole their parents' drink? Nice first impression."

"No, like I just said, Fiona took it."

"Well, she sounds like a real treasure."

"Why the hell do you care, Jo?"

"Girls, stop," Mum says. "Jo, this really has nothing to do with you. And Maeve, if everything with Lily weren't such a mess, I'd be eating the arse off you. As it stands, this is your first and only warning. Are we clear? Everyone?"

"Whatever," Jo says, and dramatically flips open the culture section again.

How did we get back here? How is it that when Mum and Dad are away, Jo can be the best person in the world, but when they're back, she acts like a total cow?

"And I don't want to hear a thing about those tarot cards again, OK?"

"But, Mum, the thing with the tarot cards is—"

"Maeve. Nothing. This is a tarot-free house, understood? They were fine for a bit of fun, but you've clearly taken them too seriously."

I hold my head in my hands, the pounding headache back.

"OK," I say weakly.

I spend the rest of the day in my room, trying not to think about the cards. I'm terrified of taking them out of the top drawer, suspecting that the moment I do, Mum or Dad or Jo will walk in and they'll be taken away again.

My relationship to the cards has changed. Something physical, something molecular has happened between us. Us. As though the tarot were a person. It's like there's some kind of electromagnetic force holding us together. Only I can't tell if I'm the metal or the magnet. If I go to the bathroom, or downstairs to make a cup of tea, it's like there's an invisible string that's being stretched too far, yanking on my fingers and toes. I used to feel like I was the master of these cards, the only person capable of interpreting their true message. Now I feel like they're the master of me.

In the afternoon, I take Tutu for a walk down by the Beg, the cards in my coat pocket. I don't know what I'm trying to achieve, exactly, but somehow it's the place I need to be. This is where Lily was last seen alive and where I encountered the Housekeeper in my dreams.

As I walk towards the old underpass, I see a flash of scarlet in the rapidly darkening evening, a tousle of shining dark curls winking under the lamplight. It's him. It doesn't feel surprising to see him here. He must have found out about the milkman yesterday, too. Maybe he even had the same dreams I did. Maybe he woke up feeling like his lungs were filled with river water.

"Hi," I say timidly.

He lifts his eyes from the ground. I may not be surprised to see him, but he is very shocked to see me.

"I'll go," I say. "Sorry. I just heard about ... you know. So I wanted to come down."

We watch one another for a moment. Wary, like two wild animals trying to see if the other will attack first. His eyes look darker in the wintery light, free from the emerald glint they flash in the day. We make eye contact for so long that I start wondering what he sees in mine. Does he watch for the grey-blue of my eyes, noticing their shift? Is that too much to expect from someone who hates me as much as he does?

I turn to go, clicking my tongue at Tutu nervously, uttering a "C'mon, boy," under my breath.

"No, Maeve, don't go," Roe says. "I'm sort of glad you're here."

My heart thumps like a grandfather clock being kicked over. "Really?"

"Yeah. I feel terrible for blowing up at you like that on Friday. I was way out of order. You didn't deserve that."

"I did. Everything you said was true, y'know?" I say, digging my hands into my jacket pockets. "I should have been a friend to Lily. And to you. But believe me, the only reason I wasn't in touch was because the school and my parents kept saying not to. You give families privacy at times like this – or something."

Roe frowns. "So I heard. Do you know, I think people only say that to make themselves feel better for not phoning or texting or whatever. I keep hearing that this is a time 'for family' but I have far less to say to my Aunt Jessica than I do to you. Frankly, I wish *you* were the one staying in the spare room."

"Thanks," I reply, uncertain and flustered. A genuine warmth bubbles through me, picturing myself back in the O'Callaghans' house. Not as Lily's friend, but as Roe's girlfriend. A sudden image of myself appears in my head, sitting up in the guest bed, his body sliding in next to mine.

I look at the floor, certain that he can see me thinking this, that I have turned his innocent comment into a fantasy about sharing a bed with him. My fingers wrench at the lining of my pockets, tearing at the string.

"Sorry," he says, "I, er … I didn't mean to make you uncomfortable."

"No, not at all," I bring my cold, chapped hands to my face, and realize that my cheeks are burning red. "Have you met Tutu?"

"I haven't," he says, bending down to scratch the dog's ear. "What is he, labradoodle?"

"Or cockapoo. I can't remember which."

I can remember, obviously. He's a cockapoo. But to contradict Roe at this point, even on the breed of my own dog, feels too dangerous. It's like I'm defusing a bomb, and one wrong tug on a wire could send us both sky-high.

"He looks more like your family than you do."

"Yeah," I laugh. "Another effortlessly charming blond Viking, aren't you, Tutes? Maybe I'll get a gnarly old tomcat so I feel like I have a friend in the house."

"That bad, huh?"

"Hey, I don't want to complain about family problems in front of you."

"Ha! Wow, you're right. I am Mr Family Problems." Roe's grimace is edged with a smile. "No, but seriously. Tell me about it. Give me something to think about that isn't Lil."

"Well, fine. It's my sister. Joanne? Do you remember her?"

"Of course I do. She took us to that marriage-equality rally a few years ago."

I had completely forgotten about Roe being there. I remember standing with Jo, yelling at the idiot with the "family values" speech, but I had forgotten that Roe was sometimes adjacent to my Lily memories. He was always her gawky, moody brother. Quiet and pale. Behind his back, we called him Colin, as in, the awkward shut-in from *The Secret Garden*.

"Oh yeah. I forgot you were there."

"It meant a lot to me, that day."

I say nothing. It feels like he's about to say something else, and I want to give him a chance.

"Anyway…" he continues. "You're having issues with Jo."

"Yeah. She's just always trying to be my parent, y'know? She thinks she can tell me what to do."

"Why do you think that is?"

"I don't know. I suppose she probably feels weird about living at home still, even though she's in her twenties. Maybe she feels … inadequate and that her life should have started by now. So she's trying to find some weird sense of purpose by being overbearing with me. Or something."

"It doesn't sound like it's 'or something'. It sounds like that's the whole deal."

I shrug. "Yeah."

"You're pretty smart at reading people. I can see why your tarot business went so well."

"Until it didn't," I finish.

"Yeah. Until it didn't."

I clasp at the cards in my pocket, wondering if now is

136

the time to tell him. About the Housekeeper, about the dream, about who took Lily.

"I want to talk to you about something," he says, just as I'm about to fish out the cards. "I have … a theory about what's happening with Lil."

I bite the inside of my cheek hard, and my hand clasps even tighter on the cards.

"OK. Tell me."

"Can we walk and talk? I feel … weird staying in one space. It's better when I'm moving."

"Sure."

So we walk, and he talks, and Tutu sniffs around us. Every so often I look up at him, his skin bluish, our heads almost level with one another. Girls in my class are always talking about height. All the boys from St Anthony's, regardless of how unbelievably average or boring or stupid they are, get a free pass if they're tall. They automatically become fanciable. Maybe that's why Roe has never cropped up in conversations before, when games of Who Has a Hot Brother? spread through lunchtime discussions. As a non-tall non-athlete, he was probably disqualified from the jump.

But surely I can't be the only person who noticed that he's gorgeous? When did that happen, and where was I when it did?

"So, on Friday. You saw that weird protest, right? At Basement?"

"Yeah. Fiona and I were there when the Children of Brigid guys showed up. We were trying on dresses when they came in to complain about the window display. Then a couple of hours later, they've managed to summon this huge crowd. It was bizarre."

"Right, so, you saw that everyone was really, really young, right?"

"Yes. It was crazy. Like *our* age. Fiona and I tried to research them but hardly anything came up."

"Right? For some reason, Children of Brigid have managed to keep their name out of the papers, but there have been all these weird reports lately about a spike in young people going religious. Joining 'organizations'."

Roe puts the word in bunny ears. This literally stops me in my tracks. *Organizations.* Where have I heard that before?

"It's like … it's like there are journalists who either want to find something but can't, or want to say something and they're not allowed to."

"Like Scientology? Aren't those guys famously into hounding people with their lawyers?"

"That's what I'm thinking. Anyway, they seem to be really good at attracting young, vulnerable teenagers. I'm thinking that maybe they managed to … to lure Lily away."

"Oh," I say, genuinely dazzled by this reasoning. I fidget. Yes. This sounds reasonable. Far more reasonable than, say an evil child-snatching witch summoned from a tarot card reading.

I suddenly feel very silly, and very young.

"What do your parents think? And the Gardaí?"

"They ignore everything I say." He shrugs. "They keep talking about 'minimizing my trauma', as if that's something you can just … *decide.*"

"It must be really lonely for you at home right now,"

I say, and the urge to touch him on the arm is so strong that I have to pinch my right hand to stop it from happening. "Have your parents gone crazy strict, like everyone else's?"

"The opposite. Weirdly enough, it's like they've stopped seeing me entirely," he says. "The funny thing is that they used to be so *strict*. Family dinners every night, no hanging around town after school. Homework done before TV. All that. Now, it's like they've realized that none of it ... mattered."

Roe stops walking and scoops his hand in the dirt. He picks up a stone and smooths it between his thumb and forefinger. It's so small and black that it almost looks like the necklace Dad got me from Portugal.

"I think they're still in shock. Like they've forgotten they have another kid. Last night, I just walked out of the house at 10 p.m. and didn't come back until after one. I don't think they even noticed. My mum was just sitting in her armchair, staring at nothing."

Turning to face the river, he unleashes the stone and lets it skim on the water's surface. It bounces once, twice, then sinks.

"And where were you?"

"Just walking. I actually went down to the Salvation Army to see if they knew anything about CoB. They didn't. Then I just walked around for a bit. Listened to music."

"If you really think there's something to this CoB story, you should join their Facebook group. That seems to be where they do most of their organizing. Fiona and I tried to join it, but as far as I know they haven't replied. I think they're ... choosy."

139

I show it to him on my phone. He pulls out his own, finds the group and clicks "join group".

"I'm going to go to one of their meetings," he says. "I'll play the vulnerable artsy teen card. Make them think I need help or whatever. Maybe it'll get me closer to Lily. Honestly, I wouldn't be surprised if she's at some Jesus Camp somewhere, wearing a sack dress and picking beans."

"Sure," I reply. "Finding the Virgin Mary's face in a carrot. I can see it."

We laugh, and it feels good. Good to imagine a different outcome for Lily. Good to think of this as a story that could be funny some day, a thing we all look back on and laugh about together.

And that's how we spend the evening. Walking the length of the river until we're on the outskirts of the city centre, talking about who we are, and who we were when we first knew each other, as sibling-of-friend, as friend-of-sibling. We dig out isolated moments from our adjacent childhoods. Snatches of time where we were briefly aware of each other, our lives like planets whose orbits could only briefly synch with one another.

I get two texts, one from each parent. Both of them are frantic, as if suddenly conscious that they haven't seen me in a few hours. I message back, and tell them I'm on a dog walk with Fiona.

DON'T BE LATE, Mum messages back.

"There was a birthday party," Roe says. "Lily was going through some kind of Enid Blyton phase and she'd read about that stupid game. That reverse hide 'n' seek English kids played."

140

"Ah, how charmingly Protestant of her," I nudge.

"Hey," he says, rolling his eyes. "I get enough of that in a Catholic boys' school."

He wrinkles his brow. "Anyway, what was that game called again?"

"Sardines?"

"Yes!

"I remember."

"We were under my parents' bed."

And then, suddenly, I really do remember it. Lying stiff under a cast-iron bed, my limbs rigid, lolling my head sideways to look at him. Him. Shrimpy and black-haired. Buck-toothed, with his pointer finger on top of his closed mouth. *"Ciúnas!"* he whispered. *"Ciúnas."*

"You told me to shut-up in Irish," I tell him. "You told me, *'Ciúnas!'* Like you were my teacher. I hated you so much for that."

"Oh my God, I was such a prissy little kid," he says, rolling his eyes at the memory. "I'm sorry."

"No, don't be. It was great that there was someone to feel cooler than."

"Y'know, sometimes I forget what a cow you are, but there you go and remind me."

Mum phones to ask where I am. I reply that I'm still out with the dog and she says, *"Still?"* in a suspicious way, so we turn back.

We have to walk through the tunnel underpass again, a place so devoid of light that I can't even see my hands when I wave them in front of my face. It's narrow: about the width of a wardrobe. Tutu charges through it, preferring to sniff at the riverbank on the other side. Roe and I have to plod. It's too narrow for both of us to walk through comfortably side by side, so I fall in behind him. I try to keep my pace up to match his, but my foot catches on a beer bottle left rolling on its side.

I stumble forwards, arms flailing in front of me, crashing into Roe's shoulder in the darkness.

"Hey, hey!" he says, catching me. He puts his arm around my shoulder to steady me.

He leaves it there.

We stand, for a moment, in total darkness. My left side against the clammy stone wall. My right side wedged into his warm frame. I can feel his ribcage softly, silently moving with his breath.

I don't move. I don't think.

A lie.

I *do* think.

I think: if he were going to kiss me, now would be the moment. All he would need to do is turn his head slightly, to angle his body just a couple of inches, and we would be nose to nose, lip to lip. A movement that, if you rounded it down, would be hardly a movement at all, but would change everything.

I feel his body turn. Now we are facing each other. I still can't see anything, but can feel the slight huff of his breath on my lower lip. He places a hand on each of my shoulders.

My skin is screaming to be touched. Pleading with me in a way my body has never pleaded before. Making its case like a lawyer in court. *Miss Chambers, I think you'll see, based on the evidence provided, that this boy wants to touch you, and you*

should respond by jumping on him, wrapping your legs around his
waist and kissing him until he falls over.

Someone driving on the road must be using their headlights, because in an instant, we are shot through with the
electric white light that fills the tunnel.

The light breaks something. It gives him sense. He
takes half a step backwards, and lets his hands slide from my
shoulders, to my elbows and then away altogether.

"Well," he says, finally, "look who's playing sardines
again."

And for the second time in our new friendship, Roe
O'Callaghan leaves me, rejected in a tunnel.

CHAPTER SEVENTEEN

I DREAM ABOUT THE HOUSEKEEPER AGAIN THAT NIGHT. A cold snap hits and I wake up with clouds of my own breath hanging in the air.

I'm following the Housekeeper along the Beg, but she is perpetually a step ahead of me. I snatch at her gown, her wet hair, her icy, sculpted fingers, but I can never get a grip on her. When we reach the underpass, she turns around to face me. That's when the water comes. The muddy river water that fills up my stomach and lungs, spilling out of my mouth, dirty and tasting like copper.

Sometimes I get a sense that Lily is there, watching somehow. It's not something I can explain or point to, just a general feeling that only makes sense in the slippery dream logic of the Housekeeper's world. Lily is there, but not visible.

On Monday morning, I see Roe on the bus.

"Hey," he says, moving aside to make room for me. "Wow, are you OK?"

"Yeah," I reply abruptly, scanning my uniform for stains. "Why?"

"You look like you haven't slept. And believe me, I know what *that* looks like."

"I haven't," I say, and for a moment I consider telling him about the dreams, and the Housekeeper, and the sense that Lily is close but unable to show herself. But it's too much. Too weird. Too silly. And his theory about CoB is solid, even if it doesn't exactly ring true in my head.

"I'm just worried about her," I say, truthfully. "And … I don't know, I just have this feeling that she's near by."

Roe nods, looking relieved to have a partner in melancholy.

"What are you doing tonight?" he asks.

"Nothing."

"There's a CoB meeting in town. They approved my Facebook request. Do you want to come?"

"Uh … sure. If you think it's safe."

"What? Are you afraid of getting brainwashed, Chambers?"

Oh God. He's used my last name. Lord protect me from beautiful musicians who call me by my last name.

"No," I reply, my voice a whole octave higher than I want it to be. "Let's do it."

"The meeting is at eight. Meet you at the river around seven? We can walk in together."

"Sure." Great. The river. The site of nightmares and constant sexual rejection.

That day, the story of the woman with Lily is around the whole school. It sours the glamour for people, I think. Running away with a strange man, or even being kidnapped by him, has a hot tinge of danger to it. Running away with a strange woman is a different proposition.

"Huh," I hear one girl say. "I guess it makes sense she was a lesbian."

"Oh, come on," says another. "*Everyone* knew Lily O'Callaghan was a lesbian."

145

"Have you seen her brother?"

"I know. Clearly it runs in the…"

I walk out of the room. I don't think anybody notices.

At lunch, I tell Fiona about the almost-kiss in the underpass. She is furious, which is comforting.

"You can't just *do* that," she rails. "You can't just… What did he do, again?"

"Sort of … nothing. He steadied me from falling over and then his face was, I don't know … very close to mine."

"Huh. It sounded sexier the first time. Go through it again."

So I do. The darkness. Our bodies touching. The slight warmth of his breath on my lower lip. The way he said we were "playing sardines again".

"Ughhhhhhh, kill me. Kill me dead."

"Why do you think he's being so … I don't know, such a *tease*?"

"Wow, problematic."

"You know what I mean. He seems to really like me. And he wants to spend all this time with me. And…"

"Maeve. His sister is missing. Can you imagine how screwed up his head is right now?"

I don't have to imagine it. I've had the nightmares, felt the guilt, hung on to the desperate, cosmic pull of the tarot cards. I still can't banish the idea that the cards have something to do with Lily's disappearance.

But Roe is smart. I keep reminding myself of that. Much smarter than me – and he might be onto something with his CoB lead.

And let's face it, at this point, if he asked me to spend the evening with him at a maggot lovers' convention, I would say yes.

I get home at half four, and make a plan to do my homework, walk the dog, eat dinner, and head out. None of that happens, though. Instead I spend the whole afternoon in my room, looking at my eyebrows with a pocket mirror, plucking two hairs, and then feeling guilty that I am taking any care with my appearance at all.

This is not a date, Maeve.

I put down the tweezers, my skin red and throbbing. How can things be going well and terribly at once? On the one hand, I have a new, incredibly fun friend who seems to really like me. A hot boy wants to spend time with me. On the other hand, my best friend is missing, my entire school thinks I'm a murderous witch, and I haven't slept in days.

It's too cold to make any kind of effort with clothes. It is virtually impossible to look sexy and mature when you're three jumpers deep. I feel like a toddler when I meet him, layered up in a blue duffel coat and wooly hat.

"Hey," he says. "Your nose is all red."

"Oh, what?" I start touching my nose, as if that's going to do anything, and he smiles.

"You look like Paddington Bear."

Ouch.

"Thank … you?"

"Have you got marmalade sandwiches packed?"

This isn't flirtatious banter. He's scared out of his mind, filling the freezing evening with nervous Paddington references.

There's some indecision about whether we should get

the bus in or not, but after three minutes waiting for it and hopping from leg to leg to keep warm, we give up. We trudge into town, the evening black, the grass frosting and crunchy underfoot. The closer we get, the quieter Roe becomes. The stupid jokes drain away. Eventually, he pipes up.

"Maeve."

"Mmm?"

"Tell me about her."

"About who?" I reply, playing dumb. He doesn't even dignify it with a response.

I sigh and kick the ground in front of me.

"What do you want to know?"

"I don't know. We saw so little of each other the past few years. Y'know, Mum and Dad were always so big on activities and schedules that even when we were small, it always felt like we were in different time zones. She was either at cello or in her room or off with you."

He sighs, and I almost feel like apologizing for Lily and me. For how insular we were. It had never even occurred to me that Roe would have wanted to hang out with us.

"I'm not *blaming* her," he continues. "I've been hiding in my room with my guitar for a good six years. I never showed an interest in her world, either. But ... I *regret* it, Maeve. She's my only sibling. We didn't even fight. No one fights in our house, not even my parents. Everyone just ... glides past one another."

That was always the pull of going to the O'Callaghans'. The fact that you could watch your cartoons in one room while the grown-ups watched the news in the other. The cool, clean, quiet rooms. The way Lily and Roe's toys were

148

never broken, or handed down. And when it all got too sedate, me and Lil could always go to my house. I'd never considered that Roe didn't have that option. That Roe, now that I properly think about it, didn't ever have any friends.

None of this is actually my business to say, of course. So instead, I just talk about Lily.

"Do you know how she was left-handed?"

"Oh, come on, Chambers! I said we weren't close. I didn't say she was a stranger."

"No, I mean, obviously, she was left-handed, but did you know that she taught herself how to be right-handed?"

"What?"

"Yeah. When we were like, eleven?" I pause a moment, trying to remember. "She said she wanted to have a second form of handwriting that she could fall back on, if she ever needed it."

"What could she possibly need that for?"

"I don't know. Maybe … maybe she planned on a life of forgery. Maybe she always sort of knew she was going to end up on the run."

"You think she's on the run?"

"I know she left your house willingly. You know that. With that … woman."

With the Housekeeper. Say it. Witches know things by their true names.

"Right. With that woman."

He slows down, takes his phone out of his pocket, then reorients himself based on the blue arrow on his screen.

"Are we almost there?"

"I think so. The invite says 'Elysian Quarter' but I don't

149

know where that is, and Google Maps doesn't seem to have a clear idea either."

We're standing on a narrow street at the edge of the city. Every building seems to be an anonymous-looking apartment block. There's a pub winking yellow light in the distance, but nothing that looks remotely like a meet-up space.

I shiver and stamp my feet. "I hope it's warm inside."

"I know, right? They said it might snow later."

"It never snows properly here."

At that moment, two boys and a girl push past us, bullish and hurried. We shrug at each other and fall in casually behind them as they turn into a courtyard and hit a buzzer on one of the apartment buildings. The trio eye us critically, but don't say anything.

"Hi," I say, unable to maintain the tension.

"Hey," one of the boys says evenly. He's a couple of years older than me, but has the kind of red-rimmed watery eyes that you initially mistake for tears and then realize, no, that's just his face.

The buzzer sounds and the door to the apartment building pops open. We trail into an elegant lobby and look for the lift.

Roe flashes his phone at me. *Apartment 44, Floor 8, Elysian Quarter.*

We're definitely in the right place. We get into the lift with the other three, hugging our elbows to our ribs in the cramped, mirrored box. Roe hits the "8" button. It's only then do I feel comfortable getting a good look at our companions, peering into the mirror rather than directly into their eyes.

The girl reminds me of Lily, although I can't figure out why. She doesn't look anything like her, but there's some quality the two of them share that I can't quite put my finger on. A squirming discomfort. A sense of being unable to relate to the physical world.

"Are you guys here for the meeting?" I offer.

They don't say anything, but the girl unconsciously nods and Roe smiles at her.

"I'm really excited for it to start," he says, maintaining careful eye contact with her, and she smiles back.

"Is it your first one?"

"Yep. Just got the invite today," Roe replies smoothly. "I'm so glad they let me join the Facebook group."

"How long did you have to wait to be accepted?" she responds, her eyes round and excitable.

"Two days."

The two guys look at each other sharply and the girl makes an "oh" shape with her mouth.

"Two days!" she gasps. "I had to wait *two weeks*."

The lift doors open and we trail up the halls. It smells like chlorine. The girl sees me sniffing and grins at me.

"It's because we're near the roof," she says, glee in her voice. "There's a pool on the roof and in the summer, we're going to be allowed to use it!"

When we get to Apartment 44, the boys knock on the door, and I'm expecting some kind of secret password to be uttered. None comes. Instead, the door flings open, and a tall, blond man in his mid-twenties welcomes us in. He's all smiles, and I immediately recognize him as one of the men from Basement.

"Clara! Ian! Cormac!" he says, ushering them in.

He takes an extra moment considering us. "Rory –" he smiles benevolently – "I'm so glad you were able to come. I'm Aaron, the chapter leader. Please, make yourself at home."

He shakes Roe's hand rigorously, the whites of his knuckles glowing.

"And you brought a *guest*," he says, his eyes scanning me. "You know, we have a very strict policy here around guests. Especially on your first meeting. We don't allow it, Rory."

"Yes, I'm sorry," Roe says, grappling for an excuse. "I didn't realize, and, I just thought that Maeve might benefit from…"

The man puts his hand up. "Don't worry, Rory. We can make an exception this time."

He turns to me. "Hello, Maeve. I'm Aaron." He takes one quick look at my blue duffel and smiles. "Can I take your coat?"

I shrug it off and give it to him.

"Wow," he says, his voice mildly flirtatious. "And here was me, hoping you had a wedding dress on under there."

CHAPTER EIGHTEEN

ONCE, YEARS AGO, ME AND LILY WATCHED A DOCUMENTARY about cults. It was on very late on the Bravo channel, and it was advertised for weeks as *"a disturbing look at how one man could drive ordinary American girls … to murder."*

The thought was electrifying. Someone could just *make* you commit murder? How?

It was on at 1 a.m., so we had a sleepover at my house and watched it. I don't remember much about it, but there was definitely an interview with a former cult leader who was known for recruiting teenage girls. The interviewer asked him how he recruited his followers. Simple, he said. He just approached groups of girls at shopping malls, singled one out and told her that she had beautiful eyes.

"If she said 'thank you', or even just laughed, I would move on," he said. *"But if she tried to deflect the compliment or looked down at the ground, I would ask her for her number. Because that girl is the one with the hole inside of her."*

That is what it is like inside the apartment at Elysian Quarter.

I am standing in a room full of people with a hole inside of them.

There's about thirty of them all together, ranging from mid-teens to early twenties. Everyone is drinking orange juice out of wine glasses and they have that kind of nervy, tremulous energy that makes them cover their mouths when they laugh and bite their lips as they listen. There's nothing individually *wrong* with anyone, just a collective sense of unease. They're all standing in groups of threes and fours, their shoulders slightly hunched. Absolutely nothing in their body language suggests, "Hey, come talk to us."

The apartment is big, open and airy, like living rooms are on sitcoms. There's a large window overlooking the city that we gravitate towards.

"What did that guy say about wedding dresses to you?" Roe asks quietly.

"Oh," I say, my face turning red. "Fiona and I were in Basement trying on wedding dresses the day of the protest. We saw him there, trying to give out to the shop manager."

He looks at me in confusion.

"As a *joke*, like," I say hurriedly. "We weren't trying on wedding dresses *seriously*. Fiona told them she didn't believe in God."

"Wow."

A small, flutey voice suddenly pipes up from behind us. "I didn't use to believe in God."

We turn around and a tiny girl with a long fringe is beaming at us. She's about seventeen.

"Hello," I say uncertainly.

"I used to think it was all crap. And when I learned about the Magdalene Laundries and the way they put girls in these horrible prisons just for getting pregnant, I thought, *Wow, the Catholic Church has ruined Ireland.*"

"And then what ... you changed your mind?" Roe asks.

154

"I realized that it wasn't the Church that ruined Ireland. Bad *people* ruined Ireland."

I want to ask her a little more about this, but at that moment the man who let us in stands in the centre of the room and taps his wine glass full of orange juice with a teaspoon.

"Circles, everyone. Circles."

A hush falls over the room as everyone forms a circle by sitting cross-legged on the floor. Roe and I copy them. I'm desperate to blend in, to be inconspicuous. But I already feel as if there's a big red dot on my head, singling me out as a non-believer. The girl next to me edges away slightly. She can tell I don't really want to be here.

"Hello, everyone!" Aaron says. He's the only one standing. He's not wearing the suit I saw him in on Friday, and, without it, he looks far younger. Twenty-five or -six. He's dressed casually, in jeans and a navy Hollister hoodie, with red Converse on his feet. "How are y'all today?"

A mumbling of "good" and "fine" fills the room.

"Oh, come on. I know we're all better than fine. How ARE y'all today?"

A grateful laugh rises. "GREAT!" one guy shouts, and another, louder laugh shoots up like a flare.

"Great! We're great? C'mon, everyone. Are we great?"

The room is feeling looser now, like stretched-out chewing gum.

"YEAH!"

"That's more like it." He smiles. "Now, I know we have a few new faces here today, so, as always, I thought we'd start with a game to warm up our circle time. That sound good to y'all?"

"Yeah!"

The 'y'all', full of Southern home-town charm, feels impossibly glamorous in this beautiful Irish apartment. But every instance feels rehearsed, dropped just at the right time to create a family barbecue atmosphere.

"All right, all right, let me think." Aaron places his thumbs and forefingers together to make a triangle in front of his face, like loose prayer hands. "All right. I've got it. Who knows Two Truths and a Lie?"

A slightly, uncertain worried hum comes from the circle.

"Relax, guys! It's not as scary as it sounds. Basically, you say two true things about yourself, and one lie. We all have to guess which is the lie. They do this in drama school all the time and it's a great way to get to know each other. Like, OK, I'll go first."

He does the triangle in front of his face again and pads around the circle, smiling to himself.

"OK, so... My name is Aaron. My parents are divorced. I really love Billy Joel." He swings around and points at the very short girl. "Katie. Which one's the lie?"

"You ... love Billy Joel?" Katie says hopefully.

"Nope." He smiles. "I really, really love Billy Joel. My parents are, however, still happily married. Twenty-two years."

Katie goes beetroot-red and everyone titters again in appreciation.

"OK, now you guys go. Let's start with a new face. Let's start from ... Rory."

"Er, OK," Roe says. "Um ... I play the guitar. My birthday is in June. And my sister is a fish."

Another laugh from the group. Aaron grants us a quick, dry smile.

"Nice first try," he says. "I can't wait to meet your sister. Enid."

Enid is sitting to the right of Roe and Aaron is moving clockwise, so I won't have to think of my two truths and a lie for absolutely ages. She is dark-haired and would be pretty if her forehead wasn't in a perpetual furrow.

"OK," Enid says. "I'm twenty-one next week. I'm double-jointed."

Enid says this very quickly, as though she is psyching herself up for something major. You can feel the whole group leaning in, hungry to hear. Then, it all comes out, slick as an oil spill.

"And I've had unprotected sex with a man twice my age."

Silence. I try to catch Roe's eye, in a sort of "all that build-up, for *that*?" expression.

Aaron crouches down on the floor in front of Enid. He looks at her very closely, making the kind of intense eye contact that feels like it's between two people that know each other very well.

He reaches out to her lap, where her hands lie dormant.

"Enid," he says softly. "May I?"

She gives him her hand and he holds it, very tenderly, in front of everyone. I can feel the eyes of all the other girls goggling and realize that they have all wanted a moment like this. To hold Aaron's hand. To feel the full wattage of his American attention on them. I am close enough to see that Enid's hand is shaking, and her face has gone bright pink.

I turn away.

After a moment of silence, Aaron speaks again, softly massaging Enid's palm with his thumb.

"Oh, Enid. You're not double-jointed, are you?"

"No," she says, her voice soft. She sounds like she is about to cry.

"That's OK, sweetheart. That's OK. It's not what you wanted. It's not your fault."

I start to wonder if I'm missing something. Enid is *twenty*. Sure, having sex with a man twice your age isn't great, but surely it's not *that* big a deal, is it?

He puts an arm around her, cradling her, and she slowly begins to sob in his arms. Enid suddenly goes from being nervous and squirming to looking like a lamb suckling on a baby bottle. A golden calm settles over her. She is safe, cosy, warm, loved.

We all watch, our breaths held. Roe and I look at each other, dumbfounded. I don't know what we were expecting, but it wasn't this.

In a loud whisper, clearly intended for everyone to hear, Aaron tells Enid that he will check back in with her at the end of the meeting, and that they'll talk about this properly. He disentangles himself and moves down to the next person in the circle.

"Cormac," he says. It's one of the silent boys who came in the door with us. "Two truths and a lie."

"I ... play GAA. My favourite superhero is Ant-Man. And ... um..."

"Go on, Cormac. It's fine."

"Once, I, uh, I..."

"Come on, now."

"I, uh, shaved my legs. Just to see what it would feel like."

Roe's eyes are like saucers. If tensions were high when Enid spoke, they're at the ceiling now.

"Hey, man." Aaron claps his hands together in delight. "Cormac! Is that *all*? Dude! What are you *worried* about? That's nothing. That's just curiosity. Look. You're an athlete, right? Right?"

"Uh-huh."

"Swimmers shave their legs, did you know that? And, like, tons of other athletes. It doesn't mean anything. It doesn't mean you're gay. C'mon. You know that, don't you?"

"Yeah," says Cormac, his voice still uncertain.

"Man, you know as well as I do that there's no such thing as being *naturally* gay. I mean, nature would just break down completely, if that were the case, right?" He starts looking at the group, his palms up, giving a "these are just the facts" tone to everything he's saying.

"Animals wouldn't reproduce. People wouldn't reproduce. So if you're having feelings like that, it's because there's a bogey in your radar, y'know what I mean? It's because there's all this weird, negative, confusing gunk on your windscreen, and you just need to clear that gunk off."

He shrugs and smiles. "I mean, otherwise, how would you *drive*?"

Everyone laughs, and Cormac laughs hardest.

My muscles tense, my fingernails digging half-moon crescents into my palms. I remember talk like this from a few years ago, during the marriage equality referendum. But it always came from the mouths of old men. Never twenty-something Americans in hoodies and Converse.

Aaron keeps going around the room, and the revelations get more and more intense. When Enid first said her piece, I thought she was the one playing the game wrong. But no: it's Roe "my sister is a fish" O'Callaghan who was playing it wrong. This isn't a funny game. It's public confession.

But strangely enough, Aaron barely has to work to get people to confess. They're already spurred on by the person who came before them, seduced by the concept of his full, undivided attention, his pep talks, his hugs.

A girl confesses to kissing her female best friend. Aaron soothes her, says it's not what she wanted, that she was manipulated, led astray.

A boy confesses to having suicidal thoughts. Aaron tells him it's only natural, normal, to want to take solutions into your own hands when life is upsetting you. But the true answer to finding self-satisfaction is to work on the world around you, not to hurt yourself. To channel your life into positive work.

On and on it goes. People cry. And the longer we spend there, the more convinced I am that Lily would never be taken in by this. She would never let someone tell her that gay people weren't real, or that they were "confused". Aaron's response to virtually everyone is that they are confused. Having sex is a result of confusion. Being gay is confusion. Having depression is confusion.

"Maeve?"

"Um ... I'm sixteen. I have a dog. And I ..."

I've been so focused on everyone else that I haven't prepared my piece. I haven't even thought of a satisfying lie for my "truth".

"... I pushed my best friend away, and now I'm afraid I'll never get her back."

The words fall out like copper coins spitting out of a vending machine. Thoughtless and clunky and entirely unwanted. Why did I say that? Why would I bring that here?

Aaron fixes his eyes on me for a moment. I wait for the onslaught of sympathy and motivational speaking. But it doesn't come. He just keeps looking at me, his fingers in that triangle shape again. There's a mild disgust in his eyes, a slight wrinkling of his nostrils as if picking up on a bad smell.

Finally, he speaks.

"Oh, Maeve," Aaron says simply. "I'm sure you'll find the answer somewhere."

And that's it. He claps his hands together and announces that it's time for a ten-minute break.

I can't believe it. I feel offended. Where's my hug? Where's my pep talk? Don't I deserve Aaron's attention? Shouldn't I be cradled in his love, just like everyone else?

Aaron starts making the rounds, first with Enid, then Cormac, then the boy with depression.

Roe turns to me. "Look, I know I dragged us here, but I think it was a bad idea. I don't think Lily would ever go in for this stuff. Do you?"

"Not really," I reply. "Are you sure it's OK if we just *leave*, though?"

"Yeah, that guy won't care. He's got a pretty dedicated flock as it is."

"All right, let me get my coat."

I find it hanging in a closet, and when I get back, Aaron is speaking very intently to Roe.

"You're not leaving already, Rory, are you, buddy?"

Roe looks to me nervously. "Yeah. I said I'd get Maeve home before it got too late."

"Look, the sharing stuff isn't for everyone," Aaron says conspiratorially. "But I think you're really going to like the second half. It's more action-orientated. We brainstorm on how we can be agents for change and we actually *act* on those ideas. You can have a lot of influence."

"I'm ready to go now," I say loudly, buttoning my coat.

Aaron looks at me like I'm a fly buzzing around him. He moves in closer on Roe.

"Look, Rory, I know you feel different, and a little lost, maybe like you're … *not like other guys*, but…"

I remember the TV show again. About trying to spot the holes in people. About that being the trick to controlling those around you.

Aaron has seen the hole in Roe. And, for whatever reason, he wasn't able to see it in me.

And for the first time in my life, I feel unbelievably, incandescently powerful.

"We have to go now," I say, louder again. "Thank you for inviting us."

I take Roe by the hand, clasping it firmly in my own, and pull him towards the door. He follows, and the last thing I see before the door slams are Aaron and the Children of Brigid's curious faces.

CHAPTER NINETEEN

WE GET INTO THE LIFT AND PRETEND NOT TO NOTICE THAT I am still holding his hand.

We cross the lobby, then the courtyard, and are on the street.

And.

We.

Are.

Still.

Holding.

Hands.

"Oh my God," he says, and he finally lets go. "It's actually snowing."

He turns his palms upwards, and he's right. Tiny flakes of white are falling into his hands.

"Wow," I say, doing the same. "I'm not sure what that's a sign of, but it's definitely a sign of ... something."

We walk to the bus stop, where the electronic sign says that the bus is only two minutes away. We give a grateful gasp of relief and sit on the bench.

"What *was* that in there, Maeve? It wasn't even that religious. It was just really manipulative and creepy."

"I guess they break people down and build them back up again, under the guise of some crap game. Maybe the religion stuff comes later. When you're already dependent on Aaron and his hugs."

"Do you think there are, like, dozens of identical meetings happening? Tonight? All over the country?"

"All with identical Aarons? Maybe."

"Lily would never join that. Never, never. I'm certain."

"How are you so certain, though?" I ask. "I mean, I haven't spoken to Lil properly in a year. I have no idea what she might believe now. You don't know, either."

"No," he says, with certainty. "Don't ask me why. But it's a no."

"OK. I guess we can cross that off the list."

"Yeah," he says, flagging down the approaching bus. "And now there's nothing left."

We climb onto the bus, tear our tickets and sit down. I want to tell him that no, there's not quite *nothing* left on the list. There is one big, fat something. The something that is burning inside of my coat pocket, that hasn't been more than ten feet from me since the day they reappeared in my bedside locker.

As the bus trundles along, I ease the cards out of my pocket.

"Oh Jesus," he says, a bitter laugh in his voice. "Them again."

"Do you want me to put them away? I just wanted to talk to you about one thing…"

"You know, you guys are two sides of the same coin."

"Me and who?"

"You and American Aaron."

"What in hell is that supposed to mean?"

164

My body recoils at the suggestion, as I back towards the window, and cold space opens up where our legs once touched.

"You force people to confess their problems to you, and then you hold all the power over them. You use their stories to manipulate them."

I'm dumbfounded. "You don't really think that, do you?"

"Well. No. Not really. But you have to admit, there are similarities."

"I don't *force* anyone."

"And neither does Aaron, you could say."

"Why are you saying this?"

"Why do you always underestimate yourself?"

I roll my eyes. "Is this really the time for a lecture on self-confidence?"

"No, I mean, your opinion of yourself is so low that you completely underestimate the effect you have on people. That the things you say to them – or *don't* say to them – matter."

"I said I was sorry about Lily Roe."

"I'm not talking about Lily. I'm talking about everyone. Take some friggin' responsibility for yourself, Maeve."

I stuff the cards back in my pocket and stare out of the window. Does Roe have a point? Those sessions I held in the Chokey, where half the school came and confessed their secrets to me. Did it make me feel powerful? A little, yes. But I didn't do anything with that power. I didn't abuse it. Not the way Aaron does.

Until Lily went missing, that is.

A familiar shudder of guilt washes over me. Lily is

missing. Lily is missing because of me. Because of me, and these cards, and the Housekeeper. I lean my head against the bus window.

"Hey," Roe says gently. "I wasn't being serious. It was more like ... a thought exercise. Sorry. You're nothing like Aaron."

I'm sick of keeping this to myself. I need to tell him about the Housekeeper dreams. Even if it's all nonsense, I need to lance the boil that's growing under my skin. I need to say her name out loud.

"Roe," I say, "there's something I need to tell you. It's about the tarot reading I gave Lily."

"Christ, not this again."

"Just listen, OK?" I exhale loudly, warming up. "So, in the reading, this card came up. This card that didn't belong to the deck. I'd seen it once before, but I took it out and put it in my desk drawer because there was no explanation anywhere on the internet about what it meant. And ... it scared me. It's this horrible illustration of a dark-haired woman in a wedding gown with a knife between her teeth. So I took it out. And then, when I read for Lily, the card was there again."

"Can you show me the card now? In your deck?"

"No," I say, chewing at the skin on my thumbnail. "I haven't been able to find her since. It's like she has to be ... summoned, or something. Anyway, I've been having these dreams. These dreams about this woman, and in the dreams, it's like Lily is watching. Like she's there, but not able to show herself."

I pause, trying to suss out his reaction to all of this. He just keeps staring mutely at the bus seat in front of him.

"Also," I continue. "And this bit is … well. So, Miss Harris confiscated my cards after Lily went missing. Totally banned them from the school. But on Saturday night, after my mum told me about Lily being spotted by the milkman with a dark-haired woman, the cards were suddenly in my bedside cabinet. It was like they'd never left."

"No," he says, shaking his head. "I don't believe you."

"I don't want to believe me, either. But that's what happened. That's what's *happening*."

"So, what? You think Lily summoned this demon accidentally when you gave her that reading?"

I bite the skin inside my cheek, swallowing the honest answer. The fact that I said, '*I wish you would just disappear…*' right to his sister's face. She didn't summon the Housekeeper. I did. Or we both did.

"Yeah," I answer. "She could have."

It's not a lie. It's possible that no one summoned the Housekeeper, and Lily could be shacked up with her cello teacher right now. Roe doesn't need to know what I said. In fact, it's imperative to us working together that he doesn't.

The bus stops. We're back in Kilbeg. We walk in silence for a few minutes.

"Where do you see her? In the dreams?"

"Near the … uh …" My brain wants me to say, "… the place you refuse to kiss me," but I resist. "Near the underpass. Always there."

"Well, let's go there then."

"What?"

"Maybe there'll be … I don't know, a clue there."

I look at him doubtfully. "I'm not sure…"

167

My phone buzzes. Dad.

Where are you?

Near the river. Omw home.

I type this, and then rethink. Do I really want Mum and Dad to know that I'm by the river, where Lily was last seen alive?

Delete, delete, delete.

Nearly home. See you soon. x

Be safe. Road slippy.

"Come on, Maeve. I have to try everything, no matter how bizarre it is. Everything."

"OK," I say uncertainly.

We trudge in silence, the snow falling on our hair and shoulder blades. I can't remember the last time I saw snow like this in Ireland. Five or six years, at least. We're too near the Atlantic. Even if it falls, snow usually melts the moment it hits the ground. But this snow is sticking and gathering in heaps beneath our feet.

The bricks at the underpass are glazed with ice, sparkling like grey diamonds.

We stand there a moment, uncertain.

"What do we do now?" I ask, tentatively.

"Can you feel Lily here? Feel her watching?"

I close my eyes for a moment, and search for … something. Some nameless, shiftless presence or sign that she's near. I burrow down into the deep black nothingness of myself, in the hopes I'll dredge up a fossil of Lily.

"No," I reply, opening my eyes. "Sorry. It's just a dream. I don't know why I brought it up."

"Read my cards."

"Here?"

"Yes. That's how you summoned this … thing. Maybe we could summon her again."

"Roe, I don't know. I haven't done this in a while. And the last time I did the results were … well…"

"I don't care, Maeve. Just read me, OK? You read me before, remember? Just do this. I'll never ask you again after this. I swear."

His voice is so desperate, his eyes shining with tears. The winter light is so dark that his lips, so full they look almost like they're pouting, appear purple.

How can I say no to him? What right could I possibly have?

"Grand," I say. "Let's get into the tunnel, though, it's too wet out here."

We sit, crouched and uncomfortable, our phone torches the only source of light. Every couple of minutes a car drives past, sending vibrations in the air around us, filling our ears with noise. People are driving carefully, slowly in the snow, and when the crunch of wheels rumbles past, we're forced to stop talking, and just stare at one another.

"Shuffle," I say, handing him the cards.

The minute he touches them, the magnetic pull I feel with the cards grows even stronger. Like the deck has a rope attached to it, and the other end is wrapped around my ribcage. The cards slip through his fingers as he shuffles, falling through the empty dark space between one hand and another. My chest tightens with each movement. My lungs feel like they're working at half capacity.

"Are you OK?" he asks, passing them back to me.

169

"Yeah," I murmur. It would be too much to tell him about this. Too much weird stuff for one day.

"Right, I think this will work best if we invent a spread. For finding Lily."

"Right. Great. Good plan. What does that mean?"

"It means we decide what each card means. Like, one card could be 'where Lily is' and another could be 'what's blocking her from coming back' and another could be 'what we need to do to get her back'."

"Yes. This is all good. Is this how it works?"

"I don't know. I'm sort of making this up."

"Well, it sounds legit. So should I pick the cards?"

"Yeah, go on."

I fan the cards out in front of him. His hands, now red from the cold, hover over each card. He plucks three and lays them face down in front of me.

I flip over the first card. The "where Lily is" card. It's the Four of Swords. The card shows a knight in full armour lying on top of a tomb. Stained-glass windows are winking in the background and three swords are hanging above him, the points facing down. The fourth sword is lying by his side.

"Jesus," Roe says, panic in his voice. "She's *dead*?"

"No, no. This is good. This is positive, I think. It means rest. Of prolonged, enforced rest. Look, the sword is still at the knight's side: he's going to get up and fight; he just can't right now."

"OK," Roe says, picking up the card to peer at it closer. As his fingers pinch the card, I feel the pull again. A slight fizzing beneath my skin, like my blood has changed its direction of flow.

I blink my eyes a few times, trying to steady myself.

From where I sit opposite him, I can only see the back of the card, a plain red square pattern. But between blinks, I can suddenly see the card from his point of view. I see the knight on the tomb. I see my own face, looking tired and desperate.

I am Roe, and I am watching myself blink like a startled rabbit.

What?

I blink again. It's gone.

"Are you OK?" he asks. "You look like you're going to be sick."

"Uh, yeah. Let's ... let's turn over the next card."

"Which one is this?"

"This one tells us what's blocking Lily from coming back."

I flip the card over and immediately put my fingers in my mouth.

It's the Devil. Not a Halloween devil, either. This is an old-school biblical devil, with horns and goat legs. Alongside him trail two people, a man and woman, naked and in chains.

Neither of us says a word.

"Maeve," Roe prods. "This is the part where you tell me that this card isn't as bad as it looks."

"Um..."

"Maeve."

"I'm thinking! I'm rusty at this, remember? So the Devil is mostly about something having control over you. It's usually about addiction or being unable to break out of a bad relationship. But in Lily's case, it could be the Housekeeper."

He picks it up and peers at it again. Again, the tug, the nausea, the sense that my body is connected to the cards and therefore connected to him.

"Roe, stop it."

"Stop what?"

"*Touching* them."

"But … why?"

"I don't know. It's making me feel sick."

"I don't understand. Are you all right?"

"Give me a second, OK. Just give me a second."

I line my back against the tunnel, close my eyes and breathe in and out, in and out. The wall is cold and damp, its grey wetness soaking through my coat and raising goose pimples on my spine.

Another car passes. Another flash of headlights, dancing on the thin skin of my eyelids.

A split happens inside my own head, like a TV screen divided into two. I am lost in the darkness of my own head, but I am also watching myself from the other side of the tunnel, seeing my head loll. Beads of sweat gather on my forehead, illuminated by the passing car.

"Maeve," Roe says. Or I say. I can't tell. I can feel my mouth saying my own name, but it doesn't feel like *my* mouth.

I bury my face in my knees, wrapping my arms around my legs. Am I going to be sick?

Please don't let me be sick. Please don't let me be sick.

"Oh, shit, Maeve. Don't pass out. C'mon, let's get out of here."

172

He wraps an arm around my shoulder. "C'mon, Maeve. Get up. You can get up."

"Mmmmno," I mumble.

"OK, well, grand, I'll just sit here with you until you can."

He props himself against the wall, his arm still around me. I fall against him, snuggling into the crook of his neck. Through the sickening nausea, I can still pick up his smell. Smoky and sweet, clean clothes and faded deodorant. The faint hint of the O'Callaghans' house underscoring everything. The ripeness of fresh sweat.

His hand starts stroking my hair, twisting a long brown length between his fingers.

I make a mental note to treasure this moment for when I don't feel so dreadful.

After a few minutes, the nausea starts to lift. I still feel heavy and disorientated, but not quite as much like I'm about to vomit.

"You smell nice," I say.

"Thanks."

"I like that you don't reek of boy."

He laughs. "And what does that smell like?"

"Like Lynx Africa and Hugo Boss."

"Ah," he chuckles again. "No, this is a concoction of my own making."

"Really?"

"Yep." I can feel his face stretching into a grin. "Sure for Men and Chanel No. 5."

We laugh together, the low chuckle of a secret reverberating through both our bodies.

I press my face deeper into his neck. "I just think you're so cool."

I can't believe I've said it. Just like that. The word "cool" so ridiculous in my mouth, like an eighties throwback.

His chest expands and he lets out a long, low sigh.

"No one's ever said that to me before," he says. "I think you're cool, too, Maeve. But you knew that already, didn't you?"

"No."

"Oh, come on. You've been cooler than me since you were eight."

"Well, that is true."

"C'mon," he says. "Let's go home. Your parents will be freaking out."

I feel the warm, firm pressure of his hand in mine.

"Oh, hey," he says. "We forgot the last card."

He turns over the final card in the Lily spread and a tremor I mistake for passing traffic rushes through my head. A flash of light fills the tunnel, and I hear a scream that could be my own, or Roe's, or that of a million people all screaming at once.

Spots form at the front of my eyes. Purple, blue, gold splotches that circle my vision. Within seconds, I feel the cold gravel embedding on my forehead. And I'm gone.

CHAPTER TWENTY

MY FINGERS WORK UP AND DOWN THE GUITAR FRETBOARD. As I press each string, I keep waiting for the sting of steel to prick at my flesh, but it never comes. The guitar feels natural. The strings an extension of my hand.

But I don't *play* the guitar.

Examining my hands as they pluck out a jaunty, repetitive tune, I see that my hands are not my hands. For one thing, my fingernails are painted azure blue. For another, they're about twice their normal size.

Holy crap, I'm in Roe's bedroom.

Holy crap, I'm in Roe's *head!*

I am sitting inside of his body like a spectator. His eyes are my cinema screen, his brain my armchair. The window is open and the vague flapping of laundry drying is just barely audible from the garden outside. It is summer. Last summer. It is nine months ago.

There's a knock at the door. "Yeah," I call, as way of welcome, and Lily comes ambling in. We might share the same gene pool, but she looks nothing like me. Never has. She's all long and loping and fair. Skittish and strange like a springbok. I'm stocky and dark, a limping badger that fantasizes about life as a giraffe.

At that moment, I feel my Maeve voice crowding in,

trying to break into Roe's flow. *How could he say that,* it interrupts. *How could he not know he's as gorgeous as he is?*

Lily sits cross-legged on the floor in front of my bed. I'm adjusting the truss rod on the guitar, determinedly not making eye contact with her.

"Mum is freaking out," she says amusedly.

My Maeve voice says, *About what?* but my Roe voice just laughs bitterly.

"Do you want me to say anything to them?" Lily asks, peeking through her long fringe. "Tell them that it's not a big deal, or whatever?"

"Nah, it's fine. You don't have to do anything."

"OK," she says.

We sit in silence. I start fiddling with the guitar. Just as Lily is about to excuse herself, my mouth – or, Roe's mouth – starts moving.

"Do you think I should have denied it? Said it was … a computer virus, or spam, or whatever?"

Lily shakes her head. "No. They would have believed it, but no."

"It would make for an easier life, though."

"Easier for who?" Lily asks. "For them? So they can pretend they have a straight son?"

Oh, comes the Maeve voice.

"I guess."

"Look," she says, with a half-shrug. "Lots of people are bi."

"Not everyone. Not O'Callaghans."

We laugh, exhausted. We know we have good parents. But we also know that our mother and father look at their two weird children with a sense of growing unease. As if the sea monkeys they had acquired have evolved, too quickly, into parasites.

Parasites, giraffes, badgers. I never knew your head was so full of animal metaphors.

Get out of my head, comes the response.

CHAPTER TWENTY-ONE

THE SNOW HAS GROWN HEAVIER NOW AND IS FALLING sideways into the underpass when I wake up.

Roe runs his hands through his curls in an attempt to get the mud out. We sit and gape at one another, unable to think of anything to say. Or at least, anything appropriate.

We look at each other, confused, and even though I'm no longer in Roe's head, I know we're both thinking the same thing: *Did that really happen?*

We have both, in a sense, been outed. I know that he's bisexual. And he knows what I think of him. He could feel the long ribbons of adoration swirling around him as I lived in his head.

His face is mottled with confusion. Revulsion? I can't tell. Oh God, somebody speak, somebody *please* speak.

"That's why you wanted to leave the CoB meeting," I say, finally. "You knew that Lily would never join a group that was that homophobic."

Roe nods.

"I'm sorry your parents were rubbish," I say. "About the ... the queer stuff."

"Thanks," he says, his voice limp. "Sorry, Maeve. I don't know if what just happened to you happens all the time, whether that's a side effect of your tarot readings or whatever, but I'm going to need a bloody minute."

"Sure. Of course," I reply hurriedly. "Only, that's *never* happened before. Ever. Brand new. I have never lived in anyone else's head before. I didn't plan it! Oh God, do you think I planned it?"

"I don't know *what* I think."

Roe turns away from me. I scoop the cards up from the ground, the edges wilting. I brush them off on my coat, still protective of them despite all the drama they get me into. I chase after the final card in the reading as it tries to blow away down the tunnel, finally snatching it in my hands. This, the troublemaker.

The Lovers.

Oh Jesus.

I tuck the card back into the pack.

I am somehow extremely clear on *what* has just happened, but flummoxed as to *how*. I sat inside Roe's mind like a guest, and lived his memories as though they were my own. His hands were mine. His reactions were mine. Yet at the same time, I could feel present-day Roe living through past Roe *with* me. We were all an orchestra: me, him and him in his bedroom.

We duck out of the underpass, the snow still falling heavily.

"Ever since I got the cards back, I've felt this strange … connection with them. Like there's an invisible chain between me and them. And when you started touching them, I started feeling weird. It was like the chain grew another link, and you were it."

"So you think this has to do with ... her? The Housekeeper?"

"Maybe? Maybe it's the cards in general. They're haunted or something. Cursed."

"Haunted. Cursed. Jesus Christ, what TV show are we on?"

"I don't know," I say miserably. "A hidden camera one?"

"You were in my memories, Maeve. You were inside my head."

"I didn't mean to be!"

"I have to go," he says, massaging his temples and pacing in circles. "I have to go home."

"Don't!" I plead. "I mean ... do, if you want to. But don't stop talking to me over this. Please. It's silly. And also, I don't care that you're bi. Like, at all. So if that's a concern..."

"Jesus Maeve, will you shut up? For one minute will you just *stop fecking talking*?"

I nod, my eyes filling up with tears. I turn away and look at my phone. A message from Dad pops up.

Everything OK?

I stare at the screen. It's only been twenty minutes since I texted Dad to say I was on my way home. We were only unconscious for a couple of minutes. Possibly seconds.

Yep. 5 mins away.

"I'll walk you back," Roe finally says.

"You don't have to."

"No. I do."

Silently, we make our way to my house, the cosiness between us evaporated. I stare at the glistening leaves and frosted hedges miserably. This might be the most romantic

Kilbeg has ever looked, and I am being punished by the boy I like for psychically occupying his brain. No way did those old *Bunty* annuals have *this* in their problem pages.

When we get to the driveway, I'm fully prepared to rush indoors and end this horrible awkwardness between us.

"Bye," I say, turning away.

"Maeve, wait. We need to talk about this."

Oh, *now* we need to talk?

"Look ... I don't know what's happening. With us, with Lily, with your ... cards. But I know that we're linked to all of this, Maeve. I'm positive."

"I think you're probably right. And whenever I see ... *her,* the Housekeeper, I mean, she's always by the river. Always. Maybe some combination of you, me and the river made our brains come together in this weird way."

Roe nods, so I keep talking, keen to build out the theory. "The memory we just ... uh, *shared* ... maybe these are breadcrumbs we're meant to be following. And at the end, we'll find Lily."

Roe allows himself a small smile of relief. "That must be it," he says. "You know, for someone who's always beating herself up about being stupid, you're pretty sharp, Maeve."

"What do you mean always? I don't go around wearing a dunce cap, or anything."

"Get away out of that. You've got this big chip about your so-called brilliant siblings. You really think you're *that* hard to read?"

"Yes," I say, sulkily.

"I'm just saying, you don't need to compare yourself or beat yourself up. You're pretty good as you are."

And he smiles at me, and my chest feels like it's about to burst open.

"Will you meet me tomorrow? Same place again?"

"Of course."

"OK." He smiles thinly. "Maybe we can grab the bus together, too."

"Yeah. Sounds good."

"I'll text you?"

I'm so relieved that we're still talking – that we're still in this – that I throw my arms around his neck and hug him as tightly as my body will allow.

"Easy, woman!" He laughs, taken aback. "You'll break me."

I don't care. I breathe in.

Sure for Men, and Chanel No. 5.

CHAPTER TWENTY-TWO

THERE'S TALK THE NEXT MORNING OVER WHETHER SCHOOL should be cancelled due to the snow, which is still falling in thin, misty drifts. Mum drives me to the bus stop and I wait in the car with her, warming my fingers off the heater.

"Let's give it ten minutes," she says. "If there's a bus within ten, then it's safe for you to get to school."

"But I could slip on the ice and break my neck."

"A chance I'm willing to take," she says, tuning in the radio. Alan Maguire's show is on, and the weather is his guest of honour. He cannot stop effusing about the snow: the unlikeliness of it, the weight of it, the trouble it's causing, the fact that it's only in this part of the country. There hasn't been a freak snowfall in Kilbeg, he says, since the year 1990.

"1990 was the year I was pregnant with Cillian," Mum says. "I remember that snow. I was on bed rest and couldn't take Abbie out to play. She was livid."

There's the beginnings of a snowball fight happening on the tarmac as the bus pulls up outside school, people scraping dirty handfuls off car bonnets and pelting it at one another. Some of the St Anthony's boys are hanging around, stuffing snow into each other's necks and into the girls' school bags.

I wonder, for a moment, whether anyone will throw

snow at me. I walk through with my breath held, my hands on the straps of my rucksack. Nothing touches me. People run around. Through me, around me. Gasping, red, laughing with their teeth showing and their breath visible. The snow has brought something, some return to innocence that they've all been craving. This is the first real *thing* that has happened since Lily went missing two weeks ago, and it's broken the tension of the moment.

Of course, no one's going to hit me with a snowball. No one wants to remember I exist.

At lunch, I do my best to explain everything to Fiona. She's fascinated by the Children of Brigid meeting.

"Two Truths and a Lie!" she gasps. "We used to have to play that in acting classes. Some people would take it way too far. They would, like, use it as a way to confess everything they'd be holding in. I used to feel strangely guilty for not having any painful secrets."

"This was exactly the same! There was this weird pressure for people to not just confess, but feel this profound guilt for completely harmless things. One guy almost broke down because he shaved his legs. Then Aaron gave a big speech about how gayness doesn't exist."

"Jesus Christ. What did you say?"

"That's the odd thing. I found myself ... playing along. Like ... like I wanted to *impress* him."

I immediately regret saying this, thinking that Fiona will judge me for it. You're not supposed to want to impress guys like Aaron. You're supposed to tell them to piss off.

But Fiona just nods solemnly. "My ex was like that. The one I told you about," she says. "I didn't actually respect anything about him. I mean, I felt like a genius compared to him. But … I don't know. I still wanted him to think I was … you know, cool. Fun. Insert vaguely positive adjective here."

"Yeah," I say. "I know."

I decide, after a brief pause, that it's time to tell her.

"Fi," I say, testing the words out like you test your tongue against an open gum. "You know how Lily was spotted with that woman? By the river?"

She nods. Everyone has heard about the milkman sighting.

"I think … I know who she was."

Fiona stares at me, her eyes practically popping out of her head, her lips pursed in complete confusion.

"And you … you've decided to keep that information to yourself, then?"

"It's not as easy as that. No one will believe me."

"Why?"

"Because the woman isn't … a woman. She's a…"

I break off. How are you supposed to explain this to anyone who hasn't had the Housekeeper dreams? Who hasn't found the Chokey cards back in their bedside cabinet?

"She's a demon."

Why aren't there any less insane words for this?

"A demon," Fiona repeats.

"Yes."

"Not a ghost? Not a witch?"

"I don't know. Either. Both. All I know is that me and Lily accidentally summoned her the day of Lily's tarot reading. I mean, I literally said, '*I wish you would just disappear…*' while the Housekeeper was staring at us."

Fiona winces. "Oh God, I remember. That *was* bad."

"And the night I got home from your party, I started dreaming about her. When I woke up, the Chokey cards were back in my bedroom."

"The ones Harris took from you?"

"Yep."

"Maeve. This is crazy."

"That's just the start," I say, and explain what happened in the underpass with Roe last night. I tell her everything about the reading and the inside of Roe's brain, skipping the part about Roe's sexuality.

Fiona listens intently, her hands pressed together in prayer position, her thumbs tucked under her chin. After I'm done speaking, she's quiet for a long time.

"So ... what do you think?" I break the silence.

"I think," she replies slowly, "we need to talk to my aunt Sylvia."

"Your *aunt*?"

She nods. "She used to do fortune telling in Manila, while she was training to get her degree. There was this salon where they would do nails and tell women's fortunes. They're pretty casual about it over there."

"I don't know," I say nervously. "I can't imagine telling an adult any of this and them just accepting it."

"Maeve, you've got to understand," she says, shaking her head, "ghosts and stuff are sewn into my tita's belief system. She considers God and magic as sort of ... on a par with each other."

"So she'll believe me?"

"I don't know. At the very least, she'll listen to you."

"OK," I reply. "I mean, I trust you."

"Great. Come over tonight. I'm babysitting my cousin, so she'll be around at, like, six to pick him up."

"I'm supposed to be meeting Roe. We were going to go back to the underpass."

"Well, *hello*."

"Not like *that*," I snap, before adding, "unfortunately."

"Well, bring him. Maybe Sylvia can cast you two a love spell or something."

"Oh, aren't you *funny*?"

"I'm hilarious, actually."

"You're being very ... chill about this," I say, cautiously. "Considering you're a passionate atheist and everything, you're accepting the notion of a spirit demon very ... gracefully."

"Yes," she says, surprised by her own reaction. "Let me think about why that is."

She's silent then, pressing her fingertips to her mouth, pondering.

"Are you analysing your own motivations?" I ask, needling her. "Wow, your mum is right. Acting school has made you pretentious."

"Mmmhmm," she replies, barely registering this accusation any more. "The thing about being atheist is that I don't have a problem with *belief*. I just don't like religion."

"So witchcraft is fine, but God is not."

"Sort of, yeah," Fiona continues. "I can accept that you accidentally summoned a demon to take away your best friend, but I can't accept the concept of original sin."

"It's not definite that I summoned her," I correct her,

remembering my lie to Roe. "We could have both done it."

"But you were the one who said the words—"

"I know. I know. But … Roe doesn't."

Fiona nods slowly. "Ah."

"Yeah."

"Are you going to tell him?"

"Right now, I think it would just upset him."

"You mean it would make him upset with *you*."

"And what good would *that* do?" I counter. "He would go off on his own and we'd be no closer to finding Lil."

We sit with the facts for a minute, mulling over whether Roe should be told.

"Let me draw a card," Fiona says, and I hand her the pack. She plucks out the Star and smiles at me.

"Hope," we both say. The bell rings, and lunch is over.

CHAPTER TWENTY-THREE

I RING FIONA'S DOORBELL AND A WAVE OF PANIC RUSHES over me. Roe and I are squeezed into the narrow patio between the glass screen and the front door, our shoulders touching as we try to avoid tripping over the plant pots scattered around us. The panic, to my great shame, isn't about Fiona's aunt Sylvia or what she might tell us about the Housekeeper.

It's about the simple, unavoidable fact that Fiona is beautiful and witty, that Roe is handsome and smart, and that I, Maeve Chambers, suddenly feel like I have very little business with either of them.

"We don't have to stay long," I suddenly blurt out. "I'm sure Fiona will be busy."

"Sure," Roe says.

"All of her friends are older, you know. Her last boyfriend was twenty."

"OK."

"So she might want to head out with them. We shouldn't keep her too long."

"Isn't Fiona your best friend?"

I glow with pride. She is, in a way. She's certainly the person I spend the most time with these days. The feeling is immediately dimmed by the fact that I have effectively

189

replaced my last best friend, a girl who is currently under the possession of a demon I summoned.

Life.

Fiona's cousin José opens the door, gnawing on a soggy Pom-Bear. He's about three. God, why don't I ever know what to say to children?

"Uh ... is Fiona there?"

He turns around, letting the Pom-Bear drop to the ground. "FIIIIIFIIIIIII!"

He turns back to us. "I did a poo in the snow today."

"Did you ... like that?"

Fiona jogs to the door in sweatpants and a horse T-shirt that is too small for her. For some reason, this feels like the height of rock 'n' roll.

"Hey," she says, folding her cousin into her arms. "Did Jos tell you about his snow poo?"

"Yes."

"He was very proud of himself. Me, less so. C'mon in."

She quickly nods at Roe. "Hey, Roe. You can leave your shoes here."

The last time I was in Fiona's house, there were at least twenty people in it, so it feels bizarrely spacious now. The living room has three guitars leaning against the wall, an upright piano and a music stand.

"Wow, I thought your mum was just into the saxophone."

"That show-off? Please. She used to be in a cover band. They even toured in America before she came here. Do *not* ask her about it. She won't stop once you get her started."

"So *that's* where you get it from. The performance stuff."

190

"I guess. Did I tell you I got Desdemona? The director texted."

"Wow! That's amazing. Congrats."

I can't help beaming with pride. Not just for Fiona, but for the fact that I am here talking to Fiona, and Roe is here, listening.

Roe starts tracing his finger on the neck of a steel guitar.

"You can play it if you want," Fiona offers. "Mum won't mind."

"No, that's fine," Roe responds, his face glowing with hope. He is willing her to say, "*No, really, it's OK,*" and a moment later, she does. He gently picks it up and starts playing a melody.

"I've never played one of these before," he says, unable to keep the grin off his face. "They're mostly for bluegrass and country music."

He starts playing a tune. Fiona cocks her ear and listens. She smiles, opens her mouth and starts to sing. There's no warm-up. No tentative talk-singing while she gets the feel of it. She immediately announces the song with a Southern drawl.

"*Aiiiiiiiiii am a maaaaaaan of constant sorrow,*" she sings. "*I've seen trouble all my day.*"

And then, to my great horror, Roe starts singing along. Fiona's singing is high and sweet, the kind of voice a sea witch would try to steal. Roe is less controlled, but every bit as affecting. His voice has points and edges, scratches and yelps. But it's good. There's no denying that.

Fiona and Roe are singing. They are singing *together.*

They look at each other and smile, communicating

191

something that I have no way of possibly accessing. Why don't I do music? Why don't I know songs?

Their voices blend together, and they're harmonizing. *Harmonizing.*

And suddenly, I imagine myself giving a speech at their wedding.

Well, I always knew they were meant to be together when I stood in Fiona's living room and listened to them harmonize after five minutes of knowing one another.

I want to be sick.

"Fifi!"

The sound of the front door slamming in the hallway. Roe puts the guitar down sheepishly. Thank *God.*

Marie is in the doorway in her uniform, smiling but clearly exhausted from her shift at the hospital.

"Fifi! Are you in a *band*?" Marie says, looking as though she may explode with pride.

"No. Definitely not," Fiona says, her face flushed. "Mum, this is Roe, he's Maeve's … *friend.*"

We hear the words "snow poo" and Aunt Sylvia is standing in the doorway with Jos in her arms.

"Tita, my friends wanted to talk to you about tarot cards."

Sylvia looks perplexed. She's younger than Fiona's mother, in her late thirties or so.

"Fifi, I'm not making anyone a *gayuma.*"

Marie suddenly bursts out laughing.

"What's a *gayuma*?" asks Roe.

"A love potion."

The three of us are silent. Marie and Sylvia clearly find this very, very funny.

"Mum! Do you know the story of the missing girl from my school? Lily?"

"The girl by the river."

"Yes."

The air in the room is immediately changed. Marie's face looks stricken.

"*Ni*, you said you didn't know that girl."

"I don't. But Maeve does. And she ... she wants to talk to Sylvia about it."

Marie and Sylvia exchange a few words in Tagalog, their voices low and concerned. Fiona rolls her eyes irritably, and it's clear that this is a language primarily used to keep things from her.

"OK," Marie finally says. "I'm going to start making dinner. You can talk to Sylvia in here, but I don't want you asking her to make anything. No silly stuff."

"OK," Fiona agrees.

"And I'm keeping the door open."

"Mum!"

She puts one finger up. "It's my house, and I have the right to stop this at any time. I don't want Maeve and this nice boy going home with stories about what 'those crazy Filipinos' get up to."

Marie puts her hand to the soft spot of her temple. "Not that you would, Maeve. But you know how it is."

I do not know, but I nod anyway. Sylvia watches us both in wary respect of her older sister.

"You don't mind, Sylvia?" Fiona asks.

"It's fine." She nods. "Let me give José a snack first, though. And I don't have any cards with me, you know."

"It's OK, Maeve has hers. And I gave him a snack."

"Crisps," Jos says happily and Sylvia looks sharply at Fiona. "Crisps, Fifi?"

"Traitor," Fiona grumbles.

Twenty minutes later, Jos has eaten his way through a bowl of carrot sticks and we are sitting on the floor of Fiona's living room, my cards spread out face up on the carpet. Sylvia is studying each one.

"It's a nice deck."

"Thank you," I say, proudly.

"Old, too. Maybe 1960s, 1970s. You might get a hundred euro for them on eBay, Maeve."

"She wouldn't sell them," interrupts Roe, who is immediately embarrassed by his sincerity. "Well, you *wouldn't*."

"You say ... there is a card missing?"

"Yes. The Housekeeper card. She showed up the day I gave Lily her reading and then never again. Except in dreams. Nightmares, really."

Sylvia runs her hand through her hair and thinks for a minute.

"Did she look like the other cards? The same red border? The style?"

"She looked different. No border. And the style was creepier, less blank-faced than these."

Sylvia nods, her face creased as though trying to work out a puzzle. "So, she isn't *of* the deck. The Housekeeper visits the deck."

"Yes."

"Or," Sylvia says, her tone measured, practical. "She's summoned *to* the deck."

194

"Yes."

"Have you ever seen this before, Tita?" Fiona asks.

Another silence from Sylvia. She traces her finger across her bottom lip, concentrating.

"Not exactly," she says finally. "Describe to me what she looked like."

I tell her. The long black hair. The white gown. The knife. The dog. The sense of her as being human-ish, rather than human: the hair that doesn't curl when wet, the un-lined skin.

"What you're describing is familiar, Maeve."

"Familiar? You know her? Who is she?"

"Everyone knows her. Black hair, white dress. In the Philippines, we would call her the Kaperosa. But versions of her exist everywhere: the Malay have the Pontianak, in Brazil it's the Dama Branca. Every culture you can think of has some version of the White Lady. Google it if you don't believe me."

"Why?"

"I'm not sure. It's just one of those unusual things. Do you know that the story of Jesus existed, almost word for word, within the Egyptian story of Horus? He even had twelve disciples."

"So ... the Christians copied the Egyptians?" asks Roe, trying to grasp her point.

"Maybe, but what I think is much more likely is that there are some stories or figures or places that are so powerful that cultures are just pulled towards them. It's like gravity."

Sylvia slowly brings her closed fists together, imitating gravitational force.

"OK, so she's everywhere," Fiona says, clearly losing patience with this cultural history lesson. "But is she *real*?"

"Yes."

"Well, OK." Fiona replies. "You … answered that pretty quickly."

"Anything people come together to believe in is real. Any intense, passionate energy that is focused on one spot will create something."

"No, I don't mean in a, like, pretend way. I don't mean, 'Is she real?' in the sense of 'Is love real?' I mean, is she *literally* real?"

"And I'm telling you, Fifi, *yes*."

Sylvia doesn't just say it, she spits it. This calm, level-headed woman is suddenly antagonized, irritated by her niece.

"Why do you think people believe in ghosts, Fifi?"

"Because they're sad and they want to believe their husband is still alive, or whatever."

Sylvia's nostrils flare and Fiona rolls her eyes again. Roe and I exchange an uncomfortable look. One that says: *Ah, I see we have stumbled into another person's long-standing family argument. Time to excuse ourselves and make a run for it.*

"It's because only very powerful emotions can create very, very powerful energy. Ghosts linger after grief because it's one of the most powerful things a person can feel. People don't see ghosts because they're sad. The sadness *makes* the ghost."

"What about the White Lady? What makes her?" I ask.

"It could be anger. Betrayal. Revenge."

I swallow hard.

Anger at Lily for showing me up in front of our class, for making me feel guilty.

Betrayal, like when I ditched her to be friends with two girls I don't truly even like.

Revenge, for just existing, for being an ever-present reminder of all the things I try to deny about myself. The silly games we played for too long. The slow-reading group at school. Licking books in Waterstones.

Tick all that apply.

Sylvia is staring at me, but I can't meet her eye. I can't let this nice woman know that I am capable of feeling that kind of emotion. I look at my hands.

"I don't know about this Housekeeper," Sylvia says, standing up gingerly. "I only know what I believe. And I believe that collective human feeling brings these spirits into existence. We like to think that the emotional world and the physical world exist separately, but that's not even *nearly* true. Have you ever cried because you were sad, and then felt exhausted afterwards? Have you ever felt so hungry that you got cranky? *Fiona?*"

"Oh, come *on*."

"Everything is balance, weights and counterweights. Like a see-saw, you know? If your left leg hurts, your right leg carries the weight. Right?"

"Right," we all say at once.

"It's the same thing with energy." She makes a see-saw with her arms. "If energy on one side is moved, energy on the other will come to meet it. Grief calls to spirits. Fear calls to demons."

"What about happiness?" Fiona asks.

"Happiness –" Sylvia smiles, looking from me to Roe – "calls to love."

"Oh Christ, Tita! Stop *embarrassing* them." Fiona buries her forehead in her hand.

"*Sssh*. Come on, your mum will have dinner almost ready."

Roe and I take this as a cheerful hint that it is time for us to leave.

"Sylvia," Roe says politely. "Do you think … that something like the White Lady, or the Housekeeper, or whatever – do you think my sister could have *willed* her into existence?"

I bite my lip. Lily didn't will the Housekeeper into existence. I did. I said the words. I wished she would vanish. But Roe can't know that. He'd never speak to me again. Fiona sneaks a glance at me but quickly fixes her face back to neutral.

Sylvia gives Roe a look of concerned surprise; this is the first time we have referred to Lily as Roe's sister. This, I realize, is intentional. Fiona knew that her mother wouldn't have allowed a speculative conversation about the occult if she knew a direct family member was sitting right there.

"Oh, love. I'm so sorry. I'm sure she's going to be fine."

"Thank you," Roe says mechanically, already exhausted by strangers' sympathy. "But do you think that maybe the Housekeeper…"

"I think your sister is probably trying to find her way home to you right now, and you should focus on being with your family."

"Yes, *but*," Roe stresses, "if you believe that the physical

198

and the emotional world can overlap, the way you said, do you think that my sister could have summoned the Housekeeper? Even without meaning to?"

"Jos!" Sylvia calls, looking around for her son. "Where are you? Have you washed your hands?"

Sylvia could not be in a bigger hurry to leave the room.

"Tita," Fiona says, tugging her sleeve. "Please. He's so worried."

Sylvia looks at him pleadingly, begging him to not ask her anything else.

"I don't want to make you uncomfortable. I just ... I just want to know what it is you think."

"I think, in answer to your question, that the physical and emotional worlds are much more connected than people think, yes. And I think sometimes the spirit world – the thing in our souls that creates ghosts and demons and hellhounds – I think that world sometimes serves as a bridge between the two."

"Right," Roe says, his brow furrowed. "OK."

"Please don't ask me any more, Roe, I don't want to ..."

"No," he says putting his hand up. "I know."

"We'd better go," I say. "My mum wants me home for dinner tonight, too."

Sylvia smiles at me, the grateful small smile of someone who has been let out of a corner.

"Thank you for telling us about the White Lady, Sylvia. It was really interesting."

And it was. It's almost too big a thought to keep in my head.

We say goodbye to Fiona and make our way through

the kitchen, where Jos is hovering around Marie. He turns to look at us.

"Sausages," he says, sternly.

"OK."

I awkwardly go to pat his head and miss it entirely. I smile at Fiona's mother. "Thanks for letting us come over, Marie."

"Any time, Maeve! You too, Roe."

Roe nods. We go through the narrow hallway and I have one hand on the front door when we hear it. Marie's singing voice. Completely different from the high, flutey sound of Fiona's Disney Princess voice. This one is low, gravelly but completely controlled. A voice that could easily pass for Amy Winehouse, travelling aimlessly out of Fiona's kitchen.

We cock our ears.

"Ladies, meet the Housekeeper card."

Roe looks at me sharply, his eyes like saucers. He puts his finger to his lips: that *ciúnas* signal again.

"Now, she can be your downfall,
or she can be your start…"

Marie is singing about the Housekeeper. *Singing.*

"And she only wants the best for you,
like she never got for herself.
She sees you at the bottom,
and she's coming down …"

We burst back through the door, Roe and I practically falling over each other to get to Marie.

"… to help."

CHAPTER TWENTY-FOUR

"It's a song," Marie says, puzzled by our astonished expressions. "It's a country song."

"Did you hear us talking about that, Mum? The Housekeeper card?"

"I don't know. I was only half paying attention, Fifi. I must have."

"Where did you learn it?"

"America. We learned all kind of songs when we were over there. This is why I keep saying that music is better than plays, ni. There's an exchange. You learn more about the world."

"Could you write down the lyrics, Marie?" I ask, trying to stop the conversation developing into a debate about the performing arts.

She furrows her brow. "I don't know, pet. It's been so long. I think I just remember the chorus. Anyway, Fiona, your daddy will be home in a minute. Set the table."

"What about after dinner, Mum? Do you think you could sit down with a pen and paper and try to remember the rest?"

Marie looks at her daughter slyly. "If I didn't have to clean up, maybe."

"I'll clean. But you'll sit down? You'll write it up?"

"I'll try, Fifi, but later. Now stop crowding me."

Roe and I leave, our minds boggling.

"I can't believe it," he says. "We thought this was some mystical magical thing, but it's a song? A friggin' *song*?"

"I mean, it could be both."

"What were the lyrics again?"

"She can be your downfall,
or she can be your start."

"Where does that leave Lily?"

"How do you mean?"

"Well, is this her downfall? Or is this her start?"

The idea lightens us for a moment. The notion that Lily could be not just surviving, but thriving. Starting again somewhere. Better, just without us.

"Do you really have to go home for dinner?"

"What? Oh no, I was just saying that. My mum has late tutorials on Mondays, so it's very much a grab-and-go situation."

"Do you want to head back to the river?"

He says it nervously, as though asking if I wanted to have a sneaky cigarette by some bike sheds.

"If you want to. But do you think we should – I don't know – talk about what I saw? In your bedroom?"

"Oh. That." Roe tugs at his hair again, twisting the dark curls into his fist. He doesn't say anything for a while.

"We don't have to," I say, my palms up. "I'm not trying to out you or anything, but if you want to…"

He hides his chin in the zipped-up collar of his jacket for a moment, and I assume the subject is closed. Suddenly, he speaks. "When my parents found out that I was…"

"Bisexual?"

"I don't know. Sure. Bisexual is fine, I suppose. It makes me feel a bit like a specimen, but whatever."

I briefly imagine this beautiful boy in nail varnish, hidden jewellery and Chanel No. 5 pinned to a frame like a dead butterfly.

"But that day was something I had agonized about for months. Before Lily went missing, that was like … the worst day of my life. And afterwards, after you made me relive it … I don't know … it didn't feel like this big burden any more. I had this weird feeling of clarity. Like I finally got how dumb my parents were being with me that day."

"A problem shared is a problem halved? That kind of thing?"

"I guess," he says, sounding unconvinced. He kicks at a stone.

"What happened that day?" I ask. "The day your parents found stuff on your computer."

"What do you think happened?"

I open my mouth, ready with the answer *"Gay porn?"* but am completely unable to say it.

He looks at my face and bursts out laughing. "You look like a fish," he says. "Relax."

"My dad was using my laptop and my texts were synched to the laptop. And there were some messages coming through from a friend."

"A friend?"

"Yeah. Someone in the band. They were talking about coming out to their parents, asking me if I had any plans to do the same. Which, ironically, *became* coming out to my parents."

"Oh, shit. I bet your friend was kicking himself."

"Themself."

"What?"

"They. Miel is non-binary."

"Ah. OK."

Miel. *Miel.*

"Is … is Miel their name like Roe is your name?"

"Do you mean, did Miel name themself?"

"Yes."

"Yes."

We walk along in silence as I try to puzzle this out, turning out of Fiona's road and down the street towards the river. A bunch of kids are hanging around Deasy's takeaway, eating chips with gloves on. It's a strange sight.

Miel. Who is Miel? Are they in a relationship? Or is it just a band thing? Are they both in some kind of gender-queer club that I will never be a part of?

Roe stops and turns to look at me. "I know what you want to ask me," he says. "And the answer is, I don't know."

"OK," I reply. "I just … I don't really know how it works."

"Non-binary people?"

"Yeah," I say, nervous. "So is it like being trans? You were born in the wrong body?"

"It's not about being born in the wrong body. I think that's just like, an easy thing to say for people who don't really get it."

I feel a moment of shame at being someone who, apparently, doesn't really get it.

"Can you explain it to me?"

"I'm not sure. I feel like..." He stands still and closes his eyes. "A pinball machine."

"Right."

We turn onto the riverbank. It's quiet, the sky turning purple. I miss the sun. I look at the snow under my feet. It's not the pure white mound of sugar crystals it was this morning. Hundreds of schoolkids and commuters have turned it to grey sludge.

He's so much more Irish-looking than me. The curly hair. The thick shoulders. The wire frame. The ruddiness in his skin, high in his cheekbones, scarlet to his ears. He's like an old drawing of some Celtic warrior.

"Like I'm this tiny metal ball that is just racing around this giant thing, colliding with all these levers and bumpers and bits of machinery. Except the bumpers are all labelled things like 'dresses' and 'naked women' and 'Keanu Reeves'. And each time I hit something, it's proof of either one thing or another."

He smiles then, clearly amusing himself with the metaphor.

"Like, on the days I hit the things a guy is *supposed* to like, it's like, *Oh wow, the guy side has won.* But some days the girl side wins, and it feels weird, but I like it, too. Am I making any sense?"

"No," I say, dumbfounded that anyone could have thoughts this detailed about their gender. "I mean, sorry, yes, of course you are. I'm just so impressed that you have this ... this thesis on all this stuff that I just..."

"Take for granted?"

"Yes."

"I guess it all feels natural to you. I'm jealous," he replies. Then he pauses. Thinks about it. "Except, actually, no. I don't think I am. I used to be. But the more I let myself just *exist,* the more fun it gets. So I try not to question it or label it. I'm trying to just see everything as … negotiable."

"Negotiable."

"Yeah. *Negotiable.*"

We laugh nervously, turning over the weirdness of the word. Our laughter tapers off, and all I can hear is the lapping of the water where the river meets the low stone wall.

I stare at him, in awe that he could know so much about himself, and at the same time, be so comfortable in *not* knowing.

He stares back.

For once, I am determined not to break eye contact. Not to change the subject. To prove to him that I'm capable of understanding him, or at least looking like I do. I hold his gaze in my own.

"And … when you imagine the pinball machine," I say, my words slow and deliberate. "Where am I, Roe?"

"What do you mean?"

"What side am I on? Am I a bumper? A lever?" I tear my eyes away as he looks at me, confused.

"Never mind," I say, certain I got the metaphor wrong.

"Maeve, you're not on the machine," he says, taking a step closer. "Lately…"

He bows his head slightly, and I can see the space between the back of his neck and his school shirt, the leather string holding my rose quartz just barely visible.

"Lately, you're due north."

206

And he kisses me. Softly. His lips are cold and full, like fresh blackberries in a white enamel cup.

I don't move. Part of me is convinced that this is yet another one of his jokes. That, until his lips are firmly on mine, he is still likely to walk away and leave me gaping after him.

He pulls back, checking my expression for ... for what? Disgust? Discomfort? Rejection? Worry flickers across his face.

I move closer to him and trace my finger gently up his school jumper, to his collar, to the soft warm skin of his pale neck. And with one finger, I loop the string of rose quartz and pull it out, the stone warm like a heart.

"I just remembered," I murmur. "I just remembered what this one is supposed to mean."

I pull the string. I pull the string and Roe follows. His mouth is on mine, his hands cupped around my face. I keep the stone tight in my palm.

And I'm satisfied, despite all the many thousands of things I have yet to understand about Roe O'Callaghan, that I know exactly what he means by the pinball machine.

CHAPTER TWENTY-FIVE

LIKE ALL PERFECT MOMENTS, THIS ONE IS RUINED BY OTHER people.

The kids who were eating chips outside Deasy's start wolf-whistling at us. Roe wraps his arms around me and turns his face to them. I bury my face in his neck, planting kisses on the warm skin there, thrilled that I finally have the permission to do so.

"Piss off!" he shouts.

"C'mon," I say. "They're going to start throwing chips at us."

The shouts get closer.

"Thought you were a bender, Rory!"

He rolls his eyes. "Yeah, let's get out of here."

All roads, inevitably, lead to the underpass. Roe holds my hand, periodically bringing the back of my hand to his lips.

"We have a gig on Saturday at the Cypress. You should come."

"Will I need an ID?"

I once used Niamh's older sister's student ID to go to the gig of a boy Niamh liked. He played Ed Sheeran and George Ezra covers in a pub almost entirely frequented by accountants on their Christmas party, and it was the most boring night of my life. I bite my lip. The door to Niamh's sister's ID is definitely closed now, and there's no chance of me getting away with Joanne's.

"No, it's an all-ages thing. It's like a cabaret night. They're using it to fundraise for an LGBTQ homelessness charity."

"That's so cool."

"Yeah, it was booked in months ago but with Lily and everything I completely forgot. Miel messaged me yesterday asking if I still wanted to do it."

"And do you?"

"Honestly, I would give my right leg to do it under normal circumstances. But with all this drama at home I would give two legs. I just need something to take my mind off it."

I nod and he smiles at me. "Although I have someone right here who's pretty good at that."

"Oh, *do* you?"

I kiss him and kiss him, feeling ridiculously brazen about my new access to him. I press his back against the wall outside the underpass, curling my fingers around his hair. We stay like that for minutes, feeling the evening temperature drop to freezing, the cold bracing against our hands and faces but warm where our bodies are fixed, glued together.

"I'll walk you back," I say.

"You don't have to."

"No, I want to. You're always walking me back."

"It's fine," he says, kissing me on the forehead again. I look at him squarely, and there's a flicker of anxiety in his smile. "You should get home."

"You don't want your parents to see me, do you?"

"What? No, it's not that."

I look at him sceptically, my eyebrows raised.

"OK, it kind of is that."

"Do they … do they blame me?"

"Of course they don't blame you, Maeve. But they're not … not exactly fans of yours."

"Right. Why should they be? I'm the cow that ruined their daughter's life."

"Don't be like that."

"Roe. It's true."

I untangle myself from him, feeling sick. I *am* sick: gross or perverted, a parasite who latches on to others, then abandons them once I'm full. I took everything I could from Lily, and now I'm taking it from Roe. I turn away from him and stare at the river, the water silent and black in the darkness.

We leave each other awkwardly. He tries to kiss me again, but I can't get lost in the moment. All I can imagine is how we look from the outside. How slutty and stupid, how uncaring and thoughtless. It's been weeks, and Lily is still missing. What have I done about it? What am I *doing* about it?

He gathers me into a hug, sweeping my long woolly hair into his hands.

"Maeve," he says. "Life is so shite lately. Can't we just enjoy the good things while we can? Making yourself miserable isn't going to bring her back."

I smile weakly. "I know. I just… The more we find out about this Housekeeper thing, the more convinced I am that if it weren't for me, she'd still be here."

210

"And if I were a better brother, maybe she wouldn't have felt so alone. We can 'maybe' things until the cows come home."

I shrug. He sweeps his thumb across my cheek. "Go home and get some dinner in you. And stop torturing yourself."

I take the long way, missing the split in the path where I usually turn right to go home. I keep left, taking a detour along the riverbank. It's strange how important this place has become to me in the last few weeks. This place that was once just a walk home, and before that, just a school project. I skim stones and throw branches to watch them sink. Green scum swirls. Coke cans float. Cigarette butts gather in an abandoned coot's nest. I wrap my arms around myself and I think of my kiss, my first important kiss, my first kiss with anyone who matters, who makes my heart race and my blood warm. The first person to make me understand that attraction isn't a puzzle or an equation, of working out who the best-looking people are and working backwards from there. It's not maths. It's magic.

And I want to tell her. I want to tell her that her brother has become the most incredible person I have ever met. That I am falling, so badly, so terribly in love with him, and the only person I want to tell is the person I may never see again.

What would I even say to her? Would she be the kind of friend who would stick her fingers in her eyes, and do the whole *"Ew, gross, my brother!"* thing?

No. Not Lily. Lily is a lot of things, but she's not predictable. She's not boring. She wouldn't act like a person off an American sitcom. I close my eyes, and remember her.

I imagine she's still here, and that we're still friends, and that the last year didn't happen.

And just like that, I see her. Her long hanks of dirty-blonde hair, her eyes that are too wide, almost alien-ish. I imagine telling her while she's drawing: the quintessential Lily pose. You would talk and talk to her, and she would draw and draw, and you would almost think she wasn't listening. But then she would look up, ask one question and you'd realize she was paying perfect attention the entire time.

"The thing is, Lil, I can't even tell whether we're both just older now, and more mature, or if I've become different and he was brilliant the whole time. But the thing is, I strongly suspect he was brilliant the whole time and I was too up my own hole to even realize."

"Mmmh," she says, scribbling with a graphite pencil.

"And I know it's weird for you! I know you don't want to hear this about your brother!" I rail, spinning around her room. "But if you had a crush on one of my siblings, I would be cool about it. You don't, do you?"

"Mmm, no."

"Well, good, because they're all so old."

"It's the second one."

"Huh?"

"He's been brilliant the whole time. You have been, too, but you were so afraid of anyone who was being themselves that you were afraid of seeing it. Once you gave up on being the same as everyone, you were able to see the advantages of being different."

"Shut up. What are you drawing?"

"A duck."

"Show me."

And she would show me the duck, but the duck, importantly, would have one thing wrong with it: a mechanical beak, or a turn-key on its back. A half-robot duck.

I open my eyes, and it's just the river again. Filthy and strange and always, always there.

"Come back," I whisper. "Please, please, please come back."

That night I dream about the Housekeeper again, but she's not at the underpass this time. She's at a different point in the city, where the river is narrower. A shopping trolley has been tipped over, sunlight glinting off its metal body. It is spring. The Housekeeper's hair covers her face, and she is standing on the other side of the riverbank, pointing at something. I follow her finger.

Halfway between us, floating in the river, there is a shoe. A black suede ballet flat, to be precise, turned greenish by the water. But it's not sinking, like the shopping trolley. It's floating. Coasting along like a tiny, stylish boat. The familiar feeling of river water in my guts rises up again.

I wake up, sure I'm going to vomit. I breathe heavily, trying to control the hot surge of spit that is pooling around my jaw. I breathe and swallow, breathe and swallow. I go back to sleep but wake up again just after 5 a.m., the air so cold that I have to get another thick, fleece blanket from the hot press. I check my phone briefly as I get back into bed. There's a message from Roe.

I had a dream about the Housekeeper. She has Lily's shoe.

The message was sent at 4.55. Only a few minutes ago.

I had the same dream. Was the shoe floating?

Yes.

What do you think it means?

Bubbles appear, and Roe is "typing" for a long time. Then they disappear again. By the time my phone buzzes with his response, I'm expecting an essay.

I think it means Lily is alive.

The next day Fiona comes into school triumphant, a piece of notepaper wedged inside her homework journal. She grabs me just before registration starts.

"Toilets," she says. "Now."

We sit huddled together on an exposed pipe that almost burns our legs. Fiona opens her journal.

"My mum managed to remember the full first verse."

"That's amazing!"

"Sure, but I also had to hear about how she met Neil Young in 1994."

"A worthy sacrifice!"

"Thank you."

We pore over the page together.

She appears in rare readings / and only to young women,
And only in times of crisis / new truths shuffled into focus.
I dealt her from the deck / two times that same week,
A woman with blood on her wedding gown /
*   and a knife between her teeth.*

Ladies, meet the Housekeeper card.
Now, she can be your downfall, or she can be your start,

214

And she only wants the best for you, like she never
*   got for herself.*
She sees you at the bottom and she's coming down to help.

"Oh my God. And did she say anything else about it?"

"She said she learned it off a band they were opening for, and that band were, like, an Irish–American country rock band."

"What does that mean?"

"I think it means that they did sped-up covers of 'The Fields of Athenry'."

"Of course."

"But that made me think about what Aunt Sylvia said about every culture having its own White Lady. Maybe the Housekeeper is an Irish form of that."

"Like an Irish folklore thing?"

"Yeah. Think about it. Irish people immigrate with this story about a deadly witch demon, country musicians turn it into a song about tarot cards, someone makes the tarot cards, the cards make their way back to Ireland. And to you, in the Chokey. It is, to quote a certain mother who loves to repeat herself, all part of the cultural exchange."

"You know, you're very hard on your mum, considering she's objectively the coolest mother I've ever met."

Fiona cocks an eyebrow. "You know, you're very hard on Joanne, considering she's the coolest sister in the world."

"I take your point."

"Thank you."

We hear people shuffling into their seats and the sound of Miss Harris's voice. We get off the pipe and dash into the classroom, the lyrics wedged firmly back in Fiona's journal.

She nods and waits for us to take our seats before she starts talking.

"Girls, I'm sure it won't have escaped your notice that the weather has been … bizarre lately."

She purses her lips as thirty girls lean forward in silent, desperate attention.

"We've heard this morning that there is forecasted to be black ice on the roads by this afternoon, and many of the bus routes will be closed. In the interests of your safety and your transport …"

You could hear a mouse's fart in this room, it's so quiet.

"… all schools have been instructed to close."

The class descends into giddy chaos. Books are flung into bags and high, hyper laughter envelops us. Fiona throws her arms around me in victory.

"A day off! A DAY OFF! On a flipping WEDNESDAY."

She does a little victory dance.

"AND tomorrow too, maybe, if it keeps up! If the black ice lasts, we won't be able to get INTO school, not to mind out of it."

People are texting their boyfriends at St Anthony's, trying to arrange a meet-up. I hear one girl arguing with her boy about whose house they're going to go to, and whose parents get home from work the latest.

A red flush climbs into my face as I listen and suddenly remember that I now *have* someone to meet up with. I have a boyfriend. Or I *think* I have a boyfriend. We didn't actually discuss it.

Fiona nudges me. "Let's see what Roe's up to. We can show him these Housekeeper lyrics."

She sees my red face and her eyes go wide. "Oh my God! Did something finally happen?"

"It ... did."

"Holy crap! What a day! Tell me everything!"

I tell her everything, and half an hour later, we're all sitting in Bridey's drinking milky tea and eating too-sour apple tart. It feels weird to be eating apple tart at 10 a.m. Weirder still to be sitting opposite the boy whose tongue was in my mouth twelve hours previous, and who also happens to be having the same dreams as me.

"She's alive," Roe says flatly. "I know she is. It's the way the shoe was pointing, the way it was just sailing down the river. It was like it knew where it was going. Lily's alive."

"Not that I don't believe in ... uh, the inherent value of dreams," Fiona says politely. "But what are we supposed to do now?"

"We've got the dreams. We've got the song," Roe says, practically. "I feel like we need someone who can ... I don't know, interpret them."

"Sylvia's out," Fiona grumbles. "I got a big lecture over dinner last night about how I put too much pressure on her, and how it's not good to turn to the occult when you're feeling desperate. Sylvia says it makes people do crazy things."

"People, or me?" Roe asks.

"You, I suppose."

"Everyone wants to be protective of the little boy with the missing sister," he says, rolling his eyes. "I'm not even allowed to mention the river to my mum."

The river again. I remember my project from primary school, where I made a map of the different ports of the Beg river: what they were used for over the years; where the grain was shipped out of Ireland during the famine, where people boarded ships to America… Coffin ships, they were called. You either made it to America or you died on the way, and often you were so illiterate that you weren't even able to write to tell your family which it was.

Then, something clicks.

"We'll say it's for a school project."

They consider it.

"Sylvia won't buy that," Fiona says. "She's onto us already."

"No, someone else. She can't be the only one who knows about supernatural stuff. And really, it's more of a folklore question than a magic question."

"Who then?" Roe asks, and I see him fiddling with the string around his neck. I can't help smiling every time I see it.

I know exactly who.

We practise our story, making sure we don't sound like desperate teenagers. Which, of course, we are.

The door of Divination has a bell on a red ribbon attached to it, and it tinkles lightly as the three of us enter the shop. The woman in the balloon pants is there again.

"Maeve Chambers!" she says, and I'm slightly unnerved by how instantly she recognizes me.

"Hello!" I say cheerily. "I didn't think you'd remember me."

She looks from me to Roe and back again, smiling softly.

"Of course I remember you. You have three 'e's in your name."

"Right. Well, my friend Fiona is doing a project on folklore and I thought you might be a useful person to speak to."

"Well, of course. Fiona, I take it?"

She gestures to Fi, who already has her refill pad and a pen out.

"Hi," she says sheepishly. "I'm doing a project on shared mythologies. Like why some cultures have shared folklore. Like hellhounds. Do you know, everyone has hellhounds?"

"Sure look it," chuckles the shopkeeper. "Dogs are trained to be so vicious in so many parts of the world. People are scared of them."

"Right." Fiona smiles. "I wanted to know what you knew about this."

She passes the lyrics to "The Housekeeper Card" across to her. "I think it has an interesting parallel to the White Lady myth, don't you?"

The shopkeeper studies it in silence.

"The Housekeeper," she says slowly.

"Do you know her?"

"I haven't seen her in a good while," she says, her voice low.

"The song?"

"No, I've never heard of the song. But the Housekeeper, I'm … *aware* of. How did you find out about her, Maeve?"

The three of us look sharply to one another. This is supposed to be Fiona's school project.

"*I* heard about it from *my* mother," Fiona says, deflecting

219

from me. "She's a musician, and it's a song she sings around the house."

"I see," the shopkeeper says warily. "Well, what do you want to know?"

"Where she came from," I push. "What she is."

The shopkeeper frowns, and then straightens. "It's an old Irish legend. Have you done the 'Big House' in History yet?"

Roe, Fiona and I all make vague noises. The shopkeeper looks disappointed by our lack of knowledge.

"Back in the old days, the 'Big House' was what you'd call … well, a big house. A rich house where the wealthy English would swan about and the Irish would serve them. Some houses were all right, paid their workers fairly and all that, but some were rancid. Absolute devils. Whippings, docking wages. Inhumane cruelty."

"Why did people work there, then?"

"Sure, there was so little work around that you were to count yourself lucky if you got into a Big House. It was either that or emigrate."

"So … the Housekeeper worked there?"

"Well, I believe there was some story, some kind of disease outbreak, tuberculosis maybe. Children going down like flies. A group of female servants, mothers, pleaded with their employers to send for the doctor and … well, they didn't. And the children died. The mothers were so bereft that they didn't come to work. But do you know who did?"

"The Housekeeper," I whisper.

"The Housekeeper. A woman, or something that looks like a woman, shows up for work. The next day, the house is empty. All the gentry are gone."

220

"Where was this?" Roe asks, with scrutiny. "When was this?"

"It's a folk story," she answers simply. "It could have happened a hundred years ago, or two hundred, or never at all."

We're all silent, in total awe. Fiona pipes up.

"So was this a common thing? Did people like ... call on her?"

"Well," she says again, crossing her arms and thinking hard. "This was still an Ireland that believed in fairies, you know? There was a lot of space for magic and belief. So I imagine there was a summoning practice around it, but it would have been understood to be black magic. The price would have been high."

"What does that mean?"

"Magic like that, you have to give big to get big," she says, sucking her teeth.

"You mean like ... a life for a life?" Roe asks.

"That's a bit of a simplification, but something like that, probably. In almost all magic the sacrifice has to match the gain. That's why people give food at temples. It's not because they think the spirit is actually *eating* it. It's because you need to show that you're willing to make the sacrifice."

"Could someone summon the Housekeeper again?" Fiona presses. "By accident, even?"

The shopkeeper cocks her eyebrow. "I thought this was for a school project."

"It is."

"Hmmm," she says absently. "I need to sort some of the books out now, but you three feel free to look around."

She says it quietly but firmly, as though this were not the first time that three teenagers came into her shop asking about revenge demons.

We look around. Roe gravitates towards the crystals, Fiona to the tarot, and I end up looking at the books next to her. I watch Fi for a moment, testing the weight of the cards in her hands, trying to tell which feels right. It might be cool if she starts reading tarot, too. Something that we could do together, to make it fun again.

I pull a book out at random. *The Beginner's Guide to Spellcraft by Alwyn Prair-Felten.*

"Made-up name," Fiona says derisively, glancing over.

I flick through the waxy pages. It doesn't look particularly inspired. It's not a dusty tome with pentagrams and incantations. It is, however, very effusive about how "anyone" can do witchcraft, and it's only a tenner, so I buy it.

Here are some incantations I use, Alwyn Prair-Felten writes. *But using another witch's chants can feel a little like wearing another person's underwear. Chant what you want, just make sure that both a) you mean it and b) it's simple and memorable enough that you can say it over and over. Chants are very do-it-yourself. All magic is.*

As the shopkeeper is sliding my book into a paper bag, Fiona gets a phone call from her mum.

"School has been cancelled *tomorrow*?" Fiona squeals, covering the mouthpiece briefly. Roe and I high-five her quietly.

"Mum, *no.* It's a snow day. Basically, a public holiday. I don't see why that means I have to mind Jos. He goes to creche, for God's sake!"

A silence as Fiona dutifully listens to her mother.

"I know, I know, I know. But she was going to pay for it anyway, regardless of whether I had the day off..."

Her expression turns grim. It's clear her mum is lecturing her, and she turns around to take the call outside.

The shopkeeper is gazing at the snow falling thinly outside like shredded tea leaves. Her left hand is fiddling at the gold studs in her ears and she's murmuring something softly to herself. She seems to have completely forgotten I'm standing in front of her, my receipt still between her thumb and forefinger.

"Snow to rain, and rain to river;
We won't be fooled again. River to sea; and sea to sky;
What's now will not be then."

"Sorry?" I ask, leaning closer. Her voice is barely above a whisper.

"Sky to snow and snow to rain;
As bud is leaf and bough.
Rain to river and river to sea;
What was then will not be now."

Fiona crashes back into the shop, muttering angrily.

"Hey," Roe pipes up. "We ready to go?"

"I just want to buy these." Fiona lays some tarot cards on the table. "Look, Game of Thrones tarot. Arya Stark is the Death card."

The shopkeeper turns her head towards Fiona and smiles. She takes the tarot, bags them and then pops a stick of incense into her bag because she's a "new customer".

I look from Fi to the shopkeeper and back again. Did anyone else hear her chanting? Did I imagine it?

"What was then will not be now."

"I can't believe my mum," Fiona rages. "The second she hears I have some time off, she thinks: *free babysitter*. It's like she doesn't even care that I get straight As and do theatre and look after Jos most afternoons *already*. I never get to relax. It's so unfair."

This is the most like a stroppy teenager Fiona has ever sounded, and it's thrilling to witness.

"I mean, Jos seems pretty self-sufficient," I offer. "You can just plop him in front of cartoons. And you're so good with him, y'know?"

"I don't want to look after people, OK?" she storms. "I don't want to be a doctor or a nurse or a babysitter or a … fucking – I don't know – a live-in carer for the elderly."

"OK, Fi," I say, trying to keep my voice calm. "I didn't say you had to be."

"No, you didn't," she says, folding her arms and sighing softly. "*You* didn't."

Roe and I look at each other, and it's clear he doesn't know what's going on either.

"Are you OK?"

"It's just, that's what good little Filipino girls are supposed to do, isn't it? Become a nurse. Watch other people's kids."

I bite my lip. "Sorry," I say, searching for something useful to say. I realize that there is nothing useful I can offer, so I just opt for the plainest expression of truth I can find. "I don't know what that's like, Fi."

She takes a couple of deep breaths.

"No, I'm sorry. This isn't about you, Maeve, this is my stuff."

She smiles at Roe and me. "Can we go get a tea, or something?"

As soon as we're back in Bridey's, Roe's mother calls.

"Jesus," he says. "Looks like it's a day for badly timed mother calls." And then it's his turn to step outside.

Me and Fiona sit on the big squashy couch, and I want to ask her more about life at home. Her family are so charismatic and fun-loving, I completely missed any tension that might be bubbling under the surface.

But before I can form the words, I hear something. A voice. A familiar voice.

"Two coffees and a muffin for six euro," he says to the cashier, sunny and disarming. "Wow, you wouldn't get that kind of value in Dublin, would you?"

I turn my head around, hoping that I'm mistaken, and there's some other upbeat American in Bridey's. But no: it's Aaron. Aaron holding two steaming takeaway cups and a brown bag. I watch him for a moment, fascinated that someone like him could be making small talk over coffee, then go back to Fiona and our shared pot of tea.

"Maeve," he says, like he's just seen an old family friend. "Fancy seeing you here. You and Roe left in such a hurry the other night."

"Yeah, well, we had places to be."

"I'm glad," he beams. "Date night?"

There's something mildly sarcastic in the way he says "date night", as though Roe and I were two children playing restaurant. Fi is fiddling with her phone, barely paying attention.

"Maybe you could come back," he offers grandly. "By yourself this time."

I can't take all this faux-friendliness. I cut right to the point.

"Sure, except … I would rather die?"

It's not the most elegant thing I've ever said, but it gets my message across.

He raises his eyebrows briefly, and then moves on to Fiona. "You're Fiona, aren't you?" he says.

"Um … yes?"

It's clear she doesn't remember Aaron from our day in Basement, but I'm amazed as to why he remembers her, and why he knows her name. He studies her for a moment, and then, in a voice as soft as honey, speaks.

"You're used to people expecting rather a lot from you, aren't you?"

It is the exact way I heard him talk to the girls at the CoB meeting. The affection, the sympathy, the sense of immediate understanding. And Fiona, who still hasn't put two and two together, is completely captivated by it.

"Well," she says, raising a shoulder to her chin. "I usually deliver."

God, to have her confidence. I remember, briefly, the older boyfriend. Is this what she was like with him?

"Stop it," I say, my teeth gritted. "Stop talking to her."

Fiona looks at me, confused. "Maeve, what's going on?"

"You need to learn to be less possessive, Maeve," Aaron says, with a smile. "You can't own people."

He narrows his eyes at me, his irises darkening. "And you can't throw them away, either."

And just like that, he leaves. He walks out of Bridey's with his hoodie and his takeaway coffees, like any normal twenty-something man. I feel like I'm about to vomit.

You can't throw them away, either.

"Maeve," Fiona says, tapping my shoulder. "Maeve, are you OK? You're shaking. Who was that?"

The light in the cafe suddenly feels too strong, like a fire burning behind my eyeballs. I close them, balling my fists into my sockets, covering my face with the crook of my arm.

"Who was it, Maeve?"

I say nothing, my breath coming short. He knows everything. Everything about what happened with Lily, and somehow, everything about Fiona. He can see inside people. Whatever dark magic went into creating the Housekeeper, a shred of that exists in Aaron, too. And if it lives in him, it must live countless other places. Suddenly, the world feels too big, and I'm too small in it.

"Come on, I'm taking you outside."

The cold street air hits me in the lungs like a throwing star.

"Sit down," Fiona orders, pointing at a window ledge. "Put your head between your knees and take deep breaths."

"I don't need…"

"Do it."

I do as she says, and as I start to speak, she stops me.

"Ah. No. Breathe first. I'm going to count your breaths. *In*, one – two – three. *Out*, one – two – three. Keep your head between your legs. That's a girl. *In*, one – two – three."

She makes me do this eight times before she eventually lets me sit up and speak. I do feel better, though, strangely. It must be a nursing tip she learned from her mum and aunts.

"Now. Who was that, and what did he do to you?"

227

It's her emphasis on the word "do" that knocks the life back into me. She thinks that Aaron is some kind of ex-boyfriend, some guy I went on a date with.

"Aaron, Fiona. Didn't you recognize him? He was part of the moral mob in Basement."

She slaps her hand to her forehead. "Crap. OK. Agh, sorry, I just assumed he was one of your brother's friends or something."

She pauses. "Did you tell him about me, or something? Why did he know my name?"

"I never mentioned you to him. He has something. I don't know. Some kind of power where he's able to see the cracks in people. He knew about Lily. Did you hear that? He said I threw people away."

"So what, he has magic, too?"

"I don't know," I say again, my voice cracking. "Maybe I'm going insane."

"The month you've had?" Fiona says, sitting on the window ledge and draping her arm around my shoulder. "I wouldn't blame you."

Roe is walking back towards us, still on the phone. His jaw is tight, and he's clearly immersed in a battle of his own.

"I'm sure … I'm sure it's not related, Mum," Roe says, his voice tense. "It's nothing. Well, no, not nothing, obviously, but you know what I mean…"

He hangs up and joins us on the window ledge. Fiona and I shuffle along to fit him in.

"What was that?"

"I made the mistake of telling my mother about my

Children of Brigid theory from before. She set up a Google Alert on them."

"And?"

"And it seems that kids actually *are* leaving home to join them."

"No!" Fi and I say in unison. And then: "We just saw him!"

"Who? Aaron?"

I nod. "He knew things about us, Roe. He knows about my relationship with Lily—"

"And he knows about…" interrupts Fiona, who then stops herself short. "He knows about me."

The three of us walk to the riverbank, oddly silent.

Fiona kicks a rock into the river.

"Look," she points at the reeds. "Frogspawn."

She's right. Bubbles of translucent, foamy spawn are floating on the water's surface. Hundreds of them. Each dotted with a black speck, like a cartoon eye.

"I've never seen so much of it," I say, trying to suppress the urge to poke at it with a stick. *No, Maeve, you have a boy friend now, resist the urge to act like an eight-year-old.*

We stare at it for a moment, dumbfounded how something so calmly natural can exist at a time like this.

"It's weird," Roe says, finally, "that the river hasn't frozen over."

"Huh," I reply slowly. "How cold does it have to be for that to happen?"

He shrugs. We go back to staring.

"Look!" Fiona says again, triumphant. "A fish!"

There is a quick gleam of radiant purple as a fish briefly

bobs above the surface of the water and ducks back in again.

"Jesus," Roe says. "And another!"

We stand and count the fish bobbing. None of us knows enough about fish to know whether it's unusual for them to come so close to the surface in cold weather.

"They're called rainbow trout," says Fiona, reading from her phone. "And they ... uh, they live in Australia and America."

"Shut up. No, they don't."

"Look!" she says, brandishing her phone. "Is this or is this not the fish we just saw?"

I look at the picture of the fish with the purple stripe on its side. "It is."

"So what are they doing *here*?" Roe asks. "The water will be way too cold for them."

We stare at the river and I begin to notice wisps of steam coming off the water's surface. Like fog from a mouth on a cold day.

Fiona must see it, too, because she crouches down, her long black hair almost touching the water. She dips her fingers in. Then, her entire hand.

"Jesus Christ, Fi, what are you doing?"

She swivels around to face us. Her eyes are wide and excited, like an owl's. "Guys, it's *warm*."

CHAPTER TWENTY-SIX

"THE RIVER IS PART OF IT. I KNOW IT." EVEN AS I SAY THE words, I know how ridiculous it sounds.

"How?" Fiona and Roe say, together.

"How *anything* at this point?" I say, cracking my knuckles nervously. "It's the common thread, isn't it? All our dreams. Strange phenomena. Where Lily was last seen alive. It all revolves around the river. It's the common denominator."

We are in Deasy's now, the three of us gathered around a single large chips and a pot of curry sauce. Lily and I used to come here on Saturdays, taking one of the diner booths, piling salt on the table and making patterns with our fingertips.

"The Australian fish. The water. The frogspawn." Fiona ticks off her fingers. "Something is *happening* in there."

"There's something Sylvia said," I say slowly. "Something about the physical world and the emotional world being more closely linked than people think."

"Go on."

"Look," I say, grabbing the salt and pepper shakers.

"This —" I hold up the salt shaker — "this is emotional suffering. Say, being forced to leave your family."

They peer at me, then look at each other.

"Salt is emotional suffering, Maeve," Roe says patiently. "Sure."

231

"And this —" I hold up the pepper shaker — "this is a physical landmark. Say, the Kilbeg river."

"Uh-huh."

I turn both upside down, and the salt and the pepper pool in one spot together, creating an ashy mountain on the table.

"Don't you SEE?" I say, after a few moments of silence.

Fiona chews the end of her hair, trying desperately to understand. "The ... pepper is the *river*, you say."

"Jesus Christ, how is it that people who get as good marks as you two can be so *dense*? It's a flippin' metaphor."

"Roe doesn't get metaphors because he's a Protestant."

"Wow, *harsh*."

"I feel like you're both missing the point," I say huffily.

"Sorry, Maeve ... what's the point?"

"The Beg is this place where thousands of people experienced the most traumatic moments of their lives. You know, it's where thousands of people were forced to emigrate and say goodbye to their families for ever," I explain. "And Roe, it's where I saw ... your ... traumatic memory."

He nods and Fiona looks confused, but says nothing.

"If the spiritual world is the thing that makes up the gap between the physical and the emotional, then I think the river ... is where that world begins. I think it's a door. Or a key. Or both. I don't know."

I am suddenly very embarrassed, but I press on. "And Lily ... I think Lily is in that world. I think she's trapped in there. Maybe the Housekeeper took her there."

Fiona casts a glance at me, raising her eyebrows in a "we're still playing that game, are we?" expression. Roe just nods, urging me to go on.

"Because she was sad and mad at me, and I think … maybe the Housekeeper couldn't … couldn't…"

"Kill you for her?" Fiona says brightly.

"Right. She couldn't finish the job she came to do."

Another silence.

Two pink spots form in Roe's cheeks. "And how … how do we get her back?"

He believes me. He thinks my theory is right. A wave of confidence surges through me. I open my school bag and slam my new book in front of me.

"With this."

Fiona takes one look at it. "Made-up name," she repeats.

We start looking through *The Beginner's Guide to Spellcraft* by *Alwyn Prair-Felten* until it is time for us to go home.

Roe walks me to the end of my driveway.

"It's lucky your family is so rich and have a long driveway," he says. "It means I can kiss you without the prying eyes of the gentry."

He kisses me in the soft space below my ear and a shiver runs down my spine.

"Wait, wait, wait," I say, slightly breathless. "I am not *rich*."

"Maeve. Come on."

And suddenly, we're fighting. Roe keeps trying to get me to admit that my parents are wealthy, pointing at the size of our house, and I keep getting defensive by telling him that I have a bigger family than he does. He screws up his face a bit, as if only rich people can afford to have five kids. Neither of us want to have this fight, but neither of us can seem to find a way out, either.

"Come on," he says, "you have to have noticed that there's a difference between me and you. Between you and Fi."

"Me and Fi are at the same school."

"She's on scholarship. And so am I."

For a second, I hate him. I know he's just trying to get me to admit to having money, but he's going at it by pushing on my weakest, sorest spots. Sore spots that he doesn't know are there, because ultimately, Roe and I still don't know each other very well. If Lily were around, she would let him know. She would get it.

"Lily wasn't on scholarship," I say, and then correct myself. "Isn't, I mean."

"No, but Mum and Dad thought she would need more attention, and that she would get it in a school like Bernie's. Also, they wanted her to be with you."

"Oh, great. Load the guilt on."

"I'm not trying to make you guilty. I'm just *telling* you…"

Roe and Fiona worked hard to get into private school, and here's me, the rich idiot whose parents had to buy her way in. The way they didn't have to with any of their other children. Abbie, Cillian, Pat and Jo all went to non-fee-paying schools and all got over 500 points in their Leaving Cert. It was only me, the person who got 33% on her entrance exam, who was gently pushed into private education.

He's here with you, Maeve. Not Fiona. He fancies you, not Fiona.

A dark voice emerges from the pit of my stomach. *Would he still fancy you if he knew that you wished Lily would disappear, Maeve?*

"Hey," I say. "Do you have time for a quick tarot reading?"

"Huh? You want to read my tarot? Now?"

"I don't know. I thought we could read them together. To see … to see what's going on with this river stuff. The water turning warm. All that."

"Sure," he says, suspicious. We have, after all, been talking about this all afternoon.

"Let's find somewhere quiet."

There's a bit of green near my house where boys play football on warm evenings. We trudge through it, snow crunching underneath our feet. I don't say anything as we walk, holding his hand firmly and in silence. We find a bit of wild hedgerow that has a space you can crouch under. I tried my first cigarette in here. Lily and I found a box on the bus and took them into this bush to examine them. We decided they weren't worth the hassle.

Roe and I settle under the bush, crouching in the dirt.

"Cosy," he says, still confused.

"OK," I say, taking out my cards. I feel the familiar, stomach-churning pull as I pass them over to him. But the nausea of the cards doesn't even compare to the crunching anxiety that Roe might leave me for Fiona. That I'll be on the outside again, looking in.

I hear a faint rustle as Roe shuffles, and at the corner of my vision, I'm certain I see a sweep of white linen dragging in the dirt. *Oh God, she's not here again, is she?*

I blink hard. It's just a bit of toilet paper, trapped in the undergrowth.

He shuffles and splits the cards.

"All right, do you want to pick them together, or...?"

"You pick the first."

My head starts beading with nausea again, but I know what to expect now. I breathe, counting my breaths in like Fiona taught me. I try to control it. If I can get in his head again, I can know for sure whether he likes me.

He picks one.

Three of Cups. Three women dancing together with cups in the air.

"That looks like a nice one," he says vaguely.

"It is nice. It's all about friendship and unity."

"Then why do you look so worried?"

"I'm not."

"Do you want to pick the next one?" he asks gently.

I pick and leave it face down on the earth. Another lurch in my stomach. *Keep it together, Maeve. Keep it together.*

"I guess ... I guess I'll turn it over then."

Roe touches the card and the world falls away. Yellow and red spots dot across my vision, and I can feel my body fall away from me.

It is happening again.

It is happening again.

Ladies, meet the Housekeeper card. Keeper, meet the Houseladies card. Hades, meet the Lousekeeper card.

I open my eyes, but I'm not in Roe's head. I'm in my own. I'm in St Bernadette's, in the toilets. The same toilets where Fiona and I sit on the exposed pipe for warmth. Lily is there. Lily is crying. Lily is crying and yelling, yelling at me, and people are watching. *Make them stop watching.*

It is thirteen months ago and it is the day before

236

Christmas break. We have had, this term, no less than three talks about groups, peer pressure and the danger of not mixing with one another. We are known as a "cliquey" year. I gather that some girls have felt excluded or terrorized by the rigid hierarchies of St Bernadette's. There are the blonde sporty girls who play hockey and go to the rugby matches of their older boyfriends, right up at the top. Then the rich girls, who go to New York on the holidays and come back with brown bags that say "Little Brown Bag" on them.

Beneath the rich girls are the party girls, who get drunk a lot and are always betraying one another. And beneath the party girls are the mid-leagues: that's where Michelle and Niamh come in. Nice middle-class girls who get invited to most things and do pretty well in school, prone to occasional spots but never acne. This is the crowd I am, thirteen months ago, so desperately trying to join. Everything below that is not worth considering. The nerdy girls have an authority of their own, what with their perfect French plaits and bright futures, but I'll never be one of them. There are a few arty girls on the fringes, who view St Bernadette's as a thing to survive so they can resume their real lives. This is how I thought of Fiona until she decided, for some reason, to be my friend. But right now, thirteen months ago, she means almost nothing to me.

I don't have the confidence or the ingenuity to have a rich life outside of school. It is Michelle and Niamh, or nothing.

I need a clique to survive.

I can feel myself telling Roe this, as he sits in my head like a movie-goer who the usher is continuously interrupting with his flashlight.

The teachers have instructed us to branch out, and a Secret Santa has been arranged. The teachers insist that the pairings are random, but it's immediately clear to everyone that this is meant to be a bonding exercise, pairing high with low. Party girls with nerds. Rich, shallow girls with Fiona-types, in the hopes their depth of character will rub off on them.

I have Tanya Burke. She's getting a lip gloss set from Boots. Easy. Lily has Michelle. From the moment they're paired, I am in a state of constant anxiety. I want to protect Lily from Michelle; equally, I want to protect Michelle from Lily.

Why are you so frightened? It's just a bloody Christmas present.

In retrospect, I know that Lily is just trying to make an effort. She knows that I am trying to become proper friends with Michelle. She wants to show Michelle that, even though they're different, they're still capable of getting on.

It's easy to see Lily's good intentions in retrospect. But in the moment, watching Michelle unwrap her Secret Santa gift, all I could feel was horror at the invisible line Lily was stepping over.

Roe can see this. Roe is watching.

What is this?

Nothing. Get out. Stop.

Why is Lily crying?

Lily, acknowledging Michelle's fondness for looking at herself, has made Michelle a portrait. She has made Michelle a steampunk vision: her shoulder a giant cog, her school uniform transformed into a Victorian lady's gown, with buttons up to the collar and down the sleeves. It is an incredible drawing, one of her best, illustrated with her special watercolours.

"What's best is that I'm under the ten-euro budget," she says cheerily, announcing it to the class. "The frame is from Dealz and it was only two."

I don't say anything. I know Michelle thinks the portrait is weird.

"Er, thanks, Lily," she says. "It's really … uh, yeah."

Michelle quickly puts the portrait away, and Lily's face flickers slightly in disappointment. She shrugs it off. She has held up her side of the bargain. She has done Secret Santa.

Why on earth did you want to be friends with these gowls?

I don't know, Roe. I don't know.

At lunchtime, Lily comes back to class to find the picture back on her desk. With a word, a word I had once heard someone throw at Jo written on it.

"Well," Lily says quietly, "I don't think they mean a river dyke, do they?"

But she keeps her cool. She keeps it together. It isn't until home time, when she walks into the toilets and finds them emptying her school bag into the sink, that the penny really drops.

"Why are they doing this?" Lily screams at me. "Why do you want to be friends with these … these *bitches*?"

The white-hot rage I am so bad at containing bubbles up in me again. I am so sick of her shadowing me. So sick of her destroying my chances of legitimate friendship with girls who could actually do something to improve my miserably unhappy school life. I am sick of being on the bottom

239

rung with Lily. The time for hints is over. I need to send a message, loud and clear.

Maeve, no.

I'm sorry, Roe, I'm sorry.

Michelle and Niamh are watching me, waiting for a response. There's no use in saying they're not bitches. They are. The only thing left to do is become one of them.

And in one fluid motion, I turn on the faucet.

Lily watches, her mouth gaping in shock. The contents of her entire school bag – her watercolour pencils, her books, her stripy little scarf and hat – are being slowly drenched in cold water. She doesn't move a muscle.

Even I know I've gone too far. Further than it is possible to find your way back from. I have drenched a lifetime of committed friendship in a school sink.

"Sorry," I say lamely, and push past her, linking arms with Niamh and Michelle as I move. She stays in the toilets, watching silently as the water spills over the rim of the sink and onto the floor.

Now, she can be your downfall, or she can be your start. Ladies, meet the Housekeeper card.

Something changes then. Like a wave washing away a drawing in the sand, fifteen-year-old Lily slowly dissolves and Lily at sixteen comes to replace her. This is a more recent memory. Much, much more recent.

We are at St Bernadette's again, a crowd of girls gathered around us. The tarot cards are spread in front of us. Lily's eyes fill with tears as she stares forlornly at the Housekeeper.

Oh no oh no oh no…

Is this it? Is this the reading?

240

"Tell me, Maeve. I'm not too much of a baby to know."

"I don't know what it means."

Fiona is next to me making soothing noises, trying to defuse the situation. But it's useless. No one watching wants this moment to end. It's the ultimate in mid-afternoon entertainment: two ex-best friends spitting venom at each other over a stupid card game.

"This is so like you. This is *so Maeve*."

"Lily. Stop. I genuinely don't know what it means, OK?"

"You'll do anything for a bit of attention, won't you, Maeve? But then, when all eyes are on you, you've got nothing to back it up."

"I can't believe we were ever friends," Lily says. "You're not a good friend, Maeve."

Oh God. It's coming. It's coming. Roe. I'm sorry.

"I wish I had never been friends with you," I reply, my teeth bared. "Lily, I wish you would just disappear."

I feel for Roe in my head, searching for his presence.

Where are you? Talk to me. Please.

I open my eyes and I'm back in the hedge, my hair caked in dirt. I look around, groping for a hand to help me up.

But there's none. Roe is gone.

I scramble out just in time to catch the back of him crossing the football pitch and eventually, he disappears.

CHAPTER TWENTY-SEVEN

I CALL HIM AND CALL HIM, AND HE DOESN'T ANSWER. Eventually, he WhatsApps.

Stop calling, he writes.

I just want to explain what happened

A brief pause.

I saw what happened.

The familiar bubbles of typing and stopping, stopping and typing. After a while he gives up.

I'm sorry, I write.

You let me believe that Lily summoned the Housekeeper. But YOU did.

I am about to tap out my response, but his next message comes too quickly.

You WISHED she would just disappear? And you didn't think that was relevant information?

I know I should think carefully about what I say next, but the panic is too strong. I type and type, sending long essay-length texts full of guilt and bargaining and misery. I stipulate over and over how we still don't know what summons the Housekeeper, that it could have been both of us, or the concentrated energy of all the girls in the room. That these were all just theories, really, and we didn't have any actual proof that the Housekeeper existed at all.

Another silence.

I just want to be alone right now.

I write and delete a million messages to him over the course of the evening. **Do you still want to go out?** And, **Am I still invited to your gig on Saturday?** And, most pathetically of all, **Do you still like me?**

Thankfully, I have enough self-preservation not to send them.

There's something on the radio about global warming and gulf streams and fish migration patterns. A scientist is explaining to Alan Maguire about a warm current coming up from Brazil, and Alan Maguire is reading messages from listeners about how, in the good old days, everyone would go skating when the river froze over. *Why hasn't the river frozen over?*

Joanne is in for the evening. She hasn't been around much, lately. Her romance with Sarra is in full swing again, and she's spending every other night at hers. I have a feeling she's going to move out, and I'll be alone with Mum and Dad again. Alone for, at the very least, another two years. Who am I kidding? It's only two years if I go to a college in a different county, and at the moment it's difficult to imagine me getting accepted into any college at all. I wince thinking about Mum getting me into the local university, or using her pull to get me a job in the bookshop.

"Hey, stranger," Jo says as I descend the stairs. She's baking again. A kind of oaty, honey biscuit that's great dipped in tea. "Haven't seen a lot of you lately."

"Yeah," I shrug. I can feel the three of them being

cautiously optimistic about how much I've been out of the house lately. They still talk about me like they suspect I'm deaf. *It's good she's keeping busy*, etc., etc.

"A little birdy told me they saw you *kissing* someone."

"What? When?"

"One of the girls asked if my sister had a boyfriend. I said not that I *knew* of..."

"Oh Jesus."

"Well? What's his name?"

I say nothing, and focus instead on dabbing my finger in the flour on the countertop.

"All right," Jo says, a smug smile in her voice. "You're lucky you're straight, y'know. It's all so simple. Girl meets boy. No one has to come out as straight."

"Sure," I say bleakly. "Lucky me."

"I remember," she chuckles, laying down a baking sheet, "getting off with boys and just *desperately* trying to like it. I flung myself at them, imagining these great romances, to get away from the fact that I was completely gaybones."

Oh God. That's not what Roe has been doing all along, is it?

"What are you trying to say, Jo?"

"What?"

"That I'm just someone's pretend girlfriend, I suppose."

"That is not even slightly what I was saying."

"God, I'm just so sick of it," I say, my voice suddenly loud and cracked. "I'm sick of being everyone's third choice."

"Maeve, you need to calm down and tell me what the hell you're talking about."

She tries to meet my eye, but I can't let her see how shiny they are.

"I'm taking the dog for a walk," I announce. "Tutu? Where's Tutu?"

I find him on Pat's bed, his head buried under a pillow. He's already had his walk today, and is enjoying his evening ritual of ignoring us all until my dad comes home.

"Come on," I say, and he trots amiably after me. I fasten his lead and take him out, hoping that Roe will be hanging around the underpass again.

He isn't.

After a solid twenty minutes of staring at my phone waiting for Roe to text, I start throwing a stick for Tutu. He fetches it dutifully, a bit too old to be excited by the game. I nestle his big blond head between my hands and call him a very good boy, as though I can compliment myself out of my own problem. We got him when I was eight, after my cat Tom died. My imagination wasn't great then, either. We named the dog Tom Two, which eventually became Tutu.

We were always a cat family before Tutu. There was the other cat, the one that ran away before I was born. I've seen pictures of him. A fat black scoundrel who once ruined Christmas by climbing up on the kitchen counter, eating the turkey, and getting explosive diarrhoea on said turkey. I wasn't there for any of this, of course. But I've heard the story so many times I might as well have been.

Tutu is snuffling around in the snow, a little bored of it already. We all are, at this stage.

I throw the stick for Tutu. It ends up in the river, and he barks at it floating on a nest of green algae.

"Oh God, you don't want me to fish it out for you, do you?"

He barks.

"Fine. I suppose I don't have the luxury of pissing you off, too."

I lean on the water's edge and pluck the stick out. It's disconcerting how warm it is. Tutu gazes into the water with me, and for a moment, our reflection – him with his puzzled expression, me with my long woolly hair falling over my face – is frightening. I keep gazing, even as Tutu loses interest and wanders away. And then it hits me.

The dog. The hair.

I look like *her*.

The Housekeeper.

I think about all the things I've done today. I lied to Roe. I've shown him the ugliest side of myself. I've suspected Fiona of trying to steal him away from me, as though he were a piece of property. I've yelled at my sister for no reason at all. And why? Because I was scared. Because I was insecure. Because I felt like a girl who no one could possibly love, and I acted like a girl who no one would want to.

What if I didn't just summon the Housekeeper because I was angry at Lily? What if the Housekeeper was alive inside of me, all the time? What if the nastiest, darkest parts of me fuelled the Housekeeper?

What if the Housekeeper *is* me?

The concept comes into view like the appearance of a single star into daylight.

I dip my hand into the water again. Green algae spools around me. I push the sleeve of my coat up further so it bunches around my elbow. I lower my arm all the way, like I am reaching into the chest cavity of a giant.

I reach in, looking to tickle the base of the river. To find its beating heart.

I don't find the soft, squishy dense organs, though. Or slippery, tangled weeds. The thing my hand settles on while groping in the wet infinite darkness is hard. Metal. Jagged.

I feel around, my fingers caking in silt. Yes. Metal things. Loads of them.

Small metal objects.

Keys? Are there … keys down here?

I clasp a handful and pull out my arm, and whatever I'm holding slices through my skin. Easy, soft, quiet, like a steak knife through a beanbag.

"Jesus!" I scream, yanking my hand out and cowering over it, dragging my closed fist towards my belly. Tutu bounds over, demanding to see my hand, intrigued by the blood and river water trickling down my arm. I shout at him to go away, more out of instinct than anything else. A small, rodent-like urge to be both frightened and private.

He backs away, hurt, and goes back to examining the snow. Slowly I open my palm to try to examine the keys that have cut through me so easily.

But they're not keys. Or, at least, not the kind of keys I was expecting: these are the big brass things used to wind up old toys, shiny and yellow like they've just fallen off a factory line. There are two in my hand, along with an assortment of rusted cogs of different sizes. A world of drawings and games and tiny little promises, all in the palm of my hand.

I look from my hand to the river, and wonder how much blood I lost in the exchange.

CHAPTER TWENTY-EIGHT

I BANDAGE MY HAND ALONE IN THE UPSTAIRS BATHROOM, spraying it with antiseptic from the first-aid kit that has been sitting on the top of Mum's wardrobe for donkey's years. The cogs go in an old jewellery box. The keys are in my hoodie pocket.

In my bookcase there's a collection of old refill pads and exercise books that Mum is always trying to get me to throw out. She says I should make more room for real books. To which I answer: "Mum, *what* books?" I haven't read a novel since the second Harry Potter, when I decided that Ginny was too annoying and that I couldn't stomach reading about her any further.

Lily always told me that there isn't that much of Ginny in the subsequent books, but I never bothered regardless. Instead, I keep the bookcase as a shrine to memory. Here are the jotters where me and Lily drew maps and plans and rules for new civilizations. There are worlds within worlds in here, false fantasy universes that reflected whatever phase we were going through.

I flick through one pad, from the year we both turned eleven. It was a design for a water world. A dirty, scuzzy sort of landscape where everything is pond scum and emerald-green with algae. There are tadpoles and frogspawn, trout and mackerel. Mullet, the worst fish of all, because, according to everyone, they feed on human waste.

And there, in writing drawn to look like it's dripping out of a tap, Lily has written one sentence:

NOBODY SWIMS, NOBODY DROWNS.

I didn't know what it means. I still don't. But the drawings of frogspawn make my teeth clench. I stare at the cuts on my hand.

Did Lily send me the cogs and keys?

Or is she *attacking* me with them?

The cut on my hand begins at the base of my ring finger, where the skin goes soft and padded like a snake's belly. It jags across one of my palm lines, my life or my wisdom, I don't know which. Flexing my fingers back and forth, I can feel the skin stretching and peeling, stinging painfully. A giant, bloody sign from Lily. A big *Suck on this, Maeve.*

Painful as it is, this is better, somehow. Better to be in some kind of dialogue with Lily than to have nothing at all.

At nine, the power goes out. Each of us are in our bedrooms. We mosey out onto the landing to see what's happened. Dad stands on a chair with a flashlight to flick the fuse button, but it doesn't work.

"It's all over Twitter," Jo says, her face illuminated by her phone in the darkness. "The whole Kilbeg area is blacked out. Some trees fell on power lines, or something."

"Why?" I say, my voice high. "There hasn't been a storm, or anything. It's just snow."

"Snow falls on trees. Trees get heavy. Trees fall over," answers Jo in a sarky "I still haven't forgiven you for being a bitch to me earlier" voice. "Duh."

"Well, this is a bit of an adventure," Dad says, trying to look whimsical. "Will we crack out the candles? Ghost stories?"

"The rads have gone out," Mum says, putting her hand on the rapidly cooling radiator behind her. "Well. We're going to need double blankets on everyone's beds. Girls, I think it's best if you sleep together."

"What?"

"For warmth. This house is going to be an icicle within the next hour, mark my words."

And it is. Even with two pairs of socks on, every step on the bathroom floor sends a chill through my legs. When Jo and I refuse to sleep together, Mum insists I go to bed in a fur coat.

"Where the hell did you get this rotten old sheep's arse from?" I ask, mortified that Roe's accusation that my family is rich was probably right.

"It was your great-granny's, and it's grey rabbit fur, I'll have you know."

"Why do we have a dead woman's coat? A dead woman's amoral coat?"

"I inherited it when I was about your age. I could never throw it out. The poor old creature gave its life so she could stay warm; it feels like a crime to just bin it."

She is uncharacteristically protective in this newfound Siberia. She sits next to my bed and lights two long white dining candles, both wrestled into wine bottles salvaged from the recycling bin.

"Take one to the toilet with you if you need to go in the middle of the night," she says, settling them down on my nightstand. "I'll leave the matches here."

"Thanks, Mum."

I keep my hands folded inside the sleeve of the rabbit-fur coat so she doesn't see the cut.

"Are you warm enough?"

"As warm as I'm going to be."

"It's a funny old time," she says, and I try not to reply by saying that it's funny, her sitting on my bed like this in the first place. She had just earned her PhD when she found out that she was pregnant with me, and according to Abbie she had a full-on freak-out that she would never get to use it. So she kicked her career into hyper-drive, and sort of palmed me off on a mixture of childminders and sibling supervision. "You were an easy baby," she often says, fondly. "Like *you* would know," Abbie sometimes retorts.

But I must look uncomfortable, or like I want her to leave, because she glances at me sort of sadly and sighs.

"I know it's been hard for you lately, old beast," she says. "Lily going missing. And Jo says you have a boyfriend now, too."

"Oh God…"

"No, no, don't worry, I won't make you tell me anything … unless you want to, of course … but then again, why would you want to?"

Her eyes are suddenly glassy in the low, flickering candlelight. I don't say anything.

"You know, when I first started a family, I never felt like I had a choice. It was either work or kids. So I chose kids. But then when I went back to school, everything seemed so hopeful, like I could do anything. Sometimes I wonder if I fooled myself into thinking I could do both, and that maybe I let you down in the process."

"But I never minded. I was free to do whatever I wanted with Lily. You shouldn't feel guilty."

"I know." She smiles weakly. "I know. But sometimes I regret not being around a bit more. For you, in particular. But still. You can't regret-proof your own life, can you?"

I don't know what is suddenly compelling her to be so open with me. These are not conversations we normally have. Eskimos might have fifty different words for snow; we have zero words for expressing how we feel about each other.

"They always say you should have no regrets," I say, weakly. "That thing the French say."

"Je ne regrette rien," she says softly. "I regret nothing. It's a stupid saying."

"Is it?"

"We all treat people badly sometimes and if you're an even remotely empathetic or flawed person, you should feel regrets. The important thing is to learn from it and go on to treat people better."

I curl an even tighter fist into my bandaged hand.

"What if the thing you did is too bad?" I ask. "What if the person never forgives you?"

Mum looks at me very steadily. "Sometimes it isn't about getting people to forgive you," she says simply. "Sometimes you have to do the best with whatever they're prepared to let you have."

And under the blanket, in my good hand, I hold the little brass river key as hard as I can.

252

I fall asleep in the dead woman's coat and I dream of nothing at all. I wake up in the middle of the night anyway, the words of a rhyme half falling out of my mouth.

"Snow to rain, and rain to river;
We won't be fooled again.
River to sea; and sea to sky;
What's now will not be then."

The cut on my hand is open again. The bandage has disappeared. I bring a wine bottle candle into the bathroom, every part of my body shivering in the black, cold house. I have taken for granted, I think, the amount of tiny red lights in any room: the orange square above a power button, the red-cherry pimple light on the boiler, the charging light on the electric toothbrush. The little signs in a house that tell you everything is working the way it should be.

The water runs warm and brown for a few seconds, like river water.

This house is not working as it should be.

I am alone. Like my house is a ship floating out to sea, and I'm the sole survivor.

I start reading *The Beginner's Guide to Spellcraft* while sitting on the edge of the bathtub, my feet in two inches of warm water.

White candles, the book states, *are best for protection, peace, truth and purity.*

I flick around. The book is big on candles and herbs, and is particularly fond of phrases such as: ... *like any you would find in your garden, or larder!*

Rosemary has a strong female energy, and is good for banishing negativity, protection. Find it growing rogue in any garden!

253

Camomile is good for a pleasant sleep, and is now popular in many teas found in the supermarket!

To mend a rocky relationship, cast a simple honey spell! Any honey will do!

There's something peaceful about this cosy, motherly form of magic. I read the spells, which feel too complicated and a little embarrassing, but after every one, Alwyn leaves the same footnote.

Remember, she writes. *Magic is an art, as well as a science. Find the magic that feels true to you.*

I do not know what time it is when I go down to the kitchen. My phone went dead hours ago, and the only clock in the house is the now-dark oven display. My wine bottle candle has almost burned down, so I grab a handful of fresh ones from the pull-out cupboard below where the cutlery is kept.

In the cupboard with the dry foods there are spice jars; in the fridge there's honey. I pull stuff at random and desperately chuck them into one of the million canvas tote bags that Mum is always bringing home from academic conferences.

Back in the upstairs bathroom, I shake rosemary, sage and a tablespoon of honey into the bath. Star anise for protection against bad dreams; a basil leaf to ward off evil spirits. I add them wildly, desperately, until the tub is thick with herbs and the bathwater has cooled down so much it's almost ice.

What now? Do I get ... *in* the bath?

I close my eyes and try to follow some sort of instinct. *Magic is an art, as well as a science.*

No. You never hear of witches getting *inside* cauldrons.

I look in the book and find instructions for a protection circle. It tells me to mark each side with candles: *yellow for Air in the east, red for Fire in the south, blue for Water in the west and green for Earth in the north.* I only have my white ones. Instead, I take a red lipstick for Fire, a yellow shower-gel bottle for Air, a blue toothbrush for Water and a green sheet mask packet for Earth.

The whole thing looks crazy, but it's too late for caring about crazy now.

I soak bath towels in the water, wind them into ropes and make a circle on the floor.

I sit in the middle of the circle, and from my tote bag, pull out a knife, and a candle. I start jankily carving into the pure white stick, the wax gathering in heaps like peeled chocolate. It is not a pretty process. But slowly, the letters start to form, like a four-year-old taking her first stab at writing. I am methodical, butchering the candle slowly and without grace.

Dig, slash, carve.

Dig, slash, carve.

"L"

She was left-handed.

"I"

She was left-handed but she taught herself how to write with her right.

"L"

She was left-handed but she taught herself how to write with her right. She thought she would need it some day.

"Y"

255

She was left-handed but she taught herself how to write with her right. She thought she would need it some day and maybe now she does.

I move down the candle. I start again, smoother this time.

"L"

She was my best friend.

"I"

She was my best friend and I betrayed her.

"L"

She was my best friend and I betrayed her and now she is getting her revenge on the city.

"Y"

She was my best friend and I lost her and now I am getting my revenge on the city.

When I run out of candle space, I tug thick, curly hairs from my scalp. Wrenching them at the ends, where they hurt most. Good. Pain is good. Sacrifice is good.

Wrapping each hair tightly around the candle, whispering my made-up chant as I go. I try to copy the shopkeeper at Divination, making it rhyme so it's easy to remember, and less clunky to say.

"Retrieve Lily, protect Maeve;
Forgive a friend, her life to save
"Retrieve Lily, protect Maeve
Forgive a friend, her life to save."

I go on and on like this, wrapping and burning, carving and chanting, until I hear birds waking up. The words start feeling like wool in my mouth, and after a while I lose sense of what they even mean. Forgive who? Save whose life, exactly?

At some point, I must fall asleep.

I wake up before anyone finds me, lying in the middle of my protection circle, huddled in a ball in my great-grandmother's rabbit-fur coat. A drop of water falls on my forehead.

Then another.

And another.

Water is leaking through the old roof of our house, falling through the ceiling tiles and onto the floor.

The snow is melting.

CHAPTER TWENTY-NINE

"WELL, THANK GOD FOR THAT," MUM SAYS AT BREAKFAST. She managed to get the gas cooker working, so we are eating fried stale bread smeared with Ballymaloe Relish and drinking tea made with water boiled on the stove. "Apparently the cold snap finally broke overnight. The power should be back on at some point this afternoon."

"When?" Jo asks irritably. "I have an essay due and nothing to write it on."

"I'm sure they'll extend your deadline, given the apocalyptic weather."

"Well, if this is the Apocalypse," Dad says, heading outside with a shovel, "at least we know the scale of it."

I can barely eat my fried bread. I did this. I melted the snow. I ended the cold snap. I invented a spell.

And *it worked*.

Flexing my hand, I see that the snow isn't the only thing that has changed. The gash on my hand has papered over with fine scar tissue, the kind of scarring that usually takes at least a week to form.

Maybe I am capable of summoning demons. But maybe all this crazy Housekeeper energy that lives inside me could do good as well as bad. Maybe the same power that pushed Lily away could be part of the solution to bring her back.

I've been so angry with myself for being angry. For flying into sudden rages, for throwing the shoe in class, for having so much frustration living deep within my skin that it would occasionally just spark out in moments of white-hot fury. But what if I could take all of that, and direct it into something else? Into … well, into magic?

I pick up the house phone every few minutes, searching for a dial tone. The O'Callaghans' landline is pretty much the only one I know, aside from my own. I need to talk to Roe. He needs to know about the spell, about what I can do. I hop from one foot to another in frustration. Dad says drivers have to be even more careful, now that the snow is melting. He doesn't want me leaving the house, despite my desperation to find Roe and Fi. We could devise a spell to get Lily back. Now that I know how, it would be easy.

"You'll slip and break your back, Maeve," he says, eyebrows furrowed, hand protectively around the dog.

"Make yourself useful, Mae," Mum urges. "We need to do a big clean-out in the study. Throw out all the crap books—"

"There are no crap books," Dad interjects.

"We have two copies of *the same* Jeffrey Archer book."

"Well…"

"Frankly, I'm offended we have *one*."

There's nothing better to do and it's still too cold to sit still, so I agree. The study is a tiny room at the back of the house with floor-to-ceiling shelves and is far enough away from the TV and the kitchen that you have no excuse *not* to study in here. I still remember Joanne, the year she did her Leaving Cert, holed up in here and breaking out in tiny skin rashes all over her body from the stress of it all. Poor Jo, I think, suddenly filled with empathy for her. She's only ever doing her best. I remind myself to apologize to her for yesterday. Maybe, I think excitedly, I can even come up with a spell that will help her chill out a bit.

I get to work clearing out the books. Most of them really are a bit crap. Even I can tell. They are mostly unofficial biographies of sports stars and ex-presidents, the kinds of thing my brothers would have bought my dad for Christmas. I fish out my Walkman from the Chokey and slot it on to my waistband, weeding away at the books contentedly. Everything is going fine until a rogue copy of *The Second Half* by Roy Keane catches on my headphones and wrestles the Walkman free, smashing it on the floor.

I scream in surprise, grappling at the tape player to see if it's completely ruined. I could easily find another one on eBay, but it makes me realize how attached I am to it now. I analyse the pieces, trying to calm down from the sudden shock. It's just the plastic bit at the front, the bit that keeps the cassette in, that has snapped off. It can be superglued back on, easy. I practically wheeze in relief.

I gather the tape and the shattered pieces in my hands, trying to keep everything together while I find the superglue.

It's only then when I see it.

The tape. Or, the sticker on it. There, on the curling, yellowing rectangle of sticky paper is the thing that has been staring me in the face this entire time.

"SPRING 1990."

The year the cat ran away.

Mum had said something about 1990. In fact, she

brought it up a lot. It's family lore that she had a rubbish pregnancy with Cillian, that she was on bed rest and that Abbie couldn't go play in the snow because Mum was too ill to take her. She can't even look at cats without bringing up Kylie, who ran away in the middle of a blizzard.

A cat that runs away in a blizzard. I never questioned the logic until now.

Could this really be the first time that the Housekeeper has arrived in Kilbeg? Has she been dormant for thirty years, waiting for new prey to seize on?

The power comes back on in the evening and Dad cooks everything that was defrosted by the freezer melting. This is how we end up having chicken, sausages, black pudding and lamb chops for dinner. Even Tutu is bored of meat by the time we're done. I apologize to Jo about snapping, and she gruffly accepts and then goes to write her essay on her now-chargeable laptop. I plug in my own phone and look at the notifications I missed. There are four from Fiona, and none from Roe.

13.02: Is your power still out??? Everyone's over at my house! My titas are LITERALLY setting up an Indian fire bowl outside to cook lunch! Come!!! xxxx

14.21: OK, my phone is about to die but come over. Should I invite Roe?

14.32: Wow 1% lasts a long time. Anyway, it has just occurred to me that your battery is probably gone and maybe you haven't seen this. Text me when you're back! Roe on his way over. SNOW BARBECUE. xxx

19.12: Hey. Roe just left. Do you want to talk?

My stomach crunches with anxiety. Roe and Fiona

261

spent the afternoon together. I remember the first night Fi and I spent in her house, with a stolen bottle of wine, sitting on her bed making fake Facebook profiles.

I breathe and try to remember my breakfast epiphany: if I can cause so many sparks with anger and hatred, I can cause an equal amount being kind and empathetic. I close my eyes and think of the honey, for friendship. The white candle, for protection. The rosemary, for female energy, and banishing bad karma.

Fiona invited her friends to a party. That is all that has happened.

I stare at the 19.12 one again. Roe has obviously told Fi exactly what happened yesterday with the tarot reading. The Secret Santa. The truth about what happened at the reading.

I think of the rosemary again. You can't do anything about what you said during the tarot reading. And as for the Secret Santa thing … that was a year ago. If Roe wants to stop talking to you over something you did a year ago, well … well there's nothing we can do about that.

Here's what I can do, though. I can make a spell to bring back Lily.

CHAPTER THIRTY

I SAY GOODNIGHT TO MUM AND DAD AND JO AT ELEVEN, BUT I don't go to sleep. I'm too busy planning my next spell. The spell that will bring Lily back.

Last night I broke the cold snap and melted the snow. It's not Lily being back in her bed, but it's progress: the light trace of cracks appearing on an eggshell before it hatches. This is the one that will pull her out. I'm sure of it.

I try to refine my slapdash methods from last night. This time, I don't use random objects to represent Earth, Air, Fire and Water. I'm more thoughtful. I pocket small items from the house all evening: a box of fancy-looking hotel-room matches for Fire, some decorative seashells for Water, a quill pen from a museum gift shop for Air. I fill a freezer bag full of thawing soil from the garden. I find a picture of me and Lily in Mum's shoebox of endless unframed photos. We are eight and she is on holidays with us, her dirty-blonde hair bleached white in the Spanish sun. We are eating ice cream out of a plastic penguin's head.

At around two I creep into the bathroom and repeat the bath cauldron, throwing rosemary, honey and a bay leaf into the water. I'll have to buy more ingredients, proper ones, from Divination.

This spell is from the book. It's called the Sailor's Loss. It involves taking two ropes of white silk, and knotting them with a sailor's knot over and over again until you have one long plait. As you tie the knots, you're supposed to visualize finding a lost item bobbing in the middle of a vast ocean, and then lassoing the lost thing and pulling it closer and closer to you.

I make my spell circle – set up my shells, my matches, my feather, my earth. I'm getting good at this. I just feel a natural understanding of this stuff without having to try very hard. It comes to me like verb conjugations come to Joanne.

Before I begin, I select a few tarot cards that I think represent what I want from the spell. I pick a card that most resembles Lily's character, and decide on the Page of Cups, a noble young guy who lives half in a dream world. I lay it face up in the middle of the spell circle, and find two friends to join it. The Four of Wands, for homecoming. The Chariot for willpower, focus and mastery.

I start the plait, focusing on the photograph of me and Lily the entire time. The silk is the cord from my dressing gown, cut in half with kitchen scissors. I close my eyes. I visualize.

Lily is lying in the Beg, floating on the water. It feels like early dawn; a mist hovers over the river, pierced by an orange light in the corner of my vision. Her hair is in long mermaid strands around her; her bug eyes are staring at the sky. I am paddling towards her.

I start looping the rope around my head, like a cowboy. I focus in on this action, trying to correctly visualize what the rope would feel like if it were a proper lasso. How heavy it would be.

In the river I am lassoing, but on the bathroom floor

I am knotting, knotting, knotting. Staring at the photo. Knotting. Knotting. Knotting.

Back in the Beg, my arms are starting to ache and I'm growing weak. I'm too far away from her. A few times, I throw the rope and it splashes next to her, flecks of water landing on her face. She doesn't move, doesn't blink.

C'mon, c'mon, I urge. *Get the rope around her. Get it around her.*

Why is this so hard? It's my imagination, after all. I can do whatever I want with it. I could get a drone to fly in and bring Lily right to me. But for some reason I can't do it. I can't get the rope around her in a way that feels convincing or real. When I try to force it, my concentration just breaks and I'm too aware of myself. Too aware of being a sixteen-year-old girl on my parents' bathroom floor.

I push through.

Just make the rope go around her feet, Maeve! It's not that hard! It's your fecking brain!

I do it.

The rope loops around her ankle, and I pull her in.

But it doesn't feel real. The Beg at dawn falls away and it's a cardboard scenery version of it. The more I pull, the more the reality disappears.

A sound of a car alarm outside. A dog barking somewhere far away.

It's gone. My concentration is broken, and there's no room left to knot.

The candle has burned out.

I know the spell hasn't worked before I even go to bed, but I can't figure out why. I tie the silken knots around my

265

wrist like a bracelet. Lily and I never went through a friendship bracelet phase, strangely enough. It seemed redundant: we were the only friend the other one had, so making a bracelet seemed beside the point. I wish I had given her one. I think she would have liked it.

Before I drift off to sleep, I remember the Divination shopkeeper again.

"You have to give big to get big."

I flex my hand, looking at the delicate scar where the keys had cut into my palm. Of course. Blood was the sacrifice that turned an old shower-gel bottle, toiletries and a bathtub of junk into a real *spell*.

I need to figure out a way to give bigger.

I feel awkward with Fiona in school the next day. Luckily, Fiona is impervious to awkwardness. She plonks herself at the edge of my desk and looks me right in the eye.

"Why didn't you text me back yesterday?"

"Uh…"

"I tried to invite you over."

"Sorry, my phone was out of battery."

"Yeah, I thought that was it. When did it come back on?"

"I don't know. Eight?"

"But you didn't text back?"

"I thought the party would have been over."

"It was, but we still could have…" She breaks off, as if she is presuming too much about our friendship. After all, we haven't known one another very long.

"I thought that maybe …" I say bashfully, "you wouldn't want to talk to me."

266

"Why?"

"Because of Roe."

She scrunches her face. "I mean, I know he's not happy with you at the moment, but it's, like, a lover's tiff, right?"

"Did he tell you what the *tiff* was about?"

"He mentioned the lie," she says, screwing her mouth to one side. "But as I said to *him*, how were you to know? I mean, sure, in hindsight, maybe don't freak out at someone and wish them dead while the Housekeeper is present. Grand. We *know that now*. But how on earth were you supposed to know that then?"

"I guess," I say, the beginnings of a smile on a face.

"I mean, imagine if I was held accountable every time I wished Jos would disappear so I didn't have to babysit him. I'd be in *prison*, Maeve."

I laugh. She's right. Roe is entitled to hate me, but she's still right.

"Thanks," I say, laughing. "I'm glad I have you on my side, at least."

"You're my friend. I wasn't going to let him talk shit about you. But I wanted to make sure you were OK, because he seemed pretty depressed."

"Really?" I say, eagerly.

"Yeah. I mean. He was sound, like, same as he always is, but he didn't stay long. I kept waiting for you to text me back so we could sort it all out. But you didn't."

"I'm sorry," I say lamely. And then I remember the spell.

I grab her arm. "I need to tell you something."

Her face lights up.

267

"Not here, though," I mutter. "Art room? Lunch?"

She nods and rushes back to her seat as class begins.

At lunchtime, I tell her everything. Well, almost. I tell her about the spell that broke the cold snap, the cogs that cut me in the river, the failed spell last night.

"And so, I think, the issue is," I finish, practically frothing, "I think I have to find a bigger sacrifice? Like, maybe a little bit of blood? I could reopen the old wound? Do you think that might help?"

Fiona looks at me blankly. "You want to *cut* yourself?"

"What? No! I don't *want* to cut myself. I just think, like the lady said, you need to give big to get big, y'know? Sacrifice. It worked when I cut my hand in the river."

She does her little thinking pose again – the prayer hands in front of her mouth, a little Hollywood 'namaste'-type gesture she obviously picked up from watching Inside the Actors Studio. She closes her eyes for a second.

"Maeve. I love you."

"Oh. OK," I reply, slightly startled by the response. "I love ... you?"

"I love you, and I'm telling you this because ... you're worrying me."

This was not the response I was expecting. "You don't believe me, do you?"

She busies herself with a piece of lint on her sleeve, trying to avoid eye contact.

"Fi?"

"I just think you might be putting two and two together and making five."

"What? What does that mean?"

"The snow melting ... like, it probably just melted on its own, Maeve."

"But... It *didn't*."

"Do you have any proof of that, though?" asks Fiona, with a face like she's picking a scab off a little too soon.

I think for a moment. "Well, no," I admit. "But I know it was. I was in the circle and..."

"And the water drops fell on your head. It sounds very cinematic and everything, but..."

"Cinematic?"

"It's just hard to believe."

I'm silent. How could she think this? After everything we've been through? After everything else she's been willing to believe, this is where the line is?

"I think if you were there, you would understand," I plead. "If you cast a spell with me, you would know how it feels. Everything feels ... more real, somehow?"

"I don't think I *want* to know how it feels. It seems a bit ... deluded."

My eyes sting with hurt. *Deluded?*

"I don't understand. You believed the whole thing about the White Lady. All that. But this is too far? The fact that ... that there's real power out there, and we can access it?"

Fiona bites her nails and looks uncomfortable. "I'm sorry! I just don't believe that a sixteen-year-old girl in her bathroom can control the weather! We're not in *X-Men*."

I start packing up my lunch, throwing my uneaten banana back into my school bag.

"Maeve. Don't."

I can't sit with her right now. I love hanging out with

269

Fiona. But I spent too long stuffing myself down to impress girls at St Bernadette's. The longer I sit here and listen to her tell me that I'm not capable of magic – real magic – the more I'll believe it, and the less likely I'll ever be able to do it again. The epiphany of yesterday, the sense that I could channel the bad parts of myself into good things, is not something I can afford to let go of. Not when Lily feels so close.

"I just want to be alone, OK?" I blurt. "It's not personal."

"It is."

"OK, it is, but I'm not mad at you. You don't have to believe me. But *I have to believe me*. It's the only way I can find a way out of this."

"OK," she says reluctantly.

"Friends?" I say.

"Friends," she agrees. She smiles weakly at me in confirmation. "Just promise me you won't hurt yourself."

"I promise."

And I leave. I leave the art room. I can't believe it. It's like something from a play: *exit Maeve*. The only time I ever leave a room is to storm out of it. But I laid a boundary with Fiona, a clear one, and even if it seems objectively crazy to do so, it feels like the right step. Uncomfortable, but correct.

After school I head down to Divination to ask the shopkeeper about spell ingredients.

"Maeve," she says pleasantly. "How'r'ya keeping?"

"I'm OK," I smile back. "I'm actually getting into spells, a little bit."

"That's gas! Well done, Maeve. Congrats. Any good ones so far?"

"Well, I think…" I venture this slowly, not wanting to

convince another person that I'm insane. "I think I might have helped end the cold snap."

"Ah, now, was that you?" She smiles, her face weary. "Thanks be to God! I've been trying to work on that myself for about a week."

"Is that what you were doing the other day? When we were last here? I thought I heard you chanting something under your breath."

"I was." She nods. "I was working away on a few things, to be honest."

"Like what?"

"Ah, it's all a bit complicated. But whenever there's a shift in energy, there's always a knock-on effect, you know?"

I remember Sylvia, and how she talked about weights and counterweights in the magical world.

"Like a see-saw," I say.

"Exactly. Although I think of it more like Jenga. Or dominoes. It's all just games, stuff knocking other stuff out of the way, or pushing it forward. A bar fight between every known force in the universe, all sliding around Kilbeg. I can feel it in the air."

"And how is that –" I try to look for the most magical word I know – *"manifesting*, I guess?"

She fixes her eyes on me, considering her answer. "Well, on sensitives, Maeve Chambers. On sensitives."

My face must look idiotic and confused, because she starts laughing at my blank expression. "Now, tell me this isn't the first time you've heard *that* word."

"Sensitive?" I repeat. "Like, when your feelings get hurt easily. Is that what you mean?"

"Not quite. Being a sensitive is a word we use to talk about people who ... well, let's say they're tuned into a slightly different frequency. They're on a higher plane."

I stare at her, mute.

"I'm not being very clear, am I?" She starts again slowly. "A person who is a sensitive might have a greater natural access to magic. They might come to spells or tarot easier. They might ... I don't know, find that certain magical skills, like telepathy, come to them naturally."

I stop dead. My mouth is completely dry, and I keep flapping it open and closed. "I ... uh ... am I a ...?"

"A sensitive?" The shopkeeper smiles. "Yes, Maeve Chambers. You're a sensitive. I knew from the first day you came in."

"Are there ... a *lot* of us?"

"Hard to say. You're the first I've met in a long, long time, and I tend to run in the kinds of circles where you meet more than average. Most never get to find out. They just spend their whole lives feeling a bit too big for their own skin."

"Are you ... are you one?"

"Me? No. Heaven was, and that didn't go too well, but I'm just an enthusiast. A good study. A kitchen witch," she laughs. "A village crone."

Heaven. Her sister. She's mentioned her before, I think. The first time I walked into the shop, and she started on about having three "e"s in my name.

"But why me? How?"

She shrugs. "Why brown eyes? Why birthmarks? Accident of fate, I suppose."

"And are they ... we – are we powerful?"

The incense stick to her right burns down, the long string of ash falling to the wooden slat beneath it. She takes a new one from a cardboard box, lighting it with a match.

"Mmm, do you smell that?" she says, closing her eyes. "Night-blooming jasmine."

"It's very nice," I reply, still reeling from this new information. A sensitive. I am *a sensitive*. I ponder it for a few seconds, inhaling the thick sweet scent that I will for ever associate with this moment.

"In answer to your question, they *can* become extremely powerful. Not all great sensitives are witches, but all great witches are sensitives. And you, Maeve Chambers –" she gazes at me, her bright blonde hair doing nothing to hide her steely grey eyes – "you could be a very good witch."

She turns to a selection of pale wooden drawers behind the till, opening and closing them to reveal that they are filled with freshly cut herbs. She smiles when she sees my surprised face.

"From the garden," she laughs. "You should try growing your own herbs. So *satisfying* to make it all yourself."

"Thanks," I murmur, watching her move through the drawers with a tiny silver pail. "Maybe I'll try that."

She shovels little bits of ingredients into a leather pouch, moving between her fresh herbs and pots of spices that she pinches from. She quickly ties it closed with a drawstring.

"There we are, pet," she says, placing it on the counter. "Dandelion seeds, rosemary, aniseed and a pinch of chilli for intensity. Help you focus your energy. Hang it over your bed for a full menstrual cycle."

I must be blushing, because she smiles at me. "Oh,

sweetheart, you mustn't be embarrassed. Our menses is a big part of our casting energy, you know."

I stuff it into my pocket. "Thanks," I say, still red. "Any tips on how I can be a good sensitive?"

"The only advice for being a good sensitive is not to be a *bad* one."

"What do you mean?"

"A bad sensitive," she says, "can see where people are at their weakest, and they exploit them for it. They crowbar their way into people's hearts and minds, put all kinds of ideas in there."

I immediately think of Aaron. And how from the moment I first met him, I knew he could see the holes in people. Were we alike in some way? Both sensitives?

Roe himself had said it, on the bus home from that CoB meeting: *"you guys are two sides of the same coin".*

"Who's your sister?" I ask. "You said she's a sensitive, too?"

"Was," she says.

I nod. I don't ask any follow-up questions. This woman might feel like my friend, but she is, after all, just trying to run a business.

"I'm sorry. About your sister."

"That will be three euro fifty, if you don't mind, pet."

The air in the room has suddenly shifted, and I feel as though I should probably go.

I pay her, thank her and turn to leave. Then, a brain-wave. "Do you remember the snow back in 1990?"

A silence. The shopkeeper starts cutting some sprigs of herbs, as though she hasn't heard me.

"The snow," I venture again. "The only other time there was snow in Kilbeg, and no other part of the country."

More cutting. She opens a drawer and distils plant shards into them. She's trying to hide her face from me, but I can see her lips moving. *"Out, out, out."*

She's trying to cast me out of the shop. A wave of profound stubbornness comes over me. I clutch the silken bracelet made out of my dressing-gown cord, and start whispering, too.

"Help me, help me, help me.

You told me what I am. Now help me."

She lifts her eyes, grey and muted, and fixes her stare on me. The shopkeeper doesn't say a word, doesn't move a muscle. She slowly closes her eyes, and as she does, mine start to close, too.

An image starts to form in my head. One of her, by the river, standing next to me and watching a milk crate float downstream.

"Not yet," she says. *"Not yet."*

"When?"

"When I'm sure you won't do something reckless with the information."

"I won't."

"You will."

She is in my head, in the same way that I can be in Roe's or he can be in mine. The only difference is that she is in complete control. She doesn't need the cards to form a gateway. She can do this at will.

Just as I'm sure she's about to dismiss me, she says one last message. Sends it without even moving her lips.

One more tip for being a good sensitive, Maeve. Don't bite off more than you can chew.

And then all of a sudden, it's over. We're back in the shop, all four eyes open. The bell on the door rings, and a woman starts asking about essential oils.

"Goodbye, Maeve," the shopkeeper says.

I go.

CHAPTER THIRTY-ONE

I HAVE NO IDEA WHAT TO WEAR TO THE GIG AT THE CYPRESS. All Roe said was that it was an LGBTQ all-ages thing, which means … what? I can't wear the blue dress I wore to Fiona's barbecue, it's way too "meet the parents" for that. But I don't have anything cool to wear, either. Being a sensitive has not, evidently, made me sensitive to dress codes.

I should be thankful that I'm even allowed go. Parents, en masse, are still holding the reins very tightly. Mum and Dad weren't going to let me go to the gig at first, but Joanne stuck up for me. She said it was important that I support the charity. I was amazed at how hard she went for it.

"I'll drop her off and pick her up. You guys know what's happening in the world right now," she said. "We need all the allies we can get."

I go through Joanne's wardrobe, but her style is too practical, too fresh, too sporty. I need grunge, not pink polo shirts. I manage to find some black fishnets that she wore at Halloween, but that's the best I'm able to do. Abbie's old room isn't much better. The only stuff she's left here are hanging-around-the-house clothes, all soft joggers and hoodies. I do, however, find one deep plum lipstick that looks quite good against my dark hair.

I hit the jackpot in Pat's room, where I find a big black

Kate Bush T-shirt. And I actually know some Kate Bush songs, so I won't feel like a complete imposter wearing it. I cut up an old pair of black jeans into shorts and put the fishnets on underneath.

After a good hour of scrutinizing the mirror, I decide that I look like someone who belongs at a gig.

Now the only trouble is going downstairs.

"Oooooh, look," says Mum.

"Oh, look at *you*," copies Jo.

"Rocker chick!" Dad cries enthusiastically. "Rocking girl!"

"Please stop," I plead.

"No," says Dad. "Shan't."

"Maeve, that shirt is *miles* too big on you," Mum says, with scrutiny.

"That's the point," I say uncertainly. "Jo, can you bring me in now please?"

"Yup," she says draining her coffee. "To the les-mobile."

She's quiet in the car, but keeps smiling over at me.

"Stop."

"I can't help it. You look so cute. My baby sister!"

"Jo, I swear to God…"

"Is your boy in the band then?"

I am silent. Roe and I have still not spoken. I wonder whether it's a good idea to go to his gig at all, but the only thing worse than going at this point would be not going.

"Still all this secrecy? Jesus, it must be serious."

"I actually…" My voice cracks. "I don't know whether we're still together."

"Oh no! Why?"

"I think I screwed it up. I was too … *myself*."

"What does *that* mean?"

I laugh hollowly. "You know."

"I don't."

"Angry. Jealous. Bitchy. Manipulative. Whatever."

"Ah."

"Yeah."

"Well, being yourself can mean more than that. You're also funny. And confident. And you know your own mind."

God. This is rare. And suspicious.

"Why are you being nice?"

"I'm just telling it how it is. I wish I'd had your confidence when I was sixteen. I wish I had your confidence *now*."

"I'm not confident."

"Maeve, you're wearing your older brother's sweaty T-shirt to a gig. That's confidence."

"Oh shit," I say, panicking and smelling the armpits of Pat's T-shirt. "Do I smell?"

"You smell fine." She smiles, pulling the car over. "Go on, get out, be young, support the baby queers. God, I can't imagine what life would have been like if we'd had queer all-ages gigs when I was your age."

"Do you think I shouldn't be there?" I say, suddenly very worried. "You know, because I'm not…"

"No," she says firmly. "Community is important, no matter who it is. As long as you're supportive and don't, I don't know, ask anyone weird intrusive questions about their gender or their sex life. We need support. Especially the way things are turning."

279

"What do you mean? The way what is turning?"

"The world, Maeve. Hate crime is still very much a thing. The other day me and Sarra were holding hands at the sandwich counter in Centra and a boy not much older than you started screaming at us. I mean *screaming*."

"What?" I say, alarmed. "Why? You never said anything."

"I wouldn't say it to Mum and Dad. They'd only get upset."

"Jo, that's *horrible*."

"It is," she agrees. "Now, I'm parked in a bus lane – get out."

She turfs me out onto the street. I'm still reeling with the thought of someone screaming at my sister – *at my sister!* – in a Centra.

I pay my seven euro to get into the gig, climb the narrow rickety stairs to the venue and nervously buy a Coke. Everyone here is colourful, with pink glitter in their eyebrows and interesting, gender-unspecific haircuts. A bearded drag queen in a turban is making the rounds, saying hello to everyone. No one is doing the stupid 1990s grunge look I'm doing.

Roe and I haven't spoken since the disastrous tarot reading. What if he doesn't want me here? What felt like a gesture of loyalty in my bedroom now feels like an insane suicide mission.

I scan a poster as a way of not making eye contact with anyone, and realize that I don't know the name of Roe's band.

I don't know the name of my own boyfriend's band.

This, surely, is the confirmation I need that I never actually had a boyfriend. Girlfriends know their boyfriends' band names! That's just a fact! There's someone called Miel in the band, but that's all I know. I haven't even got a clue what music they play or anything. God, I'm rubbish. I need to leave. I *should leave.*

I head to the door and make my way down the stairs, pushing past people on their way up. Suddenly I hear Fiona's voice.

"MAEVE!"

I whip around, my heart melting with gratitude. Fiona's here, and she's wearing black jeans, a Penelope Pitstop T-shirt and her big leather jacket. She has a little bit of winged eyeliner on. She's infinitely cooler than I am, but at least we look like we belong together. I throw my arms around her.

"You're here!" I squeal. "I'm so glad you're here!"

"I'm so glad *you're* here!"

We grin at each other, happy to be doing normal things, like going to gigs together. We will not discuss witchcraft, or spells, or sensitives. Not tonight.

"Did he…?" I begin, trying to smooth the spikes of jealousy in my voice. "Did he invite you?"

"Roe? No. A couple of the drag queens performing are in *Othello* with me. I only found out Small Private Ceremony were playing today."

"Who?"

"Small Private Ceremony," she repeats. "Roe's band?"

"Oh, sure," I reply quickly. "Of course."

Fiona knows Roe's band. Fiona. Who has only met him

281

a handful of times, as opposed to me, who has known him for ten years.

The room goes dark and a single spotlight falls on the bearded, turban-wearing drag queen who is hosting the evening.

"Hello, hello, hello," she purrs into the microphone. "Guys, gals, and those of you beyond the binary! How are we? Are we well?"

Roars of approval.

"Welcome to a night of queer musical cabaret. I'm your host, Avoca Reaction – because that's what great drag should do. Now, mic check. My name is WHAT?"

"Avoca Reaction!" the crowd calls back.

"Because WHY?"

"That's what great drag should do!"

"That's right! I'm your friendly neighbourhood bisexual non-binary intergender drag entity. Now, is there anyone here who has never been to a cabaret before…?"

Small Private Ceremony aren't on until third, and despite my hideous nerves at seeing him, me and Fiona still have a brilliant time. We scream for the kings and queens and almost cry laughing at the comedy, and we don't talk very much at all except to grasp each other and whisper, "Would you *look?*" and "I am *dying…*"

And then he comes onstage.

Standing in black Doc Martens and a floor-length, deep-red velvet gown with a split up the leg is Roe O'Callaghan. His hair is curlier than ever and pushed forward, so his eyes are barely visible under the thick mop. And with lips so painted they look swollen, he starts to sing, slowly at first. Softly. I only notice that he's holding a guitar when, three lines into his song, he takes a single, jerked stab at it.

The lights come up, and the rest of the band are now visible. A blond bass player with a page-boy haircut that I assume is Miel, wearing a white vest and black waistcoat. The drummer is a ginger boy with glitter in his beard, and the lead guitarist is a big girl with bubblegum-pink hair and a buttoned-up Victorian nightgown on. None of their outfits go together, but weirdly that's what makes them look like they belong to one another.

They play mostly covers at first, Roe going from Karen O to the Corrs in the same song. I can tell, even objectively, that he is an absurdly talented performer. He can make songs that should be embarrassing and mawkish into these slick punk numbers, and slick punk numbers into sentimental ballads. Then, they start singing their own material. It's easy to tell when Roe has written a song: it's full of his dry wit and sincerity, full of colour and story and metaphor. He sings a song about a Russian spy that, it's clear, is pretty well-loved among the twenty or thirty people here who know the band well.

> "You're a tripwire trap
> In a house that's tapped
> With a telephone trigger that's rigged to blow;
> When the ringing sounds,
> I won't wait around.
> I will pick it up and say 'hello'."

And people are singing along, yelling "tripwire trap" and then "hello" every time the chorus comes around. By the final chorus, he's screaming it. Clusters of people are screaming it back.

Roe has fans! I think in amazement. *My boyfriend has fans!*

"All right everyone," Roe says, finally addressing the crowd. He starts retuning his guitar, and I can see a tremor. His hand is shaking. He is sick with nerves under all that velvet, trying so hard to keep it together. "How are we doing?"

Fiona and I shout loudest. His head jerks in my direction, his eyes meeting mine and then journeying down to my enormous T-shirt. His mouth twitches slightly, an almost-smile playing on his red lips.

God, he's so sexy. How is he so sexy?

"This is a new song," he says simply. "I hope you don't mind that it's a bit slow."

And he starts.

"How long have we been here?
And do I say too much?
These days I'm mostly vacillating
In and out of touch…"

His eyes focus and settle on me, and every hair on my body is awake and standing on end. He is singing this song at me, to me. It feels startlingly intimate in such a full, sweating room. The only music is an occasional strum of a chord and the thud of a kick drum.

"In and out of focus
Always trying to construct
These aimless conversations
as a substitute for trust…"

Roe's eyes are boring into me, to the point where a few people in front of me are turning around to see what he's

284

looking at. The snare drum kicks in. The chorus explodes as the girl on lead guitar starts playing a high, tinkling riff that vibrates my blood.

> *"And then there's you, in livid blue*
> *Come seeping through the silence;*
> *If you're not dangerous, then how come I hear sirens*
> *And is everything just violence?*
>
> *"And then there's you, in livid blue*
> *Come wading through the weather;*
> *But if we've got to live in hiding,*
> *least we're stuck in here together..."*

I'm completely breathless. What does this mean? Does Roe love me? Is he scared of me? Is it both?

But I don't have time to figure it out, because at that moment, a glass bottle sails across the room and hits Roe in the mouth.

CHAPTER THIRTY-TWO

AT FIRST, I'M SURE IT'S AN ACCIDENT, OR A JOKE.

It is neither of these things.

The lights suddenly go out, and the room is plunged in darkness. There's some kind of fight happening near the door, and I hear Avoca Reaction's voice, loud and defensive.

"You need to get out of here. No, you're not welcome. No. No. Get out. Get *out*, before I call the…"

I can't hear what happens next. The room, which moments previously was alight with the happy, joyous shouts of singing teenagers, is now full of horrified screams. I grab Fiona next to me.

"Where's Roe?" I yell. "What's *happening*?"

A crowd of people heave backwards, crushing me and Fiona against the wall. I hear her screaming as a boy falls backwards on top of her. I crouch to pick her up and am almost trampled in the process. I haul her to the side of the stage and manage to stand up on top of it, trying to see what's happening.

A group of people have wrestled their way into the gig. Most of them are about our age or a few years older. The biggest ones, the biggest men, are shoving people backwards and screaming in their faces. A few others are carrying things. I get on my tiptoes to try to see.

Carrying ... *buckets?*

No one is actually punching or hitting, just pushing, pushing, pushing. There's about twenty of them, and the closer I look, the more I see how familiar they are.

Fiona, recovered from the initial shock, is standing on top of the stage with me.

"Maeve," she says, pointing. "Look."

I follow her finger and see a tall blond man in a soft grey sweatshirt and navy peacoat standing with his back to the wall.

"Isn't that the guy from the cafe?"

And it is. It's Aaron. Aaron has brought the Children of Brigid here, to Roe's gig. To a queer charity cabaret night. He's not moving. He's not even speaking. Just standing, watching the fury impassively. For a moment, our eyes meet, and I'm sure that Aaron can see me for who I am. The other sensitive. But his eyes rove on as he keeps scanning the room.

"Where's Roe?" I shout over the din. "Can you see him?"

A drag queen has taken her shoe off and is clubbing someone with it. The pink-haired lead guitarist from Small Private Ceremony is shoving a CoB member back, yelling at him to hit her with his best shot. The CoB kids aren't doing anything except pushing and shouting: shouting the worst kind of words you can think of, words that were probably thrown at Jo and Sarra last week when they were in Centra queuing for a hot chicken roll.

And then, somebody gets grabbed. A fourteen-year-old boy who I had noticed on the way in for having better make-up than a Jenner sister is held by the back of the head, and dragged to the doorway where the people with the buckets are waiting.

"What's in the buckets?" Fiona yells. "What are they *doing*?"

My mind goes to the worst. Piss? Blood? Animal poo? What on earth could they possibly have in there?

The boy's face is pushed into the bucket, held there and, a few seconds later, is pulled out again dripping wet.

Water. I think it's water.

His mascara is running down his face, his foundation an orange mess. He is pushed back into the crowd, shell-shocked and crying.

They're taking his make-up off.

They're trying to take *everyone's* make-up off.

As the realization sparks and carries, the room goes wild. Punches are thrown. Blood starts to spatter. The cabaret crowd start to fight. And that's when I see him. Roe, his mouth coated in blood, his dress torn at the shoulder. He is trying to get to Aaron, but he is being stopped by a boy I recognize as Cormac, the boy from the CoB meeting who played GAA and shaved his legs. Roe pushes past Cormac and manages to square up to Aaron, who seems calmly surprised that Roe wants to speak to him. He gives a "who, me?" look of indifference, as if Roe has wrongly recognized an old neighbour.

I stare at Aaron's face and realize that this is exactly what he wants. He wants the cabaret crowd to descend into violence: he wants them to throw punches, to stab with stiletto heels, to go out of control. He wants to be able to maintain that all CoB did was show up with a few buckets of water.

He intentionally brought only twenty or so Christian teenagers with him, against a crowd of one hundred. He wants it to look like an uneven fight. He wants to lose.

This, I realize, is a PR exercise. And Roe, screaming and shaking Aaron by the shoulders, is doing exactly what Aaron wants him to do.

Gay mob descends on Christian charity group!

'Art' collective goes wild!

Life's a Drag: how the city's drag scene turned violent!

I imagine the pieces in the paper, the segments on the radio, Aaron giving perfect soundbites to the press, the endless talk panels. *"Yes, of course, the CoB shouldn't have been there in the first place, but I think we can agree it's all gone a bit too far..."*

The crowd is too thick for me to be able to get over. Fiona, who seems to have realized the intention to all this at the same time I have, is recording it on her phone. "These guys have showed up and started attacking people," she shouts over the din. She is on Instagram Live. "They're attacking queer people."

Above the wall where Aaron stands, there is a framed photo of the Cypress the year it first opened.

And then I see her. The Housekeeper is standing by Aaron, river water trailing off her. Her dress is wet and plastered to her body.

By now, it seems normal for her to make an appearance. When an imbalance occurs in the world, something else must rise to meet it. Aaron came to Kilbeg because he spied a hole in the fabric, the hole the Housekeeper cut for him. But whose side was she on? Was she here to support Aaron, or to support me?

I hold on to my bracelet. My sailor's knot. I keep my eyes on the frame. I try to remember the spell, and imagine myself tying a lasso around the picture frame and bringing it forward. I picture it smashing on Aaron's head. I breathe. I start a chant.

"Tip the frame, tip the scales.

Where Roe wins, Aaron fails."

I keep it up, over and over, faster and faster. Roe keeps shouting at Aaron, Aaron keeps his shit-eating grin up. Another kid gets grabbed and thrown into some water.

"Tip the frame, tip the scales.

Where Roe wins, Aaron fails."

"Maeve, what are you doing?"

The frame is wobbling. It's *moving*.

"Fi, give me your hand."

"What?"

"I said, give me your fecking hand."

She gives me her hand, and I slide it into the sailor's knot bracelet. The white satin of my dressing-gown cord is netting us together in a single spell.

"Just hold it. And watch the frame. Watch the frame, Fiona. Above his head."

You're a sensitive, Maeve. You can do this.

I start the chant again, and soon Fiona starts it, too. We do it together, urgent, frantic.

"Tip the frame, tip the scales.

Where Roe wins, Aaron fails."

And then it happens. The wood frame falls heavily on Aaron, glass shattering around his shoulders, a crimson wound opening at his temple. For a moment, everything in the room stops as people flinch at the sound and instinctively move away from the glass. The Housekeeper, like a speck of dirt in the corner of your eye, is gone with a blink. Still tethered by the sailor's knot, Fiona and I dive into the crowd, fighting to get to Roe.

"Jesus Christ, Maeve," I hear her call. "Jesus *Christ*."

I clamp my free hand on Roe. He turns, his eyes wide and panicked, like an animal.

"Are you OK?"

We both say it at the same time.

At that moment, the Gardaí fly through the door. I recognize Griffin immediately.

"Maeve," she says, then her eyes fly to Roe. "Rory."

I can see her making a million tiny judgements, levying a thousand questions and answers in her brain.

"Get out of here," she says. "Now. Neither of you can afford to be taken home in a squad car. Your parents have been through enough."

I nod and barge past her, Fiona in tow.

"We can't just go," Roe says. "We can't just leave them."

"We have to. Do you really want your parents to see a squad car outside their house? Tonight? With you dressed like this?"

He nods.

"Fine."

And we fall down the stairs, into the street, and to the sounds of sirens outside.

CHAPTER THIRTY-THREE

THE THREE OF US ARE IN DEASY'S WITH OUR ORDER OF CHIPS and curry sauce. We're not diving in, fighting for the big chips. We're just staring into space, beginning sentences and then having no idea where to end them. Families are picking up their Saturday night order of fish and chips.

"What ... what time is it?" Fiona suddenly asks.

Roe looks at his watch. "Just gone eight."

"*How* can it have just gone eight?" she says, dazzled.

"I know," I agree. "Hate crime always feels like much more of a *late* evening thing."

We laugh, despite everything. Despite the fact that there's blood drying on Roe's neck. Despite the fact that Fiona and I just crashed a photo frame on a man without even touching it. Despite the fact that we have no idea what's going to happen to the kids at the cabaret, or how Roe is going to go home without a spare change of clothes.

We laugh. Imagine.

"Do you think this is all part of Children of Brigid's plan then?" Fiona asks. "To cause riots? Civil unrest, and all that?"

"I guess so," I shrug. "My sister said that she was attacked recently. In Centra, of all places."

Roe sinks his head into his hands, pushing his hair back

off his face to reveal two pearl earrings. "What am I going to do?"

"You can come to my house. Pat has clothes you can borrow before going home."

"No, I mean, what am I going to *do*?" he says, his voice breaking. He gestures to himself in his ripped red velvet. "How am I supposed to live?"

Silence. Neither me nor Fiona can find the words right away to comfort him. This is, after all, not a problem we have. What is he imagining for himself right now? What kind of future is he picturing? One where he gets assaulted in public for being who he is?

This is how bad sensitives prey on people. They make them afraid. This is exactly what Aaron wants to happen. For Roe to stuff himself into as small a box as he possibly can. A butterfly pinned into a frame.

"You're going to live your fecking life," I say, trying to summon every bit of authority I can muster. "You're going to live your life, and you're going to wear a dress when you want to wear a dress, and go by whatever name you want, and we'll be here."

"Maeve…"

"No. Roe. I can't promise that stuff like this won't happen again, but I can promise that… I can promise to have your back. For as long as you want it. Or need it. And you too, Fiona. We need each other. You're the only people I have."

"I promise, too," Fiona says looking from me to Roe and back again. "I'm with you as long as you guys are with me."

293

"Plus," she adds bleakly, "you know when they're done with the gays, they'll move on to the foreigns."

Roe gives us a smile, showing his teeth bathed in blood. "All right, all right, this is our Three Musketeers pledge, is it? All for one and one for all?"

"Yes," Fiona and I both say, fiercely.

"Fine," he says, smiling even wider. "I promise, too, I'll kill to protect you two, or die trying."

We don't shake on it. We don't do anything except look at one another under the fluorescent strip lighting of Deasy's chipper. We're smiling, but I know we mean it. That we've never meant anything like we mean this.

"And we've got something else," Fiona ventures. "We've got magic."

"Oh, Mrs Cynic believes in magic now, does she?" I smile.

"It's actually *Ms* Cynic," she says, sipping her Coke. "What we did in there, Maeve – I still can't believe it... I'm sorry I doubted you."

"I'm sorry, what is it you two did?" Roe asks.

"Only saved your life," Fiona responds curtly.

"Uh-huh. How, exactly?"

I explain, as sanely as I can, the spell with the picture frame, the spell that broke the cold snap, and finally, the failed spell to get Lily back.

"Right," Roe says, slightly dazed looking. "Right."

"I believe my response to this was, *Maeve, are you insane?*" Fiona politely nudges.

"Maybe I got hit by that bottle too hard," he says, evenly. "Or maybe things have just been too weird lately."

I let out a short, barking laugh. "You want to talk about weird? I'm a *sensitive* now."

Roe and Maeve cock their heads in utter confusion.

"Oh, good," I reply, slightly relieved. "You haven't heard of it, either. When the Divination shopkeeper told me, I thought I was the only one who didn't know what a freaking sensitive was."

"Well, what *is* it?" Roe asks irritably.

"It basically means that you're born with a kind of … natural knack for magic-y things."

"That doesn't sound very … specific," he says, his brows furrowed.

Fiona looks thoughtful. "Nobody could have made that crappy book work," she says slowly. "Unless they had magic in them already."

Roe still looks unconvinced.

"I think it's just an explanation for why … I don't know…" I'm suddenly flustered. I'm not used to being the special one. *They* are the special ones.

"Like, how I'm good at tarot, and how the Housekeeper is … attracted to me, and how I can sort of be in Roe's brain. And the spells. I think I just have, like, one per cent more of a natural flair for it than regular people. That's all."

"One per cent!" Fiona says, outraged. "More like, fifty."

"Eleven, Fiona. Eleven per cent."

"I won't take a penny less than thirty per cent."

We all laugh, and making it into a dumb joke helps me to normalize this strange new fact about myself. It's a bit like being in some elusive thirteenth house of the zodiac.

"But the woman at Divination, she also said that … bad

sensitives exist, and I think Aaron might be one. She seems to think that Kilbeg is at the centre of some kind of energy shift."

"Like the Housekeeper is throwing everything off," Roe says slowly.

"Yes! And I guess the Aarons of the world ... the bad sensitives, prey on that sort of thing. They get into people's heads."

Could it be possible that some grand Jenga match of forces and energy were thrown out of whack when I woke up the Housekeeper? Could the Housekeeper, who was awakened by spite and pain and anger, be feeding everything in the city – even a Christian fundamentalist group that has nothing to do with us?

I picture the river, flowing through the entire city like a blue vein. The river, filled with rainbow trout and cogs and keys. The river carrying the winds and currents and the secrets of a missing girl.

"So Lily's disappearance doesn't exist in a vacuum. It's part of everything else," Roe says, suddenly. "The Housekeeper is just the start of a big chain reaction. I *knew* we were right to see a connection between those CoB creeps and Lily."

Fiona starts to nod slowly.

"Remember when Sylvia said that strong human emotions are what create ghosts and demons?" she says. "Well, what if it can work the other way around, too? What if all this anger and resentment caused the Housekeeper, and now it's spewing out anger and resentment, too? And Aaron is just ... *channelling* it?"

"Some people are just assholes," Roe interjects. "Aaron was clearly born an asshole."

"A *sensitive* asshole," Fiona corrects.

"Sure. But what if the Housekeeper just makes everything – I don't know – more heightened?"

"We have to break the Housekeeper," I say, nodding in agreement. "I'm not strong enough to do it by myself. We have to do it. Together."

"How?"

"I don't know. But I know we're close. I know it."

Roe gets a phone call and steps outside, and Fiona checks her Instagram Live from the gig.

"Oh, God, I have like fifteen DMs. Two of them are from journalists."

"What?"

"Yeah, looks like this thing is going viral already. Or, y'know – Irish viral."

"Are you going to talk to them?"

"No, Mum would go ballistic. I'll just say they can use the video."

Roe steps back into the chipper, and the few people who are having their food in look up, startled. They take in his dress, his black dockers, the blood. It's amazing how quickly I've gotten used to him in his new clothes.

"That was Miel. The band all got out OK."

"What else did they say?"

"That a few people were hauled off. A couple of the queens were taken into questioning – I think partly because they are all over eighteen."

"Oh, God. I hope they're all right."

"I'm sure they are," Fiona says. "I've never met a drag queen who doesn't know her rights."

"We get it Fiona, you know drag queens," I tease.

They turn the music off at Deasy's and we take that as our cue to leave. Fiona hugs us both and heads south back to her house, and we head north towards mine. I don't know what to say to Roe now that we're alone. Despite all our pacts and promises to one another as a group, I still have no idea where he and I stand.

The feeling is clearly mutual. Roe is suddenly nervous of me. This exotic creature who I just witnessed fighting a Christian fundamentalist while wearing a velvet dress is now too anxious to look me in the eye. As we walk, he daubs at the cut on his lip, touching it with a wet napkin stolen from the chipper. His face is starting to swell. I want to touch the puffy skin, where the crimson of his lipstick meets the flush of new wounds.

"You were incredible back there," I say, briefly squeezing his arm. "I'm sorry you needed to do it. I mean, I'm sorry those guys crashed the evening. But y'know, you should be proud. I could never be that brave."

He is silent.

"And the gig!" I burst out, desperate to get him talking. "The gig was so great! I had no idea how good you were."

"You don't have to do that," he says, finally.

"Do what?"

"Pretend like … like you're still…" He trails off.

"Like I'm still what?"

"Like you're still attracted to me, I suppose."

I look at him, clearly confused.

298

"I saw your face when I was onstage," he snaps. "I know how it is. When we're in our school uniforms and we're on the bus and I have a little bit of nail varnish on, it's all cute. I can pass for ... for *boy*, I guess. But when you saw me dressed like this, you looked so shocked, and I knew that any chance of us..."

I start to laugh. Roe looks hurt.

"You think I don't *like* this?" I ask, pulling playfully at one of the pearl drops hanging from his ears. It falls into my hand, falling off his lobe with a faint click. "Roe, I love this."

He furrows his brow. "I saw you from the stage. Your face. You looked horrified."

"I was surprised, sure," I said. "I mean, it took me a minute, but..." I fumble for the words. I want so badly not to ruin this.

"I thought you were magic tonight, Roe. Like no one I've ever seen before. Which makes sense, because you're like no one I've ever met before."

He is so close to me now. My fingers nudge against his in the dark. The balled-up napkin is still in his fist. Gently, I ease the wet pulpy material from his hand and into my own. I start gently daubing his lip. Roe. My poor Roe.

"And," I venture, "I thought you were ... extremely sexy."

"You did?" Roe asks, as if this is a trap.

"I did," I confirm.

We are silent then, standing in the dark. I step forward and trace the edge of his cheekbone with my finger. He doesn't back away, but he doesn't move towards me either. Taking this as encouragement, I lightly kiss the skin above his lower lip, making sure I don't graze his cut. Roe closes his eyes. I lean forward again and kiss the empty ear lobe where the clip-on pearl just sat.

"Maeve," he murmurs. "No."

No?

His eyes flick open. "I'm sorry."

"No?" I repeat uncertainly.

"I just think … we should focus on getting Lily back. For the time being."

I can't help it. I feel the embarrassment and rage bubble and spill inside of me. "Well, if that's how you feel, Roe, why did you just interrogate me on whether or not I find you attractive?"

"Um, well…"

"And why –" my voice is getting shrill now, I can hear it – "why were you singing songs to me onstage about how we're in hiding together? What is *that* about?"

"Look, I'm confused, too," he says in desperation. "But … that thing you showed me – the tarot reading. I can't forget it. The Secret Santa, the way you and Lily shouted at each other, you turning on the tap and drenching her stuff… It was dark, Maeve."

"I'm sorry, Roe. I don't know how I can…"

He puts his hand up. "I know. It's fine. Fi has already given me an earful. Obviously, you weren't to know what was going to happen. But every time I think about you like *that,* I just feel so angry and guilty."

He looks at me mournfully, as though I were a game that he's been dying to play. "And when we're … together, like this, I thought … I thought I could forget about it."

300

"But you can't," I say, tears rising to my eyes. "You can't forget about it."

"You're so important to me," he says. "More important than anyone. But I can't … I can't have this big romance with you and sleep at night. Knowing that my sister is still … wherever she is."

"OK," I say, my voice flat. "I get it."

And I do. I do get it. In the same way that I needed to draw a boundary with Fiona about witchcraft, Roe needs to draw one with me. I don't like it. But I understand it.

"Come on," I say. "Let's get you some clothes."

CHAPTER THIRTY-FOUR

BY MONDAY, THE GIG AT THE CYPRESS HAS BEEN ALL OVER the media. A few people from the gig have even been on RTÉ, explaining how the violence broke out.

"This was a targeted attack on the queer community," says one queen. *"And this was an attack on our visibility. Children of Brigid specifically went after young, vulnerable kids who had found a safe space where they could express their gender orientation. This needs to be taken seriously as a hate crime."*

"I see," the host replies. *"And, in the interest of balance, we're also going to be hearing from a rep for Children of Brigid, who are an after-school organization that primarily arrange charity events—"*

"The cabaret was a charity event," the queen interrupts. *"And there's also evidence that these people are funded by the same American organizations that supported the anti-choice movement during Repeal the Eighth. These people are literally enemies of progress."*

"We'll be back after a short break." The host smiles.

Fiona, Roe and I watch the whole programme in Fiona's house. Jos keeps running in and out of the room, waving a broken toy phone around and screeching his disapproval.

"Is that true?" I ask. "The bit about the funding?"

Fiona nods. "There was a piece on the *Irish Times*

website about it. There's this whole thing where this group of wealthy white Irish Americans want to keep Ireland all pure and holy. Their ideal version of a motherland, or some bullshit."

"OK, wow. At least the media are reporting it, though."

"It was a tiny feature, mind," Roe counters. "It only made the online version. The media emphasis is still very much 'these troublesome queers won't calm down'."

I make a silent, slightly shameful note to myself that both of my friends read the *Irish Times* and that I do not. I write READ THE PAPER into my phone as a reminder.

"Look, it's back on," Fiona says, pointing at the screen.

To the surprise of absolutely no one, Aaron is the rep speaking on behalf of Children of Brigid. When the show comes back after the ad break, he is sitting on the couch, wearing a suit.

"I hate him for being so TV-pretty," Fiona says, throwing a Dorito at the screen.

And he is. He's all golden sunshine and white teeth, charming the hosts and assuring everyone that it is a "true pleasure" to be on the show. The drag queen in her pink wig and sequinned dress shoots daggers.

"*I just think we need to be conscious,*" Aaron says, "*of how young children are being sexualized. Why should a twelve-year-old have to think about their gender? Or their sexuality? Is it naive to think that childhood should last a few more years?*"

"*Perhaps it is,*" the host says, with a faraway look.

"*When I was twelve, all I cared about was riding my bike and playing on my Nintendo 64.*"

"*I loved my Nintendo 64.*" The host smiles, and the two of

303

them are locked in a tight, nostalgic romance.

"This isn't about sex or Nintendos," the queen says, confused. *"This is about letting these kids be who they are without fear of violence."*

"That's exactly what I'm saying." Aaron smiles. *"Exactly. Let kids be kids. Without it being sexual."*

"I have to say, I agree," the host says. *"It's all gotten so complicated now."*

"I can't watch this," Roe says flatly. "Can we turn it off?"

"Sure," Fiona says, and switches it off. We're silent for a moment.

Fiona has dug out the spell book from my school bag.

"It's all a bit suburban, isn't it?" Fiona says, flicking through. "I mean, where's the intense stuff?"

"I don't know if we really want to go messing with black magic," I say. "According to every movie ever, it usually doesn't go well."

"How about we take your sailor knot spell, and just … you know, joosh it up a bit?" says Roe, his voice bending strangely on "joosh".

"Joosh it up?" I say flatly. "Please explain."

"So, more white satin, more of us tying the knots. We could take it all to the river," he says. "Look, here, it says that the new moon is the most powerful time for casting spells that are trying to *'banish unwanted entities'*. When is the new moon?"

"March sixth," says Fiona, searching on her phone. "Five days away."

Roe and I look at each other silently.

"What?" Fiona says.

"March sixth," I say. "Lily went missing on February sixth."

"I can't believe it's been a month," Roe says glumly. "I can't believe so much can have changed, but we still haven't found Lil."

Silence. How *can* so much have changed? In a month I have gained and lost a boyfriend, discovered witchcraft and been involved in a riot. A month for the country to have publicly embraced homophobia and survive a snowstorm.

Jos looks up from an imaginary call on his toy phone. "You all have to go home now," he says. "I'm for bed."

We laugh, wash our cups in the sink and go.

On Wednesday morning Fiona and I are sitting on the radiator in the bathroom when Miss Harris marches in.

"Maeve," she says. "My office. Now."

"What? Why?"

"Now, Maeve."

I shrug at Fi and follow Miss Harris through. What's this about? I haven't "acted out" once. I've been carrying on doing the bare minimum to get by, and my grades haven't become any better or any worse. Not that they could get much worse.

I'm sitting in front of her desk, and my face is blank. For once, I have no idea what I've done wrong, rather than just pretending I don't know what's wrong.

"Maeve, I think you know why you're here."

"I don't, Miss. Genuinely."

"I take stealing very seriously, Maeve. It can be grounds for suspension."

"I haven't stolen anything," I say, still confused.

"Please, Maeve, lies will only make things worse."

She breathes heavily and massages the bridge of her nose. "Maeve, when I took those tarot cards from you, it was for your own good."

Oh.

Oh, crap.

"Miss, I didn't take them," I respond, truthfully.

"Maeve, no one else knew that I had them. They were locked in my bottom desk drawer. I only opened it today to get a file from there, and you can imagine my surprise to find that they were gone."

I say nothing, and just bite down on the inside of my cheek.

"I didn't take them," I repeat. How can I explain to someone like Miss Harris that the cards just reappeared in my bedside locker weeks ago?

"Well, then, Maeve, who did?"

"I don't know," I say, the tears rising to my eyes. God, why do I cry so much lately? I never used to cry before.

"Look, I don't care about the cards, Maeve. I just need to know how you got the key."

"Miss, I promise, I didn't touch it." A tear rolls down my cheek. "Genuinely."

She looks at me, hard. "Well, Maeve, I don't know what to say. You're the only one who knew where they were."

I lower my head and imagine myself coming home with another note from school. And Mum and Dad are so convinced that things are looking up for me.

She sighs. "But I suppose I have no proof."

I look up.

"All right, Maeve. I'll forget about this whole thing, the tarot cards and all, if you stay after school and help with some odd jobs again. You did such a great job with the Chokey the last time. Deal?"

"Deal," I say eagerly. I'm terrified she's going to open up my bag and find not only the tarot cards, but my bags of crystals too.

"Right," she says brusquely. "Be here at 4 p.m."

I nod and get back to class like a cat with a hot arse.

CHAPTER THIRTY-FIVE

MISS HARRIS TOLD ME I HAD TO DO ODD JOBS.

She did *not* tell me I had to do them with Sister Assumpta.

"Miss, no," I protest. "Look, if I can just clear out one of the old classrooms myself, I can get it done way faster than if Sister is supervising me."

"I'm not leaving you unsupervised in this building again, Maeve. We all know what that leads to. Just do what she says."

"But…"

"Do as she says. And have some respect, for God's sake."

I wait in Sister Assumpta's lemon-walled office until the old nun eventually wanders in. She's over a foot shorter than me and is wearing her habit, something that comes and goes depending on her mood. She hasn't been a nun in years and years, but I think she got used to wearing it. Or maybe she just wants to remind people that she's still, in her heart, married to Jesus.

"Hello, Sister," I say in my most respectful voice.

She gazes at me suspiciously.

"I'm Maeve," I say. "I'm going to be helping you today."

"What did you do wrong?" she asks, her voice rasping.

"Nothing," I say staunchly. "I'm just helping."

"You did *something*," she corrects, looking me up and down. "You did something wrong."

And for some reason, I don't think she's talking about today.

"Here," she says, brandishing a handheld vacuum cleaner at me. "Run this over the *gluaisteán*."

I look at her in confusion, trying to remember my Irish.

"The *car*," she snaps in frustration.

I am marched out to Sister Assumpta's powder-blue VW Bug in the car park, the one that always has the passenger window cracked open. The back seat is filled with rotting leaves, the windows stained with bird poo. It's a mess.

"There are buckets in the basement," she says, and wanders back into her office.

Great. I've been tricked into valeting a nun's car.

I wonder, as I'm hoovering out the back seat, if Miss Harris was just sick of having this disgusting car sitting in the car park and bringing down the desperate upper-middle-class attitude of the school. Maybe she noticed that the tarot cards were missing weeks ago, but was just waiting until she needed a favour to cash this chip in.

After I'm done hoovering, I fill two buckets up with soapy water to wash the outside. As I'm trodding back out to the car park, Sister calls from her office. "Don't forget the boot!"

"OK!" I call back.

"I beg your pudding?"

"I mean, yes, Sister."

I pop the boot, preparing to give it a quick sweep. Inside, there are rows and rows of black velvet jewellery cases.

309

It's a jarringly familiar sight. These are the boxes filled with cheap costume jewellery that Lily and I were forced to carry into school during our first week at St Bernadette's. We laughed at the strangeness of it. Strange in a way that reminded us of ourselves. Why would a nun have this much flashy jewellery? And what was it doing in the school?

I lift a case gingerly, expecting it to be heavy. It isn't. Curious, I unfasten each silver clasp on the side of the box. Inside, there's no jewellery at all.

Just paper.

Newspaper, photographs, doodles, essays. Sister Assumpta wasn't using these boxes to take jewellery *into* the school. The soft, satin-lined boxes meant for keeping delicate necklaces and bracelets in perfect condition were being used to store delicate memories instead.

There are a dozen boxes, and I carry them all into the back seat of Sister Assumpta's car. I picture Jo's face looking disapproving, saying something about respecting the property of others. But I figure I'm cleaning this woman's car for free. I deserve a bit of a nose around.

Most of it is just glowing write-ups about the school and records of the achievements of former pupils. *"ST BERNADETTE'S TOPS LEAVING CERT RESULTS, BEATING BOYS' SCHOOL AGAIN"* is one, and *"CHILDREN'S AUTHOR SAYS BERNIE'S WAS HER INSPIRATION"* is another.

It's all very sweet, really. I've never really considered Sister Assumpta as a woman capable of sentiment. She's been so old the entire time I've been at St Bernadette's that I just know her for rasping complaints at everyone. I've always been vaguely aware that she's considered to be a trailblazer in the city, using her inheritance for good, trying to get Catholic girls an education, blah, blah blah. But there's something heartbreaking about all of those memories and achievements stored in little black boxes in the back of a car filled with leaves.

All of the boxes are labelled on their underside with white stickers and tiny, chicken-scratch handwriting. There is no order or sense to the labelling system. *"1970–79"* is one, but *"ATTIC EXTENSION"* is another. I look around for a *"SPRING 1990"* box but don't see anything.

What I do find, though, is a box called *"HARRIET"*.

Harriet's box starts in September 1985.

"ST BERNADETTE'S WELCOMES FIRST CROP OF SCHOLARSHIP STUDENTS…"

It's a small item on one of the local free papers, and includes a big toothy photo of four girls grinning in front of the school. Sister Assumpta is there, nun habit on, hands on her hips.

"PICTURED L to R: Harriet Evans, Sarah Byrne, Nan Hegarty, Catherine O'Faolainn."

There's a condescending article about how these girls are being given *"the chance of a lifetime"*. The journalist asks Sister Assumpta whether she's worried about bullying, given *"the obvious lifestyle differences between the scholarship girls and the fee-paying girls"*.

I cringe, sinking deeper into the back seat. I've never once thought about this issue before my fight with Roe. I never thought that Fiona might feel there was a difference between her and "fee-paying girls". Maybe that's why she didn't

311

properly mix with anyone else in school before we became friends. I had never suspected she might feel left out, too.

I gaze at Harriet Evans. She's a big, pretty girl, with nice brown eyes and thick, curly hair like a woman from an Edwardian painting. She has winged eyeliner and a big smile. She looks like fun.

I move to the next clipping, from 1986. It's a picture of some kind of demonstration, or protest. This one doesn't mention Harriet at all, and I have to squint to see her in the crowd photo. Harriet is mid-scream and carrying a *"VOTE YES"* sign over her head.

"CATHOLIC GIRLS' SCHOOL JOINS DIVORCE DEMO

"Today thousands joined a pro-divorce protest in Bishop Stanley Square, with schoolchildren leaving school in order to voice their wish for a 'yes' vote. Teenagers too young to vote in the June referendum are in favour of divorce being legal in Ireland, which many pundits are saying is due to the influence of American films and television. Most surprising of all was the addition of St Bernadette's Catholic Girls' School, a school known for its conservative policies. Sister Assumpta, the former nun and founder of the establishment, was quoted as saying that she had her 'head turned' on the subject of divorce after 'sound and passionate pleas from the students who this issue affected'. There have been concerns raised from parents of students, saying that the school's 'yes' stance is a sign of its wavering commitment to morality."

"Commitment to morality"? I let out a harsh, hollow laugh. Is that what St Bernadette's was known for? As long as I've been here, it's been known for slightly dippy posh girls with delusions of grandeur.

312

It's funny how often I forget that divorce in Ireland is relatively new. We didn't get it until 1995, only ten years before I was born. Mum had three kids by then.

I move on. Now I'm on 1989, and Harriet is my age. She has the glowing confidence of a senator, her wide shoulders are back, her chin jutting out.

"SCHOLARSHIP GIRL WOWS WASHINGTON IN INTERNATIONAL ESSAY CONTEST

"St Bernadette's scholarship winner Harriet Evans, sixteen, has another win under her belt – only this time, she's going stateside! The talented student has won the UN's 'Together for Change' contest with her essay on divorce in Ireland. 'I wanted to highlight the sheer number of people affected by this issue,' explains Evans. 'I did a huge amount of research on women living in refuges, almost all of whom believe that their lives would be different if the 1986 referendum hadn't failed.'

"Evans is set to present her essay at the 'Together for Change' youth conference in Washington, DC, at the end of the month. Are her parents proud? 'My mother and sister are over the moon,' Evans says."

At this point, I'm actively trying not to resent Harriet Evans. A politically active genius who wins essay competitions? Also, who says "all of whom", like she is a grammar book? Give me a break. Still, it's weird that with all the impressive students that St Bernadette's has had, Sister Assumpta has chosen to focus on Harriet Evans. I mean, there's been some actually famous pupils. We have an Olivier Award-winning actress, and she doesn't have her own velvet jewellery case. I wonder if Fiona will ever get her own one.

The last thing in Harriet's file is a school photo from

1990. It's her graduation photo, A4-sized. She's lost a lot of weight since the essay competition win, as well as her Greek statue shine. She looks huddled and inward, not like the screaming girl in the divorce referendum photo, or the proud one in the competition win.

I stare at the photo for a long time, feeling dissatisfied. I've just lived through this entire girl's school career … but why? What's the ending? Why is it here?

And then I turn the photo over, to find the Housekeeper staring right back at me.

CHAPTER THIRTY-SIX

HARRIET'S DRAWING STYLE IS NOTHING LIKE LILY'S, BUT IT'S undeniable that she has talent. This Housekeeper is in water-colours, dusky yellows, deep greys and murky greens. But it's definitely her. The dog at her feet looks bruised but protective, his head lolling against her thigh. The Housekeeper is as expressionless as she always is in my dreams, human-ish but not truly human. I remember again what Sylvia said about how people manifest spirits and ghosts when their emotions have nowhere else to go. That's what the Housekeeper in Harriet's drawing looks like. Like a pool where hate gathers, but not where it originates.

My hands shake as I begin to realize: *I have Harriet's Walkman. I have Harriet's tape.*

A stone hits the bottom of my stomach like it's being flung down a well.

I have Harriet's cards.

Harriet summoned the Housekeeper in 1990. Harriet's conjuring brought about the 1990 cold snap and the runaway cats; mine brought the snow, the rainbow trout, the surge in public aggression. Harriet was a sensitive, too. Maybe even a witch. Two sensitives, thirty years apart.

Harriet must have done something to end it. And Ireland got divorce eventually: not for five years, but it happened.

I can't wait for Lily for five years, though. I need her now. Or, at the very least, by the new moon on Saturday night.

I put the jewellery boxes full of memories back together, carefully slipping Harriet's one into my school bag.

I finish cleaning the car as quickly as I can, then bring the buckets back to the basement. *This changes everything,* I keep thinking, sometimes whispering it out loud. "This changes *everything.*"

Even as I'm making my way out of the basement, I have one hand on my phone, googling Harriet Evans. Maybe she's on Facebook. If she was seventeen in 1990, how old is she now? Forty-seven? *Definitely* on Facebook, then.

My blood is bubbling with excitement. Maybe she still lives in the area. Maybe I could walk right into her living room and ask her how to lift the curse. I start searching the Facebook app for Harriet Evans. My heart sinks. There are thousands. I'll have to enlist Roe and Fi to help me message them, but we could do it. Then, there's always the possibility that Harriet got married and changed her name. Suddenly, the job doesn't seem so simple.

With my head still in my phone, I end up colliding right into Sister Assumpta, leaving her office.

"Oh," I say. "Sorry, Sister. I didn't see you."

She blinks at me behind her owl glasses, her pupils huge, her skin puckered and thin, like wet tissue. Intellectually, I know that no one is born old. But looking at Sister Assumpta, I find it impossible to imagine her as anything other than the doddering old founder, keeping herself busy at the school because she has nothing else to do. I remember the newspaper clippings: I force myself to confront the fact that Sister isn't just a cardboard cut-out of a person, but a *real* person. A person who knows Harriet Evans.

"Sister," I say, as respectfully as I can. "Would you mind if I asked you something?"

"Skirt lengths must fall no higher than one inch above the *knee*," she says sharply. "And strictly no trousers. I don't care how many signed petitions you have."

We've had optional trousers as part of the school uniform for about four years, but I don't correct her. No one wears them, anyway.

"No Sister, I have no problem with the uniform. I was wondering if I could ask you about a former pupil."

Her face softens. "I always knew Anthea Jackson would win the Olivier for *Streetcar.*"

"No, Sister, not Anthea Jackson. I'm talking about someone else. A non-famous pupil. I was wondering if you remembered a Harriet Evans."

The old nun stares at me, her eyes glistening. It's hard to tell if this is emotion, because her eyes are always a little wet. We are, for a moment, in a silent stare off. The more I look into her big swimming pool eyes, the more I notice a glimmer of something. A pale white that could be a shadow, a ghost, or a cataract.

Slowly, she begins to speak.

"How do you know about Harry?"

There's no way of answering this truthfully without admitting that I was snooping in Sister Assumpta's car.

"I'm looking to do a project," I say quickly. "About the legalization of divorce. I thought she might be a good person to ask?"

317

"Harry wrote an essay," she says fondly. "They sent her to America to read it."

"Yes," I urge. "I've heard. Maybe you could dig out the essay. Or, maybe you could give me her phone number?"

Sister's face screws up in confusion. She looks like she has just eaten a bad grape.

"No," she says, then looks at me as if she's just seen me for the first time. "Harriet's not with us any more."

"No, I know that Sister, she graduated a long time ago, but…"

Sister Assumpta shakes her head again.

"She died."

Silence.

"What?"

"She died," Sister repeats, her voice cracking. "She died, and that gurrier father of hers, that *lout* – he didn't even come to our memorial service. The poor mother shows up with both her eyes black. The little sister, Fionnuala Evans bawling her eyes out. I ask you. I *ask* you."

She takes a long inward breath, and closes her eyes.

"Mind, he didn't last long either. He was dead a fortnight later. Fell in the river drunk, and good riddance."

I am certain that Sister Assumpta is about to start crying, and I wonder whether I should hug her.

She's fidgeting, her right hand fumbling in her skirt pocket. She starts pulling at something, her fingers rotating and moving within the material. Her eyes are still closed. She starts to murmur softly.

Oh my God, what is she doing?

I see a brown, beaded string hanging out of her clothes.

Rosary beads. *Oh, thank God for that.*

"Sister?"

But she doesn't hear me, she just moves her fingers up the beads. She is saying a decade of the rosary. I wonder if this is my cue to leave. But I know that this chance might not come again. How often do you get Sister Assumpta alone, with no one else around?

Instead, I wait.

She opens her eyes. I know I need to tread carefully. That Sister Assumpta is not the kind of person you can ask direct questions.

"Do you pray for her, Sister?"

She nods slowly. "I do," she says. "I try."

Then, a long sigh. "I don't know if it will do much good."

"Why is that?"

"People like Harry don't get to be with the Lord."

What?

"What do you mean by that, Sister?"

"They don't get to be with the Lord," she repeats. "So I pray. I pray for Harry. I pray that she gets to be with Him."

"Who?" I ask instinctively, and then almost slap myself. *Him.* God.

She turns away from me, either bored or upset by the conversation. She puts a hand on the handle of her office door.

"I think He will forgive her," she concludes. "The God I know forgives."

And she hobbles back into her lemon-walled office, and closes the door.

I wander to the bus and get the 5.15, hoping that Roe won't be on it. I need to process this on my own, without the pressure of performing the information for him. So much of being around him is such a fog now. I'm glad we're friends, but there's an awkwardness with just the two of us. We're a Scooby Doo gang now, and I'm Velma to Fiona's Daphne.

"They don't get to be with the Lord. So I pray. I pray for Harry. I pray that she gets to be with Him."

I hold on to my knees, a wave of nausea sweeping through me. Did Sister Assumpta mean witches? Sensitives?

Either?

Both?

Am I also barred from heaven for practising witchcraft, or is this just the suspicious ramblings of a deeply religious old woman?

I look through Harriet's news clippings again, feeling a little guilty for having stolen them. I'll just photocopy them on Dad's scanner, and bring them right back. I start writing down everything in my refill pad, trying to get everything straight in my head. I don't want to risk forgetting anything that Sister Assumpta has told me. I draw it out, like a flow chart quiz at the back of a magazine.

Harriet was a divorce activist, and the reason she was a divorce activist was because her father was beating her mother. She went to America, bought a (*"haunted???"* I write) tarot deck, and probably summoned the Housekeeper to bring justice to her dad. She threw the whole city out of whack, making the snow fall, making the cats run away. Then she died. And her father died quickly afterwards.

Life for a life: it's straightforward black magic, isn't it? Give big to get big.

But how does that apply to me and Lily? I never wanted Lily to die. I just wanted her to go away, and even then, it was just a split second of idiocy, not a lifelong grudge match. If Harriet had died, why hadn't I? Did that come later? If we got Lily back, would the Housekeeper take me instead?

No. No, that didn't make any sense. Especially as Harriet's father died *after* Harriet did.

I google, Harriet Evans death, 1990, and find one listing on RIP.ie. My dad checks it every day. He has that Irish obsession with death, seeing it as a weird Duck, Duck, Goose game that he has managed to stay duck on. "Nora!" he'll yell across the house, "you'll never guess who died!"

There's one entry for Harriet, but it doesn't give much detail. A seventeen-year-old who was tragically taken too soon, blah, blah, blah. The family requests that you do not send flowers. The service will be family only, but the school will be holding a memorial Mass.

That's it. That's all there is on Harriet's death. No cause, no explanation. Just that she was taken too soon.

My head is so buried in my phone that I don't look up until I'm almost at the front door and realize there's a Garda car in the driveway. My stomach turns to ice. What *now?*

I wait outside the house for a moment, trying to calm myself with long, concentrated breaths. They're probably just here to get a statement from me about the cabaret gig last week. Maybe Detective Griffin had second thoughts; maybe she wants to question me about Children of Brigid. Well, if that's the case, then fine. I will gladly tell her everything I know about Aaron. In fact, it's good that he's being investigated. Finally, an end to this nonsense.

But what if it's not about that? What if it's Lily? What if she's turned up dead, floating in the Beg with her lips blue? And in that case, why would the Gardaí be at my house, and not Roe's?

I stick my keys in the door and hear a sound from the living room. Animal, guttural, feral.

I cock my ear.

It's my mother.

It's my mother and she is crying.

I rush in and everyone's there: my mum, my dad, Joanne and two police officers. And one other person, a person it takes me a second to recognize at first, partly because I don't know her very well, and partly because she is covered in blood. Sarra.

Jo, I realize, is purple in one eye, her irises dyed cranberry. Someone has hit her. Someone has hit them both.

"Maeve –" my dad stands up – "Maeve, I think you should go to your room."

"What happened?" I ask.

"Darling, I think it's best if you…"

"What HAPPENED?" I shout. "Jo, what happened to you?"

Jo looks at me mutely, utter despair in her eyes.

"Maeve," Detective Griffin says, as softly as she can manage, "I'm so sorry that we keep … meeting like this."

"Tell me what happened," I say, panic rising in my voice.

Griffin looks at my parents. My mother is still crying, my father looks completely shell-shocked. He gives her

322

a tiny nod of confirmation. A nod of "go on, you might as well tell her".

"Your sister and Miss Malik were attacked," she says simply. "We are certain that it was ... an act of intolerance."

"Where?"

"At college," Jo suddenly blurts. "Literally at college. We were just sitting in the Student Union. Having a fecking hot chocolate. A *hot chocolate*," Jo spits the words out, then laughs to herself. "I wish it was something stronger. If I'm going to get attacked for being gay, I might as well be drinking whisky. They'd love that, wouldn't they?"

"They," I say. "Who are *they*? The Children of Brigid? The same people who crashed the gig?"

"They were pushing pamphlets in our faces. About how we were undermining the natural order, blah, blah, blah. All this 'hey, can we engage you in a thoughtful conversation about how you're scum?' I told them to piss off."

"And I told them," says Sarra, her voice croaky, "that they could shove their propaganda up their holes."

"Then one of them pounced on Sarra. Saying that as a 'woman of colour' she should be 'extra-conscious' of what kind of 'example' she was setting for the younger girls in her 'community'. Oh, they were very pleasant about it."

"I said, what *community*?" Sarra gives a dry laugh. "The basketball team?"

"Then one of the men just swung for her."

"What?" I splutter. "They went from zero to punch-up in sixty seconds?"

"To be fair, I don't think it was part of their plan," Sarra says grimly. "Maybe a brown girl answering back was just

323

a little too far for this guy. Jo hit back, and after that it was a free-for-all. All bets were off."

I don't know what to do, where to look, where to put my hands. I can't stop staring at Sarra. For so long, I've had her written off as the girl who hurt Jo by cheating on her. The girl who was eventually going to steal my sister away from me. Like Sister Assumpta, I've never really thought about Sarra as a person in her own right. With her own battles.

Griffin asks me to step outside so she can finish taking their statements. I go up to my room and bury my face in Tutu's blond fur.

For as long as I can remember, Jo has been gay. I don't remember her coming out. I don't remember any discussion about it. When she was eighteen and I was eleven, she came home holding hands with a girl called Kris and that was it. Mum and Dad looked at each other and raised their eyebrows, and Abbie gave some condescending declaration about how proud she was of Jo. But that was it. Kris had dinner with us and she hung around for a few months, and then she was gone, and then a few years later Sarra started showing up. There might have been other relationships, too, but I don't know. Jo's not the sort to just open up about that kind of thing.

But in all that time, I never once remember Jo coming home bleeding, or crying, or upset about any hate she received. Once in a blue moon someone would yell something on the street, particularly when she was campaigning for the equal marriage stuff, but she brushed it off. It didn't mean anything to her. But there was never anything like this.

I hold Tutu close.

I did this. I was the one who threw the energy of the city out of whack. I pulled the Jenga brick out of the tower and the whole thing started to wobble. The snow, the river, the hate, the blood. Aaron, and his strange ability to both sense and exploit the weakness in Kilbeg. It's all pouring out of the hole the Housekeeper ripped open in the world, and I am the one who gave her the knife. I squeeze my eyes shut and see my sister's bleeding eye, the lens of crimson flowering out of her irises. Sister Assumpta's glowing, moon-like cataract. Harriet Evans and her winged eyeliner.

I have to fix it.

I have to fix it.

I have to fix it.

CHAPTER THIRTY-SEVEN

WE HAVE A HALF-DAY ON THURSDAY AND FIONA SENDS ME with a shopping list to Divination. She's still in play rehearsals, so her free time is at a premium right now. It's hard not to accuse Fiona of treating this spell as another new hobby she has to master, yet another string on her ever-growing bow, but I'm trying not to be irritated by it.

"Maeve Chambers," the shopkeeper announces as I walk through the door. It's the only place in the world where someone is guaranteed to call me by my full name. Today there's a dreaminess to the way she says it, like she's not completely focused. She's moving some dried herbs between her fingertips, lavender flowers shredding in her palm.

"Hey," I say, unfurling my list. I don't want or need to fall into another psychic conversation with her. I just need to get some candles and other supplies. I pluck what I need from the various sections. I'm so accustomed to this shop now that I'm half convinced that I could run it for an afternoon, if she ever wanted me to.

The silence between us is unsettling. I'm used to her chatter, her advice, her weird tidbits about my menstrual cycle. Instead, she has drifted to the window and is staring listlessly at the passers-by. Her blonde hair is messy, falling out of its ponytail. She looks exhausted.

"So, I was thinking about what you said about sensitives," I say warily. "You know those Children of Brigid people? I think the reason they're so powerful right now is because Aaron – he's, like, their leader, I guess – is one. A bad sensitive."

She says nothing. In fact, she doesn't even register that anyone has spoken.

"They got to my sister," I say, trying to provoke some kind of reaction out of her. "My sister and her girlfriend."

The word "sister" seems to shake her out of her stupor.

"You have to look after your sister," she says, her voice croaky and tired.

"I know."

"Don't let her slip away, Maeve. Don't ever let your sister slip away."

"I ... won't?"

This is extremely strange now. I'm used to weird declarations from the shopkeeper, but usually there's a thread I can catch and follow to the source. She gazes off again, out of the window.

"Do you know what they used to sell in this shop, before I took over?"

"No."

"Statues of the Virgin Mary. And the Infant Jesus of Prague."

"Is that the one holding the little egg thing?"

She doesn't answer me. Sometimes it's easy to forget that, for everyone over thirty at least, religion has played a huge part in their lives. Mum has stories about nuns who used to terrorize her, and Abbie had a famous phase where she was obsessed with becoming a child saint. But no one my own age thinks or talks about the Church at all, even though we're constantly preparing at school for some Mass or another. But even that is just singing and Hail Marys. Occasionally cracking out the Beatitudes for a special occasion.

"I didn't think I should take over the lease. Not after everything that happened."

Her eyes go back to the window. I feel I should leave, but I won't have a chance to come again before the ritual. And we need this stuff, if we are to have any hope of this spell working. I quietly locate the items on my list. Hemlock and mandrake, Saturday's plants. Black candles for the new moon. I get stuck when it comes to the tanzanite crystals, for communication with the spirit world. There's a huge display of them by the door, but not all of them are very clearly marked. I keep googling tanzanite and holding the images up to various rocks, but I'm having trouble finding anything that looks like the blue stone on my screen. Eventually, I find a little pot filled with rough, fingernail-sized stones that look like they *might* be what I'm looking for. I take photos and send them to Fiona for confirmation.

"Do you work here?"

I jump. A delivery guy in a red DPD coat is standing patiently with a cardboard box.

"This is a tracked delivery. From Italy. I need you to sign for it."

I look around, and see that the shopkeeper is gone. She must have slipped out while I was comparing and contrasting crystals. My notepad still in my hands, I realize that the delivery guy must think I'm taking inventory. I feel a bit

328

proud, thinking I look old enough and cool enough to work in a shop like this. Thank God I changed out of my uniform at school.

I peer at the box. Judging by the packaging, it's a shipment of tarot. Italy has the best tarot in Europe. Fiona and I have already started talking about convincing our parents to let us do an exchange there. Even though, as I keep grumbling, it would mean having to speak Italian.

The man is still looking at me, waiting for an answer.

"Um…" I cast a glance around again. "Sure, I can sign for it."

Now he's sceptical. "You *do* work here, right?"

"Yes. This is my mum's shop." Wow, what a surprisingly easy lie. "I help her out."

He shrugs and hands the electronic pad over. I scrawl something vague and he doesn't even look at it. The machine spits out a little receipt and he hands it to me along with the package.

"All right, have a good day, Miss Evans."

I stiffen. *Miss Evans?*

Somehow I manage to put the box on the counter, without letting it fall to the floor, and just nod at the DPD guy until he leaves the shop.

I read the label on the package.

Fionnuala Evans, Divination, 56 Peter's Street, Kilbeg.

Evans. The shopkeeper's last name is Evans. Harriet's sister? No, that can't be. She's told me her sister's name before. It was something witchy. What was it? Willow?

Fionnuala Evans. *Evans.*

Maybe not a sister. A cousin? A coincidence?

329

What was her sister's damn name? She mentioned it again when we had that conversation about sensitives. Yes. I was standing right here, beside the crystals. What was it? And where *is* she?

My hands start to sweat, soaking the receipt in my hands. Finally, I put the box on the counter and lay the delivery receipt on top of it. That's when everything clicks.

F. EVANS. F. EVANS.

I line it up in my head like an algebra equation.

H. EVANS.

Heaven. The shopkeeper called her sister Heaven.

All this time, I've assumed that the shopkeeper was keeping her own name a secret because of some kind of business-like privacy. Her way of saying: *Hey, I like you, kid, but don't get too close.* I remember the last thing she said to me when we were stuck in that psychic vision together, right after she tried to cast me out of her shop.

Don't bite off more than you can chew.

Clearly, Heaven, or Harriet, had done this and lost her life in the process.

"Maeve."

She's back. The library of freshly cut herbs, I realize, is also a hidden door. Fionnuala is standing next to it as it hangs ajar, and a dark stairwell is just about visible behind it. She must live upstairs. She might even own the whole building.

"I signed for your package," I say, my voice quavering. "Fionnuala."

She sits down at the stool perched behind the till and looks bleakly at the box.

330

"Thank you," she says limply. She looks like she hasn't slept in days. I'm beginning to suspect she went upstairs for a quick power nap, or possibly to take some kind of medication.

"Why…?" I don't know where to begin. Why anything, at this point? I stop. Recalibrate.

"You knew I summoned the Housekeeper. From the day we came in."

"Asking about that silly school project. Yes."

There's so much pain, so much exhaustion in her voice. I can't even summon the good sense to be angry with her.

"What's *wrong* with you?" I finally ask in frustration.

She laughs a little then. Not a cruel laugh, by any means. More the laugh a heart surgeon might give if you asked her what, exactly, she got up to all day.

"I've got nothing left, Maeve. I'm out."

"Out of *what*?"

"Of everything. Of magic. Of power. Of energy. Of my mind. I've spent the last three weeks using everything I have to protect you, and I've got nothing left. As I said before …"

She drifts a little, as if she's about to fall asleep right there on the stool.

"… I'm just a kitchen witch. Not a sensitive. Not a sorceress. Just a garden-variety middle-aged Wiccan with a little stolen magic trying to help a girl who can't help herself."

"What do you mean? What … what have you been *doing*?"

"Haven't you noticed that the nightmares have begged off? That you seem to be able to slip out of dangerous situations a little too easily? Jaysus, the sweet arrogance of

331

youth. What I wouldn't do to get it back."

I think for a moment. The nightmares ... they *have* stopped. There was the one I shared with Roe, where we both saw the shoe floating down the Beg, but I hadn't had any nightmares about the Housekeeper by myself in ages. Even the shoe dream wasn't a nightmare as such. It was a warning, a clue, a poster on the great cosmic bulletin board. I had assumed that I had just gotten stronger by myself, but no, Fionnuala has been shielding me.

"You've been casting protection spells on me?"

She nods. "Every night. I only know when I see you whether they've worked or not."

I think for a moment, carefully sifting through the last few weeks. "There was a riot at the Cypress. People were hurt. Badly hurt. But I walked out of there without even giving the police a statement."

A brief smile, a slight roll of her eyes. "Well, isn't that nice?"

"Why? Why were you doing this? You barely even know me."

"Because, Maeve, I'm old enough to know when history is repeating itself. Every day of my life I have to live with what happened to Heaven. Do you know what that's like? To have failed your own sister, and then to see another sensitive come waltzing in thirty years later? It rattles you, pet. It rattles you."

"And ... you knew about the Housekeeper? Straight away?"

"I had my suspicions. Especially when the weather started to turn, and all this craziness with those fundamentalists started kicking off. You're right, by the way. That boy, that blond boy…"

"Aaron."

"Aaron. *Aryan*. Jaysus. It's like his parents knew he was going to be Hitler Youth."

I laugh a little, despite everything. She smiles back, pleased to have found the energy to make a small joke.

"He smelled the weakness. The *imbalance*. Like a shark smells blood in the water. Children of Brigid was a tiny, hateful little speck, based way up the country. They had about five followers. And suddenly, this boy and his American money shows up here, just as the weather turns. I knew something was happening. And I didn't want another teenage girl to be at the centre of it."

"When I first met Aaron," I say, puzzling out the memory, "he would barely interact with me. Even when I was at his gross meeting, playing his emotional blackmail games … it was like I smelled of bad milk."

Roe. Roe was the one he had wanted. And I thought that my strength and self-confidence were the reasons he wouldn't come close. God, she's right. I really *am* that arrogant.

"He could smell the protection spell. Or sense it, anyway. If he knows what he is, you can bet your life he knows what *you* are. He's probably been waiting for weeks for whatever is protecting you to run out of juice."

He remembered me. Straight away, he knew me as the girl in the wedding dress, even though I had been at the back of the shop the whole time. Even though Fiona was the beauty, the fire, the one with her bare leg out, the one everyone was looking at as she shouted about atheism.

A terrifying thought crawls into my head on its belly. My conversation with him at Bridey's. My boyfriend's gig. My sister at college. Aaron has been circling me. He can't get *to* me, so he's going for the people who are closest. Slowly weakening my barriers until I give up or give in.

"Why didn't you talk to me?"

"Because I knew the more I told you, the more you knew, the more you'd get involved. So I just thought that maybe – oh, I don't know – that if I kept a bubble around you, the phase would pass without you doing anything stupid. The balance would correct itself. It often does."

"It hasn't, though."

"No," she says, massaging her closed eyelids with the tips of her fingers. "And I have nothing left to give you."

"What does *that* mean?"

"Magic isn't endless. It's like a crop. It has to have time to renew. And I've spent every last ounce on you, Maeve Chambers. So you don't end up like Heaven."

"Why do you call her—?"

"It's time for you to leave, Maeve."

"What?" I almost screech. "You can't tell me all that and then expect me to go home."

"Nevertheless, I am. Leave now. I don't want to see you in here for at least a week. And for the love of God, don't do anything before then. I don't have what it takes to protect you."

"OK," I say slowly. "I'll just buy these then." I put the candles, the crystals and the herbs on the counter.

Fionnuala grits her teeth fiercely. "Maeve," she says, her

voice low and authoritative. "If you think I am selling you anything for a ritual, you obviously think I'm a much stupider woman than I am."

"But Fionnuala…"

"Sweetheart. I'm too weak to stop you. I'm only just about strong enough to ask, so I'm asking you now: please, please do not try to end this in a ritual. Don't overestimate your own power."

"You don't understand. The Housekeeper, she has my…"

Fionnuala puts up one finger to silence me. There must be a drop of magic still left in her, because somehow, it does. My mouth clamps shut.

"I cannot stop a ritual I do not approve of. But I *can* refuse to profit off it. I will not line my pockets with your mistakes, Maeve. Now go."

And, empty-handed, I leave.

The nightmares start again the same night.

CHAPTER THIRTY-EIGHT

TEXT MESSAGE FROM FIONA.

SPELL SUMMONING CHECKLIST:

SATIN: I got us a TON from the dress material shop. Also, I've been practising knots!

HERBS: Roe, lol that your mum actually does have a herb garden. Protestants!!! Lots of rosemary y/n?

CHANTS: MAEVE, I'm depending on you to give us some real Lizzo level chants. Rhythm! Energy! SASS!

Fiona went back to Divination herself on Friday afternoon and tried to buy the supplies. Fionnuala was not convinced. Apparently, she was basically monosyllabic with Fiona, despite Fiona's pretence that this was once again for a school project.

Fiona, Roe and I have gone over Fionnuala's warning again and again. Picking at it from all sides, biting it like a prospector checks for gold.

"Surely," Fiona began, full of passion, "if her protection spells aren't working any more, then that's even *more* incentive for us to finish the Housekeeper? Right? Clearly, Aaron is working his way to you, Maeve. He knows you're a special."

"A sensitive."

"Whatever. Same thing."

Roe was quiet for a long time after I told him. Measured and logical, reluctant of Fiona's over-confident bravado.

"Heaven died," he says, simply. "We have to remember that, Fi. Heaven died."

"Heaven died. Yes," I reply, trying to mimic his mature delivery. "But Heaven was probably on her own, for one. And for two, Heaven actually *wanted* her father to die. He was beating the family. She wanted her mum to get a divorce, but the referendum didn't pass, so she summoned the Housekeeper."

"Did Fionnuala tell you that?"

"No." To my own shame, I had barely even asked about Heaven/Harriet. I had squandered my remaining time in Divination asking only about myself. By the time I got around to asking about Heaven I was already being kicked out. "But it's obvious. Sister A basically told me herself."

"And," Roe adds, "her dad died. He didn't go missing. He didn't disappear into the Beg river. It was life for a life. It's not ... nice, but it's black magic. She knew what she was doing. As opposed to you, who accidentally summoned the Housekeeper, and now Lily is accidentally stuck in a sort of ... in-between. She's not dead. So there's no swap to be made. We're just balancing the books."

The logic of this feels firm to me. It feels firm to Fiona, too. So we decide to go ahead with the ritual, crystals or no.

I think we need 3 chants: 1 for cutting the satin into ropes (I'll bring a kitchen knife), 1 for throwing the knot and 1 for pulling it in. That OK, Maeve???

I text back, **K**.

Also – can we all wear blue or black?? Saturn's colours.

And another.

I can't believe it's tomorrow?!

I put my phone on airplane mode. Sure, I'll wear blue. Or black. I'll wear whatever.

I haven't mentioned the nightmares to Fiona and Roe. It feels like I've given them enough to worry about, and this whole "sensitive" thing is already more hassle than it's worth. I've spent the last sixteen years of my life trying very hard *not* to be the kind of girl who needs a lot of looking after. The realization that I've been protected by a near-stranger for almost a month is like boasting about being really good at a video game then finding out everyone's been letting you play on easy mode.

So, no. I don't mention the nightmares. It's only the same old crap anyway. The Housekeeper. The river. The sense of Lily, near by and watching, waiting and snarling. On Saturday morning I wake up before 5 a.m., feeling heavy, hot and sick. It's still dark outside. I take my pillow into the bathtub, feeling the cool porcelain against my skin. Eventually I drift off again, drooling onto the soft cotton case.

I'm alone at the river again. It's a bright, early morning and Tutu is with me. I search around for the Housekeeper. At this stage, I'm used to seeing her statuesque, quasi-human form. It's not a comfort, but it is a guarantee. This time, I don't see her.

At least not right away.

Across the river, sitting on an upturned milk crate, is Aaron.

What is *he* doing here? Is Aaron really visiting my dreams

now that the protection spells have worn off, or is this just my subconscious, working out its growing fear of him?

There must be a beam of light streaming through the bathroom window and dancing off my closed eyelids because a rainbow is darting around on the ground in front of me. It moves as I do, bouncing and refracting off the water.

Aaron is wearing a white T-shirt and jeans, smiling easily as the morning sun plays on his tanned face. There is something in his hands. I squint. The sun is almost blinding me, and he's too far across the river to see very well. But he is definitely stroking *something* in his lap. Something dark and glossy, like a cat. A cat but bigger than a cat.

"Are you really here?" I ask. And despite the fact I haven't raised my voice, he can hear me. He looks up. "Is it really morning?"

He doesn't say anything. He just nods, and keeps stroking whatever is in his lap. Tutu starts to bark. Fiercely at first, but the noise quickly gives way to an anxious whine.

A flash of white teeth from across the river. Aaron is smiling at me.

My eyes finally adjust to the light. I can see Aaron a little better now, and more importantly I can see what he's holding.

Lying in Aaron's lap is the head of the Housekeeper.

For a sickening moment, I think it's her disembodied head, hacked clean off her body. But no: perhaps even more terrifyingly, the Housekeeper is merely resting on Aaron's lap while he slowly separates her long black hair with his fingers. Each satin band slips through his fingers like water, and there seems to be true affection in the gesture. Almost

339

tenderness. He smiles again. Another flash of white across the river.

"What are you doing? Why are you here?"

Ssssh. She's sleeping.

"What do you want from me, Aaron?"

Ssssh.

I turn around, refusing to face him. *Wake up, Maeve. Wake the hell up.*

If I were you, I wouldn't be in such a hurry to wake up. It's hard out there, y'know. It's hard for people like us.

"What are you talking about?"

He goes back to stroking her hair.

Isn't it sweet, Maeve? You are more afraid of her than anything, and she's just a pet to me.

I shut my eyes. I don't want to look at him any more.

I could smell you, you know. The first time. I could smell you from the elevator.

"Shut up."

It's going to be so interesting, he murmurs. *If you live.*

The prism of rainbow light moves and my eyes flutter open. The room is full of blinding early morning sun, bouncing off the white tiles. My entire body is shaking, my teeth crackling together like someone who is cold in a cartoon. His final words are still rattling around my head like loose change.

It's going to be so interesting. If you live.

As dispassionately as I can, I try to imagine myself dead. Another Harriet Evans, or Heaven, or Harry, or whatever she was called. I imagine being outlived by Sister Assumpta, the oldest woman in the world, and her praying rosaries for

340

me to some other idiot girl that was conned into cleaning her car. Maeve doesn't get to be with Him, so I still pray for her, my God is a forgiving God, wah, wah, wah.

My teeth start to snag on my nails. As the sweat from my dream settles and dries on my body, I feel sticky, strange.

Sister A said that Harriet Evans didn't get to be with God. Heaven didn't get to go to heaven, as it were. I remember Fionnuala, her eyes glazed as she talked about the Virgin Mary, the Infant Jesus of Prague. How she didn't want to take over the lease on the shop because it had once been used for religious gifts and memorabilia.

Names are powerful. It was the first thing she told me. Names are powerful.

Something dirty and strange starts to dredge up from my memory, like a fishing rod hauling up an old boot. Something hidden under years and years of Catholic schooling. Something I have taken for granted, never questioned nor thought about.

People who commit suicide don't get to go to heaven.

Or, not according to the Church they don't. Maybe they've changed that lately. The Pope likes to change things, rebrand Catholicism to make it seem fresh and interesting. But that was the way for a long time, wasn't it? Suicide was a sin, in God's eyes. Fionnuala called her sister Heaven as a prayer. Heaven. Heaven. Heaven.

Heaven wasn't killed *by* the ritual. She had killed herself during it.

It's going to be so interesting. If you live.

If. If. *If.*

I shred my nails down to the quick, my fingertips sore

and raw. What was I going to have to do to get Lily back? What would I have to willingly sacrifice?

I clutch my tarot cards to me, hoping that they will provide the answer.

"Will the ritual bring back Lily?" I ask aloud, while sifting their familiar weight between my hands.

I draw. The Seven of Cups. It's a weird card, a man looking at a bunch of cups, each filled with a different symbol. Jewels in one, a snake in another, a dagger in another. Gifts and curses. The man is just standing in front of them, a rabbit in the headlights of divine choice.

This card has come up a few times in readings before, and it's usually about not being able to make a choice. I try to apply that to the situation, but it doesn't quite add up. Surely, by doing the ritual at all, we're making a definite choice. We're acting; we're not staring at a bunch of cups and waiting for the world to pass us by.

I look again, and try to think of the card differently. The dagger hovering above the cup draws me in, and I press my thumb over the blade.

Maybe it's not about choices. Maybe it's about wishful thinking, and pretending there are multiple options when really, there's only one.

Life for a life. Give big to get big. It's how black magic works, isn't it?

I bite down on my lower lip and draw again. As soon as I see the card, I drop it on the floor, then immediately cover it with my foot.

"No," I whisper, looking at my toenails. "No."

342

I knock on Jo's bedroom door. It's early on Saturday morning but she's awake and propped up on two pillows, reading a book. She's not gone to college all week on Griffin's advice. "But I feel fine," Jo said. "It's not that," Griffin responded gruffly. "I mean ... it would just be safer."

"Hey," I say, hovering by the door.

"Hey back," she says, looking up. "You're up early. What are you doing?"

"I just ... wanted to check in on you."

"Are you cold?"

"Yes."

"Do you want to hop in?"

I don't say anything, just make my way across the room and climb into her double bed. The bed is so cosy, the sheets perfectly white and clean. Jo never eats in bed, like I do. I'm always in a losing war with toast crumbs.

"I've no pillow," I grumble.

"C'mon, share mine."

She reaches over for me and tucks me under her arm. I rest my head on her chest, listening to the *thump-thump-thump* of her heart.

"We haven't done this since you were small," she says. "You used to beg to sleep in bed with me."

"You'd never let me either. Cow."

"Can you blame me? You had the sharpest toenails. And cabbage farts."

"I did *not*."

What would usually be a cat fight settles into a sleepy, dozy argument, both of us staring at the ceiling.

"Are you scared?" I whisper.

She's quiet for a moment. "A little," she answers.

"That you're going to get attacked again?"

"Yes. And that Sarra is going to get it worse. And that —" her voice strains a little — "and that things are just going to get worse for everyone."

"What do you mean?"

"I think a lot of us have just … assumed that things were getting so much better. So progressive, y'know? We're in this liberal Ireland and all that. I think we all got a bit too proud of ourselves too soon."

She gulps and rubs at the tender skin underneath her black eye.

"I think this is the backlash."

I imagine my sister being screamed at, being followed, being attacked. And then Aaron on TV, distracting the host and talking about how there's two sides to every story. I hold her tight, turning my face into her shoulder, trying not to think of the Seven of Cups or the card that I trapped with my foot. The Death card is still in my room, still lying face up on the floorboards.

I know enough about the Death card to know that it doesn't mean death.

Or. Not usually.

"Hey, why are you snuffling?"

"I'm scared," I say. And then: "I'm scared for you."

"Ah, sure look it. There's no point in being scared. I'm lucky. I've got a great family and a great girlfriend and I'm smart and I'm hot. I'll be fine," she chuckles.

"But not everyone will be."

"No," she reasons. "Not everyone else will be."

344

"I love you."

She stops and looks at me, surprised.

"Are you OK, Maeve?"

I give an unconvincing nod.

"I love you too. But don't be worrying yourself about this. It has nothing to do with you. Just try your best to be there for people more vulnerable than you. Keep your eyes and ears open. Speak up if you see something messed up. OK?"

I hold her close and try to find a way to tell her that it has at least a little to do with me.

The day crawls on, sullen and heavy. The cold snap has well and truly passed, but there's now a waspy humidity in the air, close and sticky. The three of us arrange to meet at the river at midnight. Lucky for me, Mum and Dad are going to a dinner party, and Jo is at Sarra's house. The attack seems to have brought them even closer together. Sarra came over last night and they spent all evening in the living room, curled up around each other like foxes. I hope they move in together. Jo will like that.

I hug both of my parents when they leave, holding them tight. I breathe in the smell of my mother's hair. Her perfume smells like liquid gold.

"Any plans for the night, Mae?"

"I'm going to watch a film at Fiona's house," I answer mechanically, wondering if this is the last lie I will ever tell her.

"Oh? Do you need money for a cab home? I'd offer to spin you home but we won't be done till way late."

"No, I won't be coming home," I say. Already wondering, *Why did I say it like that.* "I mean, I'm going to sleep at Fiona's."

It's going to be so interesting. If you live.

"All right." Mum is wrestling to put her phone in her tiny clutch bag.

"Why don't you just leave your phone at home?" I say, encouragingly. "You don't want to be disturbed anyway, do you?"

I won't have to really do it, will I? Not when Lily isn't even dead. The Housekeeper had made that clear. She's just trapped. I won't have to do it. And anyway, I couldn't do it.

How would I even do it?

"I suppose you're right." She shrugs, and leaves the phone on the sideboard.

"Are you all right, Mae?" Dad asks. "You seem a bit ... off."

"I'm fine."

They leave, and I wander around the house aimlessly. It's only 7 p.m. My fingers trace the grooves in the wallpaper, my feet trace the skirting boards. Roe was right. I do have a beautiful home. It's funny that I never appreciated it before now. It's strange how I never understood the immense privilege, the wealth, the love that I've had the luxury of growing up with. Instead I was too busy obsessing over the friends and the grades that I didn't have. It all seems so childish now. I go in and out of my siblings' bedrooms, picking up things and putting them down again. Abbie's shelf of Jane Austen books. Pat's records. Cillian's old Subbuteo football figures, Blu-Tacked to his desk and gathering dust. I lie on Jo's bed for a while, just staring at the ceiling.

When was the last time everyone was home together? Cillian was at his girlfriend's house last Christmas, and Abbie was at a destination wedding in Tahiti. We said we would all Skype them but we never did, and instead me, Jo and Pat watched *Labyrinth* until 2 a.m. and ate a tin of Roses. Pat let me have a rum and Coke.

I remember, with a sting of shame, being glad that Cill and Abbie weren't home. Pat and Jo were my favourite siblings anyway. It was better when I had them all to myself. When the four of them were together, they all talked about work stuff and people I don't know. They treated me like a baby, and made condescending declarations about how I was "turning out". Now, I want to slap myself for having favourite siblings. For not being happy in our unit of five.

If the cards are right, we'll never be five again.

I wonder, briefly, if it would be good to leave a note. To stop Mum from blaming herself, or Dad from having a nervous breakdown. But what could the note possibly say?

Had to break a curse, brb.

I pad around the kitchen, opening drawers and closing them again. I take the sharpest knives out of the wooden block next to the stove, testing each one against my fingers. One, a long Japanese knife my dad got off the boys for his birthday, pricks my finger the moment it touches the skin. A bubble of blood appears at the tip. I suck on it. It doesn't hurt too much.

I won't have to do it. Will I? Should I?

My phone buzzes. Roe.

Hey. You home?

Yep.

347

Can I come over to yours before the spell tonight?

Sure.

Great, thanks. x

He arrives a couple of hours later in his red bomber jacket, carrying a tote bag.

"Hey," he says, smiling nervously. "Thanks for letting me come over."

I shrug. "That's OK."

He looks at me and cocks his head like a curious puppy. "Are you all right, Maeve?"

"Yeah," I say, softly. "I'm just, uh – I'm on my period."

His eyebrows shoot up to his hairline in surprise.

"Oh, you're all pro-woman and genderqueer until I start talking about my period," I say, sarky.

"No, it's not that," he says, wounded. "I'm just surprised you would bring it up."

I shrug again and make my way into the kitchen.

"Do you want a tea, or something?"

"Sure."

I flick the kettle on, and my eyes go to his tote bag on the floor. It's full of clothes.

"What are those for?"

"Oh," he says, bashfully. "I was just hoping I could change my clothes here. I wanted to … never mind."

"What? Tell me."

"I don't want to. You're in a mood with me."

"I am not."

"You are. I can tell."

And he looks so confused that my heart melts. I want to wrap my arms around him, to kiss him long and slow.

348

I want to sit him down on my couch, my legs on either side of his waist. I want to feel his hands under my clothes.

None of this is his fault. He wanted to be with me, before he found out what kind of person I am. Maybe part of him still does want to be with me.

"I'm sorry," I say, trying to hold back the emotion in my voice. "It's not about you. Really. Please tell me."

I pour the hot water and start working the bag against the bottom of each mug.

"OK," he says. "I just thought … this spell will work better the more powerful we feel, right? And I want to feel as powerful as I can. Like I do onstage."

"Are you going to do the spell dressed in drag?"

"No," he responds, a smile spreading on his lips. He holds the gown against himself. "I'm going to do it dressed like myself."

"Roe … that is *so* fecking cool."

"Do you think?" He's excited now.

"I do!" I start laughing and digging through his tote bag. I pluck out a silk navy camisole and a long pearl necklace.

"They're only glass," he says, as if he's apologizing.

"This is going to be awesome," I say, and for a minute I forget about Aaron and Heaven and all the other reasons I'm terrified.

"Do you have make-up? I don't have much."

"Not a lot. But my mum does. Expensive stuff."

We take our mugs upstairs. Roe sits on my parents' bed while I dig through her things.

"What do you have?" I ask.

"This," he says, throwing over a pencil case full of

349

pound-shop make-up. It's cakey and half-melted and looks like it's been flushed down a toilet.

"Well," I say. "Jesus."

"What?"

"Roe, I don't know much about make-up, but I wouldn't give this to my worst enemy."

"Hey, shut up. Do you know how many lipsticks I've had to suddenly flake into the bin or into the river?"

"Fair enough. Well, let me introduce you to Mr MAC."

I start working on him. I smudge a coffee-coloured shadow across his eyes, then draw an inky line across the lids, trying my best to flick upwards. I remember Michelle boring us all about "cat eyes" at school. Roe, though. He actually looks like a cat. I let him put on his own mascara because I'm too afraid of poking him in the eye. I dab a tiny bit of pearly highlighter on his cheekbones, so they glow when he catches the light.

All the while, I'm trying to avoid thinking about the fact that my skin is on his skin, my fingers on his face. I try to stop catching his eye when he looks up at me. We haven't been this intimate since the day he walked me home and made fun of my driveway. And even then, we had barely started. We were still getting to know each other's bodies, and then it was all cut short. And now I'll never know his body in that way. He won't be my first. Maybe no one will be.

"Maeve?"

"Hmmm?"

"You've gone all quiet."

"Oh. Sorry."

I pick up my mum's handheld mirror and show him his face.

"Oooh, I like it." He grins. "I usually just put on red lipstick. I haven't done this whole smokey-eye thing before."

"Lipstick is so messy," I say.

"Yeah," he says. "Hard to kiss with."

I look at him, sitting on my parents' bed with a face full of shadows and pearls, and wonder if anyone has ever been this beautiful. We stare at each other. What is he doing? Why is he throwing out lines like "hard to kiss with"?

"Yeah."

I screw the tops back on my mother's make-up and put it back on her dressing table.

"Maeve," he says, grabbing my hand as I pass him. I snatch it away.

"You can borrow some of my clothes if you like," I say quickly. "I have a fur coat you could borrow."

"A fur COAT?"

"Don't start. It's inherited from my great-grandmother, or something."

We go up to my room and I show him the coat. The room, lit by the single bulb of my bedside lamp, glows like a sunken sunset. The rabbit fur catches the light and shines a deep, steely silver. He puts it on over his T-shirt.

"You need to see the whole thing. With the silky top and the pearls and all that."

"All right," he says. "Pass me the bag."

I throw him the tote and sit down on my bed. Roe takes the fur off and slowly eases his T-shirt over his head.

And I stare. God help me, I stare.

I've never been alone in a room with a boy with his top off before. I've been to the beach. I've idly watched lads playing football in the summer, shirts versus skins. But here, in the low light of my childhood bedroom, the place I've had chickenpox and sleepovers, the place I've slipped my hand under my pyjama pants and thought about ... well, this. Him being here. In front of me. Like this.

The air shifts in the room. Roe looks at me, looking at him. I decide not to look away. This, after all, could be the last chance we get. I decide to admire him. His body, like him, is a series of contrasts. His thick, stocky shoulders against the slender, elegant collarbone. The muscled arms that have spent countless evenings lifting amps and drums in and out of practice rooms, versus the delicate arches where his stomach meets the button of his jeans. He's like a puppy now, all big paws and feet. In a few years, he's probably going to fill out like Pat did, strong and wide and thick as a brick.

He watches me, watching him. His face goes ruddy and red under the iridescent highlighter. He reaches for the navy top.

"Hey," I say, softly. "You don't have to put it back on."

"I don't?"

"No." I smile. "I like looking at you."

"I like looking at you," he responds, his voice hoarse. "But I feel a little on display here."

"Oh."

I glance down at my own clothes. I'm wearing navy, as Fiona instructed. A woolly jumper dress with thick black tights underneath. I pull it over my head, standing up as I take it off.

I am standing opposite Roe O'Callaghan in my bra and tights. I want to laugh out loud, completely unable to believe what I just did. When did I become the kind of person who takes their clothes off in front of someone?

I answer myself, and the laugh stifles. *When you decided that this could be your last day alive, Maeve.*

Aaron's right. It *will* be so interesting. If I live.

He steps forward and pushes my hair off my face, his hands following it to where it ends at my shoulder blades. Roe pulls me in closer to him, his warm body pressed against mine in the cool attic air.

"You're so beautiful, Maeve," he murmurs. "It really…"

"It really *what*?" I smile.

"It really makes life very … difficult for me."

And then we're kissing. Kisses that go from being slow and simple to frantic, urgent and hungry. We have never truly been alone together before, only ever snatching moments in the underpass or by the Beg. Our aloneness is driving us on, screaming, *Go, now, now. Before it's too late.*

I can't stop touching him. Every time I think I'm being too forward, too animal, he matches me, coming back even stronger. His hands are under my tights, his mouth is on my chest. Gravity seems to pull us onto the bed and I'm sitting astride him, his back propped against my bedroom wall.

It's all too excruciatingly gorgeous, so heart-stompingly new. Everything I do, I can't believe I'm doing it; then, I can't be satisfied with it. I need to see all of him, experience all of it.

"Woahh, woahh." Roe pulls his mouth away from mine, his voice breathless. "We need to calm down."

"Why?" I say, nibbling his ear.

"Because for one, we're due at the river soon."

"We can be done by then."

He pulls back from me, alarmed at the practicality in my voice. At the word "*done*". He scans my face, which is now blotched with his eye make-up.

"O…K. Well, even then … do you not think this is a bit too soon, Maeve? We're not even… We haven't even talked about…"

I'm getting frustrated. If only he knew that this could be our last chance. My last chance.

"I'm ready," I say, hurriedly. "Roe, I want you to be my first."

I can't even believe I'm saying this. I mean, it's true. I do want him to be my first. But I never thought it would come out like this, with me trying to convince him.

"I'm … I'm flattered. And I … I want *you* to be my … my first. But is now really the ti…"

I press my body closer to him, and I see his conviction start to wilt. It's too thrilling, all of this. Having a body. Feeling the power that comes with it. It's like everything I love about witchcraft: it's instinctual, animal, magnetic. He kisses me, long and slow, his hands pulling me towards him. He wants this as much as I do.

He breaks away again. "Maeve, we don't even have anything."

"Any what?"

"You know. Protection."

A huge wave of sadness suddenly descends over me. How can we be so connected, so physically glued to each

354

other, and be coming at this with such different points of view? Here's Roe, worried about the future, about babies, about "protection". And here's me, with all the proof in the world pointing to the fact that there probably *will* be no future – for me at least.

He starts looking at me worriedly. "Maeve, are you…?"

I get up, and reach for my dress on the floor. "Never mind," I say.

"You're acting really weirdly."

"Oh, really?" I whirl around. "You didn't think that when I was—"

"No," he interrupts, clamping both hands on my shoulders. "I mean, ever since I got here, you've been … off. Are you nervous about the spell or something? Is that it?"

"Yes," I say tightly. "I am nervous about the spell."

"Maeve, you need to tell me what's going on. I feel like you know something that I don't know."

I shrug. "It's 11.40. We should get going."

"Hey, you dropped this."

Roe bends down to pick something up off my bedroom floor.

My jet necklace has fallen between the pillows and off of the bed. I take it from him. Dad brought it back from Portugal. It was his way of saying that he wanted to understand me. It was supposed to be a protection charm.

I'm about to put it back on, but stop and look at it for a moment, smoothing my thumb over the black stone. Looks like I've had protection charms coming out of my ears lately, without even realizing it, but who's protecting Roe?

"Why don't you wear this? For the ritual?"

He smiles weakly as I lace it around his neck, the stone clicking softly against his glass pearls.

"It's for protection."

He kisses me softly and smiles. "When this is all over," he says quietly, "I would like to please take you on a date."

I laugh a little, the chuckle tinged with sadness. "We need to go."

We trudge to the riverbank, him in the rabbit fur, me with my school bag. Fiona is already there.

"Hey, you two," she says, a nervous smile on her face.

"Hey," I reply. "Let's do this."

CHAPTER THIRTY-NINE

NOT ENOUGH LIGHT IS COMING OFF THE CANDLES, BUT FIONA has torches. Four of them.

"What's the extra one for?"

"Well, one for each of us," she explains. "And one for Lily."

A glow opens up inside me. Lily. That's the most important thing to remember. Whatever happens tonight, the end goal is still getting Lily back.

We spread a blanket out on the ground, and pour a ring of salt around it.

"I purify this circle," Fiona calls, her voice loud and projecting into the dark, moonless. "I purify this circle and protect all who dwell in it."

She loves this. Loves the theatre, the performance of it. It would be easy to take the piss out of Fiona, but you can't fault her enthusiasm. Fiona simply doesn't know how *not* to try her best.

"Maeve, you're a Sagittarius. That makes you a Fire sign, so sit south." She points to a corner of the blanket. "Roe, you're Air, right?"

"Fifteenth of the sixth. Making me a Gemini."

"Great. Sit east. And I'm Taurus, which is Earth, so I'll sit " she walks around the perimeter of the salt circle and stops at the north side – "here."

"Then Lily is Water," I say, my voice low.

"Yeah," she nods, a little awkwardly. "Lily is Water."

It must be strange for Fiona to be this invested in the fate of a girl she hardly knows. As she fusses with candles and the freshly cut herbs from Roe's bag, I put my arms around her shoulders and kiss her on the cheek.

"Oh, hello!" she says, delighted with the affection. "What's that for?"

"I'm just so grateful you're doing this. And that you're my friend."

"Aww. Well. Don't thank me now, thank me when it works."

I nod. From the other side of the salt circle, I can feel Roe's careful eyes on me.

Fiona takes the white satin out of her bag and unfolds it. It's a huge length of material, as big as a duvet.

"This must have been expensive," I say, amazed.

"Yeah. Well. Better to get something right the first time, right?"

The herbs from Mrs O'Callaghan's garden are tied and burned. We each make the sign of the Goddess – a sort of three-moon drawing – in oil on each other's foreheads. Our torches are on and sitting next to us, shining a spotlight to the centre. We each pick up a candle and carve *LILY* into it, just like I did the first night.

"Wow," Fiona says when she attempts it. "This is harder than it looks."

"Yeah," I answer. Roe's eyes watch me through the flickering lights. "You'd be surprised how hard these things get."

Fiona nods, concentrating on the "Y" in her candle.

"All right, shall I start?" Fiona begins.

"Go ahead."

"Hail to the watchtowers of the North, Lords of Earth," she says grandly. "I do summon and call you to witness and protect the rites of our circle."

She looks at me. "Oh, right," I say, trying to remember the line. "Hail to the watchtowers of the South, Lords of Fire. I do summon and call you to witness and protect the rites of our circle."

"Hail to the watchtowers of the East, Lords of Air," Roe says. "I do summon and call you to witness and protect the rites of our circle."

"Great," says Fiona. "I think we did really well there."

"Are we supposed to talk?"

"There's no rules *not* to talk. Maeve?"

"Oh, right." I open up my refill pad and take out the chants I prepared. "Repeat after me and cut the satin."

I take a deep breath. *"I cut this cloth so I may find: a rope to pull, a rope to bind."*

I hold up my knife and slash through the material. The blade falls through softly, making a satisfying rip in the cold night air. It will be easy. So easy. And if I do it quick enough, it won't hurt at all.

Fiona repeats what I say, cutting her section. Roe does the same, until we each have a pair of long ropes. I take out my tarot cards and start shuffling.

"I'm going to call upon the energy of three cards to help us in this."

"Oh, *cool*," Fiona says excitedly. "Which ones?"

"The Three of Pentacles, for teamwork." I take it out from where I had stacked it, face down on the top of the deck. I place it in the centre of the circle.

"The Chariot, for mastering our power." I flip the card towards them again.

Fiona is nodding so hard now I feel like her head might fall off.

"And the Eight of Wands, for safe, quick travel from ... wherever Lily is."

Pleasant cards. Cheerful cards. Nothing too dark or foreboding. As if I am telling the Housekeeper, "Look, we can keep this simple. No harm, no foul."

"Now with the cards in place, we start tying," I say authoritatively. "I want us all to keep tying knots, concentrating on *only* the knots. Concentration, visualization and intent are the most important part of any spell."

Are they? Really? Or am I just trying to distract my friends?

"As we tie, we're going to chant this: *'I tie these knots so I may find: a rope to pull, a rope to bind.'* Because we're *pulling in* Lily but we're also *binding* the Housekeeper, right?"

"Right," says Fiona. *"I tie these knots so I may find: a rope to pull, a rope to bind."*

"That's it."

"Roe." I turn towards him. "Remember: concentration, visualization, intent. We have to believe we're roping in Lily. We all have to work together."

"OK," he says, but he is still looking at me warily.

And so we begin. We tie and we chant. The candles burn and burn. The oil on my forehead begins to dry. It feels sticky and cracked, like a scab. All we can see is the three tarot cards and our four narrow beams of light, illuminating our hands and shining bright yellow on the Beg.

Our chanting rises to a din. At first, Fiona and Roe were making an effort to enunciate every syllable, loudly and clearly. Then the simple sentences fall into a burble, each word said mechanically and hushed, like a prayer. A bud of hope starts to open up inside me. I can feel the energy changing, the vibrations in the air getting higher. It is as though we are surrounded by a thousand bees, and only I can hear them. This is what being a sensitive is, I realize. This is what Fionnuala was talking about.

Maybe, just maybe, I won't need to sacrifice anything. Maybe the strength of our combined magic is good enough. As we keep reminding ourselves, Lily isn't even dead. Just sleeping. There is no life-for-a-life here.

The buzzing gets louder, and I shift my weight slightly.

"We're going to change it slightly," I whisper. "We're going to imagine throwing the rope around Lily. Lassoing her, like in a western. We're all going to focus, and we're not going to break the chant – we're just going to change it, OK?"

Roe and Fiona don't stop chanting, but they both nod in recognition. Their voices vibrate all around me like a plucked guitar string.

"Close your eyes. Imagine the rope falling around her. Deep breaths. Hold on to the rope tightly. We're not literally going to throw it, just figuratively. Now chant: *'I throw this rope so I may send: a friend to home, a foe to end.'"*

"I throw this rope so I may send: a friend to home, a foe to end."

361

They both repeat it, strongly at first. Soon it settles into the steady chime of a few minutes ago. The candles are low now. The "Y" in my *LILY* candle is about to burn out, and the night is the darkest it's going to get.

We can do this.

"I throw this rope so I may send: a friend to home, a foe to end."

We can do this.

"I throw this rope so I may send: a friend to home, a foe to end."

I don't need to sacrifice anything! If I did, I would know by now! *We can do this!*

"I throw this rope so I may send: a friend to home, a foe to end."

I open my eyes slowly. Fiona and Roe are deep inside the spell, nestled into it like babies into sleep. A soft blue phosphorescence surrounds them, a glittering navy current of light that is looping around their bodies. It is the most beautiful thing I have ever seen.

I keep chanting, my eyes open, unable to look away from the luminescence of my friends. My brilliant, brilliant friends.

"I throw this rope so I may send: a friend to home, a foe to end."

The current of light begins to change colour. From dark blue, to sea green, to a sickly yellow, to gold. Strands of it start to pull away from Roe and Fiona and into the centre, where the tarot cards are still lying face up. The light pools and shimmers, forming a tight circle around them.

The chants continue.

The patterns on the cards begin to shift, the ink rearranging itself. I stare, the chant going dry in my mouth. My candle is moments away from drowning itself in its own molten wax.

There is still enough light left, however, to see that the three cards I had picked out – the Three of Pentacles, the Chariot, the Eight of Wands – have now all changed to three identical Housekeepers. A jackpot on the universe's worst slot machine.

I haven't seen the actual card in so long that it takes me a moment to recognize it. The wedding dress, the dog, the knife in her teeth. The splashes of blood on the end of her gown. The little touches that make her truly terrifying.

I look to Roe and Fiona, who are still deep beneath the warm, rosy, gold light of the spell. I could scream their names right now and they wouldn't hear me.

Whatever happens next, it's up to me to face it.

I bring my eyes back to the centre of the circle, and she's there. I've seen a lot of the Housekeeper lately: in moments of terror, or anger, or jealousy. But I've never been this close, and I've never been this calm upon seeing her. In many ways, it feels like we are being introduced for the first time.

Ladies, meet the Housekeeper card.

CHAPTER FORTY

I EDGE CLOSER TO HER, DIRT SCRAPING AGAINST MY KNEES. The ritual site isn't a cute project any more, a Wiccan daydream that you might find on Tumblr. It's pools of hot wax, and air so thick from burned herbs that everything smells like lamb. The white silk knots are sloppy and covered in dirt. And the Housekeeper, with a knife in her teeth, is staring right at me. I look to Roe and Fiona, whose eyes are still closed. How can they not have sensed her presence? Is she only here for me?

I gaze at her for the last time, her face strangely unlined, her lips without crease. Eyes not made for expression. Even calling her a *she* feels strange. She is not a person; she is an *it*. All this time, I've been thinking of things she might think, need or desire. But there are no thoughts, no feelings, no spite. Just a spirit with a singular purpose, briefly inhabiting human form because that is the best way to deal with humans. She is a cosmic messenger, a virus, an imbalance. She does not hate me, any more than I can hate my instinct to close a door after I open one.

I gaze into her eyes, my face a silent plea.

Please.

I wait for a reply.

Please. I'm begging you.

She gazes at me steadily and without feeling. She merely takes the knife from her mouth and gives it to me. I take it in my hand. The hilt is heavy, the blade slick. It's a good knife. A knife for killing things humanely. I measure the weight of it for a moment, and in that moment, the moon comes out.

Out, and full, and on a night where there is supposed to be no moon. Winking at me. Urging me on.

"Please," I say out loud. "Please, if there's another way, please tell me what it is."

I start to cry as I ask her, the tears making my face slick and cold. There is no point being brave about this now. Do I really have to do this? Is this really what it's going to take?

"Please. There has to be another way."

The Housekeeper's face becomes more blurred through the veil of tears. Roe and Fiona are completely still, eyes closed, as if paralysed by the Housekeeper's presence.

I feel as though time itself has slowed down, so that every micro-movement goes on for ever and ever. Brushing the tears from my eyes seems to take hours. The candlelight on Fiona's face, which flickered about her just seconds ago, lies flat as though it were a golden tattoo.

I gaze at the river. There are no quiet sounds of lapping water, and the bank is so still it looks like a black line across the earth.

"It's like Lily wrote," I plead. "Nobody swims, nobody drowns."

I hold the knife in my hands and whisper, both to myself and the Housekeeper. "Nobody has to die."

"*Yes*, they do."

Her voice is deep and young, an indifferent, exhausted sigh of someone watching yet another tourist tie yet another padlock to a buckling bridge. I don't look up in time to see her mouth move, and I'm glad. It's bad enough hearing the Housekeeper speak. I don't think I could stand anything else.

"I do this, and it's all over?" I say, following an internal sense of fairy-tale logic that you should never make a bargain unless you know the exact terms. "Lily comes back?"

"Yes," she answers.

At the sound of his sister's name, Roe starts to stir next to me.

I wipe my tears away with the heel of my hand. It's time to stop playing around.

This is it. I raise the knife, ready to cut down. To cut down, and end this, and bring Lily back.

The skin on my arm kisses the blade. Blood falls on the satin. It's crimson, and not the deep black blood I know the Housekeeper is going to want. I try to dig the blade in deeper, but start to lose strength in my hand. At least there's not much pain. That's something.

Clouds of blackness start to stain my vision, and I look up to find the Housekeeper, desperate for her approval. But she's gone, along with the golden light of the spell.

"Maeve!"

And Roe is on top of me, trying to wrestle the knife out of my hands. He pins me down, his knees on my thighs. My heads rolls in the dirt, hitting something hard.

"Roe, stop it. You don't know what you're doing."

"What is going on?" Fiona starts to scream. "Roe, why are you *attacking* her?"

"Give it to me, Maeve. Give me the knife."

In the end, I don't have a choice. He prises my fingers from around the knife's handle, and immediately turns it on himself.

"Roe, no!"

But he just stares at me, and falls, backwards, onto the white satin.

CHAPTER FORTY-ONE

THE THINGS I REMEMBER.

Fiona, tying the satin around the wounds. Making, as she called it, a tourniquet. I heard her say the word on the phone to the ambulance. She kept repeating that word through her tears, holding on to it as though it were a magic chant of its own. "I've wrapped their wounds," she kept saying. "They're bleeding a lot. I made them tourniquets."

I remember wondering whether it was painful for her, to be so good at this, when the last thing in the world Fiona wants is to look after people. I remember thinking that her mother would be proud of her.

The moon. Everywhere and everything was the moon: everything was white; everything was pearls. Cold, minty light shot through Fiona from all angles as she held her phone to her face while I watched her from the ground. Can she not see it? How is she even keeping her eyes open? I was reduced to a squint. The moon was behind her, huge and booming, like the drunkest person at a party.

The grass. It was wet, and muddy, and I pressed my face into it to protect my eyes from the glare of the moon. It felt good on my face. A balm.

Fiona, before the ambulance came, her arms around me like she was a child holding on to a too-big teddy won at the fairground. She begged me to stop pressing my face in the dirt. "Look at me, Maeve," she said, my face in her hands.

Roe's shoe. The underside of his trainer. Caked in mud, and lying lifelessly on his foot. I squeeze my eyes shut. I should have known. He knew what I was up to. He knew from the moment he saw the carving knife. *Roe. Roe. Roe.*

The river. Soft lapping sounds like a sea tide, getting louder and louder, larger and larger. I laughed to myself and thought about the cogs that had gored my hand open. It was all so obvious, wasn't it? We said it ourselves: Lily is water.

Lily is Water.

And finally: I remember the moon's light finally starting to dim, and I remember long hair tickling my face. Drops of water fell on my forehead, drops so warm and iron-rich that I first understood them to be my own blood.

"Oh, Maeve," Lily said. "What have you done?"

CHAPTER FORTY-TWO

WHEN I WAKE UP IN THE HOSPITAL, JO IS THE ONLY ONE there. She's looking at her phone, biting her nails. Her eyes are red-rimmed and raw.

"You look terrible," I say.

"Oh Jesus. Maeve. You're awake! Oh my God, let me get Mum and Dad – they're in the canteen. No, wait, how are you feeling? Are you OK? Do you need help sitting up?"

"I feel ... OK," I say uncertainly. I gaze at my arm. There's a trail of stitches, nimbly picked out in brown thread. At the top of the trail is a wad of gauze where I had tried to gouge the knife further in. Before Roe took the knife off me, and turned it on himself.

I close my eyes as tears start to spill down my face.

"Hey, don't start crying on me now," Jo says. "I'm supposed to be the crier."

"Why am I in here? How long have I been asleep? What happened?"

"You hit your head hard, Mae. Bashed your head on a rock when you fell."

"When I..."

"Fiona explained how you were ... what? Helping her rehearse? She called the ambulance and came in with you – her mum came to pick her up an hour ago."

Thank God for Fiona.

"What about Roe?"

"*Who?*"

"Rory. Rory O'Callaghan."

"He's ... not doing as well as you, but it seems like he'll eventually be OK. He had some blood transfusions. His parents don't know *what* to make of everything."

"To make of what?"

"Oh, God, I forgot. You don't know. Lily. She's showed up. She staggered home last night when her parents were already at the hospital and collapsed on her front steps. The neighbours had to ring them while they were here."

I blink, long and slow. I can't believe this. Roe and I are alive, and Lily is ... back? How can that be?

"So where was Lily?" I ask, dazed. "Where was she, this whole time?"

"I don't know. They haven't shared that with the likes of us yet. But her skin was almost blue. Hypothermia. Wherever she was must have been freezing."

"So she's in the hospital?"

"Yep," Jo says. And then, after a pause. "This hospital."

"Me, Roe and Lily are all in the same hospital," I say disbelievingly. "Alive."

"Alive," she confirms.

And I don't get another word from her, because Mum and Dad crash through the door, and I am covered in love.

They stay for hours, way past when they're supposed to. Mum treats me like I'm made of glass. I don't say a lot, and pretend to be much more tired than I am. I wait for clues, to try and make out what Fiona told them. She must be a better actress than even I realized, because the story sounds bizarre, yet Mum and Dad don't seem to have any doubts about its validity. We were rehearsing *Othello* with her, apparently: it was all Fiona's idea. The knife was there for Desdemona's death scene. Jo, who did Shakespeare as part of her Masters, says nothing. I wonder if she remembers that Desdemona was smothered, and that it Juliet who stabbed herself.

"I suppose this solves the mystery, then," she finally says.

"Of what?"

"Of who your boyfriend is."

"I don't know if we're calling it that."

But a light switches on in me, bright as the North Star. Roe lived. I lived. Lily lived. We can do anything now.

My family leave slowly, reluctantly, with promises that Pat is coming down from Dublin and that Cillian is trying to get the time off work. I nod and yawn dramatically. I'm dying for them to leave. I need to call Fiona. I need to see Roe. And Lily. How is she? How did she make it home?

The nurse comes in to check on me, and I ask her politely what room my boyfriend is in.

"Your boyfriend?"

"I'm sorry," I laugh, putting on a big performance of girlishness. "I mean Rory O'Callaghan. We came in together. The knife accident?"

Accident.

"He's on the ward," she replies. "Ward E, bed 3."

"Thank you."

I wait until everyone's asleep and sneak out, slipping on the dressing gown that Mum brought from home. I wander the dense, endless wards, my gut quaking at the thought of seeing him.

When I find his ward, it's after midnight. There are several other men on it, and it feels strange to associate him with them. Already, he feels like a different category. When I find him, I let out a small yelp of excitement. There he is. Still, if you can believe it, with his mascara on.

He's dozing, his Adam's apple bobbing softly as he snores. Roe *snores*.

I drag a chair over and sit next to him. His hand is lying across his pyjama-clad chest, and I place mine on top of it. He opens his eyes slowly, carefully, like you might cautiously unfold a broken umbrella.

"Hello," I whisper.

"Hi," he replies. His face is white, all that ruddy colour drained out of it. I can see the blue of his veins shimmering under his skin. "That was really stupid, that thing you did."

"I know," I hush back. "It worked, didn't it?"

"In a way," he reasons, his voice croaky. "I suppose it did."

"Are you OK?"

"Not really."

"How bad is it? One to ten?"

"If one was that punch-up at the Cypress, then this is … eleven hundred and four."

"Oh, Roe. Roe, I'm sorry."

"It's not your fault. Except, no wait, it totally *is*."

"It is my fault!" I say, trying not to yell. "All of it! Top to bottom, the whole thing!"

"*Sssssh*. People are trying to sleep around here."

"Lily is back."

"I know. She kind of stole my thunder," he says, grinning.

"How come … how come we both got to…?"

"Live?"

"Yes."

"I've been thinking about this. Are you cold?"

"Yes."

He moves his body over and flips back the hospital blankets. I scooch in next to him and lay my head across his chest. I think one of the men in the bed opposite is staring at us, but I don't care. We've cheated death. I don't give a crap what anyone thinks.

"Have you ever heard the story of Abraham?"

"Wow, are you Jewish *and* Protestant now?"

"Shut up," he says, picking up a length of my hair. "Abraham was a Bible guy, and he had a son called Isaac."

"Bible guy?"

"And God told Abraham to sacrifice his son. To kill him, basically."

"Scant," I say in disgust.

"I know. But when Abraham was about to do it, to kill his son, God sent a ram to sacrifice instead. He said, *It's grand, you don't have to kill your son.*"

"Why?"

"Because the fact that Abraham was willing to do it was enough. The pure intention to sacrifice was enough. I think … that's what happened with us. I think it was enough that we were willing to … to…"

"To die?" I say.

"Yes," he answers quietly. "Do you want to know something funny?"

"Go on."

He puts his hand into the shirt pocket of his pyjamas and pulls out a flat black stone.

"When I drove the knife in, it hit against something."

I marvel at the jet necklace I had given him, just minutes before we left my house. "It's jet," I whisper. "It's a protection charm my dad gave me."

"When it hit against it … it was like the blade didn't like it. I could hear the knife talking to me, if that makes sense. It was like, *Ew, gross, let's get out of here*."

"The knife said all that?"

"The knife said all that."

Silence. The low beep of a machine at the other side of the room sounds.

"Do you think," I ask softly. "Do you think that maybe … I sacrificed myself for Lily, and you sacrificed yourself for me, but I had already sacrificed my protection for you, and so…"

"This is advanced sacrifice mathematics."

"Do you think we cancelled it all out, though?"

"It's as good a theory as any. Whatever happened, no one's ever going to believe us."

"No," I say, nestling into him closer. "So it's good we have each other."

"And that you're a powerful sensitive."

"Harriet was a powerful sensitive," I say, my voice hushed. "But I guess she didn't have the friends to protect her."

We are silent for a long while then. He traces my stitches with his fingertips, winces at the big patch of gauze, and finally settles on burying his face in the crook of my neck.

"I don't want to die," I say, finally. "I never did. I like life."

"Me too," he says.

"Seems a bit obvious, doesn't it?"

"Not always," he says, a half-smile on his face. "You should go before a nurse finds you in here."

"OK," I say, getting out of bed.

"Hey, not so *fast*."

So I stay for a few more minutes, and I kiss him, and he shows me the bandages on his stomach. He lifts the corner of the white bandage tenderly, and I suck my teeth. Thick black blood has dried around a deep wound just above his naval. If he had gone just one centimetre to the left, the doctor said, he would have had to wear a bag for the rest of his life.

"To which I said –" he coughs – "Gucci or Prada?"

"No! You didn't!"

"I swear, I did."

"With your *mum* in the room?"

He nods, clutching his stomach and trying not to split his stitches laughing. "Honestly, Maeve, there's nothing like a brush with death to make you realize that your parents' opinion of you doesn't matter."

"Hear, hear," I smile. "Have you talked to Lily yet?"

"No. My parents will barely tell me a thing. Just that she's basically OK. They seem totally dazed. I don't think they've had this much excitement their entire lives."

"I can't believe she's back, Roe. It worked. We did it."

"I know. Me neither. I guess we're pretty amazing."

"Glad we're agreed."

I kiss him goodbye and turn to leave.

"Maeve?"

"Yes?"

"Nevermind."

"What?"

"It's dumb."

"Come *on*."

"No, it's the wrong moment. I hate myself already."

"Roe."

"Will you ... are you my girlfriend?"

I decide to make him wait. Just for laughs.

"Or, y'know, 'girlfriend' is a weird term. It's very binary. We don't have to gender it. Is 'partner' too weird? 'Lover'? Oh, God. Pretend I didn't say that. Please wait while I stab myself again?"

I laugh. "We are not making jokes about stabbing, Roe, as a rule."

A pause.

"And that's a rule, I insist on, as your girlfriend."

He smiles. "I accept."

I'm discharged from hospital a couple of days later. Mum comes to collect me and brings Pat with her.

"I glued that Walkman of yours back together," he says, giving me a hug. "Is this what teens are doing now? A few years ago, it was vinyl and now it's cassette tapes?"

"No," I say, remembering Heaven. "Honestly I think I'm outgrowing it myself."

I never get to visit Lily's room, even though I try to get Mum to take me. She won't even let me say goodbye to Roe. "You'll see him when he gets out in a few days," she says. "This is family time."

"You don't want *him* getting excited either. Not in his condition."

"Pat!" Mum says, disgusted.

"Mum, we were all thinking it," he protests.

It feels like it takes a long time for life to get back to normal. Cillian arrives and it's strange to watch him lump around the house with his work laptop, knowing what I do now. The brother born in the summer of Harriet. The difficult pregnancy. The year the cat ran away. He's definitely the moodiest of the five of us, and the only other one who has dark hair, like me. Part of me wonders if it touched him in some way, whether the Housekeeper is part of his DNA now. The way, I suppose, it is mine.

Mum doesn't let me go back to school until Friday. That way, she says, I only have one day before the weekend, and it won't be too much of a "shock to the system". I hug Fiona when I see her. It's awkward. Her texts have been formal the last few days, and I can't say I blame her. We meet in the art room at lunch.

"Hey," she says, holding me at a distance. "How are you feeling?"

"Uh. OK. Not too bad, really. The stitches are kind of itchy and gross, though."

"Sure. Great."

"Fiona. I'm sorry."

378

"You could have told me, Maeve."

"You know I couldn't have. And anyway, I wasn't even sure what I was going to do."

"You could have died, man! In fact, you were *planning* on it."

"I wasn't *planning* on it," I say. And because I can think of nothing else, I just repeat myself. "I was just ... willing to do whatever it took."

She says nothing, just stretches a piece of Blu-Tack between her fingers.

"It just seemed like the only way to bring her back. And to end all this ... all this horrible stuff. My sister and her girlfriend were getting attacked, Roe's gigs were ending in punch-ups, Aaron's weird influence ... it was all water flowing from the same direction. I had to be ... the cork in the bottle, I suppose."

"That makes no sense."

"It does, in a messed-up kind of way."

"No, I mean, it's an interesting theory, but it hasn't *stopped* anything, has it?"

"What do you mean?"

"The CoB are having a rally this weekend in Dublin."

"What?"

"Well. They're not calling it a rally. It's a 'city-wide festival celebrating Ireland's Catholic heritage', but it has all these creepy alt-right speakers doing events at it."

The blood drains from my face.

"Oh God. I should have waited to tell you, shouldn't I?"

"So ... nothing has changed? Aaron is still..."

"I wouldn't say nothing. Lily is back."

"But..." I rub at my eyelids. No. No, this wasn't how things were supposed to go. "That wasn't the deal."

"What deal? Did you make a deal?"

"No..." I say, trailing off.

"Maeve ... did you think that..." Fiona bites on her bottom lip, pausing to find the right words. "Did you think that you could end hate crime by killing yourself?"

"You *know* it wasn't as simple as that," I say fiercely. "But Aaron's the other sensitive. The one who's manipulating everyone. CoB's popularity was because of him. *The city was cursed*, Fiona."

"I agree that maybe the city was cursed," she reasons. "But ... did you really think Aaron could make people hateful if they weren't already?"

"What do you mean?" I ask.

"Maeve, when I was twelve, a fully-grown man screamed 'Sweet and sour chicken!' at me from a car window."

"Jesus. I'm so sorry."

"Yeah," she says. "And that was long before the Housekeeper or Aaron came to town."

I start chewing on my nails.

"He might have watered some seeds, organized some people ... but all this stuff. The seeds were already planted, Maeve. They already existed."

"I guess you think I'm pretty dumb."

"I think ... when you're looking for things that are out of place," she says softly. "You see all the things that already are."

I don't know what to say. I've never felt so stupid, or so small. But I look at Fiona, the brilliant friend who made a tourniquet from satin and held my bleeding arm together, and my heart bursts at the millions of tiny things that have happened to her. The infinite tiny interactions she's had where someone has used her race, her immigrant mother, her scholarship, her beauty, her anything, as a way to hurt her. Things she will never tell me about, but will exist nonetheless.

"I'm sorry," I say.

"What for?"

"For thinking..." But I lose the words. "For not seeing."

"It's OK," she says, and despite everything, she starts to laugh. "You're not the first person to make oppression all about themselves. And Aaron is still making this shit worse. Luckily, we have a secret weapon."

"What?"

"You, you idiot. You're the other sensitive. Glenda the Good Witch."

"I'm not powerful like he is."

"Oh, right, it must be that *other* girl who defeated a deathless witch spirit and rescued her friend. I'll go find her."

I laugh, but my skin feels tight, itchy. Lily might be back, but CoB are still more popular than ever. I start rubbing at the bandages on my arm.

It's going to be so interesting. If you live.

"Are you all right?" Fiona asks, looking at my arm. "This is always the worst bit. Your skin is probably irritated because it's not getting enough air."

I pick at the tape holding the wad of nappy-ish gauze to my arm. The angles are all weird, though. I can't get my fingernail under it.

"Here," Fiona says. "Let me help."

She removes the tape and examines the stitches on my arm. "So do you think they'll let you off homework until next week?" she says, tracing the puckered brown skin.

"I don't know," I answer, sighing at the thought. "I reckon I can get a sympathy vote for…"

But I don't finish the sentence. My eyes are on my arm, still being held by Fiona.

My stitches are beginning to disappear. The surgical thread that I was told would take weeks to dissolve start to crumble away, the broken skin puckering and joining together.

"Are you doing that?" I whisper. "Because I'm not doing that."

"Oh no," Fiona says, dropping my arm like a hot potato. "Oh no."

CHAPTER FORTY-THREE

ON SATURDAY, ROE HAS BAND PRACTICE. HE'S OUT OF hospital now, and has reassured his parents that he will keep practice short, and will sit in a chair the entire time. I go to the O'Callaghans' house carrying a plastic bag full of sweets and art supplies.

"Hello, Maeve," Mrs O'Callaghan says at the door, her voice disapproving. "Rory mentioned you might be stopping by."

"Yes, hello, Mrs O'Callaghan," I say politely. Lily always called my mum Nora. I have never not called Lily's mum Mrs O'Callaghan. "I was wondering if Lily was up for visitors."

"I'll have to ask her," she says shortly, and leaves me standing on the doorstep while she disappears inside. She doesn't even let me come in the sliding door and wait on the porch, instead leaving me to linger in the front garden. She leaves me there for so long that I consider leaving. After a while, I'm certain she's forgotten that I'm here at all.

Mrs O'Callaghan opens the sliding door. "Only for a minute," she says. "She's still not well."

I follow her up the stairs, following the progression of Roe and Lily's childhoods as I go. Tiny Roe with jug ears. Tiny Lily with drowsy, half-closed bug eyes. A few of these photos were taken by my mum at the back of our garden. There is a framed one of me and Lily jumping over a sprinkler. Not very many of either Roe or Lily in recent years. I think parents stop being so interested in taking photos of their children when they stop being children.

Mrs O'Callaghan creaks open Lily's bedroom door. "Go on," she says. "I'll come back in ten minutes."

Lily's room isn't much more than a single bed and a dressing table. I haven't been in here in almost two years, but not a lot has changed, except that the drawings on the wall are more advanced. Lily is sitting up in bed, her long blonde hair over her shoulders, drawing pad in her hand. Her eyes flicker up when I come in, but she doesn't put the pad down.

"Hi," I say. "How are you feeling?"

"Hello," she says, but she doesn't answer the question.

"I brought you some Heroes," I say, rattling the plastic bag in my hand.

"Thank you," she replies, shortly.

"How are you feeling?" I repeat, because she hasn't answered.

She puts down her pad and takes a long sip of water from the glass next to her. "Why are you here, Maeve Chambers?"

I'm startled. Why is Lily referring to me by my full name?

"I'm here because I wanted to see how you are. And I wanted to say I'm sorry."

"You're sorry."

"Yes."

"For what?"

384

"For treating you the way I did. For ditching you. For doing that stupid tarot reading that started this ... this whole mess."

I say this last part tentatively. I'm still not sure how much Lily even knows about what has happened to her. Was she just knocked unconscious for the past month, like in a coma? Or does she know everything?

She gazes at me for a moment, bored as a boy king. "You don't have to be sorry."

"Oh."

"No, wait," she says, cocking her head. "If you're sorry for anything, say sorry for bringing me back."

"What?"

"Yeah. Say sorry for ending it all. Say sorry for turning me back into this ... this *creature* in bed."

Her eyes are glassy now and beginning to brim with tears. She swipes at them aggressively, determined I don't see her cry.

"Do you know what I was thinking, on that stupid day you did your dumb tarot reading? I was thinking..."

A single, crystal tear falls down her cheek and onto her sketchbook.

"I was thinking, *God, what I wouldn't do to be anywhere or anything else*. To be away from that school. Away from you. Away from the whole disgusting business of being a human."

Something clicks in my head. "I wished for you to go away. And you wished to be taken away."

Was that what activated The Housekeeper? Two twin desires, and an enchanted deck of cards to join them?

She swipes at her face again, as more tears fall. She looks like she is trying to punch herself in the eye.

"And I was, Maeve. It worked. I was *away*."

I gaze at the new drawings stuck to the wall with masking tape. I see an overturned trolley, floating downstream. I see tadpoles hatching. I see the purple gleam of a rainbow trout.

"You were the river," I say simply.

"I was," she says, miserably. "I was."

She resumes sketching, mostly as a way of distracting herself from tears.

"I could be so huge. I could be the biggest thing. Miles and miles for ever, on and on. Or so small. Just a little stream over a few rocks..."

She pauses, and her eyes swivel towards me.

"I saw *you*," she says, fiercely. "I saw you, once."

I am now replaying all the times I kissed her brother by the riverside. "... Oh?"

"You had your hands in me."

I wince. "The cogs. The keys."

"I cut you," she says, slowly. "Your blood was in the water."

The hair prickles at the back of my neck. She's scaring me now. The Housekeeper has clearly left some long shadow within Lily, some imprint. Maybe even possessed her. This isn't Lily. This isn't the girl who would lick books and then scream laughing.

"It healed," I respond, and remember Fiona's hand on my stitches yesterday. The skin is sealed now, a red scar that should take weeks to appear. If Lily and Fiona are so changed after the ritual, then what happened to me, and to Roe? Is there something lurking in us, too?

"You can go now," she says.

"Are you tired?"

"No, I just want you to go."

"Right. OK," I look awkwardly at my plastic bag of corner-shop offerings. "Do you want me to leave these?"

She looks at me blankly. "I don't fucking care."

I race down the stairs, pushing past Lily's mum so she doesn't see that I'm crying.

"Maeve," she calls. "Maeve, are you all right?"

I walk as fast as I can down the street, my head down, my nose buried in my scarf. Lily is a monster. A monster that doesn't give a crap I almost died trying to save her, and who would rather live as a body of water than as a human girl.

As I get to the end of the street, I see Roe getting off the bus, his guitar on his back.

"Hey!" he calls, a big smile on his face. "Thank God. You can help me bring this back to my house. I'm not even supposed to be carrying stuff with my injuries."

I look at him, my eyes wet. His eyes are coated in mascara and black liner. Clearly, make-up is not just a showtime thing any more.

"I can't, Roe. I can't go back there. Don't make me."

"What? What happened?"

"Lily's different, Roe."

He sighs. "I know. But I guess that's to be expected. We can… We can't really know what she went through. It's hard to empathize."

387

"What if the Housekeeper is using her, Roe? I looked into her eyes and … and that's not Lily. That's the Housekeeper talking."

"What do you mean? You defeated the Housekeeper, Maeve. She's gone."

"Is she, though? Lily's not even a person any more. She's just this … this shell."

"Why? Why are you saying that?"

I break off, remembering the fierce, unforgiving look in Lily's huge eyes.

"The way she … talked to me."

"Oh God. Maeve."

"You weren't there, Roe. You don't know."

"Sit down, Maeve."

I look around. There's nowhere to sit, except for his neighbours' low garden wall, so I perch there. Roe puts his guitar on the pavement, kneels down and gives me a long, slow kiss on the mouth.

"Jesus," I say, when he pulls away. "What was that for?"

"That was so you don't get mad at me for what I'm about to say next."

He takes a deep breath, and sits down on the wall next to me. "Lily doesn't have to forgive you."

"What?"

"I understand what you did. I understand everything. So does Fiona. But Lily doesn't have to. Lily can hate you as much as Lily wants."

"But…" I say, grappling at this like a rope that's burning the flesh on my hands. "What I did for her? I became a witch for her. I stuck a knife into my arm."

388

"She didn't see any of it." He shrugs. "That means nothing to her."

"But she knows! I told her! You told her! Didn't you?"

"I told her everything. We're actually —" he pauses, considering this — "we're actually closer now than we've ever been."

"That doesn't make any sense," I say, petulantly.

"With all due respect, she's not your sister. Only me and Lily know what's between me and Lily. And both of us…" He trails off.

"What?"

"Both of us know what it is to feel like the body you have isn't always the body you want. I promise not to write any bad songs about it, but Lily's always going to be part of my life now. We're not going to make the same mistake again, shut each other out and just assume the other one is trundling along fine. So that means…"

"What? What does that mean?"

"It means that you two, and Fiona, are going to have to accept that."

And as he says it, a strand of light spreads, wormlike, through my mind. One that, like the night I looked at Fiona and saw the moon shooting through her, is touched with a kind of silver glow. Immediately, I am able to recognize that this is a light coming from Roe, and that it is one I can grab and hold on to, like a rope ladder dangling from a helicopter. Before I even have a chance to speak, I realize that the light is a thought, and the thought is his.

I hope she loves me enough to try.

"Maeve? Did you hear what I said? I think it's important

for Lily to have a group she can immerse in, y'know? A group like ours."

"So you want Lily to hang out with us, but you also think it's fine for her to hate me."

"I'm just saying that you need to give it time. Can you give it time? Time for her to heal, for you guys to work it out, whatever? Then we can be … I don't know. A foursome."

"Right," I grumble. "Earth, Air, Fire, Water."

"Earth, Air, Fire, and Water, yes."

"Right."

I lean my head on his shoulder and wonder just how easy life would be if I weren't in love with Roe O'Callaghan.

But, oh God, how boring.

CHAPTER FORTY-FOUR

SPRING

FIONA AND I ARE WALKING TO THE RIVER, AND SHE'S
complaining again.

"I just wish I had a gift for something I could *use*,
y'know? Like, being able to memorize huge monologues,
or dance choreography, or something. Not *this*."

Fiona has not quite accepted her newfound status as
a healer. It is possible that she never will. It's not that she
doesn't care about people. In fact, she's probably one of the
most compassionate people I've ever known. But Fiona is
butting her head up against something that, as close as we
are, Roe and I can never understand. We're not working
against a stereotype that says you should always be the girl
with the tourniquets.

"All I want is what you have," she said to me once. "The
right to be selfish."

"Yes, Fi, but then you wouldn't have saved our lives."

"What good is *that* doing my career, though?"

"I'm coming to your bloody play, aren't I, Miss Thing?"

"I suppose," she says, adjusting the canvas bag filled with
sandwiches on her shoulder. The *Othello* run went well,
even if it was just three performances. Now she's playing

the younger sister in some play about the Blitz.

"Hey, Maeve." She suddenly grins. "I'm thinking of a number."

"*This* again."

"Go on. We said you need to practise."

I close my eyes for a moment, and feel for Fiona's tail of light. "You're not thinking of a number," I say, finally. "You're thinking about whether you're going to keep being cast in the kid sister roles, and whether anyone will take you seriously."

"Well, damn."

The telepathy thing hasn't gone away. It feels mad to even call it that, especially as it's not at all how you see it in films. There, it's always this rush of a million different voices, hitting the person like a wall of sound. With me, it's never voices. It's lights. Strands of coloured lights that I grab on to and follow until I'm a tourist in someone else's brain. It takes time. It takes concentration. And it's absolutely knackering.

In the days after the ritual, Fiona and I went to Divination, mostly to reassure Fionnuala that we were OK. It wasn't an easy conversation to have, with her spinning between wild rage at having disobeyed her and extreme relief that what happened to Heaven hadn't happened to me. She made us a cup of camomile tea, and slowly, we told her about our gifts. About the healing, the lights, the scar tissue that could disappear under Fi's fingertips.

"The ritual changed you. You've seen beyond the veil," Fionnuala sighed, a tinge of jealousy in her voice. "And now you're for ever changed."

Roe and Lily are already on the grass when we get to the Beg, sitting on a blanket, deep in conversation. We waited for a long time to see whether they had gained anything in the ritual. Eventually, we gave up. Fiona and I had big conversations about the fact that we were the only ones who gained gifts afterwards, and that maybe for the O'Callaghans, surviving was a gift great enough. But then it happened.

Small things, first. A cheap padlock sprung open when Roe put his hand on it. We thought it was a fluke. Then one day I was locked out of my house, and called him round to keep me company while I waited for Dad to get home. We decided to try the lock trick again. The front door stayed put; but the back door, with its old lock and rusty brown handle, flew right open.

He said, "Oh my God."

I said, "Welcome to the club."

The vague talent he had for fixing things has flowered into a kind of strange understanding of inanimate objects, one that makes perfect sense to him, but he struggles to explain. He gave me a watch battery on the bus and told me to hide it anywhere in my house. Two days later, he walked through the front door, took one long blink, and said, "Behind the bookcase in Pat's room."

"Hey, you guys," I say, bending down to kiss Roe. "What are you chatting about?"

"It's private," Lily says. Firmly. Not crossly. A month ago it would have been snappily. Now, we are on "firmly".

"OK." I nod. "Me and Fiona have hot chicken rolls and cans."

"Angels," Roe says.

"We try," Fiona agrees. "Who wants a Game of Thrones tarot reading?"

"Ooh, me," Lily says, huddling in close to her.

I try not to take it too personally.

On the whole, Lily's mental recovery seems to be taking much longer than her physical one. The world was exhausting to her for a long time after the ritual. I think she might have given up on living entirely, if her gift hadn't appeared.

We all thought it would be water. We looked for rain and leaky plumbing. It wasn't that simple. Nothing ever is, I suppose. Then things started happening. Lightbulbs exploded. Watches stopped working. Some popcorn caught fire in the microwave. Lily kept on accidentally breaking things that Roe inevitably had to fix.

"Some gift," she grumbled.

Then a CoB head followed us down the street, demanding to know why Roe was wearing a skirt and holding hands with a girl at the same time. He shoved a leaflet into Lily's hand and immediately yelped, dropping the pile of paper on the floor. Lily froze, and we hustled her into the nearest cafe.

"What was that?" Roe asked, his arm around her.

"Sparks," she whispered. "My gift is electricity."

We sit under the trees, and Roe complains about his exams. We make grisly faces about the fact that next year, we're going to be sitting ours, and that I will almost certainly have to do night study every evening to even scrape the points for a decent college. If, as I keep qualifying to my friends and my parents, I even want to get into college.

Fiona says she'll help me, and I move my head closer to

Roe's chest. Lily's eyes rest peacefully on the Beg. She has promised Roe she won't try to go back, but I'm not sure how committed she is to keeping that promise. If Lily can find a way to become the river again, she will take it.

But I try not to think about that. I try not to think about the news, which is only getting worse. Or my sister, whose mood is only getting bleaker. Aaron, who still walks the edges of my dreams on the nights my protection spells aren't strong enough to keep him out.

I try to exist now, here, in the spring. With everything to fight for, and all our hidden gifts to help us.

ACKNOWLEDGEMENTS

The acknowledgements are the part of the book where you thank people for the part they played in your story, and for this story, it's hard to know where to begin. I could start in 2016, when my friend Harry Harris and I wrote a song called "The Housekeeper Card". We prowled around the subject of tarot for a while, but eventually landed on what we both deemed to be a killer opening line: "She appears in rare readings, and only to young women, and only in times of crisis." Or, I could start it a week later, when we showed our bandmate Ellie Cowan the song, and then practised it for an entire summer – at gigs, to our friends, in voice notes – cementing the Housekeeper as lore that I would keep returning to in my head, again and again. Thanks, to both of you, for helping to create an earworm so good it eventually became a book.

True to the song, the Housekeeper did appear again, and in a time of crisis: when, after years away, I found myself spending weeks in my family home in Ireland, waiting on bad news about my sister's health, all of us under one roof again. It was like being fifteen again: the youngest in a long line of big personalities, holed up in the smallest bedroom, waiting for something to happen. Something did happen, and it was the first ten thousand words of this book. I don't think I'll ever be done being relieved that my family are my family, so in the absence of heaped praise, let me just name them, and thank them: Peter, Noelle, Jill, Shane and Rob. Thank you.

Thank you to Ella Risbridger, who from the beginning has been the main reader and supporter of this book. Before these characters were real to anyone else, they were real to you and me. We have walked the length and breadth of south London, talking about Maeve, Fiona, Lily and Roe. I hope we keep walking, as they get older and weirder. I hope we get older and weirder too.

Thank you to Tom McInnes, for being the songwriter for Small Private Ceremony. Thank you to Wren Dennehy, for your guidance, your sensitivity, and your showtunes. Thank you to Karen Tongson for your guidance and help in researching Filipino culture. Thank you to Natasha Hodgson, for feedback and praise. Thank you to Gavin Day, because you can't write a teenage love story unless you're in one, and that's exactly how this feels.

Thank you to Walker Books, for acquiring this book and pushing to make it the best story it can be. Thank you to Bryony Woods, for loving this project as passionately as she has. And finally, thank you to an English teacher I had when I was fourteen, who went by Miss Cotter then, but who I'm pretty sure got married and is called Mrs Richards now. You liked my stories, you thought I was funny, and you introduced me to Margaret Mahy. You, I think, were there when the story really started.

Caroline O'Donoghue is an Irish writer and host of the award-winning podcast Sentimental Garbage. Her two adult novels, *Promising Young Women* and *Scenes of a Graphic Nature*, are published with Virago. She has a weekly column in *The Irish Examiner*, as well as frequent bylines for *Prospect*, *Grazia* and *Lonely Planet*. She currently lives in London with her partner and her dog. *All Our Hidden Gifts* is her first novel for young adults. Visit Caroline on Twitter: @Czaroline